The Book of Israela

The Book of Israela

RENA BLUMENTHAL

RESOURCE *Publications* • Eugene, Oregon

THE BOOK OF ISRAELA

Copyright © 2018 Rena Blumenthal. All rights reserved. Except for brief quota-
tions in critical publications or reviews, no part of this book may be reproduced in
any manner without prior written permission from the publisher. Write: Permis-
sions, Wipf and Stock Publishers, 199 W. 8th Ave., Suite 3, Eugene, OR 97401.

Resource Publications
An Imprint of Wipf and Stock Publishers
199 W. 8th Ave., Suite 3
Eugene, OR 97401

www.wipfandstock.com

PAPERBACK ISBN: 978-1-5326-5848-8
HARDCOVER ISBN: 978-1-5326-5849-5
EBOOK ISBN: 978-1-5326-5850-1

Manufactured in the U.S.A.   09/28/18

Author's Note

There is only one character in this book who is modeled on a real person: Kobi's paternal grandfather, Reb Yakov, who is based on my maternal grandfather, Naftali Tzvi Kartagener.

זכר צדיק לברכה

1

It looked, at first, like another case of Jerusalem syndrome. We'd been overrun with them since the turn of the millennium, and the epidemic had only intensified in the eighteen months since the start of the second intifada. He was a skinny fellow in white rags, with a shaved head, a scraggly beard, and a fiery insanity in his eyes. That's pretty much how they all looked. Tourists from every corner of the globe would show up in the Holy City, throw on a bedsheet, and start preaching the coming apocalypse, suddenly convinced that they were the Son of God or an ancient Israelite prophet—a brief, transitory psychosis that would resolve itself by the time they were safely home. But no, on second glance this was a case of more mundane psychosis—the oratory was in fluent, even poetic, Hebrew. A local boy. Hard to believe that someone who grew up in this obviously God-forsaken country could believe, even in a state of psychotic delusion, that the spirit of God still walked its streets.

The tension in the waiting room was palpable. Sami, our burliest security guard, was seated next to the scrawny prophet, effortlessly holding his bony arms behind his back. The young man wriggled his body as if trying to break free, but making no real effort. A pretty young woman with thick brown hair, vaguely familiar from staff meetings, was seated to his other side, whispering earnestly into his ear, though he seemed oblivious to her presence. By the exit door, two older men were engaged in a loud, emphatic disputation as to what right the hospital did or didn't have to hold people against their will. A middle-aged woman was shrieking, "Let him go! You're hurting him!" The receptionist had come out from behind her desk to shush the woman and try to calm the roomful of increasingly agitated patients.

My instinct was to march quickly through the waiting room and out the door to the stairwell, as if on urgent business, which, in a way, I was. I wanted to be home before Nava, peace-offering in hand, and had meant to slip out of the office early to stop at the jewelry shop where she had recently admired an expensive silver necklace. But something about the girl's desperate efforts made me pause. There had been a lot of grumbling about me in the office lately; it wouldn't hurt to play the gallant knight to her damsel in distress.

I walked up to the receptionist, who pretended, as always, not to notice me. It was the fireplug with the muscular arms. What the hell was her name?

"Uh . . ."

"Yael."

"Right, Yael. Whose patient is he?"

"He was brought in by the police. They found him wending his way through traffic on a busy street in Katamon, in those rags, in this horrible wind. He was calm when they brought him in, so they just left him here. The clinician on call was our new intern, Dina. She took him in for an emergency intake, but the questions must have gotten him agitated. He barged out of her office and started scaring all the patients with his fire-and-brimstone preaching. Thank God Sami was around—he's the only one who can keep these types in check."

"Has he seen a psychiatrist?"

"Dr. Barak's on call, but the patient refuses to see him. I've notified the emergency room, and they're sending up the heavies. There'll probably be a forced hospitalization." She shook her head. "I'm not sure the intern's going to hold up."

It was, indeed, a perfect chance to prove how useful I could be. A new boss had just come in a couple of months before—a puckered, no-nonsense Anglo who regarded me with a hefty dose of suspicion. It wouldn't hurt to have her hear a few good things about me.

I walked up to the girl. From up close, you could smell the unwashed odor of her disheveled patient. She was much too young to be in this position, looked barely old enough to be out of the army.

"Do you need some help?" I asked.

She looked up at me mutely, on the verge of tears.

"Dina, right? Why don't you come into my office? I don't think that talking to him right now will do much good." I turned to the receptionist, whose name had already slipped my mind. "Uh . . . can you call us when Security arrives?"

The girl sat on my office couch and cried as I fed her tissues, scrunching up her nose with every sniffle. What compelled a young innocent like her to go into this crazy field? She probably wanted to save the suffering souls of the world. Well, it wouldn't hurt to have some reality drummed in early in her career.

"What happened to upset you so much?"

"I'm sorry, Dr. Benami. I'm so embarrassed by my unprofessional behavior." She was visibly struggling to compose herself. "It's just that at first he seemed OK. He was upset, understandably, about the political situation of the country—the suicide bombings, the increasing poverty in his neighborhood. It all seemed perfectly reasonable, but as he talked, he became crazier and crazier. He told me that God speaks to him all the time, that God's angry at us, punishing us. Then he started describing these wild visions, and before I knew it he was rambling incoherently." She stifled a sob. "He was still calm; I thought I could handle it. But then, when I told him he needed to meet with a psychiatrist, he completely lost it, became mean and abusive, called me 'bitch,' described all these terrible things that would happen to me. I got really scared, told him he had no right to speak to me that way. That's when he called me a 'no-good whore' and stormed out of the office and into the waiting room." She burst into another round of tears. "It's my first emergency intake. I didn't handle it very well, did I?"

"It was a difficult case. You handled it fine," I said reassuringly.

"I feel so stupid, so naive," she sobbed, wiping her eyes with the back of her hand.

I assumed a comforting, fatherly tone. "Psychotic patients can be frightening. One of the most important things you have to learn in this field is that you're going to encounter people who are totally irrational, people you can't possibly get through to. You have to grow tougher skin—it's never personal."

"But there was something about him, when we first started talking." She scrunched her nose, fighting back the tears. "I liked him, a lot. He's genuinely distressed about the state of the country. He was so passionate and eloquent. Even his visions, they were really weird, but kind of stunning too. He described them so vividly, it was mesmerizing." Her eyes again pooled with tears. "But then, all of a sudden, out of nowhere, he became angry and abusive."

"That's not uncommon with psychotic patients," I said soothingly. "You say he's having visual hallucinations?"

"Yes, very elaborate and detailed. He sees visions of God, surrounded by ministering angels."

"Lots of schizophrenics hear voices, but seeing visions is a very serious symptom." I discreetly glanced at my watch. "The psychiatrists in the emergency room will want to hear all the details of your intake, especially how he was responding before he became aggressive. It will be a good learning experience. Do you think you're up to it?"

"Yes, I guess so," she said doubtfully.

me up half the night. Dina was obviously shaken, her hands running repeatedly through her thick hair as she spoke.

"Dr. Benami, you've been doing this work such a long time. Do you ever lose your cool? Do you ever let your patients get to you emotionally?"

"Well, no, I don't. And neither will you, Dina. With time, you'll develop good professional distance." A nice way of saying that after a while you just stopped caring.

"But I don't want to develop 'professional distance,'" she said, a worried look on her face. "I want the people I work with to know that I see them as real people, not just patients, not just a collection of symptoms. Is that really such a terrible thing?"

I smiled at her indulgently. "It's never a good idea. You can't help people if you're emotionally involved. You'll have to lose some of your idealism. Tonight was a good example; that fellow couldn't hear a word you said. You would have been better off watching the television, reading a book, letting him rant on. It might have actually helped him; he would have realized he had no audience and quieted down. More importantly, if you'd done that, you wouldn't be so wound up now."

"But he wasn't completely out of touch," she insisted. "He knew there had just been a bombing. He thinks the intifada is a punishment for our 'godless arrogance.' Maybe he isn't as crazy as he seems."

"He was totally irrational. We're at war over a piece of land. It has nothing to do with arrogance, godless or otherwise."

She leaned in toward me, and I caught the trace of a delicate perfume. "But so many of the things he was saying were interesting. Even lyrical. And thought-provoking. There was something about him . . ."

Two coffees were unceremoniously plunked down on the table by our surly young waitress. I wondered if it was run-of-the-mill Israeli rudeness or a sign of disdain for people quietly enjoying a coffee mere hours after a bombing. Dina added cream and sugar to her coffee with excessive concentration, struggling to stay calm. She finally took a sip and looked up at me with sad, frightened eyes.

"Don't worry," I assured her. "With time you'll grow thicker skin, I promise. The first hospitalization is always a little traumatic—I still remember mine from more than fifteen years ago. And to have it happen at the exact same time as a bombing downtown . . ." I shook my head sympathetically. "It's no wonder you're as upset as you are."

"I really liked him," she said. "Do you think it will help him to be shut up in a hospital ward, where no one will listen to him? I feel like I failed him."

"Dina, the guy was a full-blown paranoid schizophrenic. Any sense you made of his rambling was out of your own unconscious need to heal him. There are drugs that can help people like that." I made my voice as soothing as I could. "If you're going to be successful in this field, you'll have to work on your own countertransference issues. I'm going out on a limb here, but I'm guessing that there was someone in your own family you were helpless to heal."

"You're right," she whispered, her eyes filling with tears.

"Do you want to tell me about it?"

"I don't know. It's embarrassing."

I picked up my coffee and took a sip, watching her with a deliberately patient, sympathetic gaze. If there was one thing I had mastered over the course of the years, it was the power of strategic silence.

She looked down at her drink, gathering her resolve, then back up at me. "When I was very young, my father left my mother for a younger woman. You can't imagine how humiliating that was. My mother had to raise us alone, and she was stressed all the time, her eyes always red and brimming with tears. I wasn't the oldest, but I was the only girl in the family, and I thought it was up to me to take care of the household, to make life easier for her. One day, when I was eight years old, she started crying and crying and couldn't stop. I got really scared, and finally I called my father to ask him what to do. When he came over, he said she was having a 'nervous breakdown,' and arranged for her to be hospitalized. The whole experience was devastating." She paused, collecting herself. "She was never the same after that. I still haven't forgiven myself for calling him. If I had been able to handle things better, maybe she would have recovered on her own."

She was so young, so vulnerable. How did people like her get through life? I wanted to tell her to leave this profession, leave this war-torn country, become an accountant in a place like Sweden. She kept snuffling her tears like she'd done in my office, wrinkling up her nose in that adorable way. I reached over and took her hands in mine as she raised her watery brown eyes, large drops of liquid hanging precariously on her lashes.

"You're not the only one who went into this field to heal someone they love," I said, in as gentle a tone as I could muster. "You need to understand that very well, or it will interfere with your work. You have to separate your mother's pain—"

There was a flash of movement and I heard something clatter noisily on the table. Startled, I pulled my hands away from Dina's, staring stupidly from Nava's face to the wedding ring that had been dropped, with exquisite precision, into my empty coffee cup. She was wearing a crisply tailored maroon jacket and the brightly colored silk scarf I had bought for her birthday, tied just so. Elegant, as always.

"Don't even think about coming home tonight."

"Nava, you don't understand. This is Dina; she's a new intern at the clinic. I left you a message. We just hospitalized a patient. It took a long time because of the suicide attack, and—"

"I've understood for years, Kobi." Her voice was full of anger and pain, but her posture was poised and erect, like the dancer she was. "Right in our own neighborhood. Bombs going off in the middle of the city and you're pursuing your latest conquest. She's young enough to be your daughter. And just a month before the bat mitzvah; Yudit will be devastated." She raised her head to look out the window, as if speaking to the windswept saplings. "Don't you dare come back to the house. I'll call the police if you do. You can send someone to pick up your stuff; I'll pack it myself. The locks will be changed tomorrow." I started to speak but she cut me off. "It's over, Kobi . . . for good." She turned on her heels and with sublime self-righteousness made her way to the door, gracefully skirting the clutter of empty tables and chairs.

I frantically fished in my pocket for money and dropped a twenty shekel note on the table while scooping Nava's coffee-sticky ring out of the cup. "It'll be fine, Dina," I blurted out, grabbing my jacket. The girl looked shell-shocked, but I'd have to deal with that later. Clumsily, I negotiated my way around the obstacle path of tables to the front door.

"You only got what you deserved," cried a loud-mouthed crone, and the handful of café patrons laughed and applauded. Couldn't anyone in this country ever mind their own goddamned business? Nava must have been taking a short cut through the alley and spotted me through the window. What kind of bum luck was that? I should have been more careful after everything that had happened these past couple of weeks. By the time I made it out the door and into the cold, harsh wind, she was long out of sight. As I stood stunned on the sidewalk, wondering what to do next, I felt Dina slip out the door behind me, watched her race down the street toward the intersection of Rachel Imeinu, clutching her bag to her chest as if being chased by a thief.

I spent the night, and then the weekend, at Yossi's flat, sleepless on his foldout couch, trying to evade the whirlwind his four-year-old twin boys habitually left in their wake, and listening to his American wife, Elizabeth, extol Nava's virtues and berate me for my selfish stupidity. I called home numerous times, leaving increasingly desperate messages of apology and explanation on the answering machine, which had already been changed to erase my presence from the household. I could imagine Nava glaring at the ringing phone, explaining to Yudit in graphic detail why her no-good *abba* wasn't going to live with them anymore, Yudit's serious little face scrunched in worried thought as she took it all in.

Yossi walked over to the house Saturday afternoon to pick up my car and watched Nava hurl three garbage bags full of clothes and sundry possessions into the back seat, conveying to him with each angry toss that I should stop leaving useless messages; that Yudit was just as furious and was refusing to speak to me; that I shouldn't even consider attending the bat mitzvah. As the car pulled away she yelled out, for good measure, that she would be contacting a lawyer first thing Sunday morning to initiate proceedings for a divorce. As he dragged the garbage bags into the flat, Yossi shook his head to convey the hopelessness of it all. "That's one angry lady, my friend. You better stop calling—give her some space."

It was almost a relief when the weekend finally ended and I could return, groggy and disoriented as I was, to the stultifying routines of my job.

2

The first thing I noticed when I entered my office Sunday morning was the missing dartboard. A Chagall reproduction hung in its place, a romanticized shtetl scene with scantily clad lovers floating upside down under a garish moonlight, a cow head leering from the rooftops.

I stared at it for a few minutes in horror, then poked my head back into the waiting room. At the front desk, a receptionist was busily processing papers for a long line of waiting patients. It was the one with the copper hair and sassy hips. What the hell was her name?

I walked up to the desk and craned my head in her direction. No response.

"Uh . . ."

"Tamar." She continued to shuffle papers around her desk.

"Tamar, of course. Do you know anything about that picture someone hung in my office?"

"All I know is that the new *Americana* boss was looking for you." She tossed me a baleful glance before launching into a rapid-fire explanation of clinic procedures to the patient at the front of the line.

I went back to my office and stared at the new painting some more. Finally I picked up the phone.

"Jezebel?"

"Ah, yes, Kobi. I've been looking for you all morning. Can you come to my office right away?"

"I have a patient in five minutes. Do you happen to know—"

"Well then immediately after that. At 11:00?"

"I usually take lunch—"

"It's 9:55, and I gather you just stepped in. Your lunch can wait. Be here at 11:00 sharp."

The click of the phone was ominous. I knew she'd had her eye on me; I could have at least made an effort to come in on time. I left Yossi a message canceling our 11:15 squash game at the YMCA. The 10:00 never showed, so

I spent the hour sprawled out on my leather recliner devising clever retorts to her imagined accusations, righteously defending my professionalism and wounded honor. At 11:00, I pulled myself out of the familiar reverie and forced my way toward her open door.

She motioned me to sit while finishing her phone call, glaring at me as she spoke. When she finally hung up the phone, I steeled for the thirty-nine lashes.

"You've been at Jerusalem Hospital a long time, Kobi."

"Twelve years at the clinic. Five as chief psychologist."

"And I've only been here a couple of months. You may think it's premature for me to make judgments, but that's what I was hired to do. Things have been very lax around here."

"Well, that depends—"

"I think you'd better let me finish."

I wondered what she had looked like thirty years ago, before she'd started stuffing herself into tightly tailored suits. Had she ever had a soft edge? I tried to imagine her as a young woman but could see nothing but this click-heeled harridan.

"There's a lot of discontent among the staff," she began, her voice stern.

"People like to complain about their bosses," I said calmly. "It's human nature. You can't take that kind of thing too seriously."

"I've been hired to take it seriously," she snapped. "Caseloads are far too large. There's not enough psychiatric support, too much redundant paperwork, and no substantive training. The waiting lists are endless—the entire country is reeling from trauma, and it takes three months to get an appointment. The clinicians and support staff have given me numerous suggestions of how to make this clinic function more efficiently. They say that talking to you is like talking to a wall."

I nodded. "In this town, people find that quite effective."

She ignored my lame attempt at humor. "It's not only inefficiency they complain of. You come in late, you leave early. You disappear for hours at a time. Your caseload is a fraction the size of the other clinicians."

"Well you know, there's a lot of administrative work—"

"You're seen as, let's see . . ." She lifted her chin to perch a pair of reading glasses on the end of her beaked nose and scanned a long page of hand-scrawled notes. "Inaccessible . . . aloof . . . arrogant . . . not a member of the team . . . out of touch with the field . . ."

"I've always wondered what that phrase meant. You know, there's way too much jargon—"

She took her glasses off with a snap of her wrist. "There are charts that have been languishing on your desk since the Flood."

"Now in all fairness, that's well before my time." I grinned at my own joke, but her face remained stony.

"You showed an Arabic movie at the last staff meeting. Without subtitles. Is that your idea of in-service training?"

"It's a great film—I thought it would be dubbed. It's really an interesting case study of the Oedipal urge that underlies—"

"We are overrun with severe grief reactions and post-traumatic stress, and you're worried about the Oedipal urge?"

"Now look, you can't just ignore the fundamentals—"

A muscle moved in her jaw. "OK, forget the outmoded theories and utter inadequacy of your in-service trainings. There are other, more serious complaints—rumors of inappropriate relationships with patients."

"Inappropriate. That's another great word. If it were eliminated from the therapeutic vocabulary—"

She interrupted me again, her voice steely. "No one has yet filed an official complaint, but there's a lot of ugly gossip going around."

"I'm really shocked that you would listen to unsubstantiated rumors," I said indignantly, my mind quickly flicking through the possibilities.

"The new intern, Dina. She called this morning to say that she's quitting her internship. She won't tell anyone why." That one I hadn't expected.

"There could be any number of reasons," I stammered.

"You were the last one seen with her." She paused, watching me closely.

I regained my composure. If this was her big gotcha moment, she'd blown it. After all, nothing had happened between Dina and me! "Well of course, that must be it," I said in the no-nonsense tone I used to calm hysterical patients. "We had to hospitalize a psychotic patient Thursday night. Dina asked me to help out—she'd never been involved with a forced hospitalization. You know how stressful those can be; we were there for hours. And it was the same evening as the King George Street bombing. You can just imagine what was going on in that waiting room. By the way," I added, "we should speak to the ER about finding a more protected location for psychiatric patients. We could see and hear almost everything." I shook my head. "It was terribly stressful for her. She's awfully young, you know." I sat back and let out a world-weary sigh. "My guess is that the experience made her realize that she's just not cut out for this work. Better to realize it earlier than later." I looked at her expectantly.

Her expression had not changed. "You expect me to believe that story?"

"Why not?" I sat forward again. "What are you implying?"

"You know what I'm implying."

"But you have no proof at all . . ." My mind raced. This was insane. Of all the examples she might have given, this was the one she was fixated on?

She glared at me. "You're right. I have no proof that anything untoward happened. She won't say anything to anyone. But there's a lot of whispering going around."

"Look, this is a big misunderstanding. The receptionists don't like me very much. They start rumors. You know how that is."

"And why do you think they don't like you?"

"Oh, I don't know. An authority thing. I think there's some unconscious envy, and—"

"Kobi, I'm putting you on probation." It took a moment for the words to sink in.

"But . . . I don't think you can actually do that . . . and . . ."

"Three months. Passover begins Wednesday night. After the holiday, I'll take over all your administrative duties. You will start coming in on time and leaving on time. You will get the standard hour for lunch. Your caseload is going up by a third, and you're going to keep on top of the paperwork. Starting today, the receptionists are taking full control over your schedule— I've given them explicit instructions in that regard. I want all those charts completed and off your desk. You can use the holiday to get a jump start." She looked at me sharply. "And make sure the rumors stop. Is that clear?"

I stared at her, my mind in a daze.

"Kobi." She leaned forward and her voice took on the familiar, exasperated tone of my elementary school principal. "I hope you've been listening. You start behaving like a professional or you're fired. The hospital is undergoing major cutbacks and reorganization; I don't like it any more than you do. But your squash buddy ran this clinic like a country club, and those days are over. They hired me because I was trained in America, where productivity and accountability are taken seriously. Where people sue if they don't get appropriate treatment. That's the model the whole country is going toward, and not only in health care." She sat back again. "We all have to start getting used to it."

I continued to stare at her like a dumb kid.

"But it's not just that," she continued, her voice suddenly pressured and earnest. "At a time of such extreme collective distress, mental health clinics have a particular responsibility to the nation. We have to function in as professional and efficient a manner as possible. We owe at least that to our fellow citizens. Don't you agree?"

I nodded my head, still unable to find my voice. She sighed deeply, then got up to let me know I was dismissed.

"What happened to my dartboard?" I finally blurted out.

She shook her head in disbelief.

"Inappropriate, eh?"

"You've got three months, *habibi*."

In my office, I leaned back in my desk chair and gingerly inched my feet onto the top of the desk, careful not to dislodge the mountains of haphazardly piled charts. I took off my glasses and wearily rubbed my eyes. The Chagall was marginally more tolerable as a formless splash of color. But returning the glasses to my nose, the floating lovers came back into focus, their smitten grins as irritating as ever. I picked a rubber band off the desk and flipped it across the room, missing by a good meter the woman's upside-down breasts. What was the harm in a dartboard? I would now be reduced to shooting rubber bands like a sixth-grade boy, flipping paper clips, tossing pushpins at random targets in the room. It was an elemental male impulse, this ejaculatory thrust into the world, but what would that castrating witch know about that.

Appealing to my national duty—that was the last straw. Immigrants could be insufferable in that way. Most of them hadn't even served in the army. I had already done enough for my esteemed country, rooting out terrorists in the alleys of Ramallah. Did she really believe that providing efficient mental health services meant a damn when every bus and market and café was a target for a suicide bomb? What difference could it possibly make to the national psyche if one bored psychologist took out some of his frustrations with a dartboard?

She was right about one thing—the country was changing, and fast. It was becoming a big corporation, swallowing up the little mom-and-pop store it had been just a few years ago. People were enthusiastically pursuing the Israeli version of the American dream, throwing around words like "productivity" and "accountability," smiling polite little smiles, saying "Have a nice day" while suing each other into bankruptcy. In the old Israel, people would growl at you on the street but you could trust them with uncounted money. In the old Israel, your lunch hour could stretch into a long, lazy afternoon and no one would ever notice or care.

I randomly picked a chart out of one of the piles and glanced at the name. Havah Ashkenazi. Who the hell was that? Was I really supposed to make up years' worth of sessions and treatment plans out of whole cloth?

Nava would gloat if she heard about my probation. It was beyond me why this latest incident with Dina had set her off like that. It had all been a misunderstanding—I wouldn't really have seduced that innocent young thing. Not that it hadn't crossed my mind, but it had been nothing more than idle fantasy. Anyway, it was impossible to be a man in this field and not play around a bit. The patients were almost exclusively female, all of them hungry for some comforting male attention. Sure, there were psychiatrists, with their mind-numbing drugs; but I was the sensitive therapist, and all I had to do was stroke my chin thoughtfully and it made these women melt. It wasn't such a big deal—they were frivolous rolls on the therapy couch. I shouldn't have gotten so brazen, staying out to all hours on flimsy excuses. But I was a good father and provider, never took those flings seriously. Did none of that matter to Nava? And to bar me, now, from my daughter's bat mitzvah party? What had snapped in her that she could toss me, so thoroughly and unceremoniously, out the door?

I flung a paper clip at the doorknob and was rewarded with a satisfying ping. I stared at the upside-down lovers in the Chagall reproduction and felt another surge of hatred for the painting. I imagined coming in one day to find the weightless lovers fallen and crashed to the pavement.

The telephone made me jump.

"Dr. Benami, your 12:00 patient is here."

What the hell was that about? I never scheduled a patient at 12:00. I had already missed my squash game and hadn't had a bite of lunch.

"Are you sure it's for me?"

"Oh, yes. We've been told to schedule you in more tightly. Didn't you check the day's appointments?" Her voice was thick with sarcasm.

"Well, no. Who is it?"

"Penina Mizrachi."

The name rang a bell, but I couldn't quite place her.

"Tell her I'm running a little late. Tell her it will be at least a half hour."

A long, accusatory silence preceded the frigid reply. "I'll let her know."

I stared helplessly at the mounds of dog-eared charts for a few seconds, then angrily flipped another rubber band across the room. I had been aiming at the doorknob again but hit the lamp by the side of the couch instead, making it totter on its base. What if I broke a few things in this sterile, hospital-neat office? Without my dartboard, the office would now be littered with the detritus of my office supply requisitions, and the cleaning lady could add her lilting, Arabic soprano to the choir of voices singing out for my dismissal.

But didn't I have a goddamned right to eat lunch? I made sure the receptionist was absorbed in conversation with a patient before summoning up a forced nonchalance and sauntering out of my office. I pretended to casually check the papers in my mailbox, then took a beeline out the waiting room to the stairwell beyond.

3

When I returned to the office, I found a fuming Penina Mizrachi beached outside my door. I suggested to Penina, who I now remembered as the fat woman with the garishly dyed and braided hair, that we reschedule for another day, but she would have none of it. Once in my office, she perched on the edge of the patient's couch, clutching her oversized handbag in her lap, and launched into a long, whiny complaint about the ways in which I—like her husband, grown children, and a random assortment of neighbors—didn't afford her the respect she was due. She had been on time for her appointment, as she always was, and had seen me ever-so-casually slip out of the waiting room. Why was her time not as important as mine? I might have answered that she, unlike even minimally functioning people like myself, had no job and no schedule to keep, and what difference did it make if she spent her time in our waiting room or sunk in her couch staring at celebrity talk shows? But I held my tongue and watched her substantial bosom heave up and down with the weight of her lot, wondering at the effort and expense and poor judgment that had culminated in her odd coiffure, listening intently to the squeaking sound her breath made on the rare occasions when she took a chance and paused. She needn't have bothered, as I had no intention of interrupting her numbing monologue. Long ago she had married a man who was unabashedly in love with another woman and had kept the affair going through all the years of their marriage. Saddled with a slew of unruly kids, she had never had the confidence or self-respect to walk out on him. Listening to her, I found myself longing for Nava, thinking about her lithe body and ropy neck, the proud way she angled her head in public. Nava had dignity, self-respect—she wouldn't put up forever with a no-good philanderer. I was suddenly filled with an overwhelming sense of loss. What had I been thinking? Nava was nothing like this pathetic specimen, this Penina Mizrachi, who had let herself grow fat and lazy and reconciled to a lifetime of neglect and humiliation. I held tight to my rising grief, my face frozen into concerned listening mode, my sympathetic grunts modulating to the wavelike heaving of Penina's chronic, languishing despair.

When the session was over, I watched her dutifully get in line at the reception desk to confirm her next visit. I had barely heard a word she had said, yet she was visibly calmer. Was she really so lonely that even this pretense of caring companionship made her life more bearable? I rummaged through the piles on my desk for her long out-of-date chart, then stared at it a while, wondering what I could possibly write about this session. "Patient continues to have symptoms of depression and anxiety. Patient continues to feel unappreciated and unloved. Patient continues to lead a useless, pathetic life. Patient continues to bore husband, children, and therapist to distraction." I tossed the chart onto the floor in disgust.

The afternoon dragged on, patient after desperate patient. Jezebel was right that the intifada was causing a dramatic increase in the demand for our services, but I wasn't nearly as confident as she was that our role in the midst of this social dysfunction was entirely benevolent. Yes, we could sometimes provide superficial relief through medications, or even therapy, but weren't we just enabling all the feckless politicians on both sides who allowed this insanity to continue? My 3:00 patient was typical—an eight-year-old boy who had stopped speaking and developed violent outbursts after witnessing the Sbarro restaurant bombing in August. More than seven months later, he still hadn't said a word. His mother, frantic with worry, was herself suffering from insomnia, chronic nausea, and other post-traumatic symptoms, which her psychiatrist had been trying for months to alleviate through the right combination of brightly colored pills. But wasn't hers a perfectly normal reaction to watching a pizza parlor in downtown Jerusalem, on a hot summer day, suddenly explode into flames?

At 6:00 I thought I could finally call it a day, but the receptionists had wasted no time scheduling in extra patients, vengefully taking advantage of my predicament. They had assigned me a new patient, of all things, to the 6:00 hour. I hadn't done an intake in months—if she showed, it would mean reams of paperwork. And, as Jezebel had made abundantly clear, I'd have to complete it, too.

I petitioned whatever gods might be up there for reprieve, but being the confirmed atheist I was, my plea to the heavens was duly unheard. About ten minutes into the hour, just after I had successfully flung a rubber band over the engraved, ornamental quill pen Yudit had bought me for my forty-fifth birthday, a woman barged into the room. Why hadn't the receptionist called to tell me she was here? I flung my legs off the desk, knocking a few more charts onto the floor, but she didn't notice a thing. She was in full story before I'd even stood up.

"Dr. Benami? Thank God, I finally have someone to talk to." She was untangling herself from a huge, fringed shawl that wrapped her head like a mummy, talking all the while. "You can't imagine what it's like being followed all the time. I can't take it anymore." The tears were already starting to spring up—another desperate, weepy broad.

"Excuse me, but did you sign in with the receptionist? I'll be needing the intake forms, and—"

"I was so late, I didn't want to wait in line," she said impatiently. Her eyes flicked around the room and finally landed on me, round and dark. "His crazy friends are stalking me again. I have to dodge them whenever I leave the house, taking roundabout routes through back alleys. That's why I'm late wherever I go, but otherwise they follow me and harass me, you have no idea what it's like." She paused to push a long strand of curly black hair out of her face, fixing me with a stare. "You have to forgive me, Doctor, and you such a busy man. I know, they told me—the chief psychologist! They must realize what a tough case this is—everyone in Jerusalem knows about me." And with this she sunk into my recliner, the tears beginning to gush.

"I'm afraid you're sitting in my chair. The patient usually sits—"

"I know how busy you are, Doctor, but you have to help me!" She launched into another tirade but was so blubbery with tears I couldn't understand a word. Grandiose, paranoid, hysterical—it was going to be a long hour. I reconciled myself to the stiff couch, a stranger in my own office, noticing that the piles of charts on my desk looked particularly precarious from the patients' angle. Probably not the most reassuring sight—I made a mental note to at least arrange them into neat stacks. The woman was going on and on, sniffling and blowing her nose, complaining about her husband. Another miserable, tortured relationship. I'd heard the routine countless times from every possible angle. But this was an intake, I reminded myself; I'd have to settle her down and get at least a few details if that paperwork would ever get done. I could always pick up the forms from the receptionist at the end of the session.

"Uh, Mrs. . . ."

"Tzur. But please, call me Israela. Everyone does." She looked up at me, her eyes filled with tears, muddy brown pools of desperation.

She would have once been an olive-toned beauty. She was still attractive, but her face was prematurely etched with worry lines. Mid-thirties, I'd guess. Slim, still dressing like a hippie, in bangles and gold chains and flowing skirts, layers of flouncy material, laced leather sandals. I wondered if she shaved her legs under those billowing skirts; these gypsy types often didn't. She had dark, curly hair, long and wild, glinted with silver streaks. Her eyes were her most striking feature, large and soupy. And she was built, with full breasts straining at her white, cotton blouse. But there was something peculiar about the way she held herself, I couldn't quite put my finger on it . . .

"Doctor, what do you think I should do?" She was staring at me intently.

"Well, Mrs . . . uh . . . Israela, I think it's way too soon to start talking about solutions. I'll need to know a lot more about you before I have any idea how I might be able to help. This is an intake session, which means we're here to gather lots of information: what the problem is, when it began, your early history. Based on what I learn, we'll formulate a treatment plan. I know you're upset right now, but why don't you see if you can tell me in a few words what problem brought you here today."

She reached an arm out to pluck another tissue from the box, then grimaced in pain, rubbing the side of her neck with the other hand.

"Is something wrong?"

"The muscles go into spasm when I'm upset," she said, massaging her neck with her left hand as she dried her eyes with the right. "My husband complains about it all the time. He thinks I do it on purpose, for sympathy, or as an excuse not to listen to him. But that's totally unfair. It just happens whenever I get upset."

This threatened to release a new wave of sobs. I went to my desk, picked up a notebook and pen, and sat back down on the edge of the couch. "Israela," I said in a firm tone. "Why don't you tell me, as clearly and succinctly as you can, what makes you seek treatment at this time."

She calmed down instantly. The paper and pen was a great trick, I'd found. Helped even the most histrionic women focus, at least for a little while.

"Well, like I was telling you, my husband, he's the center of my life. He's everything to me. But the truth is, he doesn't treat me very well."

"In what way?" I jotted a note, then let the pen hover over the paper for effect.

"It's not his fault, really. He's very insecure, that's all."

"And how does he show that insecurity?"

Her eyes were darting around the room, the telltale sign of a battered wife. I'd bet my last shekel she was another bruised-up woman about to protect her beloved abuser.

"Well, for one thing, he's very secretive. He's almost never home, but even when he is, he sneaks around like a thief." She sighed deeply. "He doesn't like showing his face."

"He's that shy?" I asked.

"Oh no, not at all. He's just . . . well . . . *sensitive.*"

Yeah, right. So sensitive he'd probably kick her around the room if she happened to be standing in the way.

"I see. And does he show this 'sensitivity' in other ways as well?"

"Yes, well . . . he can be very jealous. He's always imagining that I'm having affairs. He even brags about how jealous he is to his friends, as if it were proof of how much he loves me."

I made my voice soft and sympathetic. "Does he threaten you?"

"Well, sometimes, I guess." The tears were welling up, but this time she fought to keep them down. "Yes," she whispered, "he threatens me a lot."

"What does he threaten you with?"

"Oh, terrible things. How he'll hurt me, humiliate me, destroy our house. But not directly, he never threatens me directly."

"What do you mean?" I asked.

"Well, like I said, he's hardly ever around. Months can go by and not even a word from him. He doesn't call, doesn't tell me where he is. So he sends messages, through his friends, the ones who are stalking me."

"Threatening messages?"

She nodded, absentmindedly rubbing her neck.

"Have you ever reported these stalkers to the police?"

"Oh, no, of course not. They're his friends; they're just trying to help him. And they're doing it for my own good, I know." She lowered her eyes, a delicate crease forming between her eyebrows.

"Has he ever carried out any of his threats? Has he ever gotten violent with you?" I asked gently.

"Well, sort of . . . But none of this is really his fault! I haven't been a good enough wife. I haven't been the kind of wife he wanted."

"That would hardly give him the right—"

"I know." It was barely a whisper. We sat a few moments in silence.

"When's the last time you saw him?" I asked.

"Oh, my goodness, it's been such a long time. I'm not even sure. Maybe a year? Or even longer."

That was straining credulity. "You haven't seen or heard from him in over a year? Are you sure he's OK?"

"Of course he's OK," she said. "His friends see him all the time."

There was something very odd going on here. I needed a new line of inquiry.

"What kind of work does he do?" I asked.

"He's a . . . an entrepreneur."

"What do you mean?"

"Oh, it's kind of hard to explain. He's always busy with one thing or another. Got his finger in a million pies." She smiled weakly, as if to apologize for the obvious evasion.

The husband was starting to sound like a shady character. I wondered if he might be part of the Israeli Mafia. Sometimes these Mafia types had to go underground for long periods of time, keeping their whereabouts unknown even to their wives. That would explain the lackeys with their violent threats. But was she covering up for him, or did she really not know? Now I was genuinely curious.

"Do you have any idea where he's been this past year?" I asked.

"Not really. Even before that, he was never around much. He has an office in the house, with a separate entrance. Sometimes I think I hear him shuffling around down there, but I'm never sure. The office has a couch, but I don't think he ever sleeps there anymore. Maybe his friends put him up. He must hang around with them a lot; you should see how they worship him." She looked embarrassed. "Like I said, I don't really know where he is."

"Do you think he may have another woman?" I asked gently.

She broke into a pained laugh. "Him? With another woman? Don't be ridiculous. I'm the only love of his life."

Even for a battered woman, that level of denial was extreme. I'd seen my share of absentee husbands, usually with a mistress or two in town, sometimes a slew of kids, and the wife sitting at home all innocent and surprised. Did he really sneak into his office, send threatening messages? It seemed much more likely that the guy had set up a whole new life, that she imagined his little visits, had made up the whole story about the stalking to convince herself that she was still married. Could an intelligent woman really be so blind?

And she did seem intelligent. I'd heard a lot of bizarre tales in my time, but something about her had caught my attention. There was the sharp, penetrating way she looked at me, even through her tears, that was disconcerting. I wondered if she was trying to hear my mind's commentary, to see through my pretense. It was a question that usually didn't concern me much, but I was feeling a little sensitive myself these days. It occurred to me that from the couch there was nothing much to look at other than the mess of charts; from the recliner I could always keep an eye on my reflection in the glass of the window. Without those reassuring peeks at my professional mien—the gently receding hairline, strong chin, and wire-framed glasses that made me look distinguished, even professorial—I felt, instead, naked and exposed.

"Israela, given the fact that your husband hasn't been around for so long and that he has this violent streak, I'm not clear why you would want to stay in this relationship. You could claim desertion, or abuse—file for divorce, start a new life."

"Oh, but I've given you such a terrible impression of him! He loves me so much! And he's the center of my life, he's everything to me! And we've been married such a long time. You'd really need to hear the whole story. This isn't a marriage one gets out of lightly!"

"One never gets out of a marriage lightly," I said, in my reassuring, doctor voice. It was the party line, but of course it wasn't true. Nava had tossed her wedding ring into a coffee cup, and poof, she was out. I wondered again what she would think listening to Penina or Israela, the disdain she would hold for the multitude of women who remained loyal and committed to men who abandoned and abused them. At least I'd never disappeared for months or gotten violent. Why didn't Nava appreciate what she had in me?

Israela was staring at me, a curious, almost bemused, look on her face.

I snapped myself back to my professional bearing. "Israela, it sounds like this has been going on for a long time. I'm still not clear why you're seeking treatment now. How do you think therapy will be able to help you?"

She leaned forward in the chair. "You're not the first person to tell me I should divorce him, forget all about him. All the neighbors say the same thing. But I can't. I miss him so much. You can't imagine how awful it is for me."

"But you haven't seen or heard from him in over a year . . ."

"I can't leave him!" she cried. "He'd be lost without me. I can't destroy him like that after all he's done for me! And I'd be lost without *him*. He's the one who rescued me from my horrible childhood, the one who gives my life meaning and purpose. I'll never divorce him. Do you think you can help me? Do you think you can help me be the kind of wife he wants me to be?" At this, she broke into another wave of heaving sobs.

Her reality testing was tenuous at best. The guy was happily shacked up with another woman, had practically forgotten she existed, but she couldn't leave him because he'd be devastated. *She never saw him, but he was the only thing giving her life purpose. He'd be lost without her, she'd be lost without him.* The thought of even trying to tease out the truth of this bizarre, dysfunctional marriage exhausted me.

I needed more context to figure this out. "Tell me about the rest of your life, Israela. Do you have children? Do you work? What about your family?"

"I have no family; I was an orphan," she replied. "I don't have any life outside of him; that's part of the problem. Like I told you, he's insanely jealous. I'm not to have any friends, male or female. He would kill me if I ever got a paying job; he doesn't even want me walking about the neighborhood by myself. And since the intifada started, he's even more opposed to my leaving the house—he's terribly worried that something could happen to me. You know that couple who died in Thursday's bombing on King George Street? They left two orphans, and she was five months pregnant." She paused for effect. "He totally freaks out whenever something like that happens."

"Well, of course," I said, "it affects us all. But we can't just stay locked up in our homes."

"I agree, but he doesn't see it that way. That's why I wear that enormous shawl. I sneak around like a criminal just to leave the house." Her voice went down to a frightened whisper. "He's always been obsessed with the idea that I might be having an affair, but it's not true. Don't let them tell you otherwise!"

"Don't let *who* tell me otherwise?"

"His friends, they're everywhere!" She stared out the window like a terrified child, her neck stiff, her shoulders hunched in fear, and I turned to look, half-expecting to see a spying face hanging from the fourth-floor sill. Her voice was rising with panic. "He'll be furious when he hears I came to see you. Just you wait and see. When word gets out, they'll come to see you too. They'll tell you terrible lies about me. Don't believe a word they say!"

I kept my voice calm and professional. "But if your husband's never around, how would he even know what you're doing? And how would these friends of his know—"

"He knows everything!" she shrieked, in a panicked voice. "He sees everything I do! Don't you understand?"

My heart sank. This was not, after all, some silly woman in delusional denial about an absentee husband; it was, more likely than not, a case of psychotic paranoia. I was getting the sick feeling that the day might end with another forced hospitalization. I kicked myself mentally for allowing myself to be bullied into taking on these new additions to my caseload. Didn't I have enough trouble? I should have stood up to that bitch and refused. I'd served my time in the trenches, and I was now an administrator. Didn't that count for anything? How had I gotten myself into this mess?

But even as I groaned at the hours of extra work, my diagnostic wheels were busily spinning. She was extremely dramatic in tone and mannerism, which was not typical for a schizophrenic. But then again, paranoid schizophrenics could surprise you—it couldn't be ruled out. With such a full range of emotional expression, she certainly didn't fit the pattern of a paranoid personality disorder. As a matter of fact, the most striking thing about her was her exaggerated affect, which suggested a histrionic or borderline personality disorder. Histrionics could be very loose in their reality testing, but her paranoia was extreme. And what about that neck? Histrionics often somatized their symptoms. Was this a physical manifestation of an extreme mind-body dissociation? Or maybe the whole thing was a manic episode. I needed more information.

But before I could ask another question, she offered her own reality check.

"No, of course you don't understand, it sounds crazy to you," she said. "You're probably thinking you should lock me up. And maybe you're right! I've been stuck in this insane relationship for so long I hardly know what's real anymore."

I was relieved to hear her so lucid and self-reflective. It was a good sign. "So you question your own sense of reality?" I asked.

"Sometimes," she said, her voice soft and pleading. "But if you met him, even for an instant, you'd understand. There's something about him. Once you've been in his presence you never forget it. When you meet his friends, crazy as they are, you'll see how devoted they are to him, how they love him with all their hearts. Maybe then you'll get an inkling of what kind of a man he is . . . and he chose *me*! Of all the women in the world he might have married, he chose *me*!" She turned her sad, luminous eyes toward me. "You think I'm totally crazy, don't you?"

Yes, I thought, *you're totally nuts*, but something inside me was stirred by her story. For just a moment I could feel her love, shot through, as it was, with terror and wounded pain. Despite my dalliances, I had always been attracted to my wife. I was devastated that she'd thrown me out, already missed the life we'd had together. But now I was wondering: had I ever in my life loved anyone the way Israela loved her husband, or even, for that matter, the way Nava had once loved me?

The feeling was gone in an instant, and I pulled myself back into role.

"What's his name?" I asked.

She looked away, rubbing her neck as she stared out the window.

"You don't want to tell me his name?"

She looked back at me. "Oh, no, I would, but . . . it's just . . . very hard to pronounce."

"That's OK. I don't need to pronounce it." I picked up my notebook and poised my pen expectantly.

She stared at me a few minutes longer before responding. "I call him Y," she finally said. "Everyone just calls him Y."

I let the notebook drop back into my lap. What the hell was she hiding? Was he some kind of notorious criminal whose name I'd instantly recognize? Could it be, even more bizarrely, that she didn't know or couldn't pronounce his name? Or, it suddenly occurred to me, was it possible that the husband didn't even exist?

Our time was almost up and I felt totally disoriented. Maybe it was the effect of sitting on the patient side of the room. Maybe I was just too distracted by my own problems. But I had just sat with this woman for almost an hour with nothing to show for it. I'd gotten almost no essential information, didn't even have a diagnosis. Maybe I was just getting rusty.

I debated getting an emergency psychiatric consult. The last thing I needed was word getting out that I'd failed to properly treat some psychotic patient. On the other hand, I was on the outs with all the psychiatrists, and any one of them would take perverse pleasure in the shoddy intake I had just done. She was paranoid and delusional, that was clear, but she was also lucid and calm. I decided to take the chance that she could hold on through the end of the holiday. Hopefully, she'd never come back. If she did, I'd be sure and do a full mental status exam, get a proper diagnosis. I decided to let it go.

"Israela, there's a lot more information I'll need before I can know how to help you," I said. "After Passover, I'll want to get a full life history and a broader sense of your day-to-day life. I'm going to ask the receptionist to schedule you for the first day after the holiday. Will that work for you?"

She nodded, her eyes glistening with new tears. "Passover is a hard time for me—I always miss him terribly during the holiday. I clean the house obsessively, trying to show what a good wife I can be, hoping that will draw him back to me." We sat in silence for a long minute. "It never seems to work," she finally said, "but at least the house gets clean."

I laughed, and she smiled back shyly. A sense of humor was always a good sign.

"Are you sure you'll be OK over the holiday?" I asked.

She nodded slightly, her whole upper body moving stiffly with the effort. She took her appointment slip and got up to leave, her brow furrowing as she glanced around the room.

"You know, Doctor, you should really speak to the cleaning lady. This office is littered with rubber bands and paper clips."

She wrapped her head tightly in her shawl and fearfully scrutinized the waiting room before venturing out the office door.

4

I picked up the forms from the now deserted reception area and stayed late to write up what I could remember of the intake, fudging the details I had neglected to ask. That evening, I plucked a cold schnitzel from Yossi's refrigerator and, seated at his kitchen table, combed the classified ads for cheap rentals, while the twins engaged in a raucous shoot-out in the living room and Elizabeth chided me from the bedroom, insisting loudly to Yossi that I be out before the holiday.

Even in the midst of an intifada, Jerusalem apartments were obscenely overpriced. Most of the secular, middle-class population had already fled to the coastal plain. American and French foreigners had bought up and renovated the vacated apartments, which now rented for outlandish prices—never mind that any minimally habitable flat would already be engaged for the Passover week. I decided to risk infuriating Jezebel and called in sick the next day so I could roam through the city looking at one bleak apartment after another. Desperate, I finally rented the first furnished flat I found that I could move into right away. It was a dark, ground-floor apartment on the edges of Kiryat Yovel, its empty-lot view obscured by black security bars.

I transported my three garbage bags to the new flat that very evening. It was far from both work and home but had the advantage of being a month-to-month rental. It was just a temporary arrangement, I was sure.

Two days later, as I was leaving the office on Passover eve, I found a neatly folded note in my mailbox. It was written in the oversized, boxy handwriting typical of American immigrants:

> Kobi,
>
> I appreciate your completing your intake in such a timely fashion. As you can see, the paperwork is less overwhelming when you do it quickly.
>
> Have an enjoyable and productive Passover break.
>
> Jezebel

I crumpled the note and angrily threw it into the trash. Cheap gestures of appreciation were not going to soothe the stinging humiliation of my probation or the sheer degradation of having my intakes instantly scanned as if I were a first-year intern. She had refrained from commenting on the obvious shoddiness of my work—clearly her methods were more subtle and circuitous. But it would take more than a cloyingly friendly note to transform me into her dutiful lackey. I had no intention of having a "productive" Passover break. I had as much right to a holiday as anyone else at the goddamned clinic.

I was back in Kiryat Yovel by 3:00, with just enough time to shower and change before joining the exhaust-choked pilgrimage along the Jerusalem–Tel Aviv highway. It was an unusually cold and stormy spring, and the dark, low-hanging clouds perfectly mirrored my state of mind. I was in a petulant mood from Jezebel's condescending note and in dread of the evening ahead. My parents had called to wish us a happy Passover and had been crisply informed by Nava that I no longer lived there. We had always spent holidays with Nava's family, which had riled my mother for years. I would have been happy to skip the whole rigmarole, but what excuse could I possibly give now? Not that my parents believed in any of this religious stuff, but seder was seder, and without the convenient excuse of pushy in-laws, there was no way to avoid the family gathering.

The nation was on high alert for the holiday, and convoys of soldiers were making the highway even more clogged than usual. Two international peacekeepers had been killed the day before near Hebron, and a major attack thwarted at the Malha mall. After an interminable stop-and-go ride, I finally arrived, just as the first fat drops of rain began to fall, in Petah Tikva, the faceless little city east of Tel Aviv where I'd grown up. In my childhood, the town still retained remnants of its rural past, fragrant with orange groves. But the orchards had long since been paved over, and it was now a featureless suburb, a maze of white stone buildings, indistinguishable from all the other flat, crowded little towns that sprawled across the coastal plain.

Mainly due to my own reluctance, Nava and I had rarely visited the homestead, a comfortable, third-floor flat full of overstuffed furniture. I trotted up the stairs, avoiding, as I always did, the claustrophobic two-person elevator. The door to the flat was wide open, a buzzy commotion emanating from the kitchen along with the greasy smell of frying potatoes. My father sat at a corner of the already-set dining room table grating fresh horseradish, his nose a cartoonish red, tears streaming down his face.

"You can buy that stuff already grated, you know," I said by way of greeting.

He didn't miss a beat. "That's how weak this generation is, even fake suffering is too much for them. A little bitterness in the food is beyond their tolerance. Prepared horseradish? As bitter as life with a bunion. What would they do with a Holocaust, I wonder."

"Right," I said. "That's the problem with modern Israel, there isn't enough suffering." I looked around. "Is Anat here yet?"

"If Anat was here, you wouldn't already hear her yammering?" He wiped the tears from his eyes with his handkerchief, stuffed it back in his pocket, then resumed grating. "Anat called an hour ago from the highway. The road out of Samaria is jammed. She's not the only one with the sense to escape that self-made prison for a week. Between this freaky weather and the multiplying checkpoints, it will be amazing if she gets here before dark."

"They're staying the whole week?" I asked.

"She may be a religious fanatic, but she's not crazy. You think she wants to prepare her own house for Passover when she's got a slave of a mother who'll do it for her?"

"How are you going to survive a week with Habakuk?"

"I survived Hitler, you think I can't survive Habakuk?" He shot me a look. "You were no better, you know."

"You were a bit younger then," I said.

Before he could answer, his face convulsed into another paroxysm as the horseradish made its way back up his nose. I left him whinnying and cursing at the knobby root as I ventured into the kitchen to find my mother, aproned and mitted, bustling between bubbling pots and sizzling pans, the queen of her steamy domain.

"Kobi, you made it!" She beamed at me but never stopped moving. "And with this horrible weather. To the last minute, I told your father, I wonder if he'll really come. He so hates being here, maybe he'd rather sit alone on seder night than be with his old parents."

"Ima, don't be ridiculous." I reached over and pecked her on the cheek, the steam from the open pot fogging my glasses. "Everything smells so good. What are you cooking?"

"What, on Passover there's a choice? Chicken soup, matzah balls, potato kugel, tzimmes, inedible pastries. Why do you ask? You don't even remember what a Jewish family eats on Passover? What did they feed you in that sabra household?"

"Same thing. You're right, a silly question."

She took a sip from the soup pot, then shook her head in disapproval, scanning her spice rack for options as she spoke. "Kobi, it kills me, thinking of you living all alone in some horrible flat."

"You haven't even seen it."

"You expect us to travel to Jerusalem at our age, with all that traffic? Never mind all the bombings, and the crazy *haredim* throwing stones at your car. I never understood why you wanted to live in that ghost-ridden city. You should move back to Petah Tikva, get your own flat a few blocks away. We've got plenty of crazy people here for you to cure. You could open your own practice. It's not normal for a man to live alone like that, without a wife and family. How could she do that to you? And just a month before Yudit's big party." Having spiced the soup to her satisfaction, she pulled a kugel out of the oven, slamming the oven door.

"She didn't do anything to me. It was a mutual decision," I said. There was no point trying to explain. "Did you speak to Yudit when you called the house?"

"I never speak to Yudit; she's always busy when I call. She already has a young, fancy-shmancy, Israeli-born *savta*—what does she need an old-world *bubbe* for?"

"Don't be silly, Yudit loves you."

"Yudit barely knows me, I see her so rarely. Now I'll see her even less." She sighed deeply, poking at the edges of the kugel. "Maybe she's better off that way. Our generation, we only represent suffering and shame. That's why your wife, that Nava, kept her away from us. And now we can't even celebrate her bat mitzvah."

"You're being completely unfair—Nava never kept her from you. And besides, who says you can't go to the bat mitzvah?"

She turned from the stove, brandishing her wooden spoon like an orchestra conductor. "What, you think we would go without you? So that Nava of yours can shunt us off to some distant, shadowy corner of the room? Far from her elegant, sophisticated parents? Just because their grandparents escaped the ghettos a couple of generations ahead of us, they think they can look down on us. Shtetl Jews, that's what they call us." I started to protest but she cut me off. "No, no, no—if you don't go, we don't go!"

"OK, OK, don't get upset. Although what you're saying about her parents . . ."

"It's all true, and you know it." Her face suddenly softened. "But still, that Nava was good for you. You would have never settled down without her. Kobi, what are you going to do to get her back?"

A whooping shriek saved me from having to answer. Habakuk, in a soaking yellow rain jacket, came bounding into the little kitchen, grabbing my mother's legs in a brutal grip. She tried to shake him off, but he only dug his nails in harder.

"Habe'le," she yelled, "you're hurting your *bubbe*!"

In the living room I could hear my younger sister, Anat, lecturing my father at full tilt. I peeked out of the kitchen to see her huge form rooted in the center of the living room, her raincoat dripping audibly onto the floor tiles. She was already well into a detailed complaint about the soldiers at the checkpoints who'd caused the delay. Her skinny beard of a husband was dragging in stuffed suitcases and an odd lot of water-logged paraphernalia. Habakuk zoomed out of the kitchen, flung his soggy jacket and *kipa* onto the couch, and began racing figure eights around their legs, yelling wildly into the cosmos.

I followed him into the living room. "Hey, Habakuk," I called out, grabbing him by the shoulder, wondering, as I always did, how anyone could give an innocent child such an unwieldy name. "Long time no see, buddy." He stuck his tongue out at me, wriggled free, and continued on his dizzying course.

My father and sister were fully embroiled in their usual political argument: she trying to convince him that the settlements were the only bulwark against the erosion of the Jewish soul, he trying to convince her that it was immoral, post-Holocaust, to voluntarily choose to raise a family surrounded by barbed wire.

They were obsessed with politics, those two. What was the point? The more people argued, the more the conflict spun out of control. Arafat, Sharon, Bush—who would voluntarily watch a play with such an unappealing set of characters? From my father's meager bar I searched for a stiff drink, but the Scotch had been packed away for the holiday. I settled for a shot of kosher-for-Passover vodka and sank into the omnivorous couch. Political arguments were worse than futile—they reminded the soldier in me of all the things he'd rather not think about. The terror of sniper fire. The hate-filled eyes. The children screaming hysterically as you cocked your weapon and handcuffed their fathers.

"Shalom, Anat," I interjected, when they finally came to a break in the sparring. I knew she'd never say hello if I didn't.

"Hey, Kobi. You actually have something to say about this? Some psychological insight, perhaps?" Her voice, as usual, was thick with sarcasm.

"Not really. Just thought it would be civilized to say hello."

She stared at me for a moment. "So," she said, "that wife of yours finally had enough of you?"

"Yeah, I guess so," I answered, avoiding her gaze.

"That's the way it is in the secular world. Easy come, easy go."

"Yeah, that's just what it's like."

"You'll enjoy being single. No responsibilities. You always liked the easy life."

She unbuttoned, then peeled off her raincoat, and I marveled at the way in which she could make even the most innocent gesture seem aggressive. "Kobi, don't you know what harm it does to a child to be raised without a father? There was a long article in *Yediot* last week . . ." and she was off and running on another one of her diatribes. Well, I could tolerate this more than I could stand to listen to her political views.

She rattled on for a good five minutes while my father cleared his corner of the table of horseradish scraps. Finally, he cut her off. "Enough, Anat, we have a seder to get through, and I'm not letting it go on until midnight. I'm too old for that. Besides, Kobi has to get home tonight—God forbid he should sleep one night in his parents' house. He'd rather drive through a raging storm to an empty flat in holy Jerusalem. Habi, stop that," he yelled. Habakuk had been tossing and catching green toy soldiers, which he now flung high in the air. One landed on the lip of the ceiling fixture and remained there, dangling precariously.

"Everyone sit down," my father commanded. "Let's get this thing over with."

And so we sat, my mother refusing to remove her apron despite my father's protests, Habakuk getting up every few minutes to race around the table like a drunken dreidel. The rain lashed at the windows as my father droned through the service, not skipping a word of the sacred text. Anat studied the Haggada intently, while her husband, Tuvya, stared off into space, humming tunelessly under his breath. Other than periodic attempts to get Habakuk to settle down, there was a merciful quiet behind the drone, everyone hoping to get through the evening with as little ill will as possible.

What was the point of it all? Maybe we'd been slaves a few thousand years ago, maybe not. Maybe we should figure out how to take care of our current problems instead of fetishizing ancient traumas. Didn't we have enough here-and-now tsuris, what with people blowing themselves up in our cafés and malls? I'd like to see some god liberate us from this miserable, unending war—now *that* would be a holiday worth celebrating. I listened to the singsong hum of the cloyingly familiar words, sipped the candy-sweet wine my father insisted on using, wondered what sins I might have committed in my former lives to be tied now to the hidebound rituals of this stubborn old tribe.

After we had all consumed the ritual doses of tasteless matzah and fiery, home-grated horseradish, Anat cleared the table of Haggadas as my mother handed out the first dinner course, a grayish slab of gefilte fish crowned by thin slices of overcooked carrot. I asked if there was any news from my younger brother, Gal.

My mother sighed deeply and shook her head. "You tell him, Hayim."

"Still no word. As far as we know, he's still communing with the universe in that Indian ashram. For all we know, he's merged into the Oneness and totally disappeared."

"Stop it, Hayim," my mother scolded him, "you're as worried as I am. He's such a sensitive boy, my Gali. The army was so hard on him. Remember how he moped around for months after that early discharge? Welling up with tears whenever the news came on, rescuing every little alley cat in the neighborhood? We didn't know what to do with him."

"That was years ago," I said, poking at the crumbly mass on my plate.

My mother shook her head and disappeared into the kitchen. My father glanced at my untouched fish, switched his already empty plate with mine, and continued in a low tone. "Now I look back, I should have taken it more seriously. Not normal, for a grown man to act that way. But then, when he got back from Thailand, I thought he was finally settling down. He was managing that little store in Haifa, selling all that weird junk—psychedelic fabrics, 'memory stones,' obscene statues. He'd go on and on about their mysterious powers. It was odd, but at least it was some kind of living. Then all of a sudden, just when we think maybe he'll have a semi-normal life, he quits his job and goes off to India. He can't breathe in this country, he says. What can I tell you? If this ashram in India is the only place on earth he can breathe, *zai gezundt*."

"It's a sin to leave Eretz Yisrael for any reason other than to save a life," Anat chimed in.

My father topped his second piece of fish with a thick layer of beet-red horseradish. "I'll be sure to let him know your thoughts on the matter next time I hear from him."

"Maybe this new intifada triggered bad memories," I offered.

"Spoken like a true shrink," he said. "What, any of us like this *mishugas*? More than fifty years we've had this state, there hasn't been a day of peace. You live in this country, you learn to put up with it." I watched him quickly down every bite of fish, even the soggy carrots. I had always been fascinated by the methodical way he polished off every plate of food, as if it were an onerous but necessary task.

My mother returned to the room with the huge pot of soup. She placed it on a trivet in the center of the table and started collecting the used plates. "Kobi, you've learned to eat gefilte fish! Let me get you some more."

"No, no, Ima, it was delicious. But I know there's a lot more food."

"Are you sure?" She finished stacking the plates and started ladling matzah ball soup into bowls.

"Well," I said, "I'm sorry you haven't heard from Gal. I thought he would have at least called for Passover."

My father swatted the comment away and dipped into his soup. "I doubt they're celebrating Passover in the ashram. I'm sure he's too mystically elevated to own a calendar."

"Stop being so cynical, Hayim. What with drugs and AIDS and terrorists, and all the anti-Semitism in the world, and him such a trusting soul, you think it's safe, my Gali, floating around the world in a dreamlike fog?"

"Ima, you talk about him like he's five years old," I said, annoyed. "It's no big deal—he's just getting the army out of his system. So it's taking him a little longer than most. Can you blame him for hating all the violence around here? Sometimes I wish I'd spent some time abroad myself."

"Who would have ever imagined that you'd be the success story? Such a ball of terror you were as a kid," she said, warming up to one of her favorite topics.

"Today they'd label me hyperactive and give me lots of meds and sympathy," I said, but she continued as if I hadn't spoken.

"And those constant calls from the principal. What was his name? If it weren't for the donation we gave to that big-shot rebbe, I'm sure you'd be in jail by now."

"Ima, it had nothing to do with the rebbe." I kicked myself for taking the bait. "Can't I ever get a little credit for straightening myself out?"

"And Gali was just the opposite. Sweet as a bowl of tzimmes. And look what's happened to him now."

My father put his empty bowl aside and leaned back in his chair. "Your mother thinks he's going to float off the edge of the planet. But he's a bright boy; after a while he'll get sick of all that wandering. How long can an intelligent person breathe in and breathe out without getting a little bored? Anyway, serving in the army is something to be proud of. You think '48 was a party? We didn't have proper ammunition, there was no training, they shoved a gun in your hand and told you to shoot. Half the time we didn't know what we were shooting at. But after dragging ourselves out of the camps and forests of Europe, we were eager to do it. Who was going to defend this country if we didn't?"

This launched Anat into another rant about the deficiencies of the modern Israeli army and the degradation of the Zionist dream. As she spoke, Tuvya's tuneless humming rose several notches in volume, as did the sound of Habakuk's imaginary sword fight in the living room. He was, as far as I could tell, the knight Moses tilting at the evil Pharaoh with a finely honed stalk of celery, holding his brightly colored, crocheted *kipa* to his chest like a shield, and stabbing the furniture cushions with deadly resolve. I concentrated on the greasy soup, tuning them all out as best I could.

At least Nava's family was polite and civil, if a bit boring—normal people engaging in normal conversations. As I dug into course after course of the matzah-heavy food, I remembered Nava's mother, the prior year, serving with great flourish some bizarre South American grain that she delightedly declared to be kosher for Passover. Nava had gushed about the dish, interrogating her mother in stultifying detail about cooking methods and nutritional values. I tried to imagine Nava and Yudit at their seder without me. Her parents had never been particularly fond of me—were they supporting her decision to finally throw the bum out or urging her to reconsider?

By the time we had all forced down the dry pastries, Habakuk had collapsed with exhaustion onto the living room couch, leaving no one to search for the hidden afikomen. Grumbling at his aching knees, my father pulled the crumbled matzah out from under the sofa, and we joylessly made our way through the rest of the Haggada, rotely singing every verse of the silly songs that were meant to keep the young children awake to the end. Only when every last song had been sung could the seder be declared complete.

But before I could get out the door and into the still-raging storm, my father pulled me aside for his yearly Passover admonition.

"Kobi, anything you do is your business. You're a grown man; I would never intervene. You know that, right?"

"Is it about the hametz, Abba?"

"I know we didn't raise you very religious. After the war I never had the stomach for all that ritual. But Kobi, even if you keep nothing else, you mustn't eat hametz until the holiday is over."

"I know how important that is to you," I said, pulling on my coat.

But he continued, whispering earnestly, as if I had never heard the story before.

"You know what a saintly man my father was—he should rest in peace. He was kind to everyone, never judged people for ill. I'm not like him, you know that; I inherited my mother's cynical eye and bitter tongue. But my father, he was a genuine *tzaddik*, a holy man. Even in Theresienstadt, the ruffians who shared his barracks wouldn't let him empty the slop bin. He would gladly have done it! But they knew a *tzaddik* when they saw one. 'Reb Yakov,' they would say, 'this is not work for you.'" As my father spoke, my eyes were fixed on the little green soldier hanging desperately from the ceiling fixture.

"Yes, Abba, you've told me."

"By the time we got to Auschwitz, my father was so emaciated. They had shaved his beard and *peyos*, his face scrawny and drawn. But when the air turned balmy, he started to count out the days from the new moon, trading scraps of bread for little bits of potato. And when he decided it was the full moon of Passover, for eight days no bread passed his lips. All he'd eat were the rotting potato scraps that he'd saved up. He risked his life rather than eat hametz on Passover!" He looked at me to see if his words were sinking in.

"Yes, Abba, I know."

"Me, I ate whatever little bit they gave me. And he insisted I eat the bread! He said that a child, under such terrible circumstances, was not obligated. It never made any sense to me—I was a teenager, and much stronger than he. I ate the bread, but I swore a solemn oath that if I survived, I would never, so long as I lived, eat hametz on Passover again."

"I know, Abba. You tell me this every year."

"He never made it back from that hell. It would be a disgrace to his blessed memory not to keep this one mitzvah."

"I understand, Abba. Don't worry," I said, thinking about the stash of pita I had stored in the freezer to get me through the week. I had always hated the taste of matzah.

"I trust you, Kobi. You're named after him. You even look like him— more every day. You would never desecrate his memory in that way!"

It was close to midnight before I was finally liberated for my solitary, storm-driven ride home.

5

My father called early the next morning to make sure I knew about the bombing at the Park Hotel in Netanya. I had, of course, already heard about it on the car radio during my drive home. While our family had been joylessly chanting our way through the ancient story of slavery and oppression, someone with present-day grievances had stepped out of the rain and into a crowded hotel dining hall, just as people were finding their seats for the evening's seder, and exploded a bomb hidden in an attaché case. Twenty were confirmed dead and scores more wounded. Among the many elderly dead, my father told me, was an old friend of my mother's, Libke. He whispered the name reverentially, though I'd never heard it before. My mother was taking it badly, he said, and wouldn't want to talk. Abruptly, he hung up the phone.

The following three days of the holiday dragged miserably. On Friday afternoon, a mere two hours after I had done my first real grocery shop in the new neighborhood, a bomb went off in the supermarket I had just left. Two killed, a couple dozen wounded—a minor event, by recent standards, but distinct because the bomber was an eighteen-year-old woman. I gave in to the nagging pull of curiosity and went to have a look at the glass and debris scattered throughout the cordoned-off street. The country was in a state of extreme hysteria as the bloodiest month yet of the intifada was drawing to a close, the faces of the hundred-plus dead from March attacks splashed across every newspaper. Massive incursions into the West Bank had been launched to try and rout out the terrorist cells. Thankfully, I hadn't been called up this time for reserve duty. It would all come to naught, I was sure— there was no defeating a resistance this brutal. But that wouldn't prevent the self-righteous hypocrites in Europe from staging massive protests against the country's fruitless efforts to stanch the bleeding.

The holiday had me feeling adrift; I had no idea how I was supposed to spend my days. Bored as I was by my job, at least it gave me somewhere to go each day, people to talk to, distraction from my now-vacuous existence.

I was determined, in defiance of Jezebel, not to do a stitch of "productive" work and instead spent the days walking aimlessly through the unfamiliar streets of Kiryat Yovel, the evenings trapped in my run-down flat, listening to the drone of the unrelentingly somber news reports on the television. My isolation was stark and I marveled at the extent to which my life had been orchestrated by Nava. I resuscitated the memories of holidays past: walking through the zoo with Yudit on a hot afternoon as she chattered alongside me; horseback riding on a family trip to the windy grasslands of the Golan; Nava's elegantly thrown-together dinner parties. Jerusalem was in full flower—a collage of color animated by the pervasive scent of jasmine and honeysuckle—but the sudden outburst of spring only soured my mood. Yossi was in Netanya with his visiting American in-laws, who had a luxury flat they visited only on holidays. I couldn't think of a single person to call or visit. How had I become such a helpless and dependent adult?

The hours crawled by as I obsessively brooded about my new circumstances. Foremost on my mind was what to do about Yudit's bat mitzvah. Nava had been immersed in planning the party for almost a year, and Yudit, despite heroic efforts at preteen nonchalance, was bursting with excitement. The elegant hall in the Botanical Garden had long been reserved, the handmade invitations sent out, the menu meticulously reviewed. After a widespread search throughout the city's finest boutiques, Yudit's dress had been selected, as well as Nava's own. The last couple of weeks, the two of them, giggling excitedly over the kitchen table, had been working on the final details of the handcrafted decorations for the room. I hadn't been paying much attention to the details—had thought it all a bit excessive—but was I really to be excluded from my own daughter's coming-of-age party? Nava was wrong, of course, to order me away, but if I just showed up it might create a scene and ruin the party. The bat mitzvah was only three weeks away—what was I supposed to do?

I finally decided that if I couldn't attend the party, at least I could sink my energies into purchasing a special gift—something exotic and personal that would tell Yudit how much I still cared. On Sunday afternoon I took the bus into the center of town full of purpose, but after hours of wandering the eerily empty streets, I realized that I had no idea what Yudit might want. She seemed too young for expensive jewelry, and the books and electronic devices and tchotchkes that overflowed the downtown shops seemed too small for the weight of the task. By dusk I felt exhausted and defeated. I climbed onto the bus for the long journey back to Kiryat Yovel, shutting my eyes to the pink-tinged rush of buildings whizzing by.

The bus driver had the news turned up high. The IDF had invaded Arafat's compound, the Security Council was up in arms, and there was

"I'm sorry. I should never have bothered you."

"It's OK," she said. "Not your fault. I'm a little nervous today. They find me they'll deport me. I shouldn't even be talking to you. I can't go back to that hellhole."

"To Moldova? I thought you hated it here. You'd rather stay than go home?" I felt uncomfortable prying but couldn't stop myself.

"What do you know," she said.

"Not much."

Her eyebrows rose and fell in agreement, and we sat through another long silence. Why *was* she telling me these terrifying stories? Were they true, or was she playing me? Did she want me to keep sitting there or not? I couldn't tell.

"You're incredibly beautiful," I finally said. "You know that, right?"

"Is this some kind of come-on?" Her tone was so flat. Was she insulted? Mocking me? Interested?

"No, I didn't mean it that way. Or maybe I did. I don't really know. I was just thinking . . ."

She snorted. "Another confused fancy-dress Jew, with no sense in his head."

"You really hate us."

"Everyone hates the Jew," she said matter-of-factly. "Tell me this. Why haven't they killed you off yet? They keep trying. They try every day. But you're still here. What's the secret? Tell me." She looked at me expectantly.

"I don't know," I said. "You're right. It's a great riddle."

She leaned over toward me. Without breaking eye contact, she took the scarf off her shoulder and began to wrap the scratchy fabric gently around my two wrists.

I felt a surge of warmth in my groin. She was the anti-Nava—tall and blond, foreign and merciless. Maybe I could fuck all my frustrated rage into a girl like this, strafe the Jezebels and Navas and nameless receptionists who were plaguing my life through one magical pain-feuled fuck. Maybe she was just what I needed.

"Tell me the secret," she hissed. "The secret of the Jew."

"You're wasting your time, Delia," the bartender yelled from behind his paper. He moved it aside to stare at me balefully. "This one don't belong here. He's not your kind."

"What do you know of my kind?" she yelled back. And then to me, "Don't pay attention to Pinya. He gets jealous of anyone who talks to me."

"Is he your boyfriend?" I asked. She snorted, as close to a laugh as she could probably manage, but I was disconcerted. Pinya scared me. Had he helped her escape from Tel Aviv? Did he now own her? Is that what she was doing in this rathole? I could have used another shot of Scotch, but I was frozen in place. Delia pulled tighter at the fabric on my wrists and gave me a questioning look, flicking her head toward the black corridor from which she'd emerged.

I was horny as hell, and just as scared. What kind of invitation was this? Was there a room off the back corridor for casual liaisons, or was this to be a crude bathroom fuck? Both options made me shiver with a strange mix of fear and desire. Why *couldn't* I follow this gorgeous Moldovan woman if I wanted to? But then a wave of panic flooded over me, much like the terror I'd felt on the bus. Her hatred for me was palpable—was this some kind of entrapment? Pinya was no one I wanted to mess with; I was scared to even look in his direction. Would he exact some kind of violent retribution if I slept with his girl? I'd seen too many sordid movies, and the stories about Delia's roughed-up girlfriends hadn't helped.

She pulled the scarf around my wrists tighter with one hand and reached the other under the table to feel my hard dick.

"It's not that you can't, it's that you won't," she said and unloosed the scarf from my hands. "Pinya's right, you don't belong here."

"No, it's not that. You're beautiful. It's just that . . ."

"What?" She put the scarf back over her shoulder, and I watched the rope tattoo slither on the muscles of her arm.

"Think you too good for me?" she hissed. "Think big bad Pinya's gonna beat up your soft little Jewbody if you fuck me? Maybe he would. Maybe he'd cut off your bald dick and go sell it in the *shuq*. What you think? You think it be worth anything?"

"Look, I just came in for a drink. I was . . ." Again, I couldn't finish the sentence.

"You was what? What? You're scared of me, that's all." She put her chin back in her fist and stared at me. Her voice was so low I could barely hear her. "You got some pretty little wife at home? Some fancy office job? You think they'll all find out what a horny bastard you are and your precious life will be over? Well here's what Delia says—your life's not worth the balding hair on your head or you wouldn't be here flirting with a washed-up foreigner half your age. You wouldn't be wandering this low-life neighborhood, in the middle of a Jew holiday, looking all lost and lonely. You're right, you should have let me be." She leaned far over the table, the outline of her breasts straining against the thin fabric of her dress. "You hear what happened to that asshole Zimri? Fucked the wrong girl at the wrong time. Big mistake. Ask Pinya what they did to *him*. They do the same to you if Delia tells them to. Here I am, stuck on Easter in this sewer of a pub, and you the only squirrel walking through the door. Your life's worth no more in the *shuq* than your shrunken little clipped-off dick." I could hear Pinya chuckling lightly behind his paper. How he could hear her from that distance was beyond me.

"I'm sorry to have bothered you," I said.

I got up, placed some money on the bar, and left. It had grown dark outside. I walked briskly through the gloomy, unfamiliar streets, Delia's fierce mockery still echoing in my ears. I imagined Pinya sending someone to follow me and clutched the wallet in my pocket. Only when I finally came upon a thoroughfare did I begin to feel safe, and only then did I notice my racing pulse.

I hailed a cab back to Kiryat Yovel, wondering, as the now-familiar city flew by, why I had panicked like a clumsy teenager. A good, desperate fuck would have done me well. But Delia had terrified me at least as much as the innocent boy riding home on the bus with his backpack. Who knew that Jerusalem, the Holy City, harbored pubs like Soreq's, lives as debased as Delia's? I thought we'd confined all the foreigners and lowlifes to the slums of South Tel Aviv. Did the fancy-café hoppers on Emek Refaim, the spiritual seekers of the Old City, the artists and songwriters of the Zion-romance industry, even know such places existed, here, in Jerusalem the Golden?

Back in my ugly flat, I stumbled into the bathroom and stared for a while at the face in the grimy, streaked mirror, absentmindedly rubbing the wrist that had been bound in the cheap fabric of her scarf. I dropped my clothes to the floor and went straight to bed, quickly soothed the ache in my groin, then instantly fell into a fitful sleep, my dreams inhabited by duplicitous, scissor-wielding foreigners and buildings crashing senselessly around me.

6

Yossi returned to Jerusalem on Monday night. Hearing the desperation in my voice, he agreed to meet me the next day for a game of squash and, as always, beat me handily. Not only was he almost a decade younger than me, but he also was in far better shape—short and muscular to my taller, leaner frame—and he played with a sly and ruthless energy I could never quite muster. The games had begun a few years back—when the YMCA first opened its courts, to great fanfare—as Yossi's not very subtle way of proving his alpha-male dominance at the clinic. But I had never minded losing to Yossi, had relished this rare opportunity for male camaraderie. It reminded me of the only thing I liked about being a soldier: men bonding with each other through the alchemy of sweat and sublimated rage.

We usually followed our games with lunch at Yossi's favorite hummus dive, tucked away in a back alley off Jaffa Road. But since it was still Passover week, we had to settle for a leaven-less meal in one of the few open restaurants in downtown Jerusalem. I hadn't wanted Yossi's wife, Elizabeth, to know about my conversation with Jezebel and had kept it to myself while staying in their apartment. But alone now with Yossi, I let spill all the humiliating details.

"Probation? Man, that's too much," he said, before ordering a large assortment of dishes for both of us. He had started growing a beard since I'd last seen him, adding gravitas to his otherwise boyish face.

"Kobi, you need to get out of that racket," he went on, pouring himself a tall glass of Coke. "It was the smartest thing I ever did, getting myself fired from that job. God, it's boring, sitting and listening to people's troubles all day. And the constant bitching of the staff! I'll be honest with you—I'm grateful to those bastards for letting me go. It was just the spark I needed to get my ass out of there." He downed half his drink in a long, noisy gulp.

Yossi had come to the clinic five years earlier with a reputation as a whiz kid. It was no small feat to become director of a prestigious mental health clinic at the age of thirty-two, supervising a large and experienced staff. It was clear to everyone that he had gotten the position not through any stellar clinical or administrative skills, but on the force of his impenetrable arrogance. He was so convinced of his own worth, so smooth and well-spoken, that people couldn't help entrusting him with authority. But eventually that same arrogance managed to alienate both his subordinates and the administrators who had appointed him. By the time he left the clinic, he was almost universally hated. But I had remained fond of Yossi, had always been impressed by how little he seemed impacted by the resentment he routinely aroused in others.

The dishes began to arrive, crowding every corner of the round metal table. "I tell you, Kobi, Elizabeth's father was right," he was saying. "There's nothing like being your own boss."

"So you really enjoy running that little store he bought you?"

Yossi started heaping his plate with meats and salads, talking all the while. "It's smack in the middle of the Jewish Quarter, just a few doors down from the firebrands raising money to build the third temple. It's a great location. Tourism is way down, of course, with this damn intifada. But even so, word is getting out and folks are starting to wander in."

"And you like selling knickknacks?" I scooped some food onto my plate, though I wasn't feeling very hungry.

"Her dad thought I should sell ancient artifacts," he said dismissively. "But believe me, I've got more on my mind than kitschy oil lamps. The faux antiques are great for luring in tourists who want to come to the Old City but are too scared to step foot in the Arab *shuq*. But once they're in, it's the holy-man stuff that keeps them." He put down his fork and knife and turned toward me. "Kobi, they come from all over the world, dazzled by Jerusalem sunsets and the illusion of walking on the stones trod by Jesus or some ancient Israelite prophet. They're starry-eyed, full of mystical visions and stunned realizations of how pointless their lives are. They think they're looking for a souvenir for Aunt Gretel, but before they've left my shop I've told them their futures, tapped into their greatest fears, blessed little fragments of glass or stone chosen especially for them—you know, channeled some divine energy. They pose for pictures with me, they're dropping bills on the counter without even counting. It's all part of their Holy Land experience; no price is too high." He leaned in and lowered his voice. "And you know what I've been realizing? In some ways the intifada is actually good for business."

"What are you talking about? There are almost no tourists left in Jerusalem."

He waved the comment aside. "Of course there are a lot fewer of them. But the ones who *do* come are feeling so brave, and so vulnerable at the same time. Imagine walking the streets of a foreign city—the holiest city in the world!—knowing you can get blown up at any minute. They're open to anything!" He glanced around and leaned in even closer. "It's so easy, man. I gaze deeply into their eyes, like I know their innermost secrets. A little chanting, a little mysterious mumbling, and you know what? They leave with new insight, new hope, new inspiration." He stared at me, animated and earnest. "I'm healing people of their deepest existential angst, more than I ever did with that therapy crap. This is what's missing from people's lives, Kobi—a sense of mystery, access to the unknowable powers of the cosmos, awe and terror in the face of the chasm. A connection to the infinite, the eternal, the ineffable. They come away transformed, with a new vision for their lives, and I come away with bundles of foreign currency. It's a win-win deal!" He sat back, staring at me, waiting for a response.

Could he possibly be serious? "So that explains the furry beard that's devouring your handsome mug," I said finally.

"Nice touch, eh?" He dug back into his meal. "And I've bought the coolest Bukharan cap. You should see how holy I look in it. You'd pay me a few shekel yourself if you saw me. A little palm-reading, a little dream interpretation . . ."

"Yossi, you've lost your mind. You've gone from being a highly respected professional to being a religious charlatan."

"What, I wasn't a charlatan before?" He laughed. "Come on, Kobi, you know as well as I do what bullshit that clinic is. But even so, people feel better after talking to shrinks; they keep coming back for more. You ever wonder why that is?" He didn't wait for an answer, barreling on. "Because they're lonely, man, they're alienated, they're bored, they don't know why they're spinning around on this watery little planet." He paused to let this sink in, but I must have looked as astonished as I felt. "Don't you get it? It's the same racket, but this is more creative, more powerful, *and* more lucrative. Not to mention that I'm my own boss—no more boring meetings, busybody hospital administrators, or stick-up-the-ass receptionists. You'll see," he said, nodding. "A couple more seasons and I'll make it into the guidebooks, and then the real money will start flowing in. And if we ever break this fucking intifada, there'll be no limit—I'll be sitting on top of the world. And you'll still be listening to whiny women drone on, hoping the pretty ones are lonely enough to fall for your fake-sympathy charms." He laughed again. "You calling *me* a charlatan?"

I still couldn't tell if he was being serious or pulling my leg. "You get a lot of those young, blond traveler girls?" I asked, just to lighten the mood while I collected my thoughts.

"Ah, Kobi," he sighed. "Always thinking with the same part of your anatomy. Sure, they come in, and man, are they easy. Can you imagine? A chance to fuck a real live holy man from the goddamned holiest city on the planet. They're all over me. And the ones who come to Jerusalem and wander the Old City in the middle of an intifada?" He shook his head. "You can just imagine how wild they are. A lot foxier than the bored housewives you get to lay, eh?" Suddenly, his voice became earnest and eager again. "But forget it, Kobi, I'm being careful. Those girls have no money to spend, and I've got bigger plans. I want to be a real holy man. I'm not going to screw it all up for a few minutes of bliss with a strung-out Norwegian girl. I want the rich tourists, the celebrities; I want Madonna coming to my shop to hear her fortune read. I know where the money is." He paused, as if thinking things through. "I need Elizabeth on my side here. *And* her rich American father." He gave me a sharp glance, then dug back into his meal. "No offense, pal, but I'm not making the same mistake you made."

I winced but let it go. "What does your illustrious wife have to say about all this?"

"You know how furious she was when I lost my job," he said, refilling his plate. "But now she sees how much happier I am, how much more purpose I have in my life. And she's not immune to the money potential, *or* to her father's sudden approval of me." He leaned in again, as if confiding a great secret. "I've made as much these first few months as I was making a year at the lousy clinic, and I've barely gotten established." He nodded to himself. " Elizabeth's practical, she's the daughter of an American mogul. She understands how entrepreneurship works."

He sat back in his chair with a look of deep contentment. "Holy cities need to be filled with holy men," he declared, staring off into space. "Why not me?"

I had barely touched my meal, didn't know what to make of all his crazy talk. On the one hand, it was genius. On the other, it seemed completely implausible. Could he really just transform himself, by force of will, into a "holy man"?

"How do you even know what to say to people?" I asked.

He shrugged. "I did some reading, went to a few lectures on Jewish mysticism. I even visited a couple of ashrams when Elizabeth and I were in India. Know what I realized? They all say the same damn thing." He wiped his hands on a napkin. "Go ahead, tell me a dream you've had recently."

"You can't pull that stuff off on me. I have the same shrink training you do."

"What, are you scared?" His gaze was suddenly intense. "Tell me a dream."

It was against my better judgment, but I was curious. And—as he seemed to realize—I was desperate for someone to talk to. "OK, I had one just the other night," I told him. "A woman was giving me a haircut. It felt good, it was a turn-on, her hands caressing and massaging my scalp. But then, the next thing I knew, I was in a huge room, almost like an ancient temple, crowded with people, and I was single-handedly holding up the walls. Only I wasn't holding them up, I was pulling them down. They were starting to crash around me when I woke up."

"Scared?"

"Well, yeah, kind of."

"Did you know the woman?"

"No," I lied.

He looked at me sidewise. "C'mon, she reminded you of someone."

"No, not really. But she was blond. A foreigner."

"Ah." He was staring at me intently, all the boyish silliness gone. I shifted uneasily in my chair.

"So what do you have to say about my dream?" I asked, feeling acutely uncomfortable.

He waved me aside like a gnat. "The dream is obvious. Acute castration anxiety. Not surprising, really. Between Nava and Jezebel, it must feel like the women of the world are conspiring to cut it off."

"You don't use jargon like that with the tourists, do you?" My tone was casual, but my voice now had a slight quaver.

"No, but I'm saying it to you. You have a hard time with strong women, Kobi. You're attracted to them and scared of them. You try to keep yourself safe by screwing helpless, needy women. But you misjudged Nava, completely. So pretty and petite, you never let yourself see the power in her. She's like steel, that woman."

"That's a pretty shrinky explanation," I said. "Not exactly what I'd expect from a holy man."

"So, a woman cuts your hair, symbolically takes your manhood away, and your world comes crashing down around you. The pretenses of your life don't hold up anymore. Your inadequacies are being exposed to the multitudes. You must be horrified at how little it took to bring you down."

He was right, of course, but I would never concede. "I thought you had a brand-new gig. What happened to the rapturous mumbling?"

"OK, you want mystical, I'll give you mystical." His eyes glazed over and he began to gently rock back and forth. When he finally spoke, his voice had shifted into a soft, slightly accented singsong.

"The hair, Kobi, is *Keter*, the Crown, the highest manifestation of divinity. That which is Eternal and Infinite, that which is *Ayin*, the Absence

7

For the first day back in the office, I took extra care pulling myself together, fastidiously shaving the holiday's accumulated stubble. I stopped for
a hearty breakfast and, as I made my way toward the clinic, felt a new sense
of resolve gather inside me. Today was a new day, a new start. I was going to
tackle the backlog of paperwork even if I had to make it all up from scratch.
I would pay attention to my patients, find clever and helpful things to say.
If I didn't turn over a new leaf I would lose my job, and then what would
happen to me? I had no real skills, no other way to make a living. Yossi was
right, I was too smart to let that happen. I strode into the office only fifteen
minutes late, impervious to the flinty glance of the gum-chewing receptionist, determined to start my so-called "probation" on a brand-new footing.

But by midday, my resolve was already wavering. I was as unable as
ever to concentrate on what my patients were saying or jot a coherent note
into a chart. The receptionists were nastier than ever, gloating at their ability to adapt my schedule to their whims. I rushed back from my truncated
lunch hour full of resentment, but Israela, scheduled for the 1:00 hour, was
not in the waiting room when I arrived.

Many patients never came back after the first intake session—so dis-
illusioned or so healed by the encounter, no one knew—but the thought
of Israela not returning disquieted me. As I shot rubber bands at Chagall's
leering cow, I ran through her first session in my mind. I had many patients
with convoluted histories, but her story had been particularly bizarre: married to a guy whose name she couldn't or wouldn't share; convinced they
were still a couple despite not having seen or heard from him in as much as
a year; furtively avoiding his "friends" who she imagined were stalking her.
There had obviously been a psychotic process at work, maybe more than I
had realized. I had a nagging worry that she'd had a break over the holiday.

But I had to admit that I wasn't only worried; I was also full of anticipation at the thought of seeing Israela again. After I'd twice leapt to my feet
at the sound of footsteps outside the door, I stayed standing, busying my

hands by straightening the piles of charts on my desk. She wasn't my usual type, but I was drawn to her in a way I couldn't quite define. I warned myself to be careful—I was being watched with a close, malicious eye and could afford no more "inappropriate" patient liaisons, no matter how impulsive, superficial, or fleeting.

When Israela finally did arrive—ten minutes late, slinking into the office unannounced, like a movie star evading her fans—her mood was lighthearted, and I felt my anxiety melt under a surge of relief. She flung the shawl off her head, flashed me a disarming smile, and sank into my recliner as if in her own living room.

"You seem more cheerful this week," I said, perching myself on the edge of the couch. "Did you have a good holiday?" Her dark eyes were shining. She carried with her the scent of jasmine, making the room feel small and sultry. With each breath I relaxed a little more, absurdly glad to be in her presence.

"No, not really," she was saying. "But I feel better already, just seeing you again. I can't tell you how much you helped me last time. It must be wonderful to be able to help people like that."

She was flirting audaciously, flattering me with that adoring look, familiar to me from years of therapy practice. Despite myself, it was working. I shrugged off the hazy effect her scent was having on my mind and forced myself to focus.

"Yes, well, of course," I said in my most professional voice. "But remember, we're in the earliest stages of treatment, and I still need to gather a lot of basic information in order to see how therapy might help."

"Oh, but I told you everything last time," she said, her eyes round and earnest.

I pretended to consult my notes. "Well, you did tell me a lot about your marriage. Today I was hoping to get a sense of the rest of your life." My pen fell to the floor and I bent down to pick it up. "Tell me about your holiday—how did you spend it?"

"It wasn't so great," she said, looking at her hands. "I cleaned and cleaned, cooked all his favorite meals, but he never showed up. Not that I was surprised—he never does. I don't know why I keep going through the motions every year." She looked up at me. "To be honest, it was a long, lonely week. I kept thinking of all the other families celebrating together."

"I'm sorry it was so lonely," I said.

She shrugged. "How was your holiday?" she asked. "I'm sure it was better than mine."

"It was fine, thank you," I lied, grateful for once to be able to hide behind the strict rules of therapy. "But we should continue with the intake process that we started last time. Why don't you begin today by telling me a little about your childhood?"

She sighed. "Oh, Doctor, you don't want to hear about my childhood. It was a total nightmare."

"Of course I want to hear about it. After all, that's what we're here for. What was so terrible about it?"

She looked up at me, as if to gauge my interest. "I was orphaned at a very young age," she began. "I never knew my parents. They moved to Egypt before I was born, but both of them died shortly thereafter."

I shook my head sympathetically. "What a terrible tragedy. Were you raised by relatives?"

"I didn't have any, not that I knew of. I had a terrifying childhood. I really don't think you'd want to hear about it."

She was twisting the fringed edges of her shawl as she spoke, but she'd kept her eyes firmly locked on mine. I focused myself on the task of diagnosis: there was important information here—some kind of major, early trauma—that she was not yet ready to share. But I was sure I would get to the bottom of it. I hadn't been this motivated to understand a patient in years.

"What do you know about your parents?" I asked.

"I know almost nothing about my mother. But I've learned a lot about my father from Y."

"He knew him?" I asked, hearing the surprise in my voice.

She smiled broadly. "Oh yes, he was very close to my father. He's been close to my family for years."

Her entire affect had shifted. Clearly, Y was her favorite topic.

"How did he know your family?" I asked.

"Well, it all started when he met my great-grandfather, Aba Ibra."

I kept my tone neutral this time. "You're saying that your husband knew your great-grandfather?"

"Didn't I tell you? He's much older than me. I don't know exactly how old, but older than you'd think." No name, no age. But in a way, it didn't matter. I'd come to understand that there was a layer of truth to be found even in the most bizarre delusions. There would be much to learn if I listened closely and kept my skepticism under check.

"So how did he meet your great-grandfather?"

"They met in Syria. Y was very young at the time, no more than a teenager. Much younger than Ibra, who was already married and an established businessman."

"Is Y Syrian?" I asked.

"No, Iraqi—at least I think so. Ibra was also born in Iraq, but he'd emigrated to Syria years before. Y was working in Syria as a Zionist recruiter, teaching Hebrew language and Zionist ideology, trying to get people to move to pre-state Palestine. It was around the time when the situation for Jews in Syria was beginning to deteriorate, but before there was a well-organized Zionist underground. It was very dangerous work—the Syrian government disapproved of Jewish nationalism and was not above arresting and killing Zionist operatives."

Was any of this plausible? "He was working for the pre-state authorities?" I asked.

"Oh, no. Y never works for anyone. He was an independent operator. But he's always been a fervent Zionist."

"And your great-grandfather was also an early Zionist?"

"Not until he met Y. But one day he stumbled upon Y's class on Zionist ideology, and the connection between them was instantaneous. After the class ended, Y told him that he was looking for someone to set an example for the Syrian community and that Ibra was the one he had chosen. Most Syrian Jews at the time were emigrating to America, or England, or even Latin America. But Y convinced Ibra to set a different example. He told him to summon his wife, pack up their belongings at once, and move to Palestine."

"Those early Zionists could be heavy-handed at times," I offered.

"To put it mildly. Ibra went home that very day and told his wife they were moving to Palestine. She was horrified, but what choice did a woman have in those days? Within a week they had packed up a few belongings and smuggled across the border with Y, leaving the rest of the family and their business behind. It was a harrowing journey, and dangerous. But in retrospect, it was very prescient—they left more than a decade before the Syrian pogroms and the mass emigration to Israel. Ibra claimed that he was the first modern Jew to emigrate from Syria to Palestine. I don't know if that's true, but he was proud of it for the rest of his life."

I did a quick calculation in my head: Y would have to be over eighty years old for this story to be true. It wasn't impossible—it always astonished me how many young women were attracted to older, domineering men—but it still seemed highly unlikely.

"And then," she continued, "the most remarkable thing happened when they arrived in Palestine!" Her face was suddenly bright and full of enthusiasm. "Ibra and his wife had been childless for many years, but as soon as they got here, Sana got pregnant! They were astonished, but Y wasn't surprised at all. He explained it in almost mystical terms—you know, a real Jew has to live on Jewish land, breathe Jewish air, to be fully alive. The air of the Holy Land, for a Jew, would even cure infertility." I felt lulled by the joy and enthusiasm in her voice. "It sounds preposterous, I know, but that's how people thought in those days," she went on. "Ibra was convinced that the pregnancy was entirely Y's doing, and not only because he brought them to Palestine. Y had been feeding him herbs, doing kabbalistic incantations, all meant to increase his potency. So when Sana got pregnant, Ibra acted as if she had nothing to do with the whole thing. Just like a vessel, or something. Almost like it was really his and Y's child."

The story suggested a new theory, which she seemed to anticipate.

"Ibra and Y were so close. So close . . . ," she trailed off. "Well, you'd think it was ridiculous, I'm sure. But the way he talks about Ibra, you know . . ." She eyed me closely, and I concentrated on keeping my expression neutral. "Sometimes I think it may have been more than just a friendship," she said in a guilty whisper, "if you know what I mean."

"You think it was a homosexual relationship?"

"Oh, my goodness, you put it so bluntly; no, nothing like that. I mean nothing, you know, consummated. Y's very squeamish about stuff like that. He hates gay people. Calls it a perversion."

"But I thought you were suggesting . . ."

"Well, yeah, I was. I figure it was like that, but you know, maybe without, you know . . ."

She lowered her voice to a whisper. "I always thought it was a little strange that Y stayed in Palestine after bringing Ibra over. You'd think there were other people to smuggle out of Syria. But they were so emotionally intertwined, those two."

I nodded supportively. I'd had patients before with distant or absent husbands who turned out to be gay, living a shadow life with a man. Was this one of those cases? His idealization/devaluation of his wife, in a classic madonna/whore pattern, might stem from the denial of homosexual preference and a hatred of female sexuality that could never fully satisfy; referring to homosexuality as a perversion was a transparently defensive maneuver.

Israela leaned forward. "I think it was Ibra's relationship with Y that caused the death of my great-grandmother, Sana," she said.

"She was so jealous?"

"Oh, I don't know about that. But there was this other incident, when Grandpa Itzik was a little boy. You have to understand—life in Palestine was incredibly harsh in those days. It was very demeaning for Ibra, after being a successful businessman in Syria. He was a middle-aged man, uprooted from everything that was familiar to him. He struggled to learn Hebrew, could barely make a living. There were very few Sephardi immigrants in those days, and the Ashkenazi elite looked down on them. Y was also Sephardi, of course, but he was young and spoke fluent Hebrew—it was easy for Ibra to become dependent on him. At any rate, from what I gather Ibra would do just about anything Y said."

"So what was the incident that caused your great-grandmother's death?" I asked.

She smiled and folded her hands, preparing to launch a favorite story. "Both Ibra and Sana doted on Itzik. He was their only child, born late in life and so improbably." I felt myself relaxing, my mind growing hazy from her fragrance and the rhythmic cadence of her voice. "But Y convinced Ibra that the only chance for the boy to succeed in the emerging Zionist state was for him to take over his education. He was running one of those Zionist youth villages at the time, mainly for orphans. There, he told him, Itzik would grow up surrounded by Hebrew and proper socialist indoctrination. He would learn to farm and shoot a gun, become the new type of Jew they would need when they had their own state. Y told Ibra that since he was responsible for the boy's birth, he should be responsible for his upbringing as well. So one day, out of the blue, Ibra scoops up the boy, not even a word to his wife, and heads off with him to Y's youth village on a hilltop in the outskirts of Jerusalem." I nodded. There was something oddly familiar about the story. Where had I heard it before? "Only at the last minute, just as Ibra was about to sign away all his parental rights, Y sends him a messenger telling him it was all a mistake, to take the boy home." *Wait a minute*, I thought. But Israela kept talking. "Turns out, it was some kind of hazing thing, to prove his loyalty. Y never meant to take the boy at all."

She paused and looked at me expectantly. I had the odd sensation of being half asleep, trying to remember a fleeting dream. "Israela, that's a very disturbing story," I finally said. "To even pretend to take such a beloved, only child from his aging parents."

"Y loves telling that story," she gushed. "He's always bragging about it. He thinks it shows what a loyal friend Ibra was, that he was ready to turn over his only child without a murmur of question or complaint. But Ibra and Itzik were gone for days, and the neighbors must have told Sana what was up. She was dead when Ibra got home. I figure from the shock of it all."

She said it calmly, adding to my increasing sense of surreality. I struggled to make sense of this oddly hypnotic story. Were the early Zionists really so ruthless? Or maybe it wasn't a "Zionist youth village" at all, but something far more sinister. The organized crime theory briefly flitted through my mind again. Had there been organized crime in the early *yishuv*? If so, I'd never heard of it.

"Israela," I said, trying to keep my voice even, "it sounds like your husband can be very cruel."

"Oh no, no, not at all!" she cried. "Well, I guess it sounds that way. But like I told you, he's a little insecure, that's all." She set her gaze to the window behind me. "Loyalty is the most important thing in the world to him. It's the same with me, he's always testing me to see if I'm loyal enough. And of course, I never am."

As she sat quietly, gazing out the window, my diagnostic wheels went back into gear. It was clear that in the husband we were dealing with a severe case of narcissistic personality disorder, probably with sociopathic tendencies. Grandiose in the extreme, treating all relationships as objects for his own narcissistic needs. The homoerotic relationship, whether consummated or not, fit into the picture well; narcissists often chose love objects who were weak and easily manipulated and who mirrored their own defensively constructed self-love. The whole Ibra story was obviously a fabrication, but by Y or by Israela herself? Either way, I was starting to picture this guy—a charismatic, antisocial narcissist, so incapable of any true empathy that all of his relationships would become as manipulative and destructive as the marriage Israela had described.

"Who told you these stories?" I finally asked, knowing the answer before she spoke.

"Y, of course." I nodded, but my face must have betrayed my doubt. "What, you think Y would lie to me?"

"Well, not lie, but . . ."

"Exaggerate? Of course not! Every word he says is true!"

Was it love or fear that kept her so blind? But her extreme reaction to even mild skepticism made clear that this was not a line of inquiry I could pursue at this point.

She was anxiously twisting the fringes of her shawl around her fingers. Suddenly her whole body stiffened, alert. She glanced around the room, visibly frightened.

"What is it?" I whispered. She looked as though she was being rebuked. "Is someone speaking to you?"

Her eyes refocused on me, and she lost the furtive, scared look as quickly as she had assumed it. "No, of course not. I'm sorry, I got distracted." She laughed weakly.

I had a strong suspicion that she had just hallucinated an angry voice, but it had passed so quickly I couldn't be sure. If she had, she clearly was not ready to reveal it to me. I needed to change the topic. And I genuinely wanted to hear how the rest of the ancestor tale would play out.

"Tell me about your grandfather," I said.

Her voice settled again into its mesmerizing rhythms. "A few years after Sana's death, when he was just a teenager, Itzik joined the Hagana. He was blinded by a grenade in the very first week of the War of Independence. It was a terrible tragedy. He had a weak personality to begin with, but his disability left him totally dependent on others. In fact, he agreed to marry a woman he'd never even met, a Syrian girl, just because Y picked her out for him."

It was clear that every story would lead down the same road. "Why did Y care who he married?" I asked.

"Y had promised Ibra he would stay in touch with his descendants and protect them. He'd even promised Ibra that he would one day marry one of them." She looked down demurely.

"Meaning you?" She nodded, smiling joyfully.

"Itzik lived a pretty quiet life after the war," she continued. "Y was never that involved with him, but he adored Itzik's younger son—my father."

I picked up my pen, which had fallen on the floor again. "Tell me about your father."

"Dad grew up in the rough streets of Katamonim, with a disabled father and an older brother who ran with the street gangs. On the surface he seemed like a quiet mama's boy, but he was actually quite devious. He rewrote Itzik's will to make himself the sole heir and tricked his blind father into signing it. When his brother heard about it, he was furious. Dad had to skip town or he would have had him knocked off."

That strange sensation returned, as if I'd heard the story before. "Where did he go?"

"Back to my grandmother's hometown in Syria. It was a crazy thing to do—all the Jews were frantically trying to leave, and he slipped in the other way. But he was desperate; he knew his brother would never follow him there. He lived with his uncle for many years, although that didn't end well either. They had a falling out when Dad cheated him out of some investments. Anyway, by the time he finally left Syria and returned to Israel, he was a wealthy man, married and with a slew of kids."

"And your husband was close to him?" They certainly sounded like two of a kind.

"Y knew all about my father—like I said, he always kept close tabs on Ibra's descendants. Getting out of Syria was no easy feat in those days, and it was Y who arranged for my father and his family to pass through the mountains undetected. They finally met up at the most dangerous point, when Dad was ready to cross the border. Hit it off instantly. They spent the whole night talking and drinking and wrestling—it made quite an impression on both of them. A macho bonding thing, I guess. They were so well matched as wrestlers that neither was able to pin the other down. My father ended up with a slight limp, but he wore it like a badge of honor. From that night on they were fast friends."

I could easily imagine it—two con artists, each used to having the upper hand. Or perhaps it was more than just a "wrestling match"—a savage, passionate coupling, so violent it would leave one party limping.

"I'm named after him," Israela said proudly.

"After who?"

"My father. After they wrestled to a draw, Y changed his name, out of respect, and it kind of caught on."

Typical of the sociopathic personality; conferring pseudonyms was the ultimate honor to these guys. I wondered how many fake names Y had gone through himself before just giving up and taking on an initial.

But why was I even taking this so literally? The whole narrative was ludicrous. I found myself wondering what psychic purpose could be served by the invention of such a dysfunctional family saga; most psychotic origin stories were grandiose and idealized. And even if some of her story was true, I didn't need all this detail. I'd just spent nearly an hour captivated by fanciful tales of ancestors who probably never existed. Again, she seemed to read my mind.

"You probably think we're off topic, but if you're going to understand my situation you have to know this stuff," she said. "This isn't just a marriage that can be dissolved at whim! Long before I was even born, Y promised my great-grandfather he'd marry me, take care of me forever. He can't just back out on something that sacred, and neither can I! It's like . . . like a *covenant*. You understand, don't you?"

Suddenly, I did.

8

Had I been in some kind of trance? The immigrants, Ibra and Sana; the blind Itzik, almost sacrificed as a child; the wrestling, limping father after whom she was named. What kind of spell had she cast on me that I could have possibly missed it?

I spent a restless night, and then a restless weekend, brooding about Israela and the bizarre, biblically inspired family history she had spun. If she truly believed these ancestor tales, then she was far more psychotic than she seemed. Or had she been mocking me the whole time? Perhaps it had been a critical mistake to allow her to take over the therapist's chair—by doing so, had I unconsciously ceded my professional persona and control? If so, there was something about it that felt both dangerous and liberating.

It was now obvious who the elusive, all-knowing Y was standing in for. But rather than satisfy my curiosity, I felt inundated with new questions. I couldn't wait to see Israela again. I congratulated myself for not having referred her for a psychiatric consultation in the first session. Her story was far too interesting to share, never mind subject to the sledgehammer of psychiatric medications. I wanted her to myself.

Sunday morning, I strode into the building a few minutes after 8:00. It was ridiculously early, but I hadn't been sleeping much anyway. I was determined to start attacking the moldering paperwork and get Jezebel off my back. I now had real motivation to play by the rules; I wasn't going to give that hovering hag any excuse to meddle in my sessions with Israela.

As I headed for the elevator, I noticed the Security desk was empty. The only other person in the lobby was the custodian, an ancient Yemeni who wheezed and creaked with every step. He froze over his mop when he saw me.

"Dr. Benami, it's a good thing you're here—"

I was in no mood to hear his perennial complaints. "Not now, *saha,* I'm very busy."

"But—"

I walked straight into the elevator and let it close behind me. Couldn't encourage these guys. I was so pleased with how I'd shaken him off that it took me a minute to notice the tension in the clinic waiting room.

"Dr. Benami, it's a good thing you're here!"

Well, it certainly was rare to hear that twice in one morning. For a moment I let myself hope that the staff might actually be starting to appreciate me. It was the new girl—religious and quiet. What was her name? Then I noticed what the commotion was all about.

There was an old man standing stiffly in front of my office door, as if to guard it from attack. What little you could see of his face, above the full, untrimmed gray beard, was deeply creased and weathered. He was dressed in a flowing white robe and dusty sandals, a large, knitted white *kipa* covering his entire scalp. His two hands rested lightly on a roughly whittled staff made of olive wood. But for the *kipa*, he might have just stepped off the set of *Lawrence of Arabia*. The handful of patients in the waiting room were all staring in the direction of his rigid frame. He had turned his head slowly toward me when the receptionist called my name. His voice was gravelly and deep, and he spoke slowly, as if every word that dropped from his mouth was a precious gem. "I must have a word with you, Dr. Benami."

Before I could respond, the receptionist cut in. "Doctor, he was already standing there when I opened the clinic this morning. Gave me a terrible shock." She lowered her voice, though everyone in the waiting room could still hear. "Those are the first words he's spoken. He doesn't have an appointment, he won't register, and he won't sit down."

Another homegrown case of Jerusalem syndrome? And this one had a costume to boot.

The old man's voice was low and powerful. "It's quite urgent that I speak with you," he said. "There isn't much time."

The new receptionist—eager to please and agitated by the intrusion into her still-new routine—continued to address me directly. "I've called down to Security, Doctor. They should be here any minute."

"No, that's all right," I said. "I'll let you know if I need any help." I could feel everyone in the waiting room staring at me as I took a step toward the old man and motioned to my office door. "May I?"

He stepped aside, graciously allowing me entrance into my own office, and I caught a dry whiff of the desert in his well-worn robe. He followed me into the office and stared over my shoulder. I neither sat nor offered him a chair.

"How can I help you, sir?"

"She thinks of no one but herself," he said calmly, gazing out the window, unmoving. "She lives a life of luxury, drapes herself in silk, adorns herself with gold, consumes the finest foods, the most expensive wines. She cares for nothing but her own comfort and ease."

I had been ready for psychotic thundering and was suddenly thrown off. "Who are you talking about?" I asked.

"She is full of pride and arrogance. Primps and preens, decorates and redecorates her house. She cheats and lies, shoplifts for pleasure. She has lost all sense of value and humility!"

"All right, sir," I said in my most calming voice. "I'm sure we'll be able to help you. If you'll just wait a minute, I'll arrange for whoever is on call . . ."

"I am a friend of the one she calls Y." I froze, my hand halfway to the phone.

The old man turned toward me, his gaze fierce and dignified. "I'm sorry, what?" I finally managed.

"I know she comes to see you," he declared in his sonorous voice.

Nothing remotely like this had ever happened before. I'd had a furious husband follow me to my car one night after his wife confessed the nature of our therapeutic relationship. But this man was claiming to be friends with someone who I was 99 percent sure was a figment of a patient's psychotic delusion.

I needed a minute to think. I needed him out of my office. "I'm sorry, but I don't know who you're referring to," I said.

The man continued, unblinking. "And she does need help! But you will not be able to help her unless you hear me out."

"Look, Mr.—"

His eyes flickered. "Call me Ami."

"Ami . . . look, we have strict rules—"

"You will tell me she is unhappy. How can a life of such selfishness make one happy? She spends her days reading fashion magazines, admiring herself in the mirror, filling her closets with useless frippery. She lives a tawdry, hollow life, then weeps with despair!"

Was it possible that this crazy old man really did know her? I suddenly remembered the fear that had flashed across her face in our first session when she told me people were following her. Textbook paranoia—and yet here, two weeks later, was someone claiming to know where she'd been and who she'd been talking to. Another thought suddenly struck me, sending a cold electricity through my body. Was it possible that someone powerful and manipulative enough to induce an old man to break into a clinic first thing in the morning really *was* in a relationship with Israela?

"How did you get in here?" I asked, trying not to show my alarm.

"She thinks she can live this decadent life and he will not know?" His eyes shone. "She thinks she can fool him by wrapping her stiff-necked head in a scarf?" His voice was rising ominously. "Does she know so little of him? Doesn't she understand that he sees everything she does!?"

My professional facade vanished, replaced by a burning need to know: was there a chance that Y was real after all?

"Is her husband following her? Did he tell you to come and talk to me?"

He pounded his staff on the floor. "He does not need to follow her! He knows! He knows her better than she knows herself!"

"Look, stalking is illegal—"

He silenced me with a look, but when he spoke, his voice was calmer. "Dr. Benami, I am not an important man . . . like you." He said the words with an excessive deference that I could only take for sarcasm. "I am a simple shepherd who tends his flocks in the hills surrounding Tekoa. Have you ever been there?" He didn't wait for a response, a faraway look in his eyes. "We have some of the most spectacular views in the country, of the Judean hills and the Dead Sea beyond. I would happily spend all my days on those shrub-filled, rocky slopes. But when Y came to the pastures to summon me, I had no choice but to follow."

I had never been to Tekoa, a West Bank settlement southeast of Jerusalem. But no settler I'd ever met dressed in Bedouin-like robes.

"You're a shepherd? With flocks?" I asked.

He stared past me with silent dignity.

"OK, fine, a shepherd," I said, nodding.

"Y is a very old friend of mine," he went on. "We go back to pre-state days. He is a remarkable man who is today in great distress. He insists that his wife reform herself and become a useful, contributing member of society." I opened my mouth to respond, but he cut me off, his voice rising again.

"She must change. He will tolerate this lifestyle no longer!"

I tried to take a reasonable tone. "If your friend is so upset with his wife—"

"How do you think a little orphan from Egypt came to be living in the lap of luxury?" he cried. "He saved her life! How do you suppose she affords her fancy clothes and gourmet meals? Who bought her the mansion she now lives in? How could she live this decadent lifestyle without him?" Seeing the surprise on my face, he almost smiled. "She didn't mention that, did she? Of course he supports her! She has no other source of income. The house, the furnishings, the food, the clothes—it all comes from him! She acts as if it were all her doing, this luxurious life she lives."

"But she says he's never around—" It was out of my mouth before I could stop myself. But if Ami noticed my egregious breach of professionalism he didn't let on.

"Never around?" he bellowed, eyes widening. "He devotes his entire life to her! She's too stubborn to even notice!" I wondered if the people in the waiting room could hear his booming voice through the door.

"OK, OK. Calm down," I said. I pushed Israela out of my mind and tried to refocus the conversation. "So why did you come here today?"

His faraway look suddenly vanished, and he seemed to actually notice me for the first time. I saw now that it was the bushy gray eyebrows and deeply creased face that had given him such a forbidding look; the eyes themselves were a soft, caramel brown.

"Dr. Benami, have you fully taken in the abject misery that surrounds you? The unending carnage from this bestial intifada?"

"Yes, of course. We treat many people here who've been affected by the violence. But I don't see—"

"Just last month, in my own peaceful village of Tekoa, a woman, nine months pregnant, was shot by terrorists in the stomach. Have you ever heard of anything so ghastly?" He waited for me to respond, his face etched with pain.

"Yes, of course—we all heard about that incident," I said. "Did you know her?"

"Of course I knew her. I have lived in Tekoa for a very long time. Five people have been killed in our village just this past year, including a young mother while she was sitting with her family in a car—three children, irreparably traumatized for life. And then there were the two teenaged boys out on a hike, just last year, who were bound, stabbed, and mutilated, their skulls smashed with rocks, their blood smeared on the walls of the cave where they were found." His voice remained steady. "There isn't a child in our village who doesn't suffer from terrors. We hear them screaming in the middle of the night. And are these monsters even ashamed? No, they take full credit for their crimes, celebrate their grisly deeds as a victory against the 'Zionist oppressor.' How can human beings stoop to such levels of barbarity?" He stared at me, and I found myself struggling for words.

"Well, it may be that—"

He cut me off, his voice incredulous. "You will make excuses for these ruthless child-murderers?"

"No, of course not, it's terrible, but . . ."

"Will you also make excuses for the United Nations and the screaming hypocrites of Europe? Do they think we enjoy besieging a church in Bethlehem? Fighting street-to-street in Jenin? They say nothing when our children and young mothers are butchered in the streets, but howl and scream when we try to defend ourselves. They are shameless! Less than sixty years since they tried to exterminate us themselves!"

"Well, I'm not sure there's a connection . . ."

"But forget this heinous intifada. What happened to the model society we dreamed of creating in this land? Do you even notice the wretched beggars that line the streets of Jerusalem? There are hungry children right here in this sacred city! Do you know about the trafficked women coming over our borders? As this country becomes wealthier there has been an increase in every manner of social ill, from divorce to abandoned babies to child abuse. Every day there are more unemployed, more homeless, more drugs and alcoholism, more prostitution. Outside of the settlements, which you so disdain," his tone severe and reproachful, "there is nothing left of the Zionist dream, no ideals of any kind. We have become a society that cares about nothing but chasing material wealth. Is it for this that my parents fled the pogroms of Russia?" He stared at me, his brow deeply furrowed. "And yet, with all this social distress, she flits around town following her selfish whims!"

"Well, it's hardly her responsibility—," I began.

"Whose responsibility is it?"

"Look, Ami, you have no right—"

"Whose responsibility is it, Dr. Benami?"

The stress of the preceding two weeks came crashing down on me in a sudden wave of exhaustion. I felt shaken, off-balance. Why was I talking politics with a psychotic settler, a make-believe shepherd? I had broken all rules of confidentiality by even acknowledging that I knew Israela. What was I supposed to do now? Threaten him with security guards? Try to have him hospitalized? Insist that he leave right away? But there were questions I still needed him to answer. Had he really been sent by a person calling himself Y? It would not be surprising if someone with Y's uber-Zionist background was now a leader in the settler movement. But what did all this social conscience talk have to do with the chronically absent husband, the underground crime boss, the intrepid Zionist recruiter, the obvious psychopath? Or—it suddenly occurred to me—if Y did *not* exist, were Ami and Israela both embroiled in the same biblically inspired delusion? I felt panic rising in my chest.

"May I sit down?" The quiet, deep voice had returned. He pointed to my leather recliner with a questioning look. I nodded before I had a chance to consider.

He carefully leaned his staff against the wall and lowered himself into the chair as I settled into the now-familiar couch. "Please forgive me," he said mildly. "I do get carried away at times, but it is all so terribly distressing." He suddenly noticed the Chagall painting on the far wall of the office and nodded at it reverently, as if my exquisite taste in art made up for my other obvious deficits. "It's beautiful," he said, with what almost sounded like awe.

I glanced at the painting. "I don't like it much myself," I said.

"Man and woman, floating, in harmony. Of this world and yet not of this world." He gazed at me for a moment from under his gray, caterpillar brows. "Chagall was a great genius. He captured love so perfectly, no?"

"I don't know," I said, immediately embarrassed by my response. It occurred to me for an instant that perhaps Ami knew all about my marital troubles, but I quickly dismissed the notion as ridiculous.

He paused for a moment, reflective. "He expects very little from her, really. He is happy to provide for her, to give her a life of ease and comfort. He loves her deeply and knows his duty as her husband. He wants only one thing in return—that she lead a life of compassion and service to those less fortunate than she. After all, there is no joy in materialism—in fancy clothes, gluttony, and greed. The only true joy comes from devoting your life to higher ideals, to serving others less fortunate than you. And the need in this country is immeasurable," he said, shaking his head sadly. "But I hardly need to tell that to you, one who spends his days ministering to the suffering soul of our nation." I looked into the chastening eyes and saw no hint of amusement, yet I was sure that he was mocking me. He knew exactly what kind of a fraud I was.

He sighed deeply. "Dr. Benami, I hope you understand the seriousness of this situation. If she doesn't change her ways soon, terrible things will happen."

Another surge of alarm coursed through me. "What do you mean? What will happen?"

"There will be no escaping his wrath. She wants him to return, but his return will be a terrible day of reckoning!"

"Are you suggesting that he will hurt her in some way? If this is a threat, you understand that I would be legally obligated—"

His voice rose again. "Dr. Benami, she must be warned!"

"Please, Ami, let's both stay calm," I said, my heart pounding.

"He will send messengers until she hears!"

"Why doesn't he just talk to her himself?"

He stared at me in astonishment. "He talks to her all the time! She is a stubborn, stiff-necked woman who does not listen and does not hear!"

I thought of her sudden hyper-alertness during our last session and wondered if Ami experienced the same intrusive auditory hallucinations.

"But you do?" I asked, trying to keep my voice compassionate. "How does he communicate with you?"

"What kind of question is that?" Ami asked, sounding truly puzzled. "He comes and talks to me, just like he talks to her, like I'm talking to you now."

"Then perhaps you could tell him—"

He cut me off curtly. "I only carry his messages. I do not bear messages to him."

"If he would come to a session—"

"He has spoken through me," he said firmly. "Heed my words well, and you will need no other message!"

I suddenly wanted nothing more than to have him out of the room. By clinic protocol I should have been seeking a psychiatric consult, but it was clear that he would never comply. There was no point in prolonging this meeting any longer.

"Thank you for coming, Ami," I said, standing. "But you mustn't come back."

He nodded and struggled to his feet, his voice dropping back into a soft register. "Dr. Benami, I will not bother you again."

He reached over to grasp his olive wood staff, holding it in front of himself with both hands. I now saw that the head of the staff was carved in the shape of an extended arm, the palm open and facing to the side.

"What an unusual staff you have," I said, before I could stop myself. "Did you carve it yourself?"

He looked down at it, stroked the wooden arm lovingly with his fingertips. "No. It was made for me by Y, as a special gift. It bears his logo—the outstretched arm."

"He . . . he has a logo?"

He looked at me with compassion, as if pitying my slow comprehension.

"Please understand that he does not wish her any ill," he said calmly. "To the contrary. He still believes that one day they will be reunited in harmony. He loves her deeply—he has never loved another. When she truly changes her ways, they will yet live together as devoted husband and wife." Without looking back, he walked to the door and quietly left the room.

Everyone in the waiting room watched his dignified departure—his robes trailing, his staff clicking lightly against the floor. The new receptionist's mouth was hanging open. It was only as she turned toward me that I realized how shaken I must have looked.

"Doctor, are you all right?" she asked. "Security was here, but I sent them back down. Should I call them again?"

"It's OK, uh . . ."

"Henya."

"Henya, of course." I could just imagine how bizarre this story would sound when she related it to Jezebel. "Don't worry, he did no harm," I said with all the confidence I could muster.

"Shouldn't he see a psychiatrist?" she asked, in an earnest, worried voice.

"No need," I said. "He's of no danger to anyone."

"But if he comes again . . ."

I smiled at her reassuringly and closed the office door.

9

Back in my office, I shut the door, locking it for good measure. My hands were shaking. There were no Jewish shepherds living in the Judean hills—of course he should have seen a psychiatrist. But had some mysterious figure really told him to come here? How did he know so much about Israela? I paced for a moment, then settled back into my desk chair. A box of large paper clips in easy reach, I began to work, methodically, on my paper clip flip. As I watched each silver streak somersault toward Chagall's leering bovine head, I struggled to construct a rational explanation for Ami's peculiar visitation.

If he was really a settler, as he claimed, that would explain a part of it. They were a fanatical bunch, and without them, I was sure, we would have had peace long ago. It was true that they were the last idealists left—the only ones who could still use the phrase "Zionist dream" without a hint of irony—but that made them no less dangerous. Not that I had any greater sympathy for the bleeding-heart lefties handing out care packages to the families of suicide bombers. No one in the country, right or left, had a coherent map that could steer us out of this mess. Still, the settlers—my sister included—seemed particularly unhinged. There had been a rise, as the intifada had intensified, of Jewish terrorist cells with grandiose names exacting revenge on innocent Palestinian villagers. Was that what "the outstretched arm"—Y's "logo"—was all about?

A paper clip pinged off the frame before it plummeted to the floor. If Y was real and a leader in the settler movement, how did Israela fit into this? Why send Ami to complain about what his long-estranged wife did all day?

Despite myself, I had been drawn to Ami: his passion, his eloquence, and the warm eyes embedded in that harsh, weathered face. He was right that the intifada was distracting us all from a greater rot—the social fabric of the country was fraying at the edges. I thought of Delia and my brief, humiliating glimpse into the world she inhabited. Why had Ami mentioned the women being trafficked across the border? Did he know about my sordid little excursion to Soreq's Pub? Of course not. I had to stop attributing to him all this uncanny knowledge.

Though I had to admit: Ami's scornful description of Israela had reminded me a little too closely of my own situation with Nava. It occurred to me now that if we did divorce, the issue of who would support her and Yudit was not a small one. Her dancing barely paid a slave's wage. The fact that she enjoyed pampering herself with beautiful clothes and jewelry and decorating the house with an assemblage of useless tchotchkes had never bothered me much. But how would I feel about supporting her now, with her expensive taste and low-wage career? Would I feel resentful, like Y, of supporting a wife with whom I no longer lived? Would I feel I had the right to tell her on what she could spend her money or how she should spend her time? I felt a familiar, comforting flood of indignation. Had she wondered for even a moment about her financial prospects when she'd self-righteously tossed her wedding ring into my coffee cup?

By the time Henya called to say that my 9:00 was waiting, I had smacked the floating cow face with five paper clips and convinced myself that Ami was just another atypical case of Jerusalem syndrome: an unstable, overly zealous settler, drunk on his messianic visions. A make-believe shepherd, playing the role, for some unfathomable reason, of chastising biblical prophet.

Nothing more, nothing less.

As I was leaving the office the next evening, exhausted by another harrowingly overscheduled day, I found another handwritten note in my box. I opened it, already dreading its contents.

> Kobi,
>
> Henya told me about the white-robed gentleman she discovered in the clinic yesterday morning. She said that you talked to him and that he left quietly, but needless to say, she was quite upset by the experience. I'm surprised that no intake was done, and no psychiatric consult requested. As you know, the recent surge in suicide bombings has triggered an increase in apocalyptic delusions, some of them quite unusual. It is incumbent upon all of us to handle these cases responsibly. These individuals can seem safe, even charming, but their delusions are no less psychotic and dangerous.
>
> I also wanted to briefly mention another patient of yours: the woman who calls herself "Israela." Sounds like a very interesting

case. I find it surprising that you don't comment on the blatantly delusional projection of self onto the collective story of the Jewish people. Perhaps a highly unusual form of Jerusalem syndrome, induced by the recent increase in terrorism? If her delusional system continues to be articulated within the biblical paradigm, she would make a fascinating case study for publication. Happy to talk to you more about this at some time.

Jezebel

I felt irrationally betrayed by Henya, though I could see how the whole scene might have unsettled a new receptionist. It had unsettled me too, but it had been perfectly clear to me that Ami would never have agreed to an intake or a psychiatric consult. As far as he was concerned, he'd come to deliver a message, not seek treatment. Didn't he have that right?

Heat flooded my face as I read the last paragraph again. The friendly, erudite tone; the assumption of shared professional interest—what the hell was she up to? I should have guessed that Jezebel would continue to remind me of my humiliating probationary status by instantly scanning my every note. But if she thought she could make up for this with a thin pretense of collegiality, she was sorely mistaken. I was damned if I was going to let Jezebel or the arrogant, drug-happy psychiatrists maneuver their way into the most interesting case I'd had in years. I crumpled the paper and gave it a practiced fling into the garbage on my way out the door.

When I got home, there were two telephone messages from my father. The first one informed me, in a measured tone, that my mother had collapsed that afternoon in the stifling heat of the kitchen, surrounded by her bubbling pots. He had found her on the floor, awake but dazed, with a large wooden spoon firmly in her grip. He was calling from her hospital room—I should come as soon as I could.

I was already pulling my jacket back on when the second message clicked on. "Don't come anymore tonight," came my father's voice, tired. "Don't even call. I'm going to try and get some sleep in the chair by her bed. Anat's coming in the morning. Maybe you can come too, if you're not too busy?" His Yiddish accent was thicker than I'd ever heard it.

I had a restless night, half-dreaming encounters in which Ami berated me with my father's voice. The next morning, I left a hasty, half-apologetic phone message for Jezebel and drove to Petah Tikva. My mother's room was on the third floor of Beilinson Hospital, where I found my father perched at the edge of a chair by her bedside as Anat fussed with the sheets. My mother looked frail and vacant, and there was a mild drooping on the right side of her mouth and eye. "Ima," I said and kissed her soft, wrinkled cheek. She followed me with her eyes but showed no other reaction to my presence. I sank into a chair by the foot of the bed, trying to take in the enormity of what was happening. The stroke, my father reported, had primarily affected the language center of the brain, resulting in expressive aphasia. She was unable to speak, write out her thoughts, or use language in any way. Despite her unresponsiveness, the doctors thought she could understand more than she was letting on. They were confident that with therapy her speech would return soon, although there were no guarantees.

I found myself with little to do or say. As the morning wore on, my father punctuated the uneasy silence with idle speculations about my mother's needs—"You think she's cold?"; "The sun is in her eyes"—as Anat bustled about, looking for blankets, closing curtains, brushing her hair, finding food, a perpetual motion machine of helpfulness. That left me alone, in my sticky chair by the wall, to ponder the blank landscape of my mother's face—not angry, nor frustrated, nor resistant in any way to the useless attentions of the nurses and her overly eager family. She didn't nod or frown, didn't gesture or moan. If she hadn't continually tracked our every move, I would have wondered if any consciousness was left at all. I analyzed the soft features of her face as if I had never seen them before. When I was a young child, she had never allowed me to put my hands on her face, and I had always vaguely associated her aversion to being touched in the face with the traumas of war. But perhaps that wasn't right. How could one possibly tease out the threads of the woman she might have been if she had grown up under even marginally normal circumstances?

A siren suddenly sounded, interrupting my thoughts, and the hospital hallways fell into an eerie silence but for the beeping and whirring of machinery. I was momentarily panicked by the harsh, piercing cry, thinking, for a brief second, that the hospital was under terrorist attack. My father rose, laboriously, from his chair, and Anat froze by the window, staring out. Checking the clock above the bed, which stood exactly at 11:00, I came back to my senses. With all the commotion, I had somehow forgotten what day it was—Yom HaShoah, Holocaust Remembrance Day. I rose as well, standing at the foot of my mother's bed, scanning her face for comprehension, but her blank stare was inscrutable. I had paused for this siren every year of my life, but never, within memory, like this, with them. I glanced at my father's bent form, then fought the rising sob that clutched at my jaw as the room filled, for an interminable two minutes, with the dead, the never-spoken. The clock on the wall ticked loudly through the silence, reminding me of my father's description of lying awake the last night in his childhood bedroom, before their deportation to the ghetto, listening in frozen terror to the ticking of their living room clock. By the time the piercing cry of the siren finally wound down and the scurrying of the nurses resumed, the ritualized vigil had done its work. Even Anat's frenetic energy had deflated, and we passed the rest of the day, by my broken mother's bedside, in a state of uncharacteristic gravity and calm.

They kept her for three days. Commuting to the hospital nightly after a long day's work, I found an odd comfort in observing my mother's silence, a growing relief at not having to engage with her pointless chatter. Who was my mother? My father was a font of stories—of his childhood, his parents and grandparents, the eccentric characters from the shtetl of his youth, the horrors of the war, the drama of immigration. Opinions and analyses flowed from him on every subject, but it was only dawning on me now, since this thick veil of silence had descended, what a cipher my mother had always been. The only thing that ever seemed to matter to her was caring for her family's physical needs. She had talked all the time, but never said much of anything; had worried about us constantly, yet been so oblivious to our pain. She took so naturally to silence, I wondered if she had been programmed for this from an early age, as if her mindless verbosity had been merely a curtain to the muteness that had always crouched beyond. I sat opposite her for three long evenings, wondering what had caused her to be so utterly devoid of stories.

And then she was home, as silent as the day of the stroke, having proved herself indifferent and immune to the earnest ministrations of an army of pretty, young speech therapists. Anat began to shuttle back and forth daily between her village in Samaria and the apartment in Petah Tikva, cooking and cleaning for my father as he struggled to maintain the household. Partly because I earnestly wanted to be useful and partly because I didn't want Anat to have yet another moral high ground from which to pelt me with insults, I asked my father what I could do to help. He answered instantly: "Find Gal."

I blinked. "Kobi, you have to find him," he said. "Your mother needs to see Gali. This whole incident came about from all her worrying." He shook his head. "It's all she talked about of late, especially after Libke's death. It made her so anxious, not knowing where he was. She'll never get better if she doesn't see him."

"People don't get strokes from worrying," I said, more pedantically than I'd meant to. I quickly changed the subject. "Who was this Libke? Ima never even mentioned her."

He waved my question aside. "You have to find Gal," he said firmly. I could see there was no getting away from it. If I really wanted to help, he was telling me how.

"Where was he when you last heard from him?" I asked.

"India."

"India's a big country. Anything more specific?"

"He said he was in an ashram but wasn't going to stay much longer. He had heard about a swami in another part of India. But that was at least three months ago."

"Has he been in touch with any of his childhood friends? Army buddies? Girlfriends? You know anyone I can call for a lead?" I was already annoyed with Gal—always Ima's favorite, always so ungrateful.

"He's cut off contact with everyone. Even Rami, his best friend from childhood, hasn't heard a word in months."

"I'll give it a try," I said, "but I don't have much to go on."

"You'll find him, Kobi. I know you will. You don't keep in touch much yourself, but in an emergency you'll come through. I always tell your mother that when she complains about you. 'In an emergency,' I say, 'he'll always come through.'" He nodded vigorously to emphasize the point.

"Thanks, Abba. Your trust in me is endearing."

He'd aged a decade since I'd seen him on Passover, his lips sagging, his right leg suddenly dragging behind him as he walked. He brushed it off—his sciatica was acting up, that was all. Although he was only two years older than my mother, I'd always assumed his health would go first. His whole body seemed weighted down by the unforeseen burden of caretaking. If he wanted me to find Gal, I'd do my best. But I wasn't hopeful.

The Israeli embassy in New Delhi had no record of a Gal Benami. I asked them about the most popular spiritual destinations for Israelis in India, and they laughed at the question: "You won't find a single ashram in India that's not crawling with Israelis."

On my way home from work, I stopped in a bookstore and picked up a thick paperback called *Spiritual Sites in India*. It had a couple of hundred entries. I figured if I called ten a day, eventually I'd track him down. The first call, though, wasn't promising.

"I'm looking for an Israeli named Gal Benami," I told the cheerful voice on the other end of the phone.

"You would like to meet with Swami Baba?" he asked hopefully.

"No, I'm not in India. I'm calling from Israel."

"Ah, but you must come to India to meet Swami Baba," he insisted. "You will live in the ashram for three weeks to spiritually prepare. In this time, you will do yoga and meditation and chanting and aromas and spiritual cleansing. Then you will meet with Swami Baba. It will change your life! We give lifetime guarantee."

"A lifetime guarantee? For real?"

"When do you come to India?"

"I'm not coming to India. I'm looking for my brother."

"We are all brothers under Swami Baba's roof," he said with delight.

"No, no, my real brother. The one I actually grew up with. Can't you check your records?"

"If you come, you will be so welcome," he said. "As a brother, yes. You will learn to see the radiant light that surrounds all beings. It will shine so brightly, you will wonder how you never saw it before! There is no difference among us. We are all brothers. Yes, yes, this is very good."

"I appreciate the sentiment," I said, repressing the urge to curse at his cheery voice. "But this is my real brother I'm talking about. The one who has the same mother and father. He's missing and I'm looking for him."

"We are all seekers here, every one of us," he said, and I could imagine him nodding happily. "You will find such joy here. Please bring white clothes. It will help you achieve a state of purity much more quickly. Yes, yes, we are all seekers, this is exactly right."

After four such calls, I was ready to give up on the entire quest. If Gal wanted to be found, he would have kept in touch. It was just like him to be so selfish. But I couldn't forget my mother's unblinking stare or my father's rare, earnest request that I find him. I had to keep looking.

It suddenly occurred to me that Yossi might be able to help. He had spent time in India, had visited ashrams, and was in the spiritual-seeker business himself. Perhaps there was an international network of holy men who could assist each other in these kinds of matters. Anyway, I was curious to see his shop—looking, in fact, for an excuse to visit.

Sunday afternoon, ignoring the receptionist's spiteful glare and my own deep anxieties—there had been another deadly bombing in central Jerusalem, this time in the crowded Friday afternoon market of Mahane Yehuda—I cut out of work early and made my way down to the Old City, a place I had avoided visiting for years.

Walking through Jaffa Gate always reminded me of the first time I had entered the Old City in '67, my father gripping my hand tightly. It had been a hot summer day, not a month after the Six Day War. I remembered being surrounded by tense soldiers and makeshift signs, the air dark with flies and pungent with the stench of garbage, the hostile, frightened eyes of the Arab shopkeepers, the pulsing exhilaration and fear as we made our way down the wide, sooty steps of the *shuq* toward the newly liberated Western Wall.

The area had long since been cleaned up for tourists, though it still reverberated with the wailing, just-over-your-head noise of the muezzin. I headed in the general direction of the Jewish Quarter and stopped an ultra-Orthodox man to ask if he knew the location of the third temple fundraisers. He looked me up and down suspiciously, then gave me detailed directions through the maze of Old City streets.

I arrived at the third temple storefront, upstairs from the fancy shops of the Cardo, and poked my head in for a look. A fat man with a full red beard was enthusiastically explaining to a well-dressed elderly couple the model of the third temple that filled the middle of the room. In his native, American English he showed them where the sacrifices would take place once the temple would be rebuilt, graphically depicting what would happen to the various parts of the carcass. When he saw me, he emphatically gestured for me to join them. I politely shook my head no and quickly backed out the door.

Yossi's shop was, indeed, just a few doors down. I glanced in before entering the atmospherically lit, grotto-like space, with its arched, multi-leveled ceiling and whitewashed walls. Behind a small counter, Yossi was intricately mapping with his fingers the upturned hands of an elderly woman, his brows furrowed with focus. A tall, young, very blond couple was palming a colorful array of stones, carefully weighing each one in their hands to judge its effect. Barely visible in an alcove at the far back corner of the shop was a wiry man with long hair and a sparse beard, sitting cross-legged, eyes closed in deep concentration, mouthing words under his breath.

Yossi briefly looked up when I entered the shop. His eyebrows shot up in surprise. He gave me an overly reverent nod before turning back to his customer.

The walls of the shop were lined with glass cases full of haphazardly arranged antiquities. As I waited for Yossi to finish, I scanned the cluttered shelves of oil lamps, clay figurines, and cracked pots, wondering if I might find a gift for Yudit in the jumbled mess. Here and there was a piece of jewelry made out of old coins or crystals or potsherds. I picked up a necklace glittering with an array of colorful old stones and held it aloft. Would a preteen wear something like that? I had no idea. I imagined Nava shaking her head at this latest example of my practical and aesthetic cluelessness.

As I came closer to the back of the shop, I got a better view of the long-haired chanting man. The elderly woman had left the store, and Yossi was now posing for photos with the young blond couple. I walked into the incense-filled shadows of the man's cozy nook and stared at the bald spot at the crown of his head, but he remained steeped in reverie. The first indication of a shift in consciousness was that his mouth stopped moving. With painful slowness, the face lifted and the eyes opened. Dilated as they were, I would have known those eyes anywhere, had known them since earliest

childhood. He was the only one of us to have inherited our mother's most
striking feature—her shimmering, light green eyes.

"Gal."

"Kobi," he said. His gaze was unfocused, but what unnerved me more
was that he didn't seem at all surprised to see me.

"How'd you know it was me?" he asked.

"I've known you since you were a baby. You lose a few kilos and grow
your hair long, you think I won't recognize you?"

"I have sworn off haircuts as I have sworn off wine and heavy drink.
The hair is the crowning glory, symbolic of *Keter* . . ."

"Yes, yes, I know, the divine Crown. Although you should know that
your divine crown is getting a little thin on top." The attempt at humor fell
flat, as it always did with Gal, crushed under the pervasive annoyance I always felt in his presence. Annoyance, followed instantly by guilt.

"Gal, are you OK?"

"How'd you find me?" Every word came slow and thick, as though
pulled to the surface from a great depth.

I shrugged. It *had* been extremely improbable, now that I thought
about it. "Just a lucky draw," I said. "I'm a friend of Yossi's."

His eyes widened. "Reb Yosef? You're a friend of Reb Yosef?"

"Is that what he calls himself here?" I laughed. "Well on the squash
court he's just plain Yossi."

"You play squash with Reb Yosef?" He was staring at me wide-eyed. I
felt another flash of annoyance.

"Gal, I didn't even know you were in Jerusalem. No one in the family
knows where you are. Do you know how worried they've been about you?"

He sat up straighter. "I didn't want to be found. Our family . . ." He
didn't look at me. "But I figured if I stayed in the Old City I was safe. I never
thought I'd see you in a place like this."

"You're right, it's not my usual hangout."

"But I'm glad to hear you know Reb Yosef," Gal said, nodding, his voice
full of condescension. "He's a very holy man. He could help you, Kobi. If
anyone can, it's Reb Yosef."

"His name's Yossi, and he's no kind of rebbe," I snapped. "Anyway, I'm
not looking for help; I'm looking for you."

There was a long, laden pause before he spoke. "You're the same as
ever, full of cynicism and negative energy." He resettled his posture and
closed his eyes. "I've got to get back to my practice. I was in a deep space
when you came." His brow suddenly furrowed, his eyes still tightly shut.
"Don't tell Abba and Ima you saw me. If you do, I'll have to leave the country
again, and I don't want to leave right now."

I could have strangled him. Instead I took a deep breath and kept my voice calm. "How did you get involved with Yossi?"

He opened his eyes. "I met Reb Yosef in India when he was visiting the ashram. We started talking, and I realized how much I could learn from him. You know, Kobi, so many things that I discovered in Eastern mysticism can be found in Judaism also. Reb Yosef is opening me up to a whole world of ancient Jewish wisdom . . ." He trailed off as his eyes fluttered shut.

"Gal, come back," I said. "Ima's had a stroke."

Again, the painfully slow raising of the head, the prolonged process of opening those yellow-flecked, emerald eyes—in my mother, opaque as our living room curtains; in Gal, fragile as sea glass.

"What did you say?"

"Ima's had a stroke."

He was quiet for a long time, and I wondered if he'd even understood.

"Gal, did you hear me?"

"Is she OK?" he asked finally.

"No, she's not OK. She can't speak or communicate in any way. Abba's convinced that she'll only get better if she sees you. He sent me to look for you."

He was silent, staring off into the distance, but at least his eyes were still open.

"The two of you seem to be acquainted." Suddenly, Yossi was standing next to me, the shop now empty of customers.

"So now you're bringing back acolytes from India?" I said. "That's pretty good for a freshly minted holy man. This is my baby brother, Gal. You never made the connection?"

He shrugged. "He's nothing like you."

"True enough. Although he does have the same last name—it could have been a hint." Yossi's expression remained somber, and another flash of annoyance raced through me. "He was last heard from months ago. My mother's been sick with worry about him, and now she's had a stroke. My father thinks it's because of all the worry. And all this time he's whiling away the hours chanting nonsense in your shop."

"It's not nonsense," Yossi said sternly. "Gal is on a very deep quest."

"That's some deep quest," I said, looking at my brother. "He's drugged out, evading his family, wasting his life."

Gal turned his glassy green gaze toward Yossi. "I've told you about my family, Reb Yosef. Now you see what I mean."

"Yes, Gal, I see," said Yossi, in a deep, resonant tone.

Whose side was he on? "Yossi, this is serious," I said. "I've been calling ashrams all over India trying to find the kid. No one in that whole goddamned country can hold up their end of a rational conversation. I was ready to completely give up. And here he is, hiding out in your store."

"Do you see how racist he is?" said Gal, as if from a great distance. "India is a luminous, holy place. You would never understand it."

"He's not hiding. He's studying with me," Yossi said. "He's doing the most important work a human being can do, deepening his soulquest."

"I don't care if he's in training to become the Messiah, he had no right to cut himself off from his family." My voice was rising but I didn't care. "He's had his mother scared out of her wits, and now she's lying mute from a stroke. Do you think he could take a five-minute recess from his soulquest and give his aging parents a call?"

"He's blaming me for my mother's stroke." Gal said. "Do you see what they're like, Reb Yosef?"

Yossi stared at me and responded in the same deep, all-knowing voice. "Yes, Gal, I see."

"Cut the holy-man crap, Yossi," I shouted. "I know who you are. You can't play this piety shit with me."

He didn't flinch. "I'm afraid if you continue to use that kind of language, you will have to leave my store. This is a center of holy seeking. You bring in forces of the *Sitra Achra*, the Other Side, when you speak that way." Yossi was staring at me with a fierce, accusing look. I'd known him for years, but I suddenly didn't recognize him at all.

"Yossi, it's me, Kobi," I said, "and this is my baby brother, Gal. Do you understand? I have to take him with me." I felt tears of desperation rising. "Our mother's had a stroke. OK, I agree, it's not his fault. She had a terrible shock—a friend of hers was killed in the Park Hotel bombing. Maybe that's what did it, or maybe it's all coincidence. It doesn't matter, does it? She's ill and she needs to see her son."

"I'm sorry to hear about your mother, but Gal's not a baby anything," Yossi said, his voice dripping condescension. "He's a grown man. He'll go with you only if he wants to."

"Of course I'm not going with him," Gal said flatly.

I stared at him. "Gal, what are you talking about? You can't stay here! This guy's a complete charlatan."

Gal didn't take his eyes off Yossi. "This is my brother, my own flesh and blood," he said. "I haven't seen him in almost a year. Does he seem happy to see me? No, seeing me is only an opportunity to shower me with guilt, to blame the family's misery on me."

This was madness. Did he want me to beg him? "Look, I'm sorry I'm not jumping up and down with joy at the sight of you," I said as calmly as I could. "I'm sorry. I've . . . I've been under a lot of stress lately. We all have. I . . . I'm glad to see you, Gal."

"Thank you, that was very convincing," he said tonelessly.

They both stared at me with matching expressions of calm disdain. Finally, Yossi broke the silence with his resonant, wise-man tones, swaying softly and staring at me as he spoke.

"Gal, this is how humans behave when they allow their souls to shrivel. This is what happens when we cut ourselves off from our divine essence. We are connected to the divine Source through the *chakra* in our navels, just like we are connected to our mothers until birth with an umbilical cord. In the kabbalistic system, we call this central connecting point *Tiferet*, the Glory. This umbilical cord must be massaged, nurtured, tended, so that the *Shefa*, the sacred Abundance, continues to flow, like the blood and oxygen that flows from mother to baby." His hands were tracing shapes in the air as he spoke. Gal watched, rapt. "When the *Shefa* flows unobstructed, we are in harmony, we see the sacred in every human, every creature, every blade of grass, every atom of creation. We live exalted lives of awe and compassion and gratitude for all of life's blessings. We are no longer buffeted by petty reactions, by our anger, our pride, our appetites." I was as rapt as Gal—I had to admit, he was good. "But when we ignore *Tiferet*, this umbilical cord, this vital connection to the Divine, becomes dry and shrivels up. Then we have no buffer, we are at the mercy of the petty whims of our ego. This is how your brother behaves, and I am certain that this is how your parents taught you to behave. They were survivors, no? They wanted to protect you from all the suffering they experienced, but inadvertently they taught you to be hard and cynical, to scoff at the mystery of life." I found myself nodding, despite myself. "But this can be unlearned. *Tiferet* does not die in us. It lies dormant until we reawaken it with attention and love. You must have compassion, Gal, for your parents, for your siblings, for your countrymen, for our enemies, for all creatures who have let their soul-connection shrivel. You must be a model for them on what it means to live life as a holy being."

Gal had closed his eyes and was swaying like a broken metronome. When he started chanting softly, Yossi took my arm gently and led me toward the door. I didn't resist.

I was just about to push it open when I had an intriguing thought. "Yossi," I whispered, "do you know this older guy with a beard, named Ami? He's from Tekoa. Dresses like a shepherd?"

Yossi stared at me, incredulous. "What are you talking about? Have you completely lost your mind?" For the first time all afternoon, he sounded like himself.

"No, I was just thinking—"

"Kobi, what is going on with you?" he asked, with equal parts concern and scorn. "You're hanging out with settlers now? With shepherds?"

"No, no, of course not. It was just this crazy guy who came to the clinic." I had to get out of there, and fast. I turned back toward my scrawny, swaying, soulquesting brother. "Look, Gal, you don't have to come with me," I called. "But please go visit Ima."

No reaction.

"I'm glad to see you, Gal. I am."

His eyes remained shut, and he appeared to have sunken back into his "deep space." As I stepped outside I glanced back at Yossi and saw his serene expression cut through by a broad wink. But his face reverted to holy-man mode so quickly, I wondered if it had happened at all.

10

Israela casually strolled into the office, unwrapped herself from her huge, embroidered shawl, and dropped into my chair with a big sigh. The heady scent of jasmine reached me a moment later. She was exactly ten minutes late.

"How are you doing today?" I asked.

"Not so good," she answered, her voice more resigned than unhappy. "I can't stand all these holidays, one after the other. Passover, Holocaust Remembrance Day, Memorial Day, Independence Day—it's like an emotional roller coaster. Mourning one day, celebrating the next. Couldn't they have spaced them a little?" She made a face. "I'll be glad when it's all over."

I had no trouble relating. We'd had another siren that morning—this one for Memorial Day—and the maudlin commemorations for fallen soldiers, combined with the unrelenting violence, had had a triggering effect on many of our patients, exacerbating every class of symptomology. We'd been swamped with psychiatric emergencies throughout the past week. But I had more urgent matters to explore with Israela.

"I had an interesting visitor to the clinic last week."

She sat up, suddenly alert.

"You did?"

"He called himself Ami."

"Wow, that was fast—they're wasting no time." She looked out the window, rubbing her neck. "He probably told you all these horrible things about me: I'm too proud, too greedy, too stubborn. I don't appreciate everything Y's done for me."

"Did you know he would come here?" I asked.

"It's just as well he's the first one you met. His politics can be a little extreme, but he's not a total crackpot like some of the others. Doesn't make as much of a scene, if you know what I mean."

"Israela, it seems a little strange—"

83

"You know, I'm almost relieved you got to meet him. I don't think you believed me about being followed. You probably thought I was some paranoid nut case."

"Well, I did wonder—"

"Can you see how it gets to me? Being followed everywhere, being criticized all the time? And they have such high expectations of me. But of course, they're right." She wrinkled her brow. "I should be involved in community service, political causes, acts of charity. Look at what a mess this country is! Did you hear the blast Friday afternoon, from the Mahane Yehuda *shuq*? I was shopping at the time on Jaffa Road, just a few blocks away. It was terrifying—I'm still completely in shock." She pulled her shawl tighter around her shoulders. "So many orphans, and widows, and grieving mothers, just from these last few months—it breaks my heart to think about it. I'm sure there's some way I could be helping them. After all," she went on, scolding herself, "I'm not just anyone. Y chose me as his wife! I don't know if you understand what an honor that is. And he supports me fully—maybe I didn't make that clear to you last time. All he wants in return is that I use my time constructively. I can't just spend my days pampering myself!"

I was used to patients making complicated conversational U-turns, but as usual with Israela, I felt disoriented, as in a dream. "But I thought you said—"

"Not that most people are such saints," she added quickly. "Everyone's just hunkering down, trying to survive this crazy intifada. But that's no excuse. I should be better than 'most people'! I try to be the kind of wife he wants me to be, but I'm so selfish, I fail him all the time. If I behaved the way he wants me to . . ."

Those tears again. Whether Y existed or not, it was clear that she'd internalized the narrative: how special she was because he chose her as his wife; how, even in his absence, he owned her time and her behavior.

I decided to jump straight to the question I'd been dying to ask for a week. "Israela, I was wondering if you knew anything about Y's logo, the outstretched arm."

She looked up, surprised. "Ami told you about that?"

"Well, no, not at first. But then I noticed the whittled arm at the top of his walking stick and asked him about it. I was wondering if you could tell me more about it."

She shrugged. "All organizations have logos."

"Y runs an organization?"

"He does a lot of things, like I told you. But the Outstretched Arm is one of his most important operations." She anticipated my next question. "It's a charitable organization. It helps people who are in trouble."

"So Ami is . . . an employee?"

"They're not employees—Y doesn't pay them anything. His most devoted friends volunteer for the organization. They know I'm in trouble, and they're trying to help me."

"Help you by threatening you?" I asked. She didn't respond. "Israela, if you're not safe, we can call someone . . ."

She shook her head. "You don't understand. He does it for my own good. It's how he shows his love. After a while you get used to it. He just wants me to be a better person."

She was like every abused wife I'd ever met—quick to justify any violent thing her husband did or said. The idea of Y running some shady organization that "helps people in trouble" was unnerving. Was the Outstretched Arm real or part of the larger delusion? And if the organization existed, did that necessarily mean that Y also existed? Either way, some portion of her story—some early trauma—*was* real, and I was determined to keep listening until I could figure it out.

She sighed deeply. "I know it can seem confusing. The Outstretched Arm is a complicated organization. Its methods are unusual, to be sure, but it can be quite effective. You'd be surprised how many people it's lifted up—and some of them don't even know they're being helped." She paused and studied me for a moment. "If you're going to understand, you'll have to hear the rest of my story. After all, Y first came up with the idea of the Outstretched Arm when I was a teenager, living in Egypt. I was the first one the organization ever helped."

I picked up my pen. "You were telling me last time about your father," I reminded her. "How close he was to Y."

She smiled, back in the safe territory of storytelling. "They really bonded on that trip back to Israel. At first it looked like Dad would settle down after returning from Syria, but he wasn't really the type. He had a big family to support, and he went through the money fast. That's how we all ended up in Egypt, just a few years later."

Her ancestors, if they existed, would have been pathologically oblivious to the political realities of the Middle East. "Those were terrible times for Jews in Egypt," I said.

"Yes, I know, but economically, times were tough here as well. The Camp David accords had just been signed, and my father must have thought there would be new trade opportunities. He had some crazy business scheme, I'm sure. One of his sons had gone down to Egypt and had some success, even gotten into politics. You know how it is—one member of the family does well and brings down the whole clan."

Once again, her chronology was all off. If they had gone to Egypt after the Camp David accords, she'd have to be a good ten years younger than she looked. But I knew that trying to pin her down on ages and dates would be a losing proposition.

"And so you think you were born in Egypt?" I asked.

"Oh, I know that for sure. My mother was already pregnant when they went down. I was dad's youngest. He died before I was born, that's why I'm named after him. And my mother must have died shortly after."

"Do you know what happened to them?"

"Not really. But like you say, Egypt was no place for Jews in those days. I don't know what happened to them, *or* my brother, the big-shot politician." She looked down at her lap. "It can't have been good."

"Tell me about your mother," I said gently.

She continued looking down, fidgeting with her shawl.

"Do you know anything about her? Her name? Where she came from?"

She shook her head, embarrassed. "She must have died just after I was born. Maybe even in childbirth. And something must have happened to all my siblings, because somehow I ended up on the street, just a toddler, fending for myself." She paused, a worried look on her face. "You think I made it all up," she said softly. "But I didn't. I was born in Egypt. I'm named after my father. It's all true. You have to believe me!"

I nodded. "Tell me about your earliest memory," I said.

She was silent for a long minute, as if deciding whether to trust me with something this precious. Finally, she plunged in, her voice soft and scared. "I was alone in a garbage-strewn alley, at night. I had lost whoever had been taking care of me. Maybe it was my mother, maybe a sibling, I don't know. I was cold and very scared. An old man came up to me and asked me something, I don't remember what. I don't know if I even understood him. I stared at him, not knowing how to answer his question. That's the earliest memory I have."

"Do you know who he was?"

"Yes, he was Master's father. He must have taken me to their estate in the Nile delta, although I don't remember the trip. As long as the old man was alive, life was tolerable for me. He had known my older brother—the one who had brought us all down to Egypt—and spoke fondly of him. I lived out in the servants' quarters, but the old man would come visit me, make sure I was being taken care of. I was often scared and alone, but at least I was well fed and clothed."

"Was he intending to adopt you?"

"No, I don't think so. He died when I was still very young. But I can tell you that his son, Master, hadn't known my brother and saw me as nothing more than a foreign street urchin he could exploit however he wished. He knew I was Jewish; his father must have told him. The Egyptians are terribly xenophobic. You can't imagine how cruel they can be to foreigners, especially Jews."

"What was your Master's name?"

"I don't know—we never called him anything but Master. He had other foreigners working as servants in his house and on his grounds—Turks, Filipinos, Thais—but I was the lowliest. I was just a child, and all alone, but he thought no work was too hard for me. He must have been some kind of contractor. He had me making bricks on his construction sites, backbreaking work, never any rest." The tears sprung up again, but this time, to my surprise, I believed her. There was none of the usual theatrics in her voice. "I remember the sun beating down on my head as I worked, the filth of my clothes, going to bed hungry. Wondering who my parents were and what I had done to deserve this horrible life."

I could feel the sting of tears beginning to form in my own eyes. I couldn't remember the last time this had happened to me in session. She had an uncanny way of drawing me into her story.

"Did Master call you Israela?"

"Oh, no. He didn't call me anything. He didn't dignify his servants with names. If he wanted to refer to me, he'd call me 'the little Hebrew.' I didn't even have a name. I had no idea who I was until years later when Y told me."

Didn't know who she was until Y told her. If that was true, it revealed a great deal, including the roots of her histrionic personality traits. While Israela dried her eyes with the corners of her shawl, my mind raced. Character pathology this severe was always rooted in extreme early trauma; without the early nurturing necessary to create stable ego functioning, children developed false selves that hid the chaotic, formless self that lay beneath. The total absence of identity that she had described—not even knowing her own name—would make subsequent attempts at identity formation extremely fragile. The result was the kind of labile affect, loose reality testing, and dramatic aggrandizing that characterized Israela. That would explain why she so cherished the stories of her fabled ancestors; it was not uncommon for severely traumatized children to invent an exalted pedigree to make up for the shame of being homeless, unwanted, a social outcast. Her whole sense of identity could well be built on the fragile foundation of these tales.

But what was unusual was the existence or creation of Y as a key figure in the development of this complex defensive maneuver. If this part of her story was true, she'd been some pathetic urchin off the street, with no family, no love, no story. Y—whoever he was—had not only rescued her from a degrading childhood, he'd provided her with an illustrious, biblically inspired family history full of colorful ancestors to make her feel important. He still might not be a real person—she might have invented him out of her desperate need to be saved—but either way, I was beginning to get a glimpse of why she thought she couldn't leave him. Whether in fact or in fantasy, he had literally invented her from scratch.

"Tell me how you first met Y," I said.

Her face brightened immediately. "Well, first you have to know about Musa," she said. "He lived in the house and was known to us as Master's son, but the older servants all whispered about how he was really his grandson. Master's daughter had disappeared for a while when she was a teenager, and lo and behold, when she returned there was a baby. But Master always treated him like his own son—wouldn't tolerate any scandals in the family."

She was getting that dreamy look again, and her voice was taking on the staged quality it had when she talked about her ancestors. She had been a slave in Egypt, and there would now be a savior named Musa—she was barely hiding the fabrication. But even so, there was no mockery in her tone. I had little doubt that she fully believed her story and I was getting closer to understanding the psychological motivation behind the delusion. The only possible course of action was to play along.

"What was he like?" I asked.

"Oh, he was wonderful—the only one in the whole family who treated us right. He even had to run away because Master got so furious at him for defending the servants."

"Were you close to him?"

"I barely remember him from before he left. I was very young at the time. He was gone for many years—crossed over into Sinai, joined up with a Bedouin tribe, and lived as a shepherd. It was in the desert that he met Y," she said, smiling. "And you know how it is when people meet Y—they're never the same again." I stared at her face as she talked, searching for any consciousness about the biblical resonance of her tale.

"By the time Musa returned to Egypt, I was a young teenager," she continued. "I don't remember his leaving so well, but I sure do remember his return! You can't imagine the scene in that house. The yelling and screaming and carrying on. Musa was possessed. He'd taken it as his mission in life to get me free."

"Why?" I asked.

"Y had told him that I was Ibra's great-granddaughter, the one he'd promised to marry. When he realized how I was suffering, he told Musa to return to Master's house and convince him to let me go. He said he would help him bring me to Israel, where I belonged."

What was the psychic price for a smart and sensitive woman to so utterly suspend all reason?

"Somehow, Y managed to sneak into the delta himself," she went on. "I don't know where he was staying, but close enough to create all kinds of mischief. He and Musa would concoct these wild pranks, just to make Master miserable. Releasing critters into the house, cutting off the electricity, putting red dye in the water system so it looked like blood coming out of the tap. Childish stuff, really, but it got to Master. He was in a constant rage. They dragged it out for a long time, and I tell you, I was terrified. I knew what was up, and I knew that if Y and Musa failed to set me free, my life would be even more miserable than before."

"Is that when you met Y?" I asked.

"No, but Musa kept telling me all about him. You can just imagine how he got built up in my mind, this mysterious stranger who'd come from the Jewish state, who knew who I really was, who was committed to saving me, who would marry me. It was like all my childhood fantasies come true!"

Like all her childhood fantasies come true, I scrawled in my notes. I could imagine Jezebel shaking her head at the case notes from this interview. I pushed skepticism out of my mind: the trauma was real, the details unimportant.

"And then one day it happened!" Israela was saying. "Musa and Y had been driving Master crazy with all their silly tricks. But the longer it went on, the more stubborn he became, until it looked like I'd never get out of there. But then, we got word that Master's oldest son had died in Alexandria, suddenly and mysteriously. It was probably all a coincidence, but Master was sick with grief, and got it into his head that Musa and Y were responsible. And who knows? Maybe they were! They would have done anything at that point to set me free. Master all but threw me out of the house, screaming, 'Take her, take her, I never want to see her again!' I didn't even have time to pack my few belongings—we just grabbed some stale crackers and fled.

"It was the dead of night, a fierce sandstorm obscuring the full moon, Musa and I running out of that house in a flash. Y was ahead of us, leading the way, toward the desert. I couldn't actually see him, but he was holding one of those huge industrial flashlights. Musa ran behind him, and I was in the rear, running hard just to keep up, my heart bursting in my chest." I was listening closely, enthralled. "We could hear Master behind us calling up his household—he'd changed his mind! Just when I thought I couldn't run another step, we came to a jeep that Y had waiting for us. Y jumped into the driver's seat, and Musa and I fell into the back. I'd barely shut the door behind me when he sped off, away from the lights of our little village and straight into the desert, hurtling for hours along unlit, rutted roads.

And then, all of a sudden, we came to a halt and there was a vast body of water in front of us. We stumbled down the bank to the water's edge, and Y told us that we would have to cross to Sinai on the other side. I stared at the raging waters, paralyzed in terror. Master and his minions must have been following all along, because within moments I could hear his jeep shriek to a halt behind us, could hear them getting out of the car and making their way down the embankment. I became hysterical, started screaming to Musa, 'Why have you done this to me? Why couldn't you have left me in Master's house?' But Musa and Y ignored me, plotting together under their breaths. And then . . ."

She looked at me expectantly. "Yes?"

"They were closing in on us, I was about to collapse from terror and exhaustion. And that's when it happened . . ."

"What happened?"

"It was the most incredible moment of my life. I can't possibly describe it. You'd think I was crazy."

I honestly didn't know what to think. "Tell me," I said.

"I don't know, it was like a dream. Suddenly, in that complete blackness, with the sand in my face and the wind howling in my ears, certain I was about to die, I did something only a foolish child would do—I started to walk into those foaming waters. And just as I did, I felt Y sweep me up into his arms. I couldn't actually see him, but that sensation of being swept up—I'll never in my life forget it, no matter how long I live. If I could only convey to you the *power* of that man. In that moment, I knew someone loved me, I knew I'd forever be taken care of. In that instant I fell madly, crazily in love." There was nothing forced or invented about the passion on her face or in her voice. I believed her. "Do you understand why I could never leave him?" she asked.

We sat in silence for a few minutes, she in her reverie and I in mine.

The telephone jangled us back to the present. My 2:00 patient was waiting.

11

The clinic closed early that afternoon in preparation for Yom HaAtzma'ut, Israel Independence Day. I was grateful; after my session with Israela, I had more than my usual amount of trouble focusing. But more urgently, I was getting increasingly nervous about finding Yudit a bat mitzvah gift. Now I had a few hours to go shopping, though I still had no ideas. As I sat at my desk flicking pushpins across the office, I suddenly thought of the elegant shawl that had been casually draped around Israela's shoulders as she had described her terrifying escape. I'd been deeply stirred by her story, but without consciously noticing, I had also been transfixed by its colors and fabric. It had typical red-on-black Bedouin embroidery, but with something exquisite in the flow of the material and uniqueness of the design. I smiled to myself as I imagined Yudit wrapped in the soft, luxurious fabric, holding it to her face, spinning in delight, Nava looking on with an inadvertent smile of appreciation. Nava never ventured into the Old City; a Bedouin shawl would be just the kind of mildly exotic, unique offering that I had imagined. Elated by my plan, I rushed out the door.

As I left the building, I felt a pull on my arm. A beggar who always worked the street in front of the hospital was grabbing at me, a pathetic whine issuing from his mouth. I instinctively shook him off, then turned back to look. His hand was still stretched out toward me. His face, discolored and scaly with some hideous disease, was contorted with misery and supplication, and he was mumbling incoherently under his breath. I'd always taken pains to avoid him, but I now remembered Ami's words, admonishing me to notice the beggars. I knew it was futile to give money to these scoundrels, that it only encouraged more begging, but now that I had stopped it was impossible to keep walking without a response. I fished out a shekel and dropped it into his hand, careful not to make physical contact. He could have some horrible, contagious disease, like leprosy. Did leprosy still exist? Was it still considered contagious?

The encounter with the beggar discomfited me, deflating some of my optimism. I started walking quickly in the direction of Jaffa Gate, hoping to burn off some of my now-chronic agitation. I was overworked, that was all, I told myself, and not getting enough exercise now that my squash meets with Yossi had more or less ended.

As I walked briskly down Agron, I found myself reliving Israela's story in my mind. The abuse, I was certain, was real. But how to understand the dramatic narrative of escape, the feeling of being lifted up by a mysterious force, the excitement and confusion, the sense of surreal mystery? As I crossed the large intersections at the bottom of Agron, the images of Israela's Exodus-infused childhood slowly bled into my mother's sparsely told stories. Like Israela, she too had been fending for herself at far too young an age, her father dead under circumstances she'd never fully revealed, her mother too encumbered by poverty and war and well-nurtured bitterness to tend to the mundane needs of her oldest child. For all practical purposes, she too had been an orphan, but no magical savior had ever swept her off the streets of their luckless shtetl or the crowded, pestilent ghetto that followed.

When I was very young, I had seen a child being breastfed and had asked my mother if I had been fed that way as well. She told me I had not, and although I had no memory of what explanation she gave at the time, somehow I concluded from her response that she had been shot in the breast during the war. Years later, I started to doubt if I had understood correctly and asked her if she had been wounded in that way. "No, of course not," she had said, horrified by the suggestion. "I just didn't want to breastfeed." And yet I retained, even into adulthood, a persistent belief, which I knew had no foundation in fact, that my mother had been shot by a Nazi in the breast.

The image of the injured breast had been a powerful and persistent one throughout my childhood. There were psychic wounds, I knew, that she would never share, that had thwarted me, her oldest child, in my voracious need for nourishment. What did a young woman have to do to survive the hunger, the abuse, the random slaughter? I imagined my mother as a beautiful young woman, with her shimmering green cat-eyes, walking briskly through the ghetto, hunched over, shielding her body from harm, straining for invisibility. All around me I saw the dark hauntings of wartime Poland and the muddy streets of a murky shtetl, imagined myself bent under the hail of insults and threats and rocks hurled by leering blond goyim.

Suddenly, I was staring uncomprehendingly at the swirling Arabic script of a street sign. Where the hell was I? I could smell the seductive fragrance of an Arab market, hear all around me the unintelligible gutturals of East Jerusalem. I must have been walking thirty minutes at least, continuing to walk straight instead of turning right toward Jaffa Gate. I looked into the suspicious gaze of a young Arab boy. Was it my imagination or was he looking at me with open hatred? My heart pounding, I quickly scrapped my reckless mission—what did I know about buying girl's clothing?—and hailed a cab that was slowly lumbering down the street. The driver was chubby and pale—a Jew. Slipping gracelessly into the passenger seat, I struggled to keep my voice calm as I gave him my destination.

"Kiryat Yovel."

"You should be more careful!" he scolded. "It isn't safe, a well-dressed Jew wandering through East Jerusalem, all lost in thought. Especially on the eve of Yom HaAtzma'ut—you know how that day riles them." He was driving with his left hand, his right arm gesticulating wildly. "The whole nation's on high alert. What were you thinking? There are stabbings around here all the time. Journalists, tourists looking for the consulate—they don't care. And after the bombing in Mahane Yehuda on Friday . . ." He shook his head, as if to puzzle out the secret of my appalling carelessness. The car swerved sharply, sending the air freshener hanging from the rearview mirror into mad pirouettes.

"I was just going to do a little shopping, for my daughter," I said defensively. "I saw someone wearing a Bedouin shawl earlier today, and I thought . . ."

"What, are you kidding?" He jerked the wheel, narrowly missing a young boy on a bicycle. "On Yom HaAtzma'ut, in the middle of an intifada, you're going on a shopping spree in East Jerusalem? I would have thought you had more sense than that, Dr. Benami."

I stared at him in stunned surprise. I had never seen him before in my life. He was short, overweight, and disheveled, looking like he could use a good change of clothes. And a haircut, for the wisps of hair still left on his balding head.

"How do you know who I am?" I finally managed.

He turned right and, emitting a symphony of indignant honking, forced the cab into the crush of traffic heading toward West Jerusalem. "You're the chief psychologist at that fancy hospital clinic," he said. "I was gonna go see you there later this week, but now I don't have to. I guess this is my lucky day." He grinned and laid into the horn.

Was he a former patient I had treated and then forgotten? Or perhaps it was that lecture I'd given on children of Holocaust survivors a few months back at the university. Had he been in the audience? I remembered how polished and in control I'd felt that evening, before all my recent troubles had begun. I tried to summon the feeling back.

"You'll need an appointment, of course," I said. "You can call the receptionist after the holiday and—"

"Well, now I don't need to, do I?" He grinned again. "This is really a piece of luck."

"Actually—"

"It's about your new patient, Israela."

My heart started drumming violently. It seemed that the stalking would not be confined to drop-in visits to the clinic, nor would they all fit the profile of weathered, rigid-backed shepherds. He must have been tailing me as I walked straight across Jerusalem, wondering when I would finally come to my senses and hail a cab. Even in my shock, there was a sliver of relief: at least Jezebel wouldn't find out about this one.

"It's important that we talk, Doc," he was saying. "It really can't wait." He stiff-armed the horn, then leaned out the window to yell in obviously broken Arabic at an old woman trying to wend her way through the stop-and-go traffic.

He shook his head. "I hate driving in this part of town."

"Are you also from Tekoa?" I asked, thinking of Ami.

"What are you kidding?" he asked, indignant. "I'm from Afula. What, I look like one of those crazy settlers?"

"Not really. I just thought—"

"Stop thinking and start listening, Doc. As we talk, she's out whoring all over town. She doesn't tell you about that, does she?"

I glanced at his driver's ID. The minute we got out of East Jerusalem, I'd bolt the cab. First thing in the morning, I'd report him to the taxi commission.

"Look, Mr. Be'eri—"

"Call me Hesh."

"OK, Hesh. I can't possibly discuss—"

"She doesn't tell you how she spends her evenings. She just plays the helpless victim with you, right?"

"Look, there are rules of confidentiality—"

"Just last night, I saw her going into that sleazy den, Soreq's Pub, where she hangs out all the time. You think she was wrapped in shawls and frilly skirts like she does for you? No way. Piles of makeup; short, tight skirts; hanging on Bal's arm, dripping the tawdry baubles he buys her. That's what she's up to, night after night!"

As we slowed down for a makeshift checkpoint, I slowly registered what he was saying. Soreq's Pub? The same place I had met Delia? Despite myself, I felt a surge of fascination. The soldier at the checkpoint waved us through, and we came to a screeching halt at the next red light. But though we were now safely in West Jerusalem, I didn't get out.

Hesh sensed my interest and chuckled. "She's batted those big brown eyes at you a few times, huh? You shouldn't be so flattered—she does it to everyone. She has no sense of modesty, no shame at all."

The light turned and he sped forward into the heavy traffic. I reached for my shoulder belt, but it wouldn't budge. "I know all about her type. I married one myself," Hesh was saying, weaving around the other cars as though they were standing still. "A cheating no-good whore, never even hid her affairs. Made me the laughingstock of the neighborhood. Believe me, I know what he feels!"

By a few centimeters, he missed colliding into a van full of yeshiva students. "Nothing in the world makes me as angry as a whoring wife!" he screamed. "She's like an oven in heat, a flame that's out of control!" He was careening west, toward Givat Shaul, somehow managing a breakneck speed despite the heavy holiday traffic.

"Where are you taking me?" My voice came out an octave too high.

"Don't worry, I'll get you home nice and safe," he assured me. "And I won't even charge you for the ride! I just thought I'd take a roundabout route, we should have plenty time to talk, so you can really understand what I'm getting at." He zipped into the narrow space between two huge trucks, and my stomach flipped.

"So here I am, Hesh, a captive audience," I said, gripping the sides of my seat. "Go ahead, tell me what you want me to know."

"Her husband's a great guy, Dr. Benami," he began. "He's done everything for her! He keeps her well fed, well clothed, he got her the finest house in town. He doesn't deck her out in cheap rhinestones like Bal does. He gives her the best of everything, dotes on her every need. But it still isn't enough for her." He looked at me to make sure I was listening. "She's probably told you he hasn't talked to her in over a year, but that's bullshit. He talks to her all the time! She stiffens up her neck and can't hear a word he says." He took both hands off the wheel to demonstrate.

"She claims he's never around."

"Of course not! Would you stay with a wife who's out every night with a different lover, flaunts her affairs in your face? Do you know how humiliating it is, people whispering behind your back, looking at you in that way?" The car was speeding up again. "There are folks in Afula who still can't look me in the eye, after all these years."

"It may be that you're projecting some of your own pain—"

"Don't start with the shrink talk, Doc." I cursed myself for the reckless comment, but when he continued, it was in a more reflective tone. "It's true he and I have a lot in common. After all, he set me up with Gamla in the first place, just to show me what it's like."

It certainly sounded like the same sadistic Y.

"It was the best lesson I've ever had in my life," he said, nodding, "and it brought us really close." A car moved into the lane in front of us, but he didn't honk. "I understand now how you can love a woman so much that you'll take her back, again and again, no matter how she mistreats you—no matter how much the neighbors scoff." He looked at me. "That's how much he loves Israela. That's why he sent me to talk to you; he knows I understand his point of view." The car swerved around a bend, almost hurtling me into his lap. I pulled myself upright, gripping the sides of the seat even more tightly. "I was making a good living cabbing in Afula," he said, shaking his head. "I didn't need to come to this overpriced, holy-ass city. But when a friend is in despair and asks for your help, what choice do you have?"

"You moved from Afula just to follow Israela around?"

He sighed. "What wouldn't I do for him? It's true that he's crazy mad at her, but he's also worried sick. He knows what could happen to her if this whoring doesn't stop."

"What do you mean? What could happen?" A different kind of alarm suddenly coursed through me.

"He won't just sit by and tolerate this forever," Hesh said ominously.

"Are you suggesting that he might—"

"It's not what he *might* do—it's what he *will* do if she don't stop her shenanigans," he said fiercely. "The whole town knows what she and Ashra have been up to! It's not like they're discreet or anything." My mind flashed unbidden to an image of Israela leaning into another woman in the dim light of Soreq's, the shawl slipping from her bare shoulders . . .

"I'm telling you, she's just like my ex, Gamla. There's no limit to the perversity of these kinds of broads!" He slammed the car to a halt at a red light and turned his whole body to face me. The air freshener swung madly. "He'll humiliate her, right in Soreq's, in front of all her lovers. He'll take back everything he's given her and leave her homeless and impoverished. He'll have her citizenship revoked and send her back to Egypt, where she'll have to fend for herself. He's got connections—don't think he can't do it!" His voice sounded more desperate than cruel. "Only then will she know what kind of guy her husband is!"

He turned back to the wheel and the car raced forward. I had no idea where we were. "You're not a big honcho shrink for nothing, Doc. You know I'm telling the truth. And you're a man; you understand. You know we men have no honor if we can't control our own women!"

I closed my eyes, flooded by despair. Should I have tried to stand up to Nava? Maybe she would have respected me more if I had. And what about that old bitch who was now running the clinic? I could hear Jezebel's scolding voice in my ears—I couldn't control her either. What the hell, I couldn't even assert my authority over the goddamned receptionists. All around me, women were controlling me like the helpless puppet I was. I felt a sudden surge of rage. My life was as out of control as this bucking cab. I opened my eyes as Hesh yanked the car onto a narrow side street.

"What does he want from her?" I asked.

"He wants her love, that's all. He wants her to reject Bal and that whole degenerate crowd she hangs out with. He wants the pure, innocent girl he thought he married. He wants her love and single-minded devotion—is that too much to ask?" There was anguish in his voice.

"Are you talking about Israela or Gamla?"

"Both; there's no difference between the two. You understand?"

I understood. He would never see past his own pain. But instead of dealing with it directly, he'd taken on Y's cause as if it were his own. It was less painful to think of all women as deceitful, unloving whores.

I understood, better than he knew. I thought of Nava's tortured face as she looked down at me in Café HaEmek, the pain I'd caused her with my frivolous, joyless philandering. Where were Nava and Yudit tonight? I had always done the backyard barbecuing—were they having a Yom HaAtzma'ut feast without me? And here I was, alone for yet another miserable holiday, caught up again in sexual fantasies about a woman who had come to me for help. Did I never learn? I felt confused, exhausted, guilty, disgusted with myself. And on top of it all, I still didn't have a gift for Yudit.

As the car careened through a turn into Kiryat Yovel, there was a sudden lurch and a bump. "Fucking cats," Hesh said. I turned back to look, but the car behind us obscured the pavement.

"Did you just run over a cat?" I heard the hysteria rising again in my voice.

"You're not going to start sniveling over a Jerusalem alley cat, are you, Doc? They're a menace! The city should have had them neutralized long ago."

"What? What does that mean?"

"Does it ever occur to you that cats get killed in suicide bombs too? How come no one cares about that? But God forbid you should run one over." I suddenly realized we'd turned onto my block, although I'd never specified the street or address. He knew where I lived, had probably been following me for days. But I hardly cared anymore.

As the cab rolled to a stop in front of my building, the air freshener settled into stillness for the first time. It was in the shape, I now saw, of the same outstretched arm that had been carved onto Ami's walking stick.

"The outstretched arm," I said.

"What about it?"

"It's his logo."

"Of course it's his logo."

"What does it mean?" I was suddenly exhausted by fear and grief. All my anger toward Hesh had dissolved. In the end, he was just another sad, unloved creature, no better or worse than myself.

"It means that he's there when you need him," he said. I got out of the car. As I walked to the door of my building, he leaned out the window. "You'll talk to her, right, Doc? All she has to do is ask, and he'll stretch out his arm and pick her up from where she's fallen. Things can be back like the old days. Tell her, Doc. Tell her it's not too late." As he drove away, he slammed the car into the garbage container in front of the building, sending it rolling a couple of meters, before correcting course and zooming to the end of the block.

Inside, I poured myself a Scotch, vaguely aware that I had no food in the house for dinner. Even indoors, the air was permeated by the smell of the holiday barbecues. What was there to celebrate? Fifty-odd years of trouble. I felt myself tottering on the edge of despair. Would anyone stretch out a hand and pull me up from the depths into which I was falling?

For lack of other options I went straight to bed, but lay sleepless for hours, unable to block out the high-pitched horns and distant laughter, the forced revelry that seeped through the closed, barred windows of my flat.

12

Saturday morning, depleted by my overscheduled week, I drove to Petah Tikva to visit my mother. I found her submerged in the living room sofa, calmly scrutinizing the oil painting on the wall—a frenetically colored depiction of an idealized Jerusalem—as if it held the answer to a long-hidden conundrum. Other than a slight quiver in her lower lip, she was almost completely motionless. She briefly glanced toward me when I walked through the door, then returned her attention to the painting. My father sat perched on the edge of a chair across from his wife, watching her closely. "Kobi, it's good you came. She's glad to see you," he said, nodding vigorously at this insight, his eyes never leaving her face. Gal, dressed like a high priest in white linen tunic and pants, was seated cross-legged on a pile of pillows on the terrace, his hair still uncut, his hands open to the cosmos, mumbling singsong prayers under his breath.

It was the first real heat wave of the season, and the room was oppressively hot. After depositing a peck on my mother's cheek, I reached to turn on the air conditioner, but my father grabbed at my arm before I could do so.

"Shabbat. Remember? The famous day of rest? No electricity."

"What are you talking about? Since when do you keep the Sabbath?"

His eyes flicked briefly toward the kitchen. "Anat's here to help out. So we play by her rules for a couple of days."

"How can anyone be restful in this kind of heat? It's unbearable in here. Ima's sick—can't there be a special dispensation?"

"She can't talk, but she's perfectly capable of enduring the heat. She doesn't look uncomfortable, does she?" My mother sat opposite him, expressionless.

"She doesn't look anything," I said.

"Shush, don't say things like that in front of her," my father hissed. "She understands every word you say."

"OK, sorry. But why didn't you just turn on the air before Shabbat?"

"Look at the rich man talking. A little heat won't kill you." He glanced at Gal. "And this way our holy guru can pretend he's back in India, where they know from real heat. Maybe all our brains will get fried the way his has. Maybe with enough *hamsin*, we'll all end up in some blissful state of unity."

The prayerful under-whine drew to a sudden halt. "Ima isn't the only one who can understand what people are saying," said Gal, his voice weak and ethereal, as if floating in from a distant continent.

My father looked at me wearily. A moment later, screeching noises began echoing up the building stairwell. Tuvya stumbled through the front door dragging a howling Habakuk by the collar, a prayer book and *tallis* tucked precariously under his other arm. Sweat was pouring down his reddened face into his brown-gray beard. Anat came bustling out of the kitchen to greet them, tucking a few stray hairs into her brightly patterned head scarf.

"What happened?" she asked sternly.

"This is what he's been like all morning. He embarrassed me in front of the whole congregation."

Anat gave the child an angry scowl, which made him yowl and struggle all the more to escape his father's grip.

"Someone better calm down if he's going to join us for lunch," she said slowly, shaking her head from side to side as she spoke.

Loath to witness how the scene would play out, I motioned to my father to join me in his bedroom. He glanced at my mother, then followed me down the hall, limping.

"What are they going to do about that kid?" I asked, as we both settled onto the edge of the bed. "He's totally out of control."

My father shook his head. "He's gotten much worse since that kindergarten teacher was killed in Samaria last month. She was from a neighboring village, and he knew some of her students from soccer practice. Now he's refusing to go to school every morning. Major battles, from what I hear."

"Poor kid," I said. "Are they getting him any help?"

"They're working with some rebbe. What can I tell you? Not everyone is such a fan of your esteemed profession."

I ignored the dig as the screaming in the living room intensified. "They're here for the entire weekend?"

He shrugged. "She's trying to be helpful."

"All this commotion can't be therapeutic for Ima," I said. "Abba, if you need help you'd be better off hiring a *Filipina*—they're not that expensive."

He stared at me. "I'm not hiring a *Filipina*. What, I can't take care of my own wife? If Anat feels happy puttering in the kitchen, I won't stop her. Your mother doesn't pay them any mind."

"She just sits around like that all day?"

"She gets up to go to the bathroom. If the TV is on, she watches it. If it's off, she stares at the walls. She's fascinated by all the color in that damn painting—I never liked it much myself." He paused, reflecting. "She lets me bathe her, lets me take her to bed at the end of the day. She eats whatever you put in front of her, even Anat's dry kugels, which she never would have touched before. She won't go near the kitchen. That room used to be her sanctuary . . ." He closed his eyes, putting a hand to his forehead. "She has no purpose anymore, no will."

"Abba, she's had a stroke. Maybe she doesn't fully understand—"

His brow furrowed in anger. "It was a minor stroke. The doctors say there's damage to the language centers, but her other mental functions are fully intact. She could . . ." He trailed off, then started again. "She doesn't make any effort in the speech therapy they give her. She just doesn't care anymore."

"I don't know . . ."

He looked at me. "It was Libke's death in the Park Hotel bombing that brought this on," he stated emphatically.

"But I thought—"

"It took me a while to realize it, but now I'm certain. She didn't cry and she wouldn't talk about it. I pleaded with her to go to the funeral or the shiva, but she refused. Even so, she was in deep shock. There are things those two shared, memories that her death must have triggered. And that Libke should die such a violent death, after all they'd survived . . ." He shook his head as if to dispel any doubts he might have.

"I don't know . . . really? First you thought it was worrying about Gal, now you think it's the shock over Libke's death. Strokes happen, there isn't always a reason."

"You're right, at first I thought it was about Gal. But then I saw how she reacted when he arrived. She watched him walk in the door, just like she watched you today, no expression at all. Sometimes she stares at him while he chants." He shook his head again. "Since Libke's death, nothing matters to her anymore."

"Who was this Libke? How come I never even heard of her?"

He leaned forward in a confiding whisper. "You don't remember when we visited her together? In Tel Aviv? I brought you once." I shook my head, astonished. "She had a little girl, just your age—Miki. She wanted the two of you to meet, to play together, just once. But it wasn't such a great success. The girl was a polite, mousy little thing, and you such a *vilde chaya*. Still, it meant a lot to her that I brought you that one time. I never told your mother."

A vague memory emerged of a pale little girl with a long, somber face. Me, running up and down a narrow hallway, playing soldier. A mother with a kind smile and a tightly wound bun. Something secret and forbidden.

"Who was she?" I whispered back.

He studied my face for a moment. "You know so little about Ima's history," he said.

"You're right. She never told us anything."

"So how can you possibly know what she does and doesn't understand?" He waited but I had no response. "Look at her eyes—I've lived with them all my adult life. Emaciated and desperate as she was when I first met her in the DP camp, it was those otherworldly eyes that drew me in. They're still alive, Kobi. She's still there."

Her eyes had looked anything but alive to me. "I know it's a disturbing thing to consider, Abba, but it's hard to believe that she would act this way if she still understood—"

"Enough! It's you who doesn't understand! She doesn't *want* to talk any more. She's had enough. Is that really so surprising?" This time he didn't wait for me. "A lot of things in this world are hard to believe. It's hard to believe that my saintly father, who would admonish me for teasing a classmate—we were all created in *Hashem misborach*'s image!—that he could be plucked clean like a chicken, shorn of his hair and beard, stripped of his clothes, herded into a shower, and gassed to death. It's hard to believe someone would walk into a hotel and blow himself up, killing dozens of innocent old people at a seder. A lot of things in this world are hard to believe! I've seen more than my share, and so did she. She's had enough!"

"OK, OK, calm down. Of course you know her better than I." He stared at his lap, breathing heavily, his nostrils flaring, and for the first time in my life I worried for him. How much more of this could he handle? He was looking older by the day.

"Let's talk about something else," I said. "Tell me about Gal. Is he staying with you now?"

He continued staring at his lap for a long minute, still calming himself, before replying. "He just came up for Shabbat. He's living in Jerusalem, studying with some rebbe. He barely talks to me; I'm not holy enough. He's more off the deep end than I would have thought possible. I kept telling your mother not to worry, but she was right to be worried. His eyes are glazed over, he spends all his time chanting and swaying. My Gali's gone, my wife is gone—maybe neither of them will ever come back."

"Abba," I said.

"And look at you, losing your family, living in some horrible flat at the outer reaches of Jerusalem." He looked up at me. "Nava was the best thing that ever happened to you. We were so thrilled when you brought her home—such a solid girl, we knew she'd settle you down. Now what will happen to you?" He shook his head, incredulously. "It's just a week before Yudit's bat mitzvah. What are we supposed to do? Go without you? And we were so looking forward to it."

"Of course you can go without me," I said. Riding a wave of false optimism, I added, "Anyway, Nava and I might still work things out."

"By next week?" He shook his head at this inanity and sank into another gloomy silence. Glancing around the bedroom, with its old-fashioned, European-style headboards and wardrobes, I noticed my mother's ornate jewelry box sitting on the bureau. It suddenly occurred to me that perhaps I could give Yudit a piece of jewelry from my mother, a legacy gift, something from her now-silent *bubbe* that she could one day hand on to her own children. Maybe a pair of earrings—hadn't she just had her ears pierced a couple of years before? The idea exhilarated me. Neither of my parents had even a photo from their own families to pass on to us.

"Speaking of the bat mitzvah, Abba, I've been wondering these last few weeks what I could buy for Yudit. I can't really go to the party—you know, it would be awkward, so soon after the separation—so I thought I would get her something really special and . . . well, I've been having trouble thinking of what that might be."

"A gift can't make up—"

"I know, but still. It's something. And I just noticed Ima's jewelry box and I got to thinking—maybe I could give her a piece of Ima's jewelry. Maybe a necklace, or a pair of earrings? Ima doesn't use any of it anymore. Something from when she was young, and newly married, you know . . ."

"She's not dead yet," he murmured.

"Of course not, Abba, I didn't mean it that way, but—"

"You can't just give away her things as if she were dead!" His voice was low and furious.

"But don't you think—"

"Forget it, I won't allow it!"

"OK, don't get excited. I just thought—"

"I know exactly what you thought," he said. "Kobi, I don't understand you at all. You're so clever in some ways, and then there are such basic things you don't seem to know . . ."

His words hung in the air, unfinished, as Anat rapped loudly on the bedroom door to call us in for lunch. What were the "basic things" that I didn't know? How to keep your wife from throwing you out? That it was wrong to give away your living mother's jewelry? What it was that a father ought to buy his daughter for her bat mitzvah to prove his enduring love?

As we reluctantly gathered around the oversized, sparsely set table, it occurred to me that this was the first time we'd all been in the same room since my mother's seventieth birthday, four years before. But if anyone else noticed the singularity of the occasion, they didn't mention it. Tuvya mumbled the blessings for the wine and the bread, and we silently passed around the array of cold salads and luncheon meats and kugels that Anat had prepared. Habakuk was gasping for air, his face still streaked with dusty tears, but calm enough to create and then destroy little towers of food on his plate. Tuvya was humming under his breath. My mother robotically consumed whatever was put in front of her; even before the stroke there had always been a deadness in her expression when she ate. Gal barely touched his food, swaying gently to internal rhythms. Watching him, it occurred to me that if he never married and had children—and it was hard to imagine that he would—the hallowed sea-green eyes would have no more future in our family than the Bonkowski name, which our father, upon immigrating to Palestine, had unceremoniously shed along with his threadbare religious convictions.

By the time all the plates had been filled, we had exhausted Anat's tolerance for civilized silence. "So, Kobi, your wife take you back yet?"

"No, not yet," I said, concentrating on mopping hummus onto my pita.

"She's got someone new?"

"How would I know? And what business is that of yours?"

"Just asking, don't be so sensitive. Though I can't help wondering how you're supposed to help other people with their lives when you've messed up your own so badly. Aren't shrinks supposed to have their own lives together? Who would want to go to a shrink who's in the middle of a divorce?"

My father looked up, annoyed. "Stop it, Anat. Leave him alone."

"I just never understood what made him go into that field. He's so unsuited to it."

"You're right, I *am* unsuited to it," I said, surprising myself with the bluntness of my answer.

"You see, Abba, he knows it himself," she said smugly. "So why did you become a shrink? I've always wondered."

It struck me that no one in my family had ever asked me that question before. "I don't know. I thought I should make something of myself, and this seemed like the path of least resistance. Easier than becoming a doctor or a lawyer. How hard could it be to sit around and listen to people complain all day? That's what I figured, anyway."

"It's true, you were always lazy."

"That's me—a lazy fool. And you've always been so industrious and wise."

"Leave him alone, Anat," my father snapped. "Don't we have enough problems around here? Anyway, it wasn't his fault." He put down his fork. "Your mother and I had no idea how to raise kids, didn't give you the guidance or encouragement you needed. But Kobi was a bright boy, even if he was a little wild." He looked at me sadly. "You had talents. There were things you could have done."

"Some people think being a psychologist is honorable work," I said. "Some people might even be proud of a son who is chief psychologist in a major urban hospital. But why talk about me? Isn't there anyone else's life we can dissect?"

Anat piled another round of food onto her plate as she spoke; she'd always had an insatiable appetite. "It's true, you gave us very little guidance. What did our family believe in, except not becoming victims of the next Holocaust?" She chewed her food, methodically. "Kobi, you know the things I've discovered since coming here to help out? The mezuzah on the front door was completely empty—not even a make-believe parchment. There were no Shabbat candles; we had to run out and buy them on Friday afternoon. We couldn't even find a prayer book; luckily, Tuvya brought his own. This apartment may as well be in Wisconsin, America, for all that makes this family Jewish."

"Wisconsin, America?"

"It's in the middle someplace. It doesn't matter. You get my point. We could be anywhere, living with goyim. Is this why we fought for a Jewish state, spilled Jewish blood?" She was getting louder and more emphatic. "To live like goyim? Look at Kobi, driving here on Shabbat."

My father refilled his own plate; both he and Anat would indiscriminately eat whatever was put in front of them. "Something so terrible about living like normal people?" he asked. "What your mother and I wouldn't have given just to have lived quiet, normal lives. What, living without fear, without people hunting you down, that's not enough?"

"They're hunting us here too, with suicide bombers instead of Gestapo. It's not so different, really."

"If that's what you think—"

"And after all these years, we've learned absolutely nothing. We still don't have the guts to do what it takes to stop them." Anat was almost shouting now. I glanced at my mother but her face was completely impassive. "Did you hear yesterday's news? Arafat fakes a massacre, the world yells and screams, and we pull right out of Jenin. What's the matter with this government? Why are we pulling out? So they can keep sneaking in to blow us up in cafés and buses?"

My father was not backing down. "What, you enjoy being the great pariah of the world? You enjoy sending our boys into those hellholes—"

"Who cares what the world thinks? You, of all people, have to know that they'll hate us no matter what we do."

"Well, excuse me if I refuse to live my life—"

I couldn't take it anymore, not without my mother to share an eye-roll. "OK, OK, don't start, you two," I said. "Do we have to argue politics at every meal? Can we try and pretend to be a normal family for once?" Looking for an ally I said, "Gali, what do you think the holy Reb Yosef would say about this crazy family of ours?"

He slowly turned toward me. "You know what he'd say. You heard it yourself."

Anat laughed out loud. "What, you're going to this so-called rebbe too?"

"He's no rebbe; he's my old squash buddy playing holy man. But I thought you'd approve. You and Gal have a lot in common now. You're both enamored with matters of the spirit."

"Gal isn't even keeping Shabbat," she sniffed. "What kind of rebbe would allow his disciple to desecrate the Sabbath?"

Gal's voice came down a few notches, losing its tinny distance. "He teaches about how to revive the wounded soul. You don't need to turn the electricity off—"

There was a loud crash as Habakuk picked up his plate and forcefully smashed it to the ground. Instantly, lunch was over, and the screaming commotion that had preceded the meal resumed full force. Gal walked shakily to his roost on the terrace, while my mother remained seated at the table, in her bubble of vacancy or serenity—it was hard to tell which. Was my father right? Did she really know what was going on around her? If so, it was hard to see how she could achieve such preternatural calm.

Clearing the table, trying to sidestep the broken shards and ignore the ear-splitting clamor, I pondered my uncharacteristically honest response to Anat's question. Of course I had been a fool to go into a field to which I was so obviously ill-suited, but I had never said as much out loud. Despite all the clichés of how people became psychologists to heal themselves, I had never considered how such primitive motivations might apply to me. I had done my doctoral research on the coping mechanisms of children of Holocaust survivors, thinking it a hot topic, with all of us coming of age at the same time. But somehow I had never put the pieces together. I was a bigger fool than any of them knew. We were a family of fools, a nation of fools, an entire society reeling in trauma, all of us thinking we had escaped unscathed.

When the table had been cleared, I returned to the living room, where I now noticed that the little green soldier still dangled from the ceiling fixture. My father was again seated opposite my blankly staring mother, but lost in thought, no longer trying to intuit her every thought and need. Gal was a swaying shadow against the fierce sunlight now blanching the room. Couldn't they at least close the shades? The room was becoming increasingly claustrophobic as the afternoon heat closed in. There seemed no point in staying any longer.

"Abba, I'd better get going."

"Of course, you've got a busy life." Was that supposed to be sarcastic? He pushed himself up from the chair and stiffly walked me to the door.

"Tell me, Kobi," he said, opening the door for me. "You're a hotshot shrink. You're right, an honorable profession. So tell me the truth. After everything your mother and I suffered, why did our kids have to come out so weird?"

"I don't know, Abba. I've wondered about that myself."

"Was it the war? Were we wrong to have children, so damaged as we were after the war?"

"Of course not, Abba. You did the best you could."

"But not good enough, eh?" He leaned toward me, searchingly, but I couldn't meet his gaze.

"You know, Kobi, just last night, I had the same dream I've been having for over fifty years."

"You've been having recurrent dreams?"

"Just this one, and it's only a fragment—but I have it so frequently. In the dream, I have a message for my father. It's urgent that I get it to him. I'm gripping it tightly in my pocket and running, but my shoes are sinking into the sand. So I keep running, but not fast enough. I wake up, knowing I didn't reach him. Wondering if maybe I could have run just a little faster."

"You never told me about that dream."

He shrugged. "Why would I? Over fifty years, it's exactly the same. I never know what the message is. I never reach my father. I always wake up with my heart pounding, wondering . . ."

"Abba—"

"You'd think it would get easier with time, but it doesn't. You know what, Kobi? Your mother and I, we were the real fools. We thought we could put it behind us."

13

Ireturned to Jerusalem feeling more than a little unhinged. It was a Saturday night, and in my former life Nava and I would be heading out to dinner or a movie, or to friends, or just for a stroll down Emek Refaim. Yudit was now old enough to join us sometimes or to have plans of her own with friends. What were they doing tonight? Did they miss me at all? I bought a falafel off the street, at the entrance to the city, then sat in the car trying to figure out where I could tolerate spending the rest of the evening. After a long spell of paralysis, I decided, on a kind of self-dare, to return to Soreq's and have a second look.

So mythic had the pub become in my mind that I was surprised to find it listed in a telephone directory. The whole way there I chided myself: on my cowardice, my determination to steer my life off course, my extreme lack of professionalism in going to a bar I now believed might be frequented by a patient. My inability to stop picturing Israela in a tight dress, leaning into Delia.

Arriving by car, the neighborhood seemed less threatening than I recalled, but I still had to summon all my bravado to walk down the three steps and through the door. Without looking right or left I went straight to the bar, thankful to see an unfamiliar face serving drinks. Only when seated did I allow myself to scan the huge, windowless room, which felt stiflingly hot and stale, a few propped up fans churning the listless, smoky air. There were a handful of people sitting at the rickety tables, but it was still a depressing scene, the tinny laughter and drunken ribbing all pitched several notches too high. I glimpsed neither Delia nor Israela in the dimly lit room.

The bartender was a young Arab, tall and wiry, with a vacant, wild stare. He gave me a jerky, expectant nod and I ordered a Scotch. Only when I'd downed the first drink and ordered a second did I ask him if he knew a girl named Delia.

He motioned with his chin to a dark corner booth where a girl with straight blond hair could barely be seen, slumped over the table, her head cradled in her arms.

"Delia," he called out in a reedy voice and thick Arabic accent. "Wake up, you've got a visitor." The room went silent as I felt all eyes turn toward me, and I thought I caught a few smirking glares. Delia lifted her head for a look, squinting into the darkness, then scowled darkly when she saw me walking toward her. I saluted her with my drink, straining to keep a steady gait. Tousled and unkempt, she was even more beautiful than I'd remembered.

"Look at that. The limpdick Jewboy is back," she yelled.

I sat down across from her. She wore a skimpy lavender top, the thin ribbons of fabric falling off her slumped shoulders. On the table, a cigarette was smoldering into a precarious stick of ash.

She appraised me. "Didn't think I'd see you back here. You decided to fuck me after all?"

"I guess I needed a little more abuse." I smiled weakly.

"Aaaah, you must have some messed-up life."

"That's true, I got a pretty messed-up life."

She scowled. "And you want to tell all to an exotic stranger. Go home to your wife."

"She threw me out. I kept cheating on her, for no good reason. Just to distract myself, I think. Finally she had enough."

"You? A cheating husband? You look like such a Jewboy coward."

"I am a coward. Biggest there ever was."

"You're not the biggest of anything. You here to waste my time again. Go away."

I reached over and stubbed out the ember of her neglected cigarette.

"I'm probably going to lose my job too," I said. "Bitch of a new boss doesn't like me."

"No one likes you. You're a shithead." She pulled another cigarette from somewhere and lit it. "If you were my husband, I'd throw you out too."

"And my mother's gone and had a stroke." I had no idea why I was spilling my life to her, but now that I'd started I couldn't stop. "She doesn't talk anymore. Doesn't say a word, just sits there. I think she's happier now, relieved that she doesn't have to waste her life with make-believe conversation. And you know what? I don't even much care. I don't want to visit her anymore. I can't stand being with the whole lot of them."

I thought she hadn't been listening, but she said, "A man who don't even love his mama. You're more shit than I can believe."

"My sister's a religious fanatic. My brother's a drugged-out mystic. My daughter won't talk to me. Her bat mitzvah party is only a week away, and she doesn't even want me to go."

Delia blew a cloud of smoke into my face. "You got more problems than hell's got sinners." Despite all her spitfire abuse, she seemed less spirited than the last time I'd seen her. "Listen, asshole," she said wearily, "you need to shut up. I got problems of my own. You don't belong in this shithole. Get out of here." She glanced toward the bar, and I thought I detected a momentary fear.

"What happened to Pinya?" I asked. "Does he still work here?"

She looked at me sharply. "What do you care? He didn't like you anyway."

"Just curious."

She dragged on her cigarette. "He's dead."

"You're kidding."

"Yeah, big fat joke."

"For real? What happened?"

"You didn't read about it in the papers?"

"No," I admitted. "I don't follow the news much. Was it a terrorist attack?"

She snorted. "What, that's the only way people die around here?"

"No, of course not, but—"

"The world's better off without him." She glanced toward the bar again and added in a lower voice, "Ismail's no better—don't let his youth fool you. He's wild as a bucking mule, that kid. You smart, you stay out of his way too." She fiercely ground out her half-smoked cigarette.

I decided to ask a question that had been worrying me. "Did he used to hurt you?"

She stared at me sharply. "Who, Pinya? What you asking about shit that's none of your business? You don't know anything, Jewboy. You should keep your big-nose face shut up." The mockery was gone from her voice, replaced by real anger.

I stammered, "I'm sorry, I didn't mean to . . ."

"Then stop whining about your problems. I hate people who got money and no sense. Jewish people are all like that."

"What does—"

"I bet you grew up in some shiny-clean apartment, parents falling all over you." She put on a mocking voice. "*You have enough to eat, little pussy boy? Anyone hurt your feelings today, little baby-doll boy?*"

"Well, not exactly—"

"You know I'm right. You Jews are all fucked up. Think you're so smart because you read a lot of books." She reached out and flicked the frame of my glasses, a polished fingernail grazing my face. "I bet you read all the time, all kinds of fancy-thick books. Lot of good it did you."

"Well, actually—"

"I never read any books. Never got so far as sixth grade. But so what?" She looked up, her face full of scorn. "Chosen people—ha! Chosen to get blown up in buses. Chosen to get gunned down while sitting in fancy cafés. Chosen to be hated by the whole world."

"Did Pinya—"

"You still asking about Pinya?" She laughed, but when she spoke again, her voice was icy. "You know what, asshole? Your problems are shit. I'm tired; I gotta sleep. Get lost."

She put her head down, her long, impossibly straight hair cascading over her strong, freckled arms, only partially covering her slithering rope tattoo. I watched her skinny back rise and fall until I noticed Ismail eying me suspiciously from the bar. What had really happened to Pinya? It must have been something big for an underworld murder to make national news. Was Ismail responsible in some way? The fact that Hesh had known about Soreq's made me wonder if this place was a cover for some other, larger operation. A sudden thought struck me with a cold wave of fear.

"Delia?"

She looked up. "What, you still here? Go away."

"Were you sent to me by Y?"

Her incandescent eyes flared in rage. "Y? What Y? What the hell you talking about? You making fun of me?" Ismail was staring at us. I tried to calm her down.

"No, no, of course not. I—"

"You looking for trouble, go somewhere else. You need a shrink, find a shrink." She rummaged around furiously for another cigarette. "I'm just a foreign nobody you don't even have the balls to fuck. Stop wasting my time."

"I'm sorry, I got confused," I said.

She produced a cigarette, placed it between her lips and lit it, her hands shaking. But when she spoke again, she was calmer. "You're not confused, you're just a fucking loser." She forced out a laugh. "No wonder your wife threw you out. You're even more fucked than me." She shook her head with disgust, stubbed out the barely smoked cigarette and put her head back on the table.

It had been the wrong question to ask, of course. She probably wouldn't admit to knowing Y even if she did—assuming, I had to remind myself, that Y even existed. Anyway, would a misogynist like Y ever send a woman? I should have asked if she knew Israela, or Bal, or Hesh, or if she'd heard of the Outstretched Arm. She was right, I was a fucking loser. Why had I come? Why was I still sitting here?

She had begun to snore lightly. In sleep, she looked sad and desperate, beads of sweat gathered on her temple, her face flushed, her features collapsed into a vulnerable, stricken look. I knew nothing of her world and couldn't imagine the sequence of events that had brought her to these inhospitable shores, so far from home. In sleep, it was easy to see the face of the child she had once been, someone's little girl gone lost and sour. I suddenly thought of all the mornings I'd brushed Yudit's thick wavy hair before school and was overcome with homesickness.

I sat there a long time, my face in my hands, before leaving the pub and driving home to my empty, prison-like flat.

14

"I'm sorry I'm late again," Israela said, unwrapping her shawl and nestling into my leather chair, her legs folded under her.

"Actually, you're always about ten minutes late."

"Am I? I'm so sorry. I try to be on time, but I have a very hard time getting here. I have to walk everywhere. I don't have a car—and of course I'm terrified of the buses." She gave me a long, unnerving stare. "And I had a bad experience a while back, so now I avoid taxis as well."

There was no point pretending I didn't know what she meant. "Hesh?"

"I knew it." She leaned forward, her eyes wide. "He's some wacko, huh? At least you survived his kamikaze driving."

I was torn between trying to preserve some semblance of professionalism and giving over entirely to my growing list of questions. "Israela, I can't help wondering—"

"Can you believe how much he hates me? But then, he hates all women. Ever since he married Gamla, he's on a campaign to cleanse the world of 'the harlotry of women.'" She had mimicked him so perfectly I had to smile, and she smiled back, all glowing innocence. "I hope you didn't believe him."

"Well, you know . . ."

Her face collapsed in a shock of betrayal. "You believed him."

"I'm not saying that. I'm just suggesting that—"

She wasn't listening. "He tells everyone I'm a whore! Bal and I go out for dinner, he tells them I blew him under the table. Ashra and I go shopping, he tells folks we were screwing in the ladies room. The guy's got a sick mind. All he sees is sex, sex, sex."

Feeling a flash of guilt, I tried to bring the conversation back in a therapeutic direction. "How does that make you feel?"

"What kind of question is that? How do you think I feel?" She was almost shouting. "I walk into a room and the whispering starts, the knowing glances." She stifled a sob. "And the worst is that he gets Y believing all his slander. I mean, Y has his own jealous streak, I'm not saying he doesn't, but he's got other sides to him too. But when he's with Hesh, all he can think about is how I'm cuckolding him day after day." This unleashed the watery pools back into her eyes. "I can just imagine how hurt that makes him feel."

She was radiant in her wide-eyed, teary innocence. If nothing else, she was a terrific actress.

"Your husband is never around," I started. "Some people would think—"

"But I'm *married*. After everything I told you, I thought you'd understand." She wiped her eyes with a corner of her shawl. "Why does everyone believe everything that cat-killing psychopath says?"

She took a deep breath. "It's true that I hang out with Bal sometimes. He's not as bad as Y claims. It's not that I love him, but at least he's around— at least I can see him whenever I want. And we never hang out at sleazy bars. We go to a movie, have dinner, that's all. And Ashra's been a loyal friend to me. I know people whisper about her and Y, back in the old days, but it's not true what they say! Y never dated another woman, and even if he had, he would never date an Arab. He's totally prejudiced in that way."

"Ashra is an Arab?" I could hear the astonishment in my voice.

"Yes, so is Bal. What's wrong with that?"

"Nothing, I'm just surprised." More than surprised. Hadn't she told me that she had no friends? Suddenly she has a coterie of Arab pals and lovers. Where would she have met them? Soreq's Pub? She was lonely, and her reality testing was so precarious—I could easily see her being targeted and exploited by terrorists or criminal gangs.

Once again, it was like she read my mind. "I shouldn't have told you that Ashra's an Arab. Everyone's in this country is so prejudiced! They hear Arab, they right away think terrorist or criminal. Not every Arab is a would-be terrorist! Ashra's been good to me. Arabic's my native language, don't forget." I had forgotten; her Hebrew didn't have a trace of an accent. "It took me a while to understand her—the dialect here is so different. But she taught me, patiently, and I've gotten much better at it. Sometimes I need a woman to talk to, to go shopping with, to confide in, and . . ."

She stopped. "I don't want to talk about this anymore. You wouldn't understand." She said it casually but her face was full of terror. Why? I cursed my own stupidity again. I'd have to work hard now to regain her confidence.

"We don't have to talk about it anymore," I said brightly. "Last time, you were telling me about the dramatic escape from Master's house, how you stepped into those storming waters." She was examining her nails sulkily. "It was an unbelievable story." *Emphasis on "un-,"* I thought.

"It was the most amazing moment of my life," she said. I settled back on the couch, pen in hand, ready to listen.

She closed her eyes. "I woke up on the far shore of the sea. The storm had passed, and it was a beautiful night, clear, with a full, opalescent moon. There was an exquisite stillness, as if the whole world was holding its breath." I felt myself slipping into the hypnotic rhythms of her voice. But there was one detail I wanted to hear her explain.

"The 'far shore'?" I asked.

She opened her eyes and looked at me. "We walked across."

"But I thought—"

She shook her head impatiently. "Y knows those waters well. He's passed through them a million times. There are shallow channels that you can easily cross at low tide."

I nodded. Who knew what body of water she was even talking about; on a stormy, moon-hidden night a marshy reed bed could look like a forbidding ocean. I reminded myself to keep listening to her story for what it was—a stirring, coming-of-age fantasy.

"When I awoke," she continued, "Musa was setting up camp, stringing together animal hides and acacia branches to make three little tents, and Y was checking the perimeter of the site to make sure it was secure. What I remember most is how safe I felt. When you grow up in Egypt, the desert is the scariest thing in the world. You hear dire warnings about mirages that tempt people to their death, desert demons, agonizing thirst, madness brought on from sunstroke. But there I was, at the edge of this bleak wilderness, and I'd never felt so secure. And then I remembered that I was finally free, and for the first time in my life I was flooded with pure happiness. I started to sing and dance from joy."

I smiled at the image, and she smiled back shyly. For now, all was well between us. I felt a surge of relief.

"I even got Musa to sing along," she was saying. "No small feat! He was such a serious guy, you could barely crack a smile out of him. But that night, we laughed and sang like children." She smiled at the memory. "He was terribly off-key."

"That must have been amazing, after all you'd been through," I offered.

"Yes, but the euphoria didn't last long," she sighed. "I woke up late the next morning, soaked in sweat—those little tents were deathly hot—and it suddenly made me realize that we were headed into the middle of the Sinai, with no food, no water. Once we left the shore and headed into that sun-streaked wilderness, it got pretty scary. We were in a very remote area, crawling with Egyptian military, UN troops, never mind the bands of Bedouin smugglers. Don't forget, we were technically still in Egypt, so not completely beyond Master's reach. Y kept changing the route so we wouldn't be discovered. He always acted like he knew exactly where he was going, but I was never so sure." She paused. "Sometimes I thought they'd brought me out of Master's house just to die in that forsaken desert. But Musa would tolerate no complaints—he trusted Y completely. Sometimes they'd argue, but then they'd have these long tête-à-têtes in Y's tent, and Musa would emerge all dreamy-eyed and confident that everything would be OK."

"Didn't you talk to Y as well?" I asked, already knowing the answer.

She shifted in her seat and averted her eyes. "Not directly, no."

Was she conscious of the fabrication or had my question revealed the deep flaws in a real relationship? Either way, after the earlier awkwardness, I decided to take a safer line of inquiry.

"So what did you eat? How did you find water?"

"Musa showed me how to forage for these sticky, seedlike things that accumulate on the thorn shrubs." She made a face. "They looked like bug shit to me, but if you ground them up and cooked them into cakes, they weren't half-bad. Anything becomes edible after long days of trekking through the heat. Sometimes I got really hungry and complained to Musa about how the two of them were starving me to death. Even in Master's house, at least we got fresh fish and vegetables. I should have known better—Musa never kept anything to himself. He'd go right off and report to Y that I was making trouble. I can still remember the time I overheard Musa bitterly complaining about me. He said, 'What am I, her nursemaid?' That hurt me a lot." She paused, reflecting.

"I guess there weren't many food options in the middle of the desert," I said.

"Oh, but that's not true! Y always carried a rifle. One day, after grumbling and raging and carrying on about how ungrateful I was, he went off hunting and returned with enough quail to gorge on for a month. He could have shot gazelles, foxes—there was plenty of game. I still don't know why he thought it was so terrible that I craved a little meat. It's not like he had any trouble finding it when he wanted to. And Musa could find water under any rock. Truth is, both of them had lived in the desert for years, and they knew it well. They weren't going to let me starve or die of thirst."

"Where exactly were you heading?"

She smiled. "Y was leading us to the mountain where he'd lived before he came to save me, the spot where he first met Musa. He had it in his head that we'd get married at his old mountain hideaway. He loves that place. If he hadn't been so busy evading every soldier and Bedouin shepherd, I'm sure we could have gotten there much quicker."

I wondered briefly if the Mossad had left behind a secret outpost, built into the mountains of Sinai, to monitor Egyptian troops or to have a base for rescuing the few remaining Jews left in Egypt. Could Y's rescue of Israela have been part of a larger operation? It certainly didn't sound like a very professional job, but the Mossad's professionalism was often overrated. But probably not; Israela had been adamant in her contention that Y always operated alone. More likely he was one of those under-socialized, itinerant loners, hiding from life in a mountain lair—the kind you usually hear about after they've committed some heinous crime.

"So Y just assumed you'd marry him?" I asked.

"Of course I was going to marry him!" she exclaimed. "It's true that I never really saw him during the journey—he was always off plotting the route or hunting for food. But what can I say?" Her face grew soft, loving. "I had never had any family or friends, and here was someone who had saved me from a life of servitude and had chosen to marry me. And yes, he was a lot older than me, but so vigorous and sure of himself! Don't forget, I was only a teenager, and a bit of a romantic. It never occurred to me not to marry him!"

"But why the rush?"

She waved the question away impatiently. "He wanted to make sure I wouldn't have any legal problems once we got to Jerusalem and settled in. After all, I was born in Egypt and had no papers connecting me to my family. Marrying me would make me legitimate, a proper Israeli." She paused. "But actually, I think that was just an excuse." She looked at me. "Have you ever spent extended time in the desert?"

"Why do you ask?"

"Well . . . it's hard to explain unless you've lived it. The desert is brutal, of course, but there's something to that starkness that jars the soul. Maybe because there's no tree cover, no room for subterfuge." She thought for a moment. "In some ways, I've never felt as alive as when I lived under the desert stars. I understood why he wanted to get married there. If you're going to make such a solemn commitment, you should do it somewhere austere and forbidding, to make sure that you really mean what you say." She looked up at me. "Sometimes I think that I'd be less committed to this marriage if it had happened in a Tel Aviv ballroom."

That stung a little. Nava and I had been married in an expensive Tel Aviv ballroom, every detail meticulously planned by her and her mother for over a year. The whole event had seemed vacuous—entirely her affair, not mine.

"Although at one point I thought he was going to cancel the whole thing," Israela was saying. She pulled her shawl around her. "Y and Musa were up in the cave writing out the *ketubah*. But they were gone so long, I got really lonely. Then night began to fall and I heard strange noises in the distance—I thought it might be jackals, or soldiers, or Bedouin smugglers—and I got scared. So to distract myself, I collected all the scraps I could find in the camp and tied them together, stuffing them with acacia leaves." She smiled shyly. "I created an enormous doll. I wove stems into the head to make a smiling face, then decorated the whole thing with leaves and tiny wildflowers. It was primitive, but so beautiful!" She laughed out loud, remembering. "I'd never had a doll in my life but had always dreamed of having one. I spent hours working on it and was so pleased with what I'd created. I talked to it, confiding all my fears and hopes, and fell asleep hugging it close." She shook her head, her smile fading. "But the next morning, when Musa came down from the mountain and saw what I had done, he was furious! First he ripped up the *ketubah* he'd just spent all night writing, then he made me tear the doll into shreds. I was sobbing hysterically. I thought it was over, that they would abandon me to my death right then and there."

She looked at me, perhaps expecting an expression of pity or concern, but her story had evoked an unexpected memory of my own: Yudit, age nine or ten, had created a plush fabric doll as a gift for a friend's birthday party, stuffed plump with pillow stuffing, with an embroidered, winking face. She then fell so in love with her creation that she refused to give it up, crying and holding it close. Nava eventually gave in and took her shopping, only an hour before the party, to buy a generic, plastic replacement gift. The original had remained on her bed for years; as far as I could recall, it was still there.

It was the beginning of a whole doll-making phase that for several years had taken up all her free time. She'd experimented with different methods: sewing fabric scraps, whittling strips of olive wood, wrapping string, puddling the yard with sticky mounds of papier-mâché. She created humans and animals and fanciful extraterrestrials, some in little family units, some with moving limbs. She'd decorate them with ribbon and pipe cleaners, buttons and dried flowers, markers and glitter, always scavenging the house for new ideas. An avocado pit became an old grandmother-doll's painted head; bits of electric wire became a doggy-doll's wild-fur coiffure; a painted glass door knob, festooned with purple-yarn locks, was precariously fastened to the top of a long, blue dinner candle to become an elegant Venusian goddess. There had also been a trio at some point—a mama doll, papa doll, and Yudit doll—that had hung from long hooks in a recess of the living room window. I had never much liked the papa doll, with its crooked smile and mismatched arms. She never dressed it—said she didn't know how to dress a male doll—so it looked naked and foolish, in awkward, pipe-cleaner glasses, especially compared to the elegant mama doll and the cute, pigtailed Yudit doll. Sometimes I'd see her spinning the papa doll, chattering away, and wondered if she preferred the facsimile papa to the original. At some point the ersatz family had quietly disappeared from their hooks, replaced by flowering, hanging plants.

"Dr. Benami, are you OK?"

I pulled myself out of a deep ache of loss, remembering, in renewed panic, that Yudit's party was that very weekend and I still hadn't come up with an idea for a suitable gift.

Israela had been talking throughout my reverie but was now watching me intently.

"My daughter used to make dolls," I said. Even for me, this was a serious breach of protocol.

Israela leaned in, speaking softly and intently, as if confiding a great secret. "I never outgrew my love of dolls," she whispered.

I struggled to pull myself back together. "Why did Musa make you destroy your doll?" I finally managed.

Israela studied me for a moment before responding. "I shouldn't have gotten so scared. I should have trusted them. I should have known that Y would protect me."

"Maybe they shouldn't have left you alone in the desert for an entire night," I said and then immediately regretted it.

"But they had to! Don't you see? It's as if I'd already forgotten everything Y had done for me. He would never have let anything bad happen to me! I'm still mortified at what a coward I was."

I didn't see at all. It was a cruel and ruthless logic.

"Do you see how generous Y is? He married me even after I showed how little I deserved it!"

Amazingly, the tears were dripping again. I couldn't tell if I was more shaken by the sadomasochistic undertone of her story or by the vividness of the memories it had aroused in me.

She'd gone back into storytelling mode, I noticed with relief. "There was a storm on the mountain the night of the wedding—it was eerie, frightening, but utterly enchanting. I couldn't really see Y, the cloud cover was so low, and he stood a distance up the slope. Musa was officiating, the flashes of lightning serving as a mystical huppah. I remember shaking from excitement through the whole ceremony. We didn't exchange rings or break a glass, but that's precisely what gave it so much power! It was the essence of a wedding—a deep and sacred exchange of promises."

I remembered almost nothing from my own wedding. We had stood under a flower-covered huppah while an austere, gray-bearded rabbi we'd never met before mumbled at us. The only thing I really remembered was how happy and beautiful Nava looked when she took my hand.

"What kind of promises?" I asked.

Israela's eyes were dreamy and soft. "I solemnly agreed to obey all of Y's rules, sight unseen, and he promised to protect me forever." She laughed. "It's kind of old-fashioned, I know, but it was exactly what I needed. After everything I'd been through, I was hungry for rules, structure, someone telling me what to do. After the ceremony, Musa brought me the new *ketubah*, where Y had written out the most important rules. They covered everything you can imagine. There were rules about being kind to strangers and poor people, to never treat anyone like Master had treated me. Others were about being faithful, not sleeping around, not mixing too much in the neighborhood. Like I told you, loyalty's a big deal to Y." She studied my face. "And there were many others. Y can be a little . . . obsessive."

One more addition to the diagnostic list. "What do you mean?"

"There were rules about when I should work and when I should rest. What I'm allowed to eat, and what foods to avoid. Detailed instructions on how to cook his meals." She bit the side of her lip before continuing. "I agreed to it all. I was in awe of him! That's the only way I can explain it. And after that magnificent, terrifying wedding . . . ," she trailed off. "I'd never known anything but the drudgery of Master's house. I needed a new master, but one who loved me and would take care of me. That's what Y was offering me."

I nodded carefully. What would I ask next if this were a normal patient session? "So then you moved into his tent?"

"Oh, no," she said immediately. "He would never share a tent with me."

"But I thought—"

"It wasn't like that. Not that kind of marriage, if you know what I mean."

I don't know what I'd been expecting. "It was never consummated?"

"Well, yes, but not in the way you're thinking. I mean he would come to me at times, in the middle of a moonless night. I would sense him entering the tent, feel him near me, inside me." She smiled. "It was wonderful, overwhelming really. But it was always in the dead of night when I was half-asleep; he would never come near me if I was fully awake. He's shy in that way—doesn't really like to be seen."

"Yes, of course." Why was I even asking?

Our time was up. As I handed her the appointment slip, I saw her staring at the Chagall painting, her mouth slightly agape.

"You know, Dr. Benami, this picture on your wall—it reminds me of my wedding night."

Why did everyone love this asinine painting so much? "But it's a shtetl scene, from Eastern Europe. No mountain. No desert."

"I know, isn't that funny?" She didn't take her eyes off it. "But something about the lack of gravity, the magic, the floating lovers, the upside-downness of their world . . ." She stood and turned back to me, laughing shyly. "I feel like you really understand what it all meant to me."

The adoring, expectant look in her enormous brown eyes undid me. It took all my willpower not to reach out and slip the edge of her shawl off her shoulder, to sink my face into the warm fragrance of her neck . . .

I smiled at her weakly, awkwardly, and ushered her to the door.

Just before she walked out, she turned around. The adoring look was gone, replaced by something shrewder. "Your daughter," she said. "Does she still like dolls?"

"I don't know," I stammered.

"Maybe you should buy her one," she whispered and disappeared out the door.

15

My 2:00 patient never showed, giving me an entire hour to brood on Israela's parting words. Yudit's room was still crowded with a menagerie of stuffed animals and figurines, on the bed, sitting on shelves, strewn into every corner. Some were the product of her own handiwork, but many were not. All those little faces watching from every corner had always unnerved me.

When Anat was about seven or eight, our parents had bought her a life-sized, plastic baby doll for Hanukah. My mother showed her how to rock it in her arms, pretend to feed it and put it to sleep, but it clearly left Anat—from earliest childhood, more prone to giving speeches than to playing with toys—perplexed and disinterested. Some time later—a few days or weeks or even months—my mother found the doll in Anat's room with arithmetic equations scrawled in blue ink up and down its pink, plastic limbs, even on its neck and face. When we came home from school, my mother was sobbing hysterically. She screamed at Anat—what was the matter with her, why didn't she know how to play with a doll like any normal child? I remembered Gal's terrified yowls and my sister cowering as our father restrained our mother from physically attacking her. It was the only time I ever saw my mother so utterly out of control, and it was only many years later that the significance of the tattoo-like numbers on the doll's limbs even occurred to me. I doubted that Anat understood, to this day, what she had done.

But Yudit had none of these associations. Her dolls had been beloved companions and were now—the word came to me, I'd heard her use it with Nava—part of a collection. And didn't every collection need a prize item? An image began to form in my head. What if I found her a doll that was unique and handmade—sophisticated, expressive, smartly attired—up to the high standards of a keen-eyed preteen? It would be a bat mitzvah offering that patently demonstrated, in its distinctiveness, how much her Abba still loved her, even from afar.

When I'd dispatched my last patient of the day, I headed for the shops of Nahalat Shiv'a full of anticipation, but none of the dolls I saw came close to the image in my head. They were too childish, too plain or too precious, too commercial and generic; and too many of them reminded me, eerily, of Anat's ill-fated baby doll. After a frustrating hour of being shunted from store to store, I began to despair that what I imagined even existed. I was ready to give up and concoct yet another new birthday present plan when a seasoned sales clerk, listening to my faltering description of what I wanted, knowingly nodded her head and wrote something on a slip of paper.

"That's the place you want," she said and brusquely turned to her next customer.

I walked out into the crowded street and looked down at the slip of paper. In English she had written:

Al-Quds Doll Shop
#4 al-Bustan
Muslim Quarter (nr. Damascus Gate)

I had no wish to return so soon to the Old City, especially to the Muslim Quarter. Was it really possible that no one in all of West Jerusalem could fashion an interesting doll? But I had no alternate plan.

I hopped a cab at noon the next day. I could have walked, but after Hesh's dire warnings about the many violent attacks in the area, I was too frightened to do so. After a stop-and-go, checkpoint-filled ride, we arrived at Damascus Gate, where the swarm of Israeli soldiers did little to assuage my unease.

Two steps into the Old City, I was cursing myself yet again. It was impossible that the doll I imagined could be found in this fetid warren—what could that sales clerk possibly have had in mind? I showed the address to an old Arab man, who stared at me for several unbearable moments with his rheumy, gray-brown eyes before holding up four fingers and saying, in halting English, "Four . . . streets . . . left." I thanked him and quickly made my way through the crowd of Arab shoppers. I counted four streets, then ventured cautiously into a dark, claustrophobic alley that bore no street sign. Other than a ragged tailor shop on the corner, there seemed to be no commercial properties on the narrow cobblestoned street.

Deep into the alley, a young girl, about Yudit's age, sat on a low stool in front of a black curtain, her head covered with a loose scarf. She eyed me closely as I walked back and forth looking for a street number or shop sign. As I passed her the third time, ready to give up on my foolish quest, she whispered to me in schoolgirl English, "You look for doll shop? Best doll shop in Jerusalem." Her tone made me wonder if she was speaking in code, offering me an illicit drug deal.

"Uh, yes," I admitted. "Do you know where it is?"

She stood, moved the stool from the entranceway, and parting the curtain, went up on tiptoes to pull the chain on a bare electric bulb. "Come in, please," she said, inviting me with a sweep of her hand.

I stepped into the shadows of a dollhouse wonderland.

The room was much bigger than seemed possible from the alleyway. It was filled with about a hundred dolls, all handmade of carved and polished olive wood, yet with a roughness in the finishing that was, I suspected, the signature style of their creator.

The first one to catch my eye seemed like an exact replica of my elementary school principal. I looked carefully at the exquisite craftsmanship. Tall, thin, and bespectacled, in rumpled clothes, a lock of thinning hair falling onto his forehead, his face bore the worried burden of a world spinning out of his reach. Next to him sat the spitting image of my high school girlfriend, Talia. The doll was an older version, to be sure, but unmistakably her. There was a delicate creasing in her face, her hair shorter and more dignified than I remembered, but still with that distinctive slump in her posture, looking out at the world with wary, you-will-hurt-me eyes. I felt a chill as I walked through the dim shop in a trance, recognizing and remembering the full supporting cast of actors that had wandered on and off the stage of my life: school friends, army buddies, patients, distant aunts and uncles and cousins, even the clinic receptionists whose names I could never remember, each doll slightly different from its original model—darker or paler, taller or shorter, younger or older—yet fully known to me by a telling detail in their expression or posture or pose.

I wandered like this for I don't know how long before noticing an exquisite doll, larger than most of the others. This one I recognized not as a character from my life but as the image I had formed in my mind for Yudit's gift. I stood staring in disbelief: it really existed. She was a beautiful, elegant, middle-aged woman, with distinctly Arab features, dark wavy hair, and a knowing, flirtatious smile. The eyes were wise and kind, encased in deep laugh lines, and when I looked into the dark pupils I sensed forgiveness. She was clothed in luxurious layers of silk that billowed about her—in exactly the deep shade of rose I had imagined—and wore an excess of silver jewelry that tinkled from the breeze of the standing fan.

"You like her?" A woman's voice, speaking in fluent, British-inflected English.

I turned in surprise. Standing behind me was a tall, solidly built Arab woman of about fifty, the obvious model for the doll I'd been admiring. She was dressed in the same shimmering silks, a rose-colored scarf slung carelessly over her rich, dark hair.

"I'm sorry, I didn't hear you enter. She's beautiful. She looks like you."

The woman dipped her head once to receive the compliment.

"Were you the model?"

"I am the artist," she said, smiling wryly at my surprise. "My name is Ashra. And these," she said, her arms sweeping across the store, "are my children."

Ashra? "They're magnificent," I said. "I know this will sound absurd, but I feel like I recognize every one of them."

She laughed out loud, a laugh that rippled with joy. "It's strange, isn't it?" she finally said. "I hear that all the time. It is music to a craftswoman's ears."

"Well, you're very talented. Why is your shop so hidden?"

She lowered her voice to a conspiratorial whisper. "Many Muslims don't approve."

"Oh, of course. Carving human images is forbidden. But they're just dolls . . ."

She shook her head. "These days, even dolls . . . and you are not the first one to recognize real people in my work, whether I intend it that way or not. It has become too dangerous."

"But how can you make a living with your shop so hidden from view?"

She shrugged and tossed me a carefree smile. "You found me, no? People find me. Were you looking for a gift?"

"Yes."

"For your wife? Or perhaps for a mistress?" She winked at me coyly.

"No, no . . . it's for my daughter."

"Aaah. What is she like?"

"I don't know, she's a girl. She'll be twelve on Friday."

"Such a fabulous age," she said. "Neither child nor adult. What a joy to buy a gift for a child that age."

"Yes, well . . . I haven't much time. I'm on my lunch break. I was wondering . . . how much does this one cost?"

She smiled at me, then lovingly stroked the hair of the self-portrait doll. "You have expensive taste. She is very dear to me."

I belatedly remembered the cardinal rules of bargaining in the Arab *shuq*: never appear too interested in the item you want, and never suggest that you are short on bargaining time. I had already broken them both.

"Well, there are others I like equally well," I said, a little too brightly.

Again, that joyful tinkle of laughter.

"Ah, no, *habibi*," she said when she had composed herself. "This is the one you want."

The young girl reentered the room with a tray holding a tea pot and cups, sugar bowl, and spoons. She set it down on the stool and began to pour.

"My daughter, Ishta."

"Salaam Alaikum," I said.

"Wa-Alaikum Salaam," she responded shyly, handing me a cup of tea into which she had mixed a large spoonful of sugar. Mint leaves swirled on the dark surface.

To be polite, I took a small sip of the sickeningly sweet liquid. "Thank you, this is delicious." I watched Ashra take a cup of tea into her own hands, entranced by the gracefulness of her every move. "You're right," I admitted, "this doll is exceptionally beautiful. I probably can't afford her. Is she even for sale?"

Ashra stroked the hair and fabric some more, played with the dangling necklaces, preparing herself to part from a dearly beloved child. "Yes, she is for sale. She will cost you a thousand shekel."

It was an extravagant price. She would, of course, expect me to bargain. The customary back-and-forth would take hours, and glass after glass of sugary tea, before a reasonable price would be struck. I hadn't done it in years and really didn't have the time. But I gave it a feeble attempt.

"That's well out of my price range. I could offer a hundred shekel at most."

She laughed sweetly, and I considered saying one preposterous thing after another only for the wonder of hearing her laugh. "For a hundred shekel you can have this one," she said and gently placed in my hand the sadistic army captain I'd had in basic training, the thick, black eyebrows carefully gouged to a menacing depth.

I quickly sat him back on the shelf. "Well, it's very nice, but hardly appropriate for a twelve-year-old girl." I decided to try another tactic. "I think we might know someone in common," I said casually.

She smiled at me indulgently, allowing her daughter to refill her cup. "I don't for a minute doubt it, my friend. But it won't make any difference." She took a sip. "I have all day to bargain and drink tea and exchange pleasantries. I've baked some delectable poppy cakes that Ishta can bring, and we can spend a lazy afternoon doing business. But in the end, you will buy this doll, and only this doll, because this is the doll you have come for. And it will cost a thousand shekel. Believe it or not, there is no negotiating. I spent months carving this child, and it was truly a labor of love." She put her cup back down on the tray. "I do not want to part with her, but if I must . . ."

"A thousand shekel . . ."

". . . is an extravagant amount of money for a doll, I agree. But I love this doll and you love your daughter, and you are filled with guilt and the need to atone, am I right?" I couldn't break her gaze, nor did I want to. "It's a magnificent doll—you will find none like it in all of Jerusalem. Not even in all the Middle East. Your daughter will see it and know deep in her heart how much her father loves her. A thousand shekel, and it will be worth every pruta." She smiled at me with the forgiving smile of the doll, and I knew I was defeated.

I peeled off the bills, feeling like the ultimate *freier*. No one had ever paid the asking price in a Muslim Quarter shop, not even the most naïve American tourist, but what could I do? It was true, I had to have this doll, no other would do, and I had neither the time nor the patience nor the skill for the requisite bargaining. No one would ever need to know the absurd amount of money I had spent.

The doll was huge, almost the size of a toddler. Ashra shook her head no, the laugh lines still creasing her eyes, when I asked if she had a large enough bag, but she carefully wrapped the doll's veil over its hair and face, draping the copious material of its dress over its limbs, so that its transgressive doll-ness would be at least partially hidden from disapproving eyes. I imagined Ashra laughingly retelling the story to her women friends—perhaps even to Israela—of the native-born *freier* who had paid more than triple the going price for a wooden doll. I took off through the *shuq* in the opposite direction from how I had come, toward Jaffa Gate, even more scared than before of passing through Damascus Gate now that I was carrying a huge woman-doll under my arm. I felt like a kidnapper, pressing the hidden limbs close to my body, apprehensive and ashamed lest some passerby recognize the expensive wooden doll for what it was.

In front of Jaffa Gate, a large, desultory crowd was spilling from the direction of the Armenian Quarter and into the plaza. It was a mournful procession, dotted by a handful of monks draped in black, with veiled, pointy hats and huge crosses lying heavily on their chests. The crowd was chanting and singing, with little enthusiasm, raising and lowering handmade signs in Hebrew, English, and Armenian. "Never Again" cried many of the signs, and a more useful one declared today as "Armenian Genocide Remembrance Day." I'd never even heard of it. Good luck to them, I thought, as I fought my way through the crowd, the woman-doll pressed close to my chest. It was hard to imagine that anyone in this morbidly self-obsessed country would pay attention to a genocide other than our own.

As I passed out of the crowd and through Jaffa Gate, I finally allowed myself to exhale. Only then did it occur to me to wonder how I was going to deliver my giant Ashra-doll to Yudit before the bat mitzvah. Going to the house in the evening, when both Nava and Yudit would be home, was unthinkable. I called the clinic, told the skeptical receptionist that I was caught in heavy traffic, and took another stop-and-go taxi ride to the German Colony.

It was my first time back at the house since the day Nava had tossed her wedding ring into my coffee cup in Café HaEmek. The house was at the end of a quiet alley, with a lush and inviting entranceway. Nava had a knack for adding colorful touches: wind chimes and bird feeders, hanging plants and chipped archaeological artifacts, all in seemingly careless harmony with the elegant Arab tilework that adorned the front porch. One of Yudit's handmade dolls still hung from a hook in the ceiling of the porch, a genderless nude with moving limbs, made of painted plastic piping and wire-spring hair. I gingerly seated the luxurious Ashra-doll on the fabric cushions of the porch's hanging swing. I found the "Al Quds Doll Shop" scrap of paper in my pocket and wrote, "To Yudit from Abba, with love," on the opposite side, tucking it into the doll's front collar where it could easily be seen. I wondered for a brief moment if it could possibly be stolen, but I didn't have many choices. The front door was locked, and as I'd been warned, my old key no longer worked. The porch was sufficiently sheltered from the alley by a cascade of shrubbery, and anyway, it was just a doll—who could possibly guess how valuable it was? I sat on the swing next to the doll for a few long moments, and like Yudit, like Ashra herself, had trouble parting with my doll gift. I peered one last time into its dark and forgiving eyes, gently stroked its hair and silky clothes. Finally, I planted a fatherly kiss on its smooth, wooden cheek before returning, after my almost three-hour lunch break, to the wrath of the all-knowing receptionists.

16

All afternoon I imagined Yudit's delight in coming home to the unexpected gift, and then all evening I waited for her call. But the telephone remained silent that evening and the next. All day Thursday I wondered in helpless despair how she was spending the day before her big party. Was she busily attending to final details? Fluttering with excitement? Suffering from the anxious stomach pangs she sometimes experienced before big tests? I thought of the complicated arrangements involving a few select friends that had only recently replaced the raucous balloon-and-noisemaker parties of her early childhood. Nava had always taken charge of the birthday arrangements—helping to formulate the guest list, baking the cake, buying the presents, festooning the house with streamers and hand-painted signs—and this year, though larger in scale, was no different. They were busy, that was all. But as the third day wound to a close, I had to admit the obvious: the extravagant purchase had done nothing to win me what Ashra had slyly referred to as "atonement." Perhaps it had made matters worse. Did she think that I was trying too hard, confirming my unforgivable guilt in her eyes? Or maybe she really was too old for dolls and had interpreted the gift as one more instance of my impenetrable cluelessness. One thing was clear: she was still furious at me and was not yet ready to forgive my innumerable offenses. Perhaps she never would.

That night I had a disturbingly vivid dream. I was at the bat mitzvah dinner, but the room was filled with animated dolls, all of them laughing and arguing and gesticulating with exaggerated vitality. I desperately needed to tell Nava that these were imposters, not the real guests, but I couldn't find her among the wooden faces in the room. A fight broke out at one table, and the dolls began to push and shove at each other with increasing aggression. Two particularly vicious-looking dolls in army fatigues started to strafe the room with their Uzis, and I ducked behind a chair. From my hiding place, I spotted a suicide bomber doll, keffiyeh wrapped around his head, just before he exploded, destroying an entire table of old-people dolls. There was mayhem throughout the room, some dolls shooting, others fleeing, others punching and kicking their fellow dolls, the floor littered with splinters and broken wooden limbs. I then noticed the Ashra doll begin to twirl with wild abandon in the center of the rambunctious crowd, her rose-colored garments flashing as she spun, the central axis of her body spinning into a ceiling-tall wooden pillar. The room quieted as every olive-wood eye turned in her direction. I realized that the other dolls must think this is Yudit, the bat mitzvah girl, and I tried to alert them that she too was an imposter. But the crowd was too mesmerized to notice, and no matter how I strained, no sound emerged from my voice. I awoke with a pounding heart and a cold coat of sweat, a choked scream in my throat.

It was 4:00 a.m. I lay in bed for another hour trying to calm down, then got up and, still a little shaky, prepared myself a pot of strong Turkish coffee. The silence of the apartment felt more oppressive than ever. The thought of spending Yudit's bat mitzvah weekend wandering aimlessly through the bomb-filled streets of Jerusalem, or visiting my family in Petah Tikva, or sitting alone in the flat brooding about Nava, Delia, Ashra, or the impenetrable mystery surrounding Israela—each option seemed more unbearable than the next. I had to get out of town now, immediately.

On a sudden inspiration, I decided to head south to the beaches of Eilat. A little vacation—why not? As far from Israel as you could get without crossing a border. It was hours of driving, but the very idea filled me with new energy and resolve. I showered and quickly packed the car with swimsuit, towel, and a cooler with a six-pack of beer. Just before getting in the car, on impulse, I worked the wedding ring off my finger and laid it on the bedroom bureau encircling Nava's. Perhaps it was time to let go of the illusion that I was still married.

I hit the road just as the sun was hitting its full force in the cloudless blue sky. It had been years since I'd been south of Beersheva. Nava disliked the desert, and all our family vacations had been in the north, hiking or visiting obscure archaeological sites. She seemed to revel in the stultifying layers of history that lay under every Israeli rock. I, on the other hand, longed to beach myself on a sun-bleached strip of sand and let the heat melt away my accumulated angst. I had been a teenager the last time I'd headed this far south, back when the Sinai had been Israel's backyard getaway, and I had a vague, nostalgic memory of snorkeling with high school buddies at Ras Muhammad, gazing at the Red Sea through a blanched, shimmering haze.

I remembered the Negev road as a dull one, flat stretches of grainy sand to both sides, but this time it exhilarated me. South of the Dead Sea, the austere strip of highway unfurled itself through the barren landscape like a royal carpet, a passageway to freedom. Corny Zionist songs from my youth surfaced unbidden, and I started to sing loudly, flamboyantly off-key, celebrating the miraculous liberation of the ancient desert homeland.

This is what I had wanted all along, without knowing it—a stark change of scenery. In fact, what I needed was a full transformation, more extreme than this short, weekend jaunt. Possibilities opened up in front of me, one after the other. I wasn't tied down anymore by parental obligations, the one upside of Yudit's total rejection of me. I was a complete failure as a therapist, but wasn't Yossi a lot happier in his new line of work? Maybe I too needed a new scam. Or maybe it was time to join the battalions of my countrymen who had found more serene, profitable lives on foreign shores. Why would any sane person continue to make a life in a perpetual war zone? I'd always been enamored with Scandinavia, the chilled, down-to-earth sensibility of those sparsely populated, somnambulant lands. Perhaps I could apprentice myself to someone—a cabinetmaker, say, in Denmark, or Finland, even better—who, speaking slowly, with as few words as possible, would teach me a nice, utilitarian craft. I could do work that was creative and obviously useful instead of numbly listening to people's problems all day. Everyone spoke English in those places, and my English was serviceable. I'd find some kind of commune—they still existed, I'd read about them. No one would care where I came from. I'd be valued as a dark, mysterious stranger with a lyrical accent who knew how to work with his hands. I'd find some young girl, an innocent, who would be seduced by my skills and my silent ways. A pretty wisp of a girl, who knew how to garden. Maybe the two of us would have a child, a boy, a blond little *shaygetz*, who would be enamored of his exotic, foreign-born father. An hour passed while I fantasized about the relationship I would have with my doting young wife and adorable, precocious son.

By the time I arrived at the outskirts of the city, I had convinced myself that Eilat was the perfect launching point for my new life. It was the only city in Israel still marginally full of travelers, far as it was from the mayhem of that miserable conflict. No one ever got blown up in Eilat. So why go for just the weekend? I would call in sick on Sunday—even people on probation could get sick every once in a while. Maybe this very weekend I would meet some adventurous European traveler who would, offhandedly, give me an idea that would steer me on my new course. I felt intoxicated with hope.

Singing loudly, drumming on the steering wheel, I got so caught up planning my speech to Jezebel ("Oh yeah, some Finnish friends of mine really need my help with this community they're building . . .") and imagining how much fun Yudit and I would have cross-country skiing under the towering fir trees that I made a number of false turns before finally arriving at the coast. Interrupted from dreams of leaping into icy lakes by the sauna-like heat of Eilat, I found the town completely unrecognizable. The sleepy little north coast I remembered from three decades earlier was lined now with enormous, garish, overpriced hotels. Beyond this chain of mega-monsters was a tangle of malls, and beyond that, on the once-empty southern coast—where I remembered laying out my sleeping bag below the stars—was a handful of almost as pricy, tackily themed hotels. I had imagined, at most, a messy clutter of eclectic guesthouses, but there was nothing of the kind. I stopped at three hotels, all of them laughably overdecorated, and all of them full. Coming out of the third, beginning to wonder if I shouldn't have done at least a little advanced planning, I noticed a slight, middle-aged man, in shorts and a loose T-shirt, waving at me emphatically from across the street. He had a wiry, energetic frame and a rubbery suntanned face. I looked around to see if he was gesturing to someone else, but I was the only one around. He ran up to me, slightly out of breath.

"Are you looking for a place to stay?" he panted.

"Well, yes. I didn't think it would be so hard." I glanced up the street, hoping to find another hotel I'd somehow overlooked.

He was still catching his breath. "Eilat is always full, even off-season—even during an intifada." He waved his hands vaguely at the street. "These European travelers, they aren't scared off by a few bombs. But you don't have to stay in one of these touristy places." He turned and beckoned me to join him. "Come, I have a great room for you. Fully air-conditioned." He took a few steps, hitching up his pants. Then he wiped his nose on the sleeve of his T-shirt.

This was not the life-changing encounter with a stranger that I'd hoped for.

He glanced back and saw that I hadn't moved. He stopped, squinting at me. "You look familiar," he said. "What army unit did you serve in?"

"Golani.

"Early '80s?"

"Well, yes."

"Ah!" he shouted. "I knew it! Were you in that operation in Ramallah? 1980? What a hellhole. Don't say another word, we both know what it was like." I didn't recognize him at all, and if I'd had to guess, I'd have said he was ten years older—though I might have been flattering myself. He had taken my arm and was walking me down the street. "We're like brothers, you and I. At least we missed Lebanon. Of course, you'll stay in my home—it's not far. Can we go in your car? I left mine at home. I'll give you a very good price."

Despite every scrap of logic, I trusted him. He seemed a little odd, but what he had said was true: I didn't belong in these tourist joints. And hadn't I committed to being open to whatever the universe provided? From the passenger seat, my new friend navigated us through a maze of streets until we parked in front of a modest villa with a well-tended garden. Inside, the room he showed me was small and neatly furnished, with an attached, private bath, and the price he quoted was half what the hotels were charging. I couldn't tell whether he lived in the villa alone or with a family, but it seemed well-kept and serene. I congratulated myself on having trusted the spirit of adventure; this was a lot more comfortable and homey than some touristy hotel.

In the room, I opened the cooler and pulled out a beer. I quickly changed into my swimsuit, whistling happily, though my mood shifted as I caught a glimpse of myself in the full-length mirror. Living on my own, I'd been eating poorly and exercising less—is that how I had developed the beginning of a hanging gut? Or had it been there for years without my noticing? And when had my scalp transitioned from a distinguished receding hairline to indisputable baldness? I examined my image closely. I was still tall and reasonably fit, but looked decidedly middle-aged, and more than a little ludicrous in my tiny bathing suit. I ran my hands through my scanty hair, my ring finger glaring at me in unaccustomed nakedness. I suddenly imagined the young Finnish girl laughing at my advances.

But what the hell—that didn't mean I couldn't change my life. I pulled up my chest and sucked in the gut as far as it would go. Plenty of young women were attracted to middle-aged men. But forget the woman. The point was to move to some quiet, peaceful country and grow old in a sane environment, perhaps alone. I could live in a secluded wooden cottage, building beautiful pieces of furniture in my studio or writing pithy, clever stories that obliquely captured the absurdities of life. I could learn to garden myself. Why not? People did crazier things. I switched to sunglasses, slipped on a pair of flip-flops, wrapped a towel around my waist, and headed out to ask my host, whose name, I had discovered, was Yoni, for his recommendation for the best beach in Eilat.

He was waiting for me in the kitchen, dressed now in nothing more than brightly patterned boxer shorts and a floppy hat. "Good, you're ready. You'll be my guest this afternoon, on my boat. No charge, only for special friends. Come."

"Well actually, I was hoping—"

"Come, come . . . the day is disappearing." He took my arm again and steered me toward the door. "There is nothing like late afternoon on the Red Sea. You can see Jordan to the east, Egypt to the south, the mountains of Saudi Arabia purple in the distance from the setting sun. Israelis, they travel the whole world but don't appreciate the treasures in their own backyard. Come, you need nothing but your towel—the boat is small. Pull the door shut behind you." And with that, he was already out the door, his car keys jangling in his hand.

The marina was crowded with foreign tourists piling on to large, fancy ships, a few rich Israelis lounging on yachts. Yoni's boat, on the other hand, was a tiny, scuffed-up dingy with a rusty motor hanging off the back, knocked about by its giant neighbors. The word "Tarshish" was painted in fancy script on its battered side.

"There she is, my pride and joy. A little the worse for age, but aren't we all?" He nudged me, with a knowing wink. "Come, quickly, the sun is already dropping."

I couldn't imagine a more unappealing mode of travel. I would have much preferred to lie comatose on a beach or to join the throngs of bikini-clad tourists on the large boats—a great way to meet some interesting European travelers. But I couldn't say no to Yoni; he'd shown me nothing but kindness and was already tenderly wiping seagull guano from the seats. Tomorrow for sure I'd insist on going my own way.

I gingerly climbed into the rickety little boat. As soon as I did, a mild wave of seasickness reminded me why I didn't like any kind of watercraft. But Yoni's enthusiasm, or was it impatience, left no room for second thoughts. With great fanfare he paddled us out of the marina maze, stirred the stinking, sputtery motor to life, and then launched us into the overcrowded gulf.

The sea was a frenzy of action. In addition to the large tourist boats and luxury yachts, there were sailboats and motorboats of every size and dimension, paragliders, family-filled banana boats, and water-skiers. Yoni motored us deftly through the crowds, pointing the *Tarshish* out toward the emptier space beyond.

But we were only about one hundred meters from the shore, still in the thick of the traffic, when Yoni's energy and enthusiasm suddenly evaporated. He turned off the engine, yawned extravagantly, said something mildly incoherent about the busy day he had had, then stretched himself out on the seat with his feet dangling in the water and his hat pulled low over his eyes. Without its motor, the *Tarshish* was buffeted by every swell from the larger, faster boats.

"Hey!" I called out, "I don't know anything about boats! And I'm not a very good swimmer!"

Yoni's head jerked up for a minute as he looked at me, startled and annoyed. "Don't worry. The other boats will avoid us. Be a tourist, enjoy the view." He dropped his head to the seat, and as it awkwardly lolled back, a grating snore issued from his mouth.

"Hey!" I called out again, but there was no response. I looked around for a life vest, but there were none on the boat. I began to panic, then chastised myself for my city-boy ways. Of course it was safe. He wouldn't just go to sleep in the middle of the Red Sea if it wasn't perfectly safe.

But it certainly didn't feel safe. I sat bolt upright, gripping the boat's gunwales tensely, the tiny craft rocking drunkenly from side to side whenever a motorboat whizzed by. Was it my imagination or did the people on the other boats look startled to see us? Was this normal?

A huge swell rocked the boat and filled it ankle-deep with cold water. "Hey! Yoni!" I called again, but he was out like a stone. How could he sleep through such a drenching? A huge party boat went by, blasting dance music at excruciating volume. "I'm not having fun!" I screamed, at the top of my lungs, but I couldn't hear my own words. I didn't even know how to take a normal little vacation, couldn't maneuver my way through a tourist trap in my own country. Who was this oddball I'd decided to trust so blithely? Someone who knew enough about military operations in the '80s to throw out a few names? I was no courageous, life-changing adventurer. I was an idiot in a scuffed-up boat about to die.

The next big swell did what the first had failed to do. I suddenly found myself plunging headfirst into the chilly water, then sputtered to the surface. Short of breath, I hung on desperately to the hull of the overturned boat. My prescription sunglasses and flip-flops and towel were all gone, and the watery wonderland was now a fuzzy haze. Where was Yoni? I remembered, in my panic, that the biggest danger of being capsized was getting knocked unconscious by the boat itself. And he'd been asleep—he might not have woken and reacted quickly enough. I dropped hold of the boat and opened my eyes underwater to look for a sinking human figure, but nearsighted as I was, could see nothing in the dark depths. I surfaced and gripped the boat again as speedboats and water-skiers raced by, oblivious or unconcerned about an overturned dingy. I waved my free hand frantically but couldn't see whether anyone was taking notice. Blind, chilled, and terrified, I clung to the tiny craft, my body rigid with fear.

"Hey, you!" cried a deep voice, in heavily accented English. "Not a great place for a swim."

It came from the direction of one of the large tourist boats. I could hear high-pitched exclamations and laughter in the background.

"Yes, but I don't know where my friend is . . . ," I started to answer in Hebrew.

"Ah, you're Israeli? What are you doing in Yoni's boat? Don't worry about him, he'll pop up later. You'd better get out of there—one of those motorboats will come by and slice you in two. Swim on over; you can board with us."

His words made me cling even more desperately to the *Tarshish*. I was in a strange paralysis and doubted I could swim at all with the tightness I was feeling in my belly and chest. I managed to shake my head.

"Ah, OK. You don't look so good. We'll come in closer. Hang in there." I felt the waves grow bigger as the boat moved slowly closer, and I thought I could see a blurred, colorful line of curious tourists above. What had he said about Yoni? Shouldn't I still be worried?

The boat nudged in closer. My heart beating wildly, I swam the short distance to the rope ladder and hoisted myself up awkwardly under the amused gaze of dozens of alien eyes.

"I think you'll live," said the captain, as he threw me a huge, multicolored towel.

My whole body was shaking. "We should radio someone," I managed. "Yoni."

He chuckled with amusement. "He fell asleep again. He does it every time. But I'm surprised he found you; he doesn't usually work with locals. Where are you from?"

"Petah Tikva. But I live in Jerusalem."

"Ah, the Holy City," he chuckled. "I could never live there—too many starry-eyed mystics, no? It's going to be a while before we go back to shore. Don't worry, you can enjoy the ride for free. And a drink on the house, for your terrible ordeal." He moved toward the cabin. "What'll you have?"

His nonchalance did little to calm my worry, but I accepted a large paper cup full of Scotch and removed myself to the bow of the boat, far from the bemused tourists. Huddled in the towel, I buried my head in my hands, and soon even the children lost interest in the panicky native who'd been pulled from the calm Red Sea waters. I closed my ears to the tipsy repartee as the boat slowly charted its way into a quiet cove, well sheltered from the wind. The young men began to high-dive into the water, a joyful shriek accompanying every loud, macho splash. I thought of Yoni sinking unconscious through the dark ocean depths. Was there anything I should have done? I could sense a spectacular sunset brushing the sky behind me but couldn't bring myself to turn around.

I didn't move until we finally docked in the darkened marina. Was I going to have to break the news about Yoni to anyone? I couldn't stop thinking about what would happen when I walked back into his house. But as I stepped onto the gangway, the captain nodded toward the end of the dock. There was the *Tarshish*, gently rocking—as dilapidated as ever, but none the worse for the afternoon's wear. "He'd be home by now," the captain said. "He rarely stays out this late." He gave me directions to Yoni's house and sent along his warm regards. But it wasn't until after he left that I realized I would have to find my way without money, clothes, eyeglasses, or shoes. Buzzed by the way the Scotch had hit my empty, water-shocked gut, I unsteadily walked barefoot the two kilometers back to the villa, squinting and shivering in my ill-fitting, flimsy bathing suit.

I had some trouble finding the villa in the dark, but everyone I asked knew Yoni and directed me along. Like the captain, they seemed to find it funny, or curious, that a sabra would be staying at Yoni's house. When I finally arrived, he was on the patio preparing to grill an enormous fish, whistling cheerfully as he fanned the coals.

"Welcome home! Shabbat shalom! You look cold. You must be hungry, too. You like fish, no?"

I squinted at him, shivering, furious. "What the hell happened to you?"

"Ah, I must have fallen asleep again. Narcolepsy. Something about the rocking of the water, knocks me right out." He shrugged. "Great sunset, no? Eilat can be cool at night—I hope you brought a sweatshirt. Dinner will be ready soon; you have just enough time to shower and dress. The fish I catch are always a delight, full of surprises, unlike anything you've ever tasted." He winked broadly at me. "I caught it while you were cavorting with the young European tourists."

I was still shaking, and not only from the cold. "Why didn't you warn me?"

"About what?"

"That you might fall asleep! That we might capsize! I lost my sunglasses!" I was sputtering with rage. "I'm not a very good swimmer!"

"Ah, that's a shame. Such an important skill." He turned back to the grill. "You spend some time here, you'll learn quickly."

"That's not the point . . ."

He looked at me expectantly, waiting, I suppose, for the point. But what *was* the point? That I was a helpless city boy, an inept adult, a failure in every way? I felt suddenly deflated and exposed, still standing barefoot in my skimpy suit. "Yes, you're right, I should shower and dress," I finally said.

When I returned to the patio, the table was meticulously set with a colorful array of homemade salads, artfully arranged around the sprawling fish, which looked up at us with a knowing gaze. Two bottles of expensive white wine stood at each end of the table. I was ravishingly hungry. Each bite reminded me: at this very moment, Yudit was being feted, surrounded by family and friends, and I was having dinner with a total stranger. Did she miss me? Or was she only relieved at my absence?

"So, Mr. Kobi Benami," said Yoni, after I'd polished off a plateful of fish and salads and was sipping my second glass of wine, "what brings you to Eilat?"

I was still pissed at him for abandoning me in the middle of that hectic gulf, perplexed by his disappearing act, and shaky from my ordeal. But the food and wine were beginning to mellow my anger.

"I don't know. Just thought I'd get away for a couple of days."

"Got a job?"

"Yes, but I may lose it. Boss doesn't like me very much."

"I've never had an office job—they're deadly, aren't they?" He didn't wait for a response. "I see you don't wear a wedding ring. You're not married?"

"Separated. Soon to be divorced, I guess."

"Ah, too bad. Me, I never married in the first place. What for? I live a good life here. No responsibility, no one to nag me. You may end up liking it." He grinned.

"I don't know," I said dejectedly. "It's not working for me so well."

"Children?"

"A daughter. But she's mad at me too." I took a long swig of the wine. "Didn't even call to thank me for the gift I bought for her bat mitzvah. It was expensive, too."

"Maybe you shouldn't have bothered. Children can be so unappreciative. When's the big event?"

"Actually . . . it's tonight. Happening right now."

"Oooh, that's rough," he commiserated. "Not invited, eh? No wonder you wanted to get away."

"Just for a couple of days," I said. The wine was relaxing me, and I realized how long it had been since I'd had a conversation with anyone who cared enough to ask me questions. "Actually," I went on, "I've started thinking maybe it's time for me to leave this country altogether."

He laughed aloud, a hearty, exaggerated guffaw. Seeing my look of hurt, he quickly stopped, though a half-smile remained on his face.

"More fish?" he asked. "It's a big one I caught. So big, it almost caught me. You'll have to help me finish it." He reached for my plate.

"Thank you, it's delicious. But wait . . . what was so funny? You never heard of people leaving Israel? Starting over somewhere new?"

"I'm sorry, my friend, I didn't mean to be rude." He looked genuinely sorry. "It's just that I've tried so many times."

I accepted my refilled plate. "What, to leave?"

"I keep trying, every day," he said. "Like a compulsion. Of course I want to leave! Who wants to live in a country that's constantly at war, where every stone is resonant with thousands of years of history, where the voice of God seems to echo through every desert wind? You can't live a normal life in a place like this. But you know what? It never works. Every time I try to leave, something calls me back."

"I don't understand," I said, my mouth full.

"Like this afternoon—a perfect example." He put down his fork. "There I was, on my way to the bus station to catch a bus up to Tel Aviv. That's why I didn't have my car with me. I thought I might get on a boat from Jaffa to Cyprus, or beyond. But then, there *you* were, such an obviously lost soul, needing a place to stay. What could I do? Turn my back on a comrade in his moment of need? I had to stay another night. You see what I mean?"

I swallowed. "No, I don't see what you mean. You didn't even have a suitcase with you. And you were nowhere near the bus station. And anyway, I wasn't lost at all. I'm sure I would have found another place to stay."

He waved away this logic. "Don't be silly. It was Friday afternoon and all the hotels were full. This was the only place you could have stayed." Suddenly petulant, he added, "What, you think you could have found something better? The room isn't good enough for you? Something wrong with the price? The food?"

"No, of course not—"

"Because if you think you can find something better, if this isn't good enough for you, I'll give you all your money back, right this minute."

"No, I didn't mean . . ." What was with this guy? Was narcolepsy the only condition he suffered from? I used my most soothing voice. "I'm very glad that you found me," I said.

He played with his food, sulking like a child.

"I just meant—"

"Let's forget it," he said. "You're here, and there is nowhere else you could have been this weekend. Not even at your daughter's bat mitzvah. It wasn't meant to be. Agreed?"

"Sure, yes. Agreed."

"Good. And your life, it's the same. It's the only life you could possibly have. You are where you need to be. You just don't know yet why. You'll have to come to terms with it. There's nowhere else you can go."

I didn't want to anger him again, so I nodded my head in agreement.

"There, that's settled. You'll go home tomorrow, back to all your troubles, with nothing to show for this trip but a nasty sunburn." He appraised my scalp. "You should get a hat, you know—the sun in Eilat is nothing to play around with. Agreed?"

I nodded again, all the resolve washed out of me.

In the same matter-of-fact tone he continued, "And I will try and leave Eilat again tomorrow. But something, I don't know what, will call me back. And I'll have no choice but to follow the call, and come to peace, somehow, with all the superficial, supercilious, ungrateful Eilat tourists that plague my life." He scowled at me. "You understand?"

For a shrink, I was unbelievably bad at identifying crackpots. But still: he'd given me a nice room, a thorough distraction from my troubles, and the best meal I'd had since losing Nava. By the time he had cleared the dinner plates, I'd had another glass of wine and the tension between us had eased.

Dessert was a platter bearing two halves of an odd-looking fruit that he'd plucked off a scraggly tree in the garden. It had a thick, ambrosial flavor that numbed me, sweetly. As I stood up to go to my room, my head thick with wine and fatigue, I noticed the platter's rim design: gold-plate in the shape of an outstretched arm. I was too exhausted to think anything more than: *Of course.*

17

I drove out of Eilat at dawn, having scrapped my beach plans and inane dreams of Finnish romance. The bat mitzvah was over, and I hadn't been there—what was the point of staying an extra day in that godforsaken desert? The return trip was long and uncomfortable. I was badly sunburned, and without my sunglasses, the harsh glare of the sun stung my eyes.

I filled the dull hours of the ride speculating about Yoni. He was eccentric, to be sure—perhaps some kind of illusionist, with an elaborate disappearing act for unsuspecting tourists—but he didn't seem psychotic in any classic sense of the word. Did he even know about Israela, or had the emissaries of the Outstretched Arm decided to follow me around for some other reason? If Y's operation extended all the way to Eilat, just how far did its power reach? Would he have had emissaries waiting for me in Finland? Perhaps there was no escape, and they would find me wherever I went.

The next morning, I decided to call in sick as planned. The sunburn was ugly and painful, but if I were to be fully honest with myself, the only patient I had any interest in seeing was Israela, and her appointment wasn't until Tuesday. Monday morning I did the same—Jezebel be damned. I spent both days smearing layers of aloe on my blistering burns and pacing the flat, fretting.

Monday afternoon, the empty lot behind my flat began to bustle with activity. It took me a few moments to figure it out: the children of Kiryat Yovel were assembling the makings of a giant bonfire for that evening's Lag BaOmer celebrations. They were dragging in treasures they'd been hoarding for the past week: stacks of broken cupboards, chairs and ladders, shutters and planks, scaffolding and fruit crates—all manner of discarded wooden junk. But they also created piles of dilapidated furniture and mattresses, car seats, and pillows, all interlaced with a latticework of dead branches. It brought back fond memories of my own childhood—roasting marshmallows and hot dogs in the flames, dancing around the bonfire to Zionist music, all in defiance of my parents' attempts to prohibit what they saw as a recklessly dangerous celebration of an obscure and trivial holiday.

As night fell, I watched from my window as a group of older boys gleefully lit the spark, and within minutes an enormous bonfire raged. But it appeared that the children of Kiryat Yovel were too jaded for anything as innocuous as dancing around a bonfire or even roasting marshmallows. Instead, they turned up their thumping music and played complicated, danger-defying games that involved jumping over burning logs and fencing with glowing twigs. There seemed to be no adult oversight. I dropped the shutters tightly, drawing the tattered curtains for good measure, but it did little to banish the jarring music, mocking laughter, and sickening smell of singed furniture, which lingered in the flat throughout the night and into the morning.

"I hope you enjoyed your sick days," the receptionist said on seeing me the next morning, her voice thick with sarcasm. "They seem to have left you with quite the sunburn." I ignored her and closed my office door.

The morning dragged interminably. When Israela arrived for her session—on time—it caught me off guard.

"You arrived on time today. That means that we get to have the full fifty minutes," I said, hoping that the relief, almost joy, I felt at seeing her was not embarrassingly obvious.

She swept into my chair in a sweet cloud of jasmine and shot me a look of sympathy. "There's not much point in trying to evade them, is there?"

I cocked my head quizzically.

"That's quite a sunburn—you must have met Yoni."

"Well, yes, though—"

"He probably didn't mention me," she said. "He's a bit more discreet than the others."

"I never—"

"Told anyone where you were going?" she laughed. "The Outstretched Arm has a pretty extensive network. You'd be surprised how far-flung some of their volunteers are."

"I've never even heard of them."

She shrugged. "They're effective because they're discreet. They don't want people coming to them—*they* choose the people they want to help."

"Help?" I said. "It feels more like stalking."

She adjusted her shawl. "Sometimes I like the feeling of being watched. Even being followed. Don't you?"

"No," I said bluntly. "What's to like about it?"

"Life can be so lonely," she sighed. "I don't just mean having friends or family or people to talk to. It's more than that." She reflected for a moment. "The world is so big and cold. I kind of like the idea that someone is watching over me all the time." She eyed me for a moment, then laughed and leaned forward.

"Well, I'm glad you got to meet Yoni. He's one of my favorites. He almost never threatens me."

I winced. "Israela—"

"The best part of going to Eilat is the ride through the Negev, don't you think?" She didn't pause for a response. "I spent so many months of my youth roaming through the wilderness—it's where I grew up, got married, matured into a woman. I guess that's why I can never get enough of it."

The drive home had struck me as bleak and tedious. I'd been looking for the soul-stirring hills she had described, but had only seen a barren wasteland.

"I'd like to hear more about that journey," I said, realizing that I was as eager to change the subject as she was. I knew that eventually, if the therapy were to move forward, we would have to leave the safe realm of history-taking and start talking about her present experience. But the stalkers were now making my own experience a shadow of hers, with reality and delusion ever more hopelessly entangled. And I had to admit: I knew what she meant about the strange comfort of being watched and followed by some mysterious force. It unsettled me.

"Well," Israela was saying, "the original plan was to cross into the Negev and make a beeline for Jerusalem. But in the end, it didn't work out that way."

"Why did he want to bring you to Jerusalem?" I asked. "Y doesn't sound like a city person. You could have settled in a quiet village in the Negev."

"That's true—he loves the desert, even more than I do. But back in the days of his friendship with Ibra, before the establishment of the state, Y had fallen in love with a parcel of land on the road to Hebron. At the time, it was still outside the boundaries of Jerusalem; don't forget what a very small city Jerusalem was in those days. He told Musa that it was the most beautiful piece of land he had ever seen and that once he and I were married it would be mine. Musa went on and on about how enchanting the land was—framed by the Judean hills, shady and cool, lush and fruitful. Not that he'd ever seen it, but Y had described it so vividly, and Musa had an active imagination. Y would take me to this dunam of land, build me a spectacular house, and we would live in it for the rest of our lives, in an Eden of love and harmony." She shook her head, with a wry laugh. "But when we arrived at the border, that's when I made my second big mistake."

"Second?"

"The first was building that horrible doll. I told you about it last time."

Doll. I pushed back an image of Yudit tossing my gift into a Lag BaOmer bonfire. "Yes, of course," I said.

"We were camped on a desolate section of the border, where the crossing would have been easy. There were very few soldiers there, and only a couple of small, ramshackle Israeli settlements on the other side. We were supposed to cross over just before dawn, but . . ." She put her head down, a hand to her forehead. "I'm so embarrassed about what I did . . ."

"Tell me," I said.

She lifted her head and gazed out the window. "It was early evening, and I was looking across into Israel, knowing that this would be my new homeland. I was full of excitement, but scared, too. I had never lived anywhere but Egypt, where they said terrible things about the Jewish state. I was dying of curiosity. So while Musa and Y were conferring in Y's tent, deciding when and how to cross, I snuck across myself to have a look." She massaged her neck ruefully. "It was a dangerous and foolish thing to do, and what I saw scared me half to death. The settlements were fortified, surrounded by barbed wire, and though the fields were fertile and well-tended, the people seemed rude and contentious. There were soldiers, of course, but even the civilians had rifles swung across their shoulders. Everyone I saw, from old woman to child, talked loudly and walked with a swagger. I couldn't understand anything they said, but I could see that they were different from anyone I'd ever met. Egyptians are cruel, but scrupulously polite. These people terrified me. I crossed back a little after midnight and told Musa what I'd seen. I told him I was scared we would get shot, that I would never fit into such a scrappy culture . . ." She shook her head. "Of course, the big blabbermouth had to go tell Y."

"How did he react?"

"What do you think? Y was furious. He wants me to trust him absolutely, and there I was again, doubting his promises."

You were a child, I wanted to say.

"Y decided to punish me. We packed up camp and headed back into the Sinai. He wouldn't bring me to the land until I'd been humbled and repented. I thought it would be for just a day or two, but we ended up roaming very far." The sudden change in plans tracked perfectly. How often had I heard stories of abusive spouses so afraid of their own failure that they carelessly and cruelly broke important promises?

"It probably sounds terrible to you, but in retrospect, I completely understand," she was saying. "He wanted to make sure I was ready to fearlessly enter my new homeland, preparing me to be a free citizen of an independent Jewish state." Her voice dropped, embarrassed. "I mean, it's also possible that he just got terribly lost. He never admits to making a mistake, so there's no way of knowing."

"And Musa was still with you?"

"Yes, of course. Musa was the one who was taking care of me. I don't know how long we were wandering around, but it was many months, maybe as much as a year. My feet were constantly blistered, and the monotony was driving me crazy." She looked embarrassed again. "Sometimes I got so desperate I wished I'd never left Master's house. At least there I saw other people, had some variety to my diet, had proper shelter on a stormy night." She shook her head. "But there was no talking to those two. Y was so sure of himself, always telling Musa how perfect everything would be when he'd finally allow me to go to the land he'd promised me. I learned not to complain—it just caused trouble. Once Y got so mad at me he set fire to a corner of the camp. The truth is, we were all a little testy." She paused. "I mean, it's not like I could have found my way back to Egypt on my own. And I definitely didn't want to be a servant for the rest of my life."

When she spoke again, the storytelling lilt was back in her voice. "Sometimes we'd camp at an oasis for a while, eating fresh dates and swimming in the cool water. A few times we got attacked by Bedouin bandits, and Y had to fight them off. But usually we avoided all people, all villages, all roads, passing from one desolate landscape to another. Sometimes we traveled at night, to avoid detection—never mind the daytime heat, which was oppressive. It was harrowing, bleak, and lonely, but also quite powerful. Once I got accustomed to the heat and the long hours of walking, I began to appreciate the soul-shattering beauty, the towering mountains, the infinitely varied shadings of sand and rock. To this day, I often dream of roaming through those sandy, barren hills, and it's a dreamscape that fills me with serenity and joy. Like I said, I grew from child to woman wandering that desert. When we finally came to the Jordan, I was at peace and ready to cross."

Just when I thought I'd been following. "The Jordan River? But that makes no sense. You would have had to have first crossed into the Negev and then out again into Jordan."

"I know it sounds crazy, but Y had changed his mind and decided we should cross the West Bank into Jerusalem. He thought it was a more dramatic way to enter the land."

I remembered patrolling the border on one of my reserve duty stints. "Wasn't that a dangerous plan?"

She shrugged. "People cross those borders all the time. How do you think the Bedouin smugglers manage to move their wares? Anyway, Y doesn't worry about such things. The desert is his natural habitat. He's wandered that wilderness for decades, crossed those borders numerous times. Of course there were dangers," she conceded. "I had no papers at all—wedding or no wedding—and Musa was an Egyptian national. But for Y, there's no such thing as borders, just variations of desert to navigate." She pulled her shawl tighter. "Although the final part of the journey really was harrowing. Word must have gotten out about us, and we were being pursued. We even ended up in a couple of skirmishes with Jordanian soldiers." Her eyes got soft as she again stared beyond me out the window. "But I remember so clearly when we finally got to the banks of the river. That time, I knew it was for real."

"And you weren't afraid anymore?"

"No, I was completely ready. The river was so inviting, after months of scorching heat, sand, and dust. I had no fear at all. I just wanted to run down and splash over to the other side." She gave a bitter laugh. "But that would have been too spontaneous for those guys. Musa summoned me, very sober and formal. He had to have an important talk with me before I crossed the Jordan."

"I would think they'd be just as eager to cross as you, with the Jordanian army on your heels."

"You'd think, right? But no, he had to give me this endless speech. He repeated everything—as if I'd forgotten! Starting with Aba Ibra and the promises Y had made him. Rescuing me from Egypt, our marriage vows, all the rules I had agreed to. The wandering, the promised land, what would happen to me if I didn't keep my vows . . ."

"Threats," I said.

She waved this away. "I told you, that's the way he shows his love. Oh, but that's when Musa told me the sad part," she added, "that he wouldn't be coming with us into Israel."

"Why not?"

She nodded seriously. "I've wondered a lot about that. It might have been that at this point his being an Egyptian was really too dangerous. He was convinced that he was Jewish, but what proof did he have? An Egyptian national wandering through the West Bank with no papers—he could have ended up rotting in an Israeli prison for years. Even being caught by the Jordanian army would be a lot less dangerous. But it wasn't just that . . ." She paused for a long moment, her face suddenly taut. "If Y had wanted him along," she finally said, "he would have figured it out."

"What was it then?"

She shook her head. "I don't know. They'd had some disagreement. Y was angry and didn't want him to come."

"But I thought they were so close."

"He was the closest confidant Y ever had. But you know how he is—he has such a terrible temper. If you do the littlest thing wrong . . ."

Was it possible she was getting closer to acknowledging her abusive situation? I decided not to press it. "What happened to Musa?" I asked.

"I . . . had to say goodbye to him."

"But where did he go?"

There was a long silence, as she rubbed her neck distractedly.

"Home?" I ventured.

"He didn't have a home anymore."

"Don't you think he went back to Egypt?"

She shook her head. "No. He wouldn't have."

"Maybe he returned to the shepherd's life."

She was breathing heavily now, staring out the window, her face a frozen mask.

"Have you had any contact with him since? Do you know if he's still alive?"

We sat in silence for a long time before she finally continued, her voice small and tremulous.

"You know, he was the first person who ever really cared about me. I had no parents or siblings, not that I could remember. No one thought Musa was Jewish; he could have led a comfortable life in Master's home. He had no reason to dedicate his life to freeing me. He did it because of his loyalty to Y, of course. But he also did it because . . . he was *good*."

Her eyes were brimming with tears, but without the usual histrionics. "No one ever loved me like that. No one ever cared about me in quite that way. Y loves me, of course, but he's so distant, and moody, and difficult. Musa . . . he was right there, taking care of me, devoting his life to me. He complained about me all the time, but . . . he loved me . . . like a father. And I never even understood why."

I had no idea if "Musa" was a real person, but these emotions were definitely real.

"You were lucky to have known him," I said.

"Lucky? If it weren't for him—and Y, of course—I'd be long dead. A nameless servant, worked to an early and brutal death. And we left him, in the middle of a hostile desert . . ."

"It wasn't your fault."

She nodded, her cheeks wet.

I decided to push. "I wonder, Israela, if you're angry at Y for having left Musa behind."

Her face collapsed. She began to whimper, then sob, as she pulled her legs up, curling herself into a fetal position in my leather recliner. What had she witnessed? She draped the shawl over her head as her body shook with the force of her sobs.

The crying lasted a good long while. As I stared at her trembling form, I allowed my heart to wander into the desolate inner landscape of a motherless child. Finally, she composed herself, sat up straight, used the edges of her shawl to wipe her face clean.

"He did what he had to do," she said with only a slight tremor in her voice.

I nodded.

"He sees the big picture, even when I don't. Sometimes you have to say goodbye to people, even when you don't want to. That's the way life is."

Didn't I know it. "Yes, that's true," I said. "That's the way life is."

"Sometimes they die. Sometimes you just have to leave them behind."

And sometimes they make you leave, even when you don't want to. And sometimes they shut you out, with silence, with doors. I felt my heart splitting.

"You have to keep going," she said.

"Yes, of course," I said. "You have to keep going."

She got up, her elegant, fringed shawl crumpled and twisted in her two hands, and moved toward the door.

"What happened to your wedding ring?" she asked suddenly, turning back toward me.

I looked down, stupidly, at my bare finger.

"You're still married, aren't you?" Her eyes were pleading.

"Yes, of course," I said in a cracked whisper.

"Then you understand."

She wrapped the shawl tightly around her head. "I'm sorry. I don't know why I fell apart like that."

"It's called grief," I said, and actually meant it, the bile of it rising in my throat as I closed the door behind her.

18

Israela's story was disquieting me more with each session. How could her narrative seem so crazy and so real at the same time? She was deeply grieving someone—of that I was sure—but her story couldn't possibly have transpired the way she had related it. Did she really believe that it had? I had treated scores of psychotic patients, but she just didn't fit the mold.

What made a person psychotic? I certainly knew the checklist: sensory hallucinations, distorted logic, delusional thinking, paranoid ideation. But who gets to discern what logic is distorted, which convictions are "real"? The literature was replete with studies showing how deeply illogical we all were, forever distorting the evidence of our senses to fit predetermined convictions. There were thousands of people, right here in Jerusalem, who believed every phantasmagoric story in the Bible to be literally true. Were they psychotic or sane?

I brooded on these thoughts while waiting for my 2:00 to show. By the time I realized she wasn't coming, it was too late to run out for the cup of coffee I desperately needed. The only coffee maker was in the staff lounge, a place I avoided at all costs. It could mean subjecting myself to clinical psychobabble or, even worse, the abject hostility of the receptionists. But I'd have to take the chance.

The lounge was blissfully empty. This small victory, followed by immediately locating an almost-full coffee machine and a clean mug, led me to exclaim, "Lucky day!" in a loud, goofy warble.

A motion in the corner of the room suddenly drew my attention. How could I not have noticed her? It was the receptionist who had ratted me out to Jezebel after Ami's visit. She had her back to me, her arms folded in front at the waist, her head bent forward toward the wall, her upper body swaying slowly, irregularly, back and forth, side to side. Wisps of hair from the top of her head brushed softly against the wall whenever her body rocked forward. I wondered if she was ill—or even drunk.

"Are you OK?" I finally asked.

Her body froze as she turned, puzzled. Her face was white, her eyes a little puffy as though she were hung over. She nodded slightly, then turned back to the wall.

I poured my coffee, conscious of every clumsy bump and rattle. From the corner of my eye I saw her settle into an unsteady, standing pose, her eyes shut tightly in pained concentration.

I went over to the square folding table around which the staff often gathered at lunchtime and plucked a couple of cookies from an open tin. I felt her watching me and turned around.

"I was saying *Mincha*," she explained. "The afternoon prayer."

What an idiot. "Of course. I'm sorry I interrupted you," I said, intensely aware of my fistful of cookies. I'd rarely seen a woman praying outside the synagogue. The rocking movement was less rhythmic, and much gentler, than the aggressive back-and-forth of male devotions. Still, in retrospect it was obvious. She must think I was a total imbecile.

She was still watching me.

I held up the mug. "I'll take it to my office. I don't want to bother you."

"You're not bothering me," she said kindly. "I was going to have some myself." She gestured toward the cookie tin. "I baked those last night. I hope you like them."

She went to pour herself a cup of coffee. I had wanted a few moments to myself, but it seemed rude to leave now. With adolescent awkwardness, I returned to the table and sat down. It had never occurred to me that the receptionists actually baked the cookies that always sat in the scratched-up tin. I took a sip of anemic coffee and inadvertently grimaced before realizing: she had probably brewed the coffee too.

She poured milk into her coffee, tasted it, poured sugar, tasted it, repeated the process numerous times, mixing thoughtfully until she was satisfied, then sat herself gingerly on the metal chair opposite mine.

She was about thirty and wore a sandy, overly groomed wig that signified, in the religious world, a married woman. Her face was very pale and not quite pretty, her wide-set eyes a disconcerting shade of milky gray. She was slightly plump and wore the long sleeves and skirts of the very religious. Her attire was stark and unadorned, as if she were making every effort to meld into the shabby surroundings of the room. She'd done a good job of it.

"I'm sorry," I said, "that was so stupid of me. You looked unsteady. I really thought you might be sick."

She nodded gravely. "You probably don't know a lot of religious people."

"Not really," I conceded. "Although actually, my sister has become very religious. Kind of like a fanatic, even. She lives in some militant settlement in the West Bank. But she's not like you; she's pretty crazy. Not because she's religious—that has nothing to do with it. She's very loud, autocratic. She's got opinions about everything under the sun. I don't spend much time with her. Don't see her in action, if you know what I mean."

I was literally babbling, but she nodded politely and managed an almost imperceptible smile, just enough to show her slightly crooked, very white teeth. Was she afraid of me? Offended by what I'd said? The silence felt unbearable, so I rambled on.

"My brother's become religious too now, but different, also not like you, and also not like my sister for that matter." I couldn't stop. "He's become a mystic. He chants and sways a lot. You were swaying too, but it's different. He went to India and came back with all these wild ideas about the unity of the cosmos. I don't know, maybe he understands something that I just don't get. Maybe you all do." I forced myself to take another terrible sip.

"You have an interesting family," she said politely.

"Yeah, well . . . we're a bit of an odd lot. We don't get along that well, never did." What the hell was I doing telling this saintly, cookie-baking mouse all about my dysfunctional family? Did I never know when to shut up? "But what about you? Are you from an observant family? Have you always been this way? I mean, religious?"

She barely nodded, but again gave me that crooked little smile. Was she laughing at me? Enjoying what a fool I was making of myself?

"And your whole family is religious like you?" I asked.

"I have four brothers and two sisters. I'm the oldest. We were raised to believe in God and follow His commandments. And so yes, of course, we all do."

"Why 'of course'? Not everyone stays that way." She stared at me blankly. "Not that there's anything wrong with being religious," I added quickly. "It's just hard for me to imagine what it would be like. Did you like it? Growing up like that?"

She seemed to be really considering the question. "I've never thought about it. It's just who we are."

"And you all get along with each other?"

She nodded, smiling. "I'm especially close to the older of my two sisters. She has two small children; I visit them every Shabbat. And this past Shabbat we were all together—it was my youngest brother's bar mitzvah."

"Well that's a coincidence," I observed. "This past Shabbat was my daughter's bat mitzvah too. But it was just a party, you know. Nothing religious."

She nodded, a quizzical look on her face. Panicked at the thought that she might, naturally enough, question me about the party, I quickly changed the subject.

"And you? Do you have children as well?"

She looked down at her coffee. "I haven't yet been blessed," she said in a hushed tone.

"Oh, I'm sorry. But you're young, you still may. Is that one of the things you pray for? Do you believe that God answers prayers?" The question burst out of me, leaving any pretense of small talk behind.

She looked back up at me and stared, as if she couldn't imagine how to respond.

"I'm sorry," I stammered. "You don't have to answer. I just had an upsetting session with a patient and it's made me a little . . . I didn't mean to be rude."

"It wasn't rude, just . . . surprising. Yes, I do believe that God answers prayers."

She sat there scrutinizing me, in that unnerving, inscrutable way. The silence stretched between us, but less uncomfortable now.

"You know something funny?" I finally said. "When you were swaying like that in the corner, I thought you might be drunk."

Her face broke open with a wide smile and a high-pitched laugh. She quickly covered her mouth.

"OK, I know. I guess I'm really out of it sometimes," I said.

"No, it's just . . ." She paused. "I thought I was alone in the room. I've been under . . . some stress. I've been praying very hard of late. I can see how it might have looked strange to you."

"I'm so sorry. I've been under some stress myself . . . ," I started but managed to stop myself in time.

She was still staring at me intently, but the laugh had wiped the guarded apprehension from her face. It was now a naked, gentle gaze, and it embarrassed me deeply.

"Well, I hope . . . your praying helped you," I said.

"Thank you. It does," she said shyly. Then, looking down at her cup, "I really should get back to work."

"No, wait . . . ," I said, surprising myself. Her eyes widened. "I mean, of course you should go back, but I just wanted to ask you something. It's been bothering me but . . ." I hesitated. "Maybe this isn't the time."

"What is it?" she asked.

"It's ridiculous really. But . . . you seem like a nice, normal person, you know. So I'm wondering . . . how can you possibly believe in God?" I didn't look at her face. "I mean, if there's a God, and you pray so hard to Him, then why wouldn't He already have given you everything you want? Children, or whatever? Why would you believe in a God who doesn't give good people what they need? Please don't take offense. I really just . . ."

"You're right," she whispered, standing, barely able to get the words out. "This isn't such a good time . . . for such a big conversation."

"I've just always wondered."

"Maybe you could ask your sister. Or your brother."

I nodded. "Yes, of course."

She stood there staring at me for an interminable length of time, until she finally broke the silence.

"Dr. Benami?"

"Yes?"

"Do you know my name?"

"Henya," I said. "You're Henya. The quiet, religious one."

She smiled, went to the sink to rinse out her cup, and started to the door.

"I hope God does answer your prayers," I blurted out.

She nodded politely and left the room. I dropped my head in my hands, completely humiliated. It was a mistake to ever talk to anyone in this clinic—I should have learned that by now. There was no way to get back to my office without passing her desk. I wondered when her shift would be over and if I could get away with hiding in the lounge until then.

I stared for a while at my cold, watery coffee, then got up and walked over to the corner. I took the position, arms crossed, face to the wall, willing my upper body to rock gently, drunkenly, of its own volition. I thought of Gal, swaying unevenly as he chanted. Did we all long for the soothing waves of our mothers' wombs? I closed my eyes and imagined myself as Henya, she of the deep faith and the spooky gray eyes, a sinless naïf, pleading with some invisible, benevolent being to grant her a fertile womb. I felt the soft haze of longing descend upon me, allowed myself to be intoxicated by the rhythm . . .

"Kobi! I was hoping to find you. I've been wanting to talk to you about the increasing number of Jerusalem syndrome cases we've been seeing. I've been wondering if perhaps . . ." Jezebel broke off abruptly and I turned around to her astonished face. "Are you OK?"

I unfolded my arms, and with as much calm as I could muster from my trembling legs, walked to the table and picked up my cold cup of coffee and uneaten cookies. "*Mincha*," I murmured, as I walked past her out the door.

19

After several more hours of listening to patients—depression, anxiety, loneliness, every possible variation of trauma—my nerves were shattered. I left work desperate for a drink. Fighting off the urge to head to Soreq's, I ducked into a nameless pub I had passed often on the way from the bus stop to the flat but had never even considered entering. I sat down at the bar and ordered myself a Scotch. It was still early, and the only other customers were a handful of isolated souls glaring dead-eyed into their drinks. The warm flush of the Scotch and the blissful quiet of the dimly lit room restored my balance. I returned every night that week, downing three or four drinks before walking back to my flat.

It was almost a week later, on Monday evening, as my third drink was being poured, that I noticed a young woman at the far side of the bar, already passed out. Her thick brown hair had fallen back from her face. She looked familiar, but I couldn't quite place her.

There had been a number of army raids in the past week, both in the West Bank and Gaza, and Sharon was in the United States meeting with Bush, trying, yet again, to get a peace conference off the ground. A small television was broadcasting repeated images of a dozen or so dead Palestinians lying in West Bank rubble, interspersed with urgent, talking-head commentary. There was no other sound in the room.

I decided three drinks was enough. As I walked the short distance back to my flat, the brown-haired girl's face suddenly snapped into recognition: Dina, the intern with whom I'd been sitting when Nava threw her wedding ring in my cup. I knew she'd quit her internship, and I'd been relieved not to see her again. What was she doing in Kiryat Yovel? It had never occurred to me to wonder what had become of her.

I was still pondering this when I turned onto my block and stopped short. A lanky gentleman, wearing a white shirt and a light gray summer suit, was leaning against a pillar at the entrance to my building, casually leafing through a copy of *Ha'aretz*. I felt a pulse of hope at the sight of him.

The stranger glanced up, folded the newspaper under his arm, and walked up to where I stood. He stretched out a hand to me, as if he were the host and I the invited guest. "Dr. Benami, so good to see you. I've hardly had to wait at all." He handed me a business card. "Shaya Ben Amotz, attorney at law." The card confirmed the name over a tony Tel Aviv address.

I started to ask what he was doing at my home, then remembered. "Yossi," I said.

He nodded. "So sorry to hear of your impending divorce. I know this is slightly irregular, but I'm so rarely in Jerusalem. I gave him my word I'd stop by."

So he wasn't a messenger. As I unlocked the door I said, sheepishly, "I don't know what Yossi told you. I'm not sure I'm ready for a lawyer."

He shook his head sadly. "No one ever is. There is nothing more tragic than the dissolution of love." He followed me into the flat, wrinkling his nose as he walked through the door. "What a terrible stench."

"Oh, that," I said. "There was a huge Lag BaOmer bonfire in the empty lot behind the building." I had opened all the windows on the street side of the flat, but the odor still hadn't dissipated. "It's a silly, dangerous holiday—I don't know why they even allow it."

He held back the curtains to look at the mess of ash and fire-scarred furniture that littered the weedy lot, then surveyed the shabby living room, shaking his head firmly in disapproval. "Dr. Benami," he finally declared, "this is no way for a grown man to live."

I hated the apartment too, but who was this guy? "It's just a temporary arrangement," I said defensively. I started toward the kitchen to pour myself another glass of Scotch.

"I'm always astonished by the foolhardiness of men," he was saying. "You had a devoted wife, a fine daughter, a beautiful home. Why would you throw it all away?" I stopped and turned back toward him slowly.

"Reminds me so much of a friend of mine," he continued, "only the story is reversed. It is *she* who has betrayed her husband's devoted love."

Of course. What could be more outlandish than a lawyer making house calls?

"You're one of her stalkers." I felt a rush of excitement, followed immediately by a cold, prickly sense of invasion: we were in my living room.

"I wouldn't put it quite that way. But yes, I've been sent by the one she calls Y."

"Look, Mr. Ben Amotz—"

"Call me Shaya."

"OK, Shaya. How long have you been following me?"

"I haven't been following you at all," he said with great dignity. "Do recall that you invited me, quite graciously, into your home. If you wish me to depart, I shall do so instantly."

"No, I wasn't suggesting—"

"Dr. Benami, please do not think that I am here of my own volition. This is not my usual line of work."

"What do you mean? Are you really a lawyer?"

"Of course I am," he said, slightly offended. "But this is a highly unusual case." He looked at me. "Have you ever been to the headquarters of the Outstretched Arm?"

"There are headquarters?"

"Yes, of course. Right here in Jerusalem. Underground, in the Old City. It's not easy to find, unless you've been given exact directions."

I wondered if I looked as astonished as I felt.

"Y had heard of my work and summoned me," Shaya continued. "I am not unknown in the field of human rights law, especially for my extensive pro bono work." He smiled modestly. "I was flattered, of course, but didn't fully understand the import of the invitation until I visited his extraordinary headquarters—such an ornately designed space, volunteers bustling everywhere. It's a life-changing experience." He paused briefly, his eyes glazing over. I wondered if he had entered an altered state of consciousness, but he quickly snapped back to the present. "Well, needless to say, I accepted the job immediately, and for no fee. Since then, he and I have become much more than mere business colleagues—we are now close friends and confidants." He again smiled modestly.

"So you're not really a divorce lawyer," I said. "You don't really know Yossi."

"I am and I do," he replied briskly. "I engage in some divorce work on the side. The insight I've gained into the complexities of the marital relationship is part of what commended me to Y. And your friend, Yossi, happens to be the son-in-law of a very important client. I'd be quite happy to assist you with your legal difficulties, and for a considerably reduced fee."

"OK," I said. But I knew what was coming next.

"Dr. Benami, please understand," he began. "He has been the most doting of husbands. He has provided her with everything a woman could possibly need and desire—healthy food, elegant clothes, a stately home. She is stubborn, incorrigible, unspeakably selfish, her life ruled by frivolous whims!" His diction was crisp, his posture perfect, as though he was addressing a throng of admirers instead of an exhausted, confused man who'd heard all this before. I settled onto the couch as he spoke and, to my surprise, found myself comforted by his presence, entranced by his parables and flights of poetic display, lulled by the soothing rise and fall of his voice. At some point, I dozed off.

"Look, Shaya," I said, when he appeared to be winding down. "I've already heard these same complaints from Ami, and so has Israela."

His dignified face suddenly contorted in disgust. "Ami? That zealot? He only knows half the story!"

"But I thought—"

"Do I look like a settler to you?" he sputtered indignantly. His polished tone was gone. "Those fanatics only care about their own messianic visions. They are obsessed with the historical trauma of the Jewish people. You can't possibly untangle the puzzle of this unending war if you only listen for the heartbreak of one side!"

"But—"

"Dr. Benami, have you ever spent time in an Israeli Arab village?"

"Well, yes, a few times. Before the intifada, of course." I thought about it. "There's this wonderful hummus joint in Sachnin . . ."

His voice dripped with sarcasm. "You've eaten hummus in Sachnin. Have you ever been to the West Bank?"

"Yes, of course, many times—as a soldier," I said. "And I was in a casino in Jericho once. It's really a shame that since the intifada—"

"You have eaten hummus in Sachnin, gambled in Jericho, and terrorized the civilian population of Ramallah." He dramatically shook his head a few times back and forth. "We have become utterly immune to their suffering."

"Well, I don't know—"

His polished courtroom voice was back. "Dr. Benami. Why are there Palestinians still living, more than fifty years after the war, in squalid refugee camps? Three generations without citizenship, without proper homes."

"I don't think—"

"But forget the squalor of the West Bank. Have you seen the overcrowded conditions right here in East Jerusalem? Do you know how underfunded their schools and clinics are? Why must we destroy their houses? Uproot their olive groves? Is this how we treat the stranger in our midst? How could they not be consumed with rage?"

"Well, of course, but—"

"Have you studied the history, Dr. Benami? How we ruthlessly emptied out and then destroyed the Arab villages that stood in the way of our possessing the land?"

"But there were good security reasons—"

"We wanted the land, and so we drove them out!"

"But—"

"You will blame it all on the settlers and the occupation. But the atrocities didn't begin in '67. We have never confronted the original sins of '48!"

"Wait a minute—"

"You have fully digested the propaganda they fed you in school. How they left their homes of their own volition. How the Arab armies instructed them to leave. Does this make any sense to you? But you had to obediently swallow every word. How else could you serve faithfully in the army, be a good puppet of this militarized regime?"

"Now that's a little unfair—"

"Is it fair what we did to the indigenous inhabitants of this land? Five hundred villages destroyed and ethnically cleansed. Thirty-five years of heartless occupation. The massacres of which we refuse to speak!"

"Well, the Arabs weren't exactly—"

"You will make excuses for our actions? We took their homes and gave them to Jewish immigrants! You yourself lived in an elegant Arab home— did it never even scratch at your conscience? Did you never wonder about its previous inhabitants? We pretended it was an empty land, then stole their houses and their fields! You expected them to have welcomed us with open arms?"

"Look, Shaya—"

"You don't want to hear of it. Of course not! We still terrorize their children in unnecessary midnight raids. Arrest twelve-year-olds for throwing stones. Torture and even assassinate people who have received no due process. I have devoted my entire legal career to righting these wrongs! No one in this country will open their eyes and ears to the suffering of their so-called enemy!"

I was thoroughly confused. I had been thinking Y was involved with the settler movement but here was one of his emissaries preaching to me like a lefty peacenik.

"But Ami—"

"Forget about that fanatic shepherd!"

"And Hesh—"

"A sex-crazed maniac! A heartless cat-killer!"

"What about Yoni?"

"What *about* Yoni?"

"How is it possible that all of you work for the same organization?"

"Right, left. Left, right. You will fit everything into these stifling little pigeonholes. The Outstretched Arm transcends left and right!"

Seeing my abject confusion, he softened his voice again. "It's true that we disagree about many things. But we all bear the same message. The important thing is to convey to Israela the urgency of the situation."

"But—"

"Yes, I know," he said, a resigned tone entering his voice. "She's heard it over and over, and yet she doesn't change. You're a psychologist, Dr. Benami, an expert in the intricate pathways of the human mind. How do you account for such obstinacy? A life lived thus sows the seeds of its own destruction!"

I stared at him mutely. Who the hell was he, and what did he want from me?

He coughed demurely. "Dr. Benami, I apologize for losing my equanimity. I wonder if you would be so kind as to pour me a glass of water."

"It's getting late. Perhaps—"

"Yes, you've had a long day, and so have I. But I'm not quite finished—if you would grace me with just a few more minutes of your time."

I stood up. Anything to get him out of my living room.

"You're sure you don't want a Scotch?" I asked. "I sure as hell could use one."

His eyes flared in disapproval. "Don't you think you've had enough this evening? How can you help her when you engage in the same vices as she?" Israela, drinking? I was about to ask him about this and then realized what floodgates it would open.

"Water," I said. "I'll get you a glass of water."

I went into the kitchen and pulled two glasses off the shelf. I filled one with water, intending to use the other for my Scotch. What right did this self-righteous pedant have to tell me what to drink in my own home?

But I hesitated before pulling the stopper from the bottle. He was right, in a way. How long had it been since I'd gone a single night without a drink or two or more? Even before Nava kicked me out? I usually thought of my choices as affecting me alone, but of course they had consequences for others. Dina's slumped form flashed into my mind. And Nava's enraged face as she flung her ring into my coffee cup.

I put the second glass away and returned to the living room, ashamed and irritated, intending to suggest that Shaya wrap up his diatribe right away. But as I handed him the water, I had the eerie sensation that this was not the same man who had been talking for the previous hour. There was an uncanny resemblance, to be sure, but he now seemed slightly taller, a bit younger, his features more angular, his nose more pronounced.

He took a sip of water. "Thank you, Dr. Benami. Talking so long can be hard on my throat." Even the voice was slightly different.

"Look, Shaya, it really is getting late—"

"DO NOT . . . cut me off." He was staring at me with a quiet fury in his eyes—eyes that were bluer than the pale gray eyes I remembered from earlier in the evening. Maybe I should have poured myself that Scotch after all. Was he threatening me? Mutely, I settled back into the couch and stared as he emptied his glass, put it down on the coffee table, emphatically cleared his throat, and started in again.

Shaya's language was poetic and full of visions of peace, but I now felt a palpable sense of menace slithering just beneath the surface. Perhaps I was mistaken to see these stalkers as harmless. Yoni had dumped me in the sea with a chilling disregard for my physical safety, never mind Hesh's homicidal driving. Was the "outstretched arm" one of assistance or aggression? I listened carefully to his words: threat and hope seamlessly intertwined.

And then I suddenly knew, with terrifying clarity—impossible as it seemed—that Y was somewhere in the flat.

My skin prickled as Shaya talked on. Did he know? Perhaps that was why he couldn't interrupt mid-oratory. Was his new boss watching, listening, judging the performance of his latest messenger? I felt my chest tighten, fought back the urge to open the closets, check the bathroom. It took everything I had not to stand up and throw back the curtains. I stared at Shaya, barely breathing, listening for the sound of Y's presence beneath the words, trying to calm my racing pulse.

By the time he had finished and discreetly left my apartment—minutes or hours later, I couldn't tell—my panic had been replaced by a numb exhaustion. I picked up the business card he had left on the table. It was identical to the one he'd shown me at the door, except this one was emblazoned with an outstretched arm. I could no longer summon any irritation at the audacity of this stranger—strangers?—intruding into my home.

I remained sunken into the couch for what was left of the night. Delia's curses, Ashra's laugh, Gal's chants, Shaya's poetic oratory, and Y's menacing silence echoed and harmonized in my overwhelmed brain. In my mind's eye I wandered into the endless stretches of parched desert that radiated out from the desolate road to Eilat. I felt the kind puzzlement of Henya's gray-eyed gaze upon me and allowed my head and upper body to rock gently of their own accord as I had seen her do. Shamed and confused by the images that made up the wasted self-absorption of my life, I sat on that couch until the light of dawn began to sift its way through the drapes, where I could now see that no man lay hidden.

20

"You look exhausted, Dr. Benami," she said the moment she'd settled into my chair. "Shaya must have kept you up all night with one of his interminable speeches."

"Israela, you have to explain this to me. How do you always know when they've come to see me?"

"That guy can talk, can't he? He's relentless."

"You're avoiding my question," I said, with a little too much annoyance.

"When Shaya comes around, you can forget about getting anything else done. Though his words can be beautiful. He can really turn a phrase, don't you think?"

"Yes, he spoke very eloquently, but—"

"Did they do that thing where they switch Shayas mid-oratory?" she laughed. "Really freaks people out the first time."

"So there really were two of them?"

"Some folks claim there are three." She pushed a strand of hair off her forehead. "Frankly, I'm a little bored with it myself."

I asked the question that had been gnawing at me all morning: "Was Y there as well?"

She sat up, suddenly alert. "Where?"

"In my flat."

Her voice was tense but calm. "What makes you think he was there?"

"Well, I didn't see him or hear him. But I had this strange . . . feeling."

"You did?" she whispered.

"But I was probably just imagining it."

"Yes . . . I'm sure you were just imagining it." She was staring at me intently.

"Do you think he *might* have been there?" I asked. My own voice was now down to a whisper as well.

She fidgeted with the fringes of her shawl and shook her head. "No, of course not . . . But even if he was . . ."

"What? Tell me."

She was quiet for a long time, visibly struggling how to respond.

I knew I should let her find the words, but I was too exhausted, and had too many questions, to remain patient any longer. "Israela, I don't understand . . . any of this. Does Y really exist? And if he does, why does he keep sending all these crazy messengers? Why doesn't he just come and talk to me himself?"

"Of course he exists!" she said indignantly. "Like I told you, he's very busy."

"Busy with what? I know he's secretive, but what harm would it do to come and talk to me directly?"

"He just doesn't operate that way."

"Why not?" I said, too loudly. When she didn't answer, I took a deep breath and tried another tack. "Shaya claims that the Outstretched Arm has headquarters right here in Jerusalem, in the Old City. Is that true?"

"Oh, that," she shrugged. "It's not so important. You know how people are—they love to be part of big organizations, with fancy headquarters and hierarchies, logos and mission statements, gala dinners." She waved vaguely. "The truth is, it's become a very complicated organization. I'm not even sure Y himself knows what all his emissaries are off doing."

Another answer that was not an answer. I heard my voice rising again. "How can he not know? Doesn't he care what they're doing in his name?"

"They're trying to make the world a better place!" she cried, her voice rising too. "Isn't that all that matters? The world is full of problems that no one wants to take care of. At least Y and his friends are trying!" She stared at me so angrily I suddenly worried that she might walk out the door and I'd never see her again.

"I'm sorry I made you so angry," I said, too depleted from my sleepless night to challenge her. "Why don't we pick up where we left off last time? You had been telling me how you had to leave Musa behind in the wilderness." The last thing I wanted was to hear more of her long, confabulated story, but it was the one sure way to calm her down.

I was right. "I guess I should tell you how I finally got to Jerusalem," she said sullenly. But as soon as she returned to the story, her voice fell into its lilting tone. "First we had to cross the Jordan without being noticed . . ."

I was only half listening. Today's tale centered on someone named Shua, a settler from the West Bank, who had helped sneak her across the Jordan and into Israel. Her description of Shua reminded me of a distant cousin of my father's who had been an officer in the Hagana during the War of Independence—one of those people whose whole life was defined by his wartime experience and could speak of nothing else. "Shua spoke passable

Arabic, which impressed me," Israela was saying. "Not many of the settlers did, especially back then. In the evenings, he'd grill me on Hebrew verbs, over the campfire. And then, when the study session was over, he'd tell me these amazing war stories from '48." She looked up at me expectantly. *I don't want to hear Shua's stories*, I thought, *I want you to tell me if Y is real*. But she took my silence as encouragement.

She told me about the time Shua's platoon had been protecting a small moshav that was being attacked by enemy tanks, though they had no anti-tank weaponry—just rifles and one wildly inaccurate Davidka mortar. In desperation, sure that they would be slaughtered, the civilians and soldiers had started making a huge racket—shooting the Davidka, exploding glass bottles, hollering at the top of their lungs, firing wildly, even blowing on homemade trumpets—to make it seem like there were hundreds more of them than there were. To their astonishment, the tanks turned around and fled. "Shua called it a 'modern-day miracle,'" she said. "He would brag to me about what experts at subterfuge the Hagana was—moving stealthily under cover of darkness to confuse enemy troops, sending out misinformation to deceive their intelligence services, playing the different Arab forces against each other—as if he were personally responsible for every Hagana ruse."

"Sabras all grow up on those stories," I said, hearing the impatience in my voice. I was about to change the subject, but she wasn't done.

"Yes, I know, but they were new to me," she said, and launched into more Shua stories, but of the kind we *didn't* grow up on: purging villages, terrorizing the locals so they'd flee. "I hated listening to it," she admitted, "but Shua thought I should know the truth of how the land had been con-quered. He'd go on these rants about how modern-day Israelis have gone soft—how they wouldn't be capable of the sacrifices that made this country possible." She was winding the fringes of her shawl tightly around her fin-gers. "He thought that if we'd only expelled all the Palestinians back in '48, we wouldn't have all the problems we have today. He's very cynical about the whole thing—thinks we left them here for the cheap labor. I don't think that's true, do you?" She didn't wait for an answer. "But at the time I didn't know what to think. And it's true that he was there, so maybe he understood more than I did. All I knew was my own desperation to have a home, after all the abuse I'd suffered in Egypt." She glanced at me to gauge my response.

I again opened my mouth to try and change the subject, but she was on a roll. "Shua thought that every Arab we met meant us harm," she con-tinued. "He'd ambush perfect strangers, convinced that they were coming to attack us. Sometimes he'd hide me in an olive grove, and I'd hear the shooting in the distance. Then he'd come back all puffed up with pride and tell me the road was safe for passage. To tell you the truth, I saw some things

I'd rather not talk about," she said, looking away. "But then he'd tell me that I had to trust him, that this was a new kind of warfare—that it's impossible for a civilian to tell the difference between an innocent villager and a potential terrorist. I'm sure that's true." She met my gaze evenly. "Y was with him in all those skirmishes, so I know that everything they did must have been to protect me."

Y. There was no point even asking. He would have been off ahead plotting the route, finding ways to avoid the military checkpoints, devising strategies for outwitting all their supposed assailants.

Israela kept on talking, describing her joy at leaving the desert behind her, gorging on the abundance of fruits and vegetables, the fresh milk and honey; her anticipation at finally having her own home in this lush, fertile land, in a state run entirely by Jews, where no one would ever enslave her again. She shook her head, suddenly somber. "But then we got to Jerusalem, and Y's plot of land was nothing like I'd imagined. I guess it wasn't that surprising, given how many years it had been since he had seen it and the way the city had since engulfed the whole area. It was no longer on the actual road to Hebron—it was in the middle of a crowded urban neighborhood in West Jerusalem, and there was a house already standing there. A large Arab family was living in the house, which they'd built on the property. It wasn't easy to get them out." Her voice went down to a guilty whisper. "By the time it was over, the house was a wreck."

The story was completely implausible. There were no Arab families still living in West Jerusalem at that time; they had all fled or been expelled in '48, their homes distributed to Jewish immigrant families. But that made her version of events no less chilling.

"Who owned the land, Israela?"

"Y, of course."

"Who gave it to him? The Jewish National Fund? Did he have a deed?"

"Dr. Benami, you forget, I was only a teenager. What did I know about deeds? He said it was his land, so it must have been."

"If it was his land and people were squatting, why didn't he just go to the police?"

"He doesn't work that way. Look, I know it must sound awful to you, but he did it for me! He knew how desperately I needed a home!"

"So what happened to the family who was living there?"

"I don't know. Y said they were Arabs and not worth worrying about. That they had no right being in West Jerusalem to begin with."

A common thought, to be sure, but rarely had I heard it expressed so bluntly. It didn't sound like a notion that Shaya would condone. Did he even know the political views of his so-called boss?

"So once they were out, you just moved in?" I asked.

"Actually we had to go through this whole ceremony again. This time it was Shua repeating it all—the promise to Aba Ibra to marry me, how he'd rescued me from Egypt, how I owed him my very life and my freedom—the whole bit. Including the part about how jealous Y is, how I'd be in trouble if I didn't obey him. How if I did obey his rules and be loyal he'd love me and take care of me forever. How I should never have anything to do with my neighbors. You see, I knew exactly what I was getting into, from the start. Only when I'd agreed yet again to all the terms would he let me move in."

"So was it like he said? Did he finally move in with you?"

"Not exactly . . ."

She rubbed her neck in silence. "Not that he ever left me completely alone. His friends were always around, making sure I was OK. He even appointed caretakers to watch over me . . ." Her voice trailed off.

I held my thoughts and waited.

She gazed out the window. "I thought once we moved into the house he'd be around more, that we'd finally have a normal life," she said slowly. "But actually, he was around even less than before."

She looked back at me, her expression confused and vulnerable. "It's this strange paradox," she said softly. "On the one hand, he's most at home in the desert. He loves the nomadic life. And yet, he has this almost irrational love for this one piece of land." She looked at me with profound sadness, but there was something else I couldn't read in her expression. Hurt? Resignation? Pride? "He insists that I live on this one piece of land," she finally said, "and yet, he can't settle down himself."

21

In the days that followed, the stalking picked up pace. A long-haired hippie with a guitar slung across his back accosted me in line at the supermarket; a homeless man in desperate need of a bath ruined a half-hearted pickup in Independence Park. They were an annoying but passionate crew, united by their insistent complaints about Israela, their fanatical devotion to Y, and their uncanny ability to know where I was at any time of day or night.

Yoni and Shaya had made one thing perfectly clear: whatever the stalkers might claim, they weren't only talking about Israela—they were deliberately, consciously, talking about me. It was I, after all, who was leading a selfish, decadent life, who had been whoring about, not caring how my behavior affected the ones who loved me. I was left with no wife, no friends, a daughter who despised me, and a job that had become nothing but a burden. They were warning me that if I didn't change my ways, only more suffering would await me. They were telling me that change was possible, even necessary. But what was I supposed to actually do?

My obsession was now full-blown: searching every face for the next stalker; scanning every billboard and advertisement for the logo of the Outstretched Arm; perusing newspaper crime reports for long, unpronounceable names that started with the letter Y. Since Shaya's visit, my dingy little flat had continued to feel intermittently haunted, and I couldn't quite shake the notion that Y was there, watching me.

If ever I needed to talk about a case with a supervisor, this was the one. Part of me wanted to hear Jezebel's ideas about widespread Jerusalem syndrome—could a whole organization suffer from it?—but there was no way I was going to reveal to my hawk-eyed nemesis the irrational obsession and sloppy intake procedures that had characterized my interactions with Israela. I would give her no excuse to transfer this case to another clinician.

Then, on Friday morning, an admiring profile of Yossi came out in the weekend supplement of *Yediot*, describing his growing popularity and extolling his ability to seamlessly fuse psychological methods of dream interpretation with mystical Jewish concepts and practices. There was a large photograph of his shop, part of a more extensive spread, in honor of Jerusalem Day, encouraging Israelis to visit interesting sites in the city. I hadn't seen or spoken to Yossi in a while and was still irritated at his dubious role in my brother's life. But still, you couldn't fool all the spiritual seekers all the time. He was a charlatan, to be sure, but he was also one of the smartest people I knew. Maybe he could give me some perspective on the bizarre web in which I was now entangled.

I hopped a cab to Jaffa Gate. Passing through a throng of singing, flag-waving Jerusalem Day celebrants—in the same square where that morose Armenian procession had gathered, just a couple of weeks before—I retraced my steps to the Jewish Quarter, alert all the while for any sign of an underground doorway that might lead to hidden, subterranean headquarters. As I approached Yossi's shop, I suddenly wondered if Gal might be in there, rocking and chanting. I almost turned back—asking Yossi for guidance with my brother surreptitiously listening in was more than I could handle—before remembering that he was safely ensconced with my parents for the weekend.

Glancing through the window of the third temple storefront, I saw a handful of people listening to a discourse on the function of the altar, the symbolism of the eternal flame, and the sacred qualities of priestly raiment. But instead of the fat, gesticulating redhead who had been there the last time, a scrawny, bearded man was staring intently at the visitors as he spoke. He was talking in a low mumble, his small audience hunched toward him in puzzled concentration. If he had not been facing directly my way, I would never have believed it: my brother-in-law, Tuvya.

I had never heard Tuvya say more than a couple of words at a time. He had a job as a teacher's aide in an ultra-Orthodox elementary school and was, as far as I could tell, despised and abused by all but the youngest students. He had the habit of putting his hand on his large knitted *kipa* every few minutes—as if to check that it was properly calibrated to his head—and he was doing so now, repeatedly, as he instructed his small audience on the intricacies of temple sacrifice. So engrossed was he in his exposition that he didn't even notice me staring in from the street. What the hell was he doing in Jerusalem? And how had such an unassuming schlemiel gotten mixed up with this addle-headed messianic mission? I sat on the smooth stone doorstep of the store across the street, absorbing this new bit of information and trying to decide what to do about it. Nothing, I finally concluded before continuing on to Yossi's shop.

The store was mobbed; I wasn't the only one who had read that morning's newspaper article. I elbowed my way to the counter, where Yossi was fervently blessing a tall, willowy woman, his arms straining up to clutch her thick red hair, their eyes locked in deep spiritual communion. Only after she had tearfully hugged him goodbye did he seem to notice the crush of people around him. His smile toward me was reserved, his tone firmly entrenched in holy man cadence.

"Kobi, what a surprise. You had more dreams, my friend? I'm afraid you'll have to wait your turn."

I leaned over to whisper in his ear. "Is the store ever less crowded? I was hoping we could have a word in private."

He responded loudly, to the crowd. "Thank God, I am lifting many sacred souls these days. And Friday is always the most auspicious of days."

"It's kind of important," I whispered.

This time he addressed me directly. "Come at 3:00. That's when I generally close on Erev Shabbos, but today I can stay a few minutes late. Special treatment, for special friends—for old time's sake." Again, that annoying, barely discernible wink.

That gave me a couple of hours to roam the Old City. I wandered down to the platform overlooking the Western Wall, from where I could see the plaza filled with Jerusalem Day celebrants, surrounded by a swarm of anxious soldiers. I subjected myself to the tight security check, edging my way down to the plaza and then to the Wall itself, a cardboard *kipa* perched on my head like an untethered tent.

Branded into the memory of my fingertips was the first time I had touched those cold, grainy stones, just a few short weeks after the Six Day War. I had been a young child, my father by my side, and the power of cosmic mystery and deep historical resonance had shivered my fingers to the touch. But today there was nothing but a clammy chill and a visceral revulsion for the fervently swaying, black-coated *haredim* who surrounded me.

There was nothing even remotely sacred about this wall; it was no more than a retaining wall built by that psychotic mass-murderer Herod. I watched the pigeons strutting on the edges of the stones above my head, oblivious to the sanctity of their world-famous roost. Reproaching myself for my boundless cynicism, I ran my fingers along the ridges and holes and cracks of the cold-stone facade, wondering what heartfelt yearnings might be inked into the tiny, multicolored notes that filled every crevice, trying to recapture the aura I had felt as a child.

Suddenly, I heard a commotion coming from the plaza behind me. I looked back and noticed a bevy of foreign journalists, with their cameras and their notebooks, hovering along the edges of the crowd, all but asking for a photogenic riot. Disturbances on the Temple Mount, accompanied by a hail of stones aimed at those praying at the Wall, almost always took place on Friday afternoons. The fact that today was Jerusalem Day, honoring the reunification of the city in the '67 war, made the probability of a Friday disturbance almost inevitable. I retreated quickly from the Wall, tossing the stiff, cardboard *kipa* back in the box. The noise I had heard was no more than the stirring of a restless, overstimulated crowd. But why would people insist on praying and celebrating in such a perilous spot, on such a sensitive day? Didn't any of them possess the elemental instinct to avoid danger?

I made my way into the Arab *shuq* but lasted there no longer, further discomfited by the hostile eyes of the backgammon-playing, tea-drinking shopkeepers and their half-hearted attempts to lure me into their now chronically empty shops. The impact of the upbeat *Yediot* article clearly didn't extend to the Muslim Quarter. Most of the shops were shuttered, and white surveillance cameras jutted out of every overhead pipe. There were far more soldiers than tourists, and it occurred to me that this almost-empty, main drag of the *shuq*, leading from Jaffa Gate down to the Wall, was probably one of the safest places in Jerusalem—though that made it no more inviting. A helicopter whirred overhead, and I thought I could make out the sound of tear gas canisters in the distance. Perhaps the riots had begun.

I traced my way back to the Jewish Quarter, wondering, as I did, if the headquarters of the Outstretched Arm—if such a space really existed—might lie beneath the Muslim or Christian Quarter. It would be far easier to hide the entranceway in that thicket of storefronts and alleys—Ashra had certainly hidden her shop well enough—and though it would be a precarious locale for a Jewish charity, Y didn't seem to care about such mundane perils. Back in the open expanse of the Jewish Quarter, I found a small café with a couple of outdoor plastic tables and no customers. I bought an overpriced Coke from a pale, teenaged girl with the ankle-length skirt and grim demeanor of the earnestly religious and stared at the crisp cut of the newly hewn wall-stones until a few minutes before 3:00.

When I arrived back at Yossi's shop the door was locked and the window shutters closed, but I could see through the door's tiny arched window that he was still inside. He shifted and I suddenly saw a disheveled blond head in his lap. The window was beveled, providing only a contorted view, but I could see him gently stroking the woman's long hair. It was hard to believe that he could get away with his holy-man act while carrying on, in easy view of the street, with a young foreign woman. I was about to knock, loudly, when I looked again. She was wearing a clingy lavender top. I squinted through the disorienting prism in astonishment. Those long limbs. That glittery scarf. I'd spent so many nights remembering and imagining her, I truly wondered for a moment if I was actually awake.

I pounded on the door, and Delia looked up, black makeup streaked across her face. Had she been crying? My view of Yossi's face was blocked, but they ignored my knocking, talking earnestly. I pounded on the door again, and Delia pulled herself up, rubbing her belly with her tattooed arm as she walked unsteadily to the door and pulled it open.

"You following me, Jewboy?" Her voice was flat.

"No, of course not. What are you doing here?"

"Same thing as you—looking for help. But I'm leaving; he's all yours." As Yossi rose, Delia went back to give him a long, lingering hug, her head resting on his shoulder. He murmured something in her ear. She nodded and draped a huge black cape over her flimsy clothes, brushing past me out the door.

"Wait, Delia." I grabbed at her shoulder, but she shook me off, breaking into a trot as she left the shop. I watched in amazement as she rounded the corner out of sight, her spiked heels wobbling precariously on the uneven stones.

"Yossi, how—"

"Sorry I wasn't ready for you; I was counting on your being late. You were never on time when you worked at the clinic. Is this a new development?" He smirked at me.

"How do you know Delia?" The question came out urgent and desperate.

Yossi smiled patronizingly. "Now, Kobi, you know all about confidentiality."

I snorted. "There are codes of confidentiality for holy men? You got some ethics committee monitoring your holy-man conduct?"

He responded seriously. "You're much too cynical, Kobi—have I ever told you that? The rules are the same. You happened to have walked in on something private. Just forget you even saw it." This from the man who'd once regaled me with every salacious detail of his patient liaisons.

"Stop with the bullshit, Yossi. I know that girl."

He laughed. "Lots of people know Delia. She's a spirited gal, eh?" The inscrutable wink was in his voice this time. I wanted to punch him.

"What's going on between you two?" She had looked so upset and had been rubbing her belly in that weird way. "Is she in trouble?" I asked. And then, dawning on me, "Is she pregnant?"

"Don't worry," he said. "If she is, it's not yours. That much I can assure you." He laughed again, sounding more like his old self. It didn't make me feel any better.

"Don't be an idiot, of course it's not mine. What do you mean you can assure me? Is it yours?" He had turned away, straightening up a shelf full of crystals. "Yossi, I'm worried about her," I said. "There are people looking for her. She could be deported."

"Not your problem," he said with maddening calm. "You've got a case-load full of kooky broads to puzzle over. Let me worry about this one."

"Why did she come to you? How do you know her? Do you know how she got to this country? Is there some meaning to that weird tattoo on her arm? Is she safe?"

He walked over to me. "The question is why *you* came to see me. You said it was urgent, that you needed to see me in private, so here I am." A note of impatience crept into his voice. "You want to waste my time trying to extract information about another client?"

"You're calling them clients? You've suddenly become so ethical? Talk about new developments."

He sighed. "Look, Kobi, I'm an official, *Yediot*-certified holy man now. Certain things come with the territory. I can't talk about other people's problems. They trust me, you know?" He sounded like the old Yossi again. "So what did you want to talk to me about? You finally trying to get your life together?"

Hearing an old friend ask about my life, I suddenly felt overwhelmed. "I don't know, Yossi, I'm so shaken by seeing Delia here. Never mind having just barely missed a riot at the Wall. And you know what else? When I first got here, I saw my schlimazel of a brother-in-law fundraising to build the third temple. How crazy is that? What the hell is going on around here?"

"The threads always come together, Kobi. You're finally starting to notice," he intoned, back in holy-man voice.

"What threads? What the hell are you talking about?"

He motioned me to sit. "Why'd you come to see me, Kobi? What was so goddamned urgent?"

"I don't know, it was a crazy idea. I was going to talk to you about this new patient I got, but now I'm too upset about Delia."

"They're giving *you* new patients? Man, things are out of control over there."

"They're doing everything possible to make my life hell. But that's not the point. The thing is, I've got this new patient, I've only seen her a few times, but I'm thinking about her constantly."

"A looker?"

"Well, yeah, sort of, but that's not it. Her story is so bizarre. It's the first time I've been really interested in a patient in a long time."

He nodded. "Married?"

"Yeah. You probably know her husband. That lawyer you sent me? Shaya? He works for him."

"For who?" he seemed genuinely perplexed, then shrugged. "I don't know any of Shaya's other clients. He's just a lawyer I met through my father-in-law. High-priced Tel Aviv attorney, very busy. Not that you should thank me or anything."

"He wasn't interested in my business. He just came because her husband sent him."

"Whose husband?"

"The patient I was telling you about. You really don't know them?"

"What the hell are you talking about?" I realized I was going to have to explain it out loud and didn't know where to begin.

"Yossi, it's the weirdest marriage you've ever heard of. I'm not even sure the husband exists. He's never around, sounds like some kind of underworld figure. Except he runs a big corporation, with hidden headquarters, right here, underground, in the Old City. Unless everyone's made that part up. She says it's a charitable organization, but I'm not so sure. She hasn't actually seen him in over a year. But man, he's powerful, must have some crazy charisma. He's got his friends following her around, total fanatics, threatening her, and now they're following me around. Shaya's one of them; he had the logo on his business card. Or at least the second Shaya did. The whole story is full of weird biblical references, but parts of it are definitely true . . ." I couldn't continue, hearing how inane the whole story sounded.

Yossi was nodding. "Have you been to Soreq's?" he asked.

Of course he knew Soreq's. "Well, yeah, I stopped in once. It was kind of an accident. And then I went back, for a second look."

He laughed. "An accident? That's a good one."

"What do you mean? How do you know about Soreq's? Do you hang out there? It doesn't seem like the kind of place for a holy man."

"You don't understand any of it." He was suddenly serious.

"No, I don't. I . . . I was hoping you'd help me."

He started rocking gently. "You have always lived on the surface, Kobi," he began, his voice rhythmic and soothing. "That's where most people spend their entire lives. But now, suddenly, you are flirting with the edges of the underworld. But know, my friend, that there are both underworlds and overworlds, and they aren't all that different." Despite myself, I was hanging on every word. "We are surrounded, enveloped, enmeshed in worlds upon worlds that we cannot see. Worlds in which past and future, good and evil, truth and falsehood, fold in on themselves—in which every step we take, every word we utter, every thought that enters our minds reverberates through an infinite cosmos. Worlds where there are no accidents, no coincidences, no random events. A world infused so thickly with meaning, that it drives some people mad and others to soar like eagles. You are standing at the edge of the abyss." He was facing me now, holding my gaze steadily. "But will you jump? Do you dare to fly? Do you have the courage to enter dimensions of existence you have never even dreamed of?"

Suddenly it was too much for me. This was *Yossi*. "What the hell are you talking about?" I said.

He snapped out of his reverie. "No, I didn't think so."

"Yossi, I feel like I'm losing my mind."

He got up and went back to tidying his crystals. "Have you gotten laid since Nava threw you out? That's probably all you need. Do you a lot more good than obsessing over my client and yours."

"Stop it, Yossi. What am I supposed to do now?"

He shrugged and started fussing with his keys, shooing me toward the door as he spoke. "Ignore it, Kobi. That woman sounds like just another fucked-up patient, but with a dangerous husband, so I'd keep it in my pants. The novelty will wear off soon enough and she'll become as boring as all the others. And if her husband's friends keep following you around, you should call the police—stalking's illegal, you know. And stay away from Soreq's; only trouble there. Remember, you're trying to hold onto your job. And Delia? Just another lost-soul foreigner with a basketful of problems. Nothing there, Kobi—nothing to get bent out of shape about." He put his hand on my shoulder as he steered me out the door. "You really are fucked up about women, you know that?" he added thoughtfully. "I gotta run, pal; it'll be Shabbos soon. A holy man's gotta keep up appearances."

"Wait, Yossi. Do you know where Delia lives?"

"Don't worry about Delia, she knows how to take care of herself." He locked the door behind us. "I've got errands to run, pal. Stay in touch." And with that, he shot off at a brisk pace in the direction of the Arab *shuq*.

The streets were choked with Friday afternoon traffic, and it took the cab a full hour to get me back to Kiryat Yovel. I sat in the back to avoid the driver and have time to think. I kept trying to tell myself it was none of my business, but Delia was obviously in trouble. Maybe she needed money or a doctor. I did work for a hospital, after all—perhaps I could be useful. When I got back to my flat, I washed the day's grime off my face, jumped in my car, and headed back into the mess of traffic. Just as the siren heralding the onset of the Sabbath was blaring through the dusky streets, I arrived at Soreq's.

The room had been transformed. It was as hot as the last time I'd been there, but the liquor-soaked listlessness was now replaced by a sweaty, electric energy. Amid flashing strobe lights I could make out a makeshift stage that had been set up against one wall of the room. A thin man with swarthy skin and silvery blond curls was playing a lute-like instrument and singing with a slightly foreign accent. He was wearing a skintight, sequined bodysuit that showed every ripple in his lithe, muscular form as he shimmied along to the lewd lyrics of his song. The audience loved it. Many were dancing, but others were tossing things at the performer—the olives and limes from their drinks, bras, condoms—jeering and laughing all the while.

A different bartender—a huge man, as tall as he was wide, with wild gray hair and flaring nostrils—was leaning heavily on the bar, breathing noisily, and glowering with unabashed loathing at the singer. I waited for him to see me, but he never turned his head.

"Excuse me," I said loudly.

He glared in my direction for an instant. "Go away," he grumbled and turned back to his malevolent staring. The singer caught a lime in his mouth and a pair of red lace panties on his head and, writhing salaciously, somehow managed to launch them both back into the audience.

"Can I have a Scotch?" I shouted over the roars and whistles.

I heard an angry grunt, but this time he didn't even turn my way.

Even for Soreq's, this was a new low. I was just about to walk over and get in the bartender's face when I heard a familiar voice behind me.

"Oh, c'mon, Shulik, get him a Scotch. He's a friend of mine."

I turned in surprise.

It was Israela.

22

Shulik cursed under his breath, grunted as he pulled his enormous frame upright, and poured me a drink with his beefy hands. "Only for you, girl," he said, his voice parched and raw. He pushed the drink toward me and turned his attention back to the vaudeville-like performance.

Israela looked pale and drawn, and even in the dim, flashing lights I could see the dark rings under her eyes. She wasn't dressed in the trampy clothes Hesh had described, but neither was she clad in the gypsy-like attire I was used to. She wore a simple, dark, form-fitted dress, her wild hair pushed back into a high, careless ponytail. Around her neck, collar-like, was a plain gold band. She looked older, more elegant, and despite the haggard look on her face, quite beautiful.

"So you do come here," I said, yelling to be heard above the noise. She set something carefully on the bar—a feathery purple mask—and perched on the stool next to mine.

"No, never," she replied.

"The bartender seems to know you well."

"Shulik and I go back a long way," she shrugged. "I had an upsetting week. There was someone I wanted to talk to, and I knew he'd be here."

"You came to see Bal?"

She smiled wryly. "You really did believe everything Hesh told you. No, I don't hang out here all the time. And no, I didn't come to see Bal, although I'm sure he's here somewhere." Her smile turned quizzical. "What are you doing here? Doesn't seem like your kind of place. Did you come to check up on me?"

"No, of course not." For a moment I tried to pull together a professional facade but then realized how useless that would be. "I . . . was also looking for someone," I admitted.

Israela nodded. "She isn't here."

"How do you know—"

She shrugged, as if it were obvious.

"Then you must know where she is."

"No idea," she said, looking down at the bar, as if to admit she was lying.

The singer was walking off the stage for a break, and loud thumping music filled the room, making it impossible to talk. Israela sat at my side absentmindedly twirling her feathered mask. She didn't seem to feel the slightest discomfort in running into her therapist in a sleazy bar. When I finished my Scotch, she went around the bar to pour me another. It was comfortable sitting next to her, as if in the company of an old, familiar friend. It was indisputably Israela, but without the histrionics, without the tall tales and hippie clothes—as if I had stumbled upon her on a quiet night at home.

The song changed to a syrupy ballad, and I took advantage of the relative quiet. "So who did you come to see?"

She turned her head—stiffly, in her thick gold necklace—and I saw that the singer had returned and was now flitting from one table to another, his lute slung casually onto his back, expertly working the room. We watched him glide onto the lap of a giddy young woman who squealed with delight as he slipped his hand under her shirt and buried his face in the crook of her neck. Her companions laughed and whistled. Israela watched him a few more moments, sighed deeply, then turned back to me.

"Well, I certainly won't be getting *his* attention any time soon." She flicked her chin toward an empty booth, the same one in which I'd sat with Delia a few weeks before. "I was sitting over there when I saw you come in. Why don't you join me?"

I hesitated. Even by my very low professional standards, this was crossing a line.

She laughed. "Is it considered inappropriate to share a drink with your patient in a pub?"

"Most therapists would think so."

"But you're not most therapists, right?" She had me there. This case had left the safe boundaries of the office long ago.

She donned her eye mask and led me to the booth with an unsteady gait. Apparently, she'd already had a few drinks that night. As we sat, I caught a trace of Delia's scent, and the ashtray was overflowing with lipstick-stained stubs. Israela put her mask down on the table, beside a half-drunk margarita. I leaned toward her to yell above the din.

"How do you know the performer?"

She was facing in his direction, and I turned to get another glimpse. He was now dancing to the throbbing music, twirling on the stage with exquisite confidence and grace, his face dripping in sweat. Some of the drunks in the room were spinning comically in imitation, the women tossing off their shirts to accommodate the stifling heat, "Dudu's a very old friend." She was silent for a long moment. "He used to be my caretaker, many years ago. After Shulik. You know, the bartender? The one who wouldn't serve you a Scotch?" she laughed. "Shulik was my very first caretaker."

I looked over at the bartender, still staring at the performer and muttering furiously under his breath.

"Not a very reassuring presence."

"Oh, but you should have seen him in his youth, before he got all fat and crazy. So tall and strong. And brave, too—not scared of anyone." She sipped her drink. "Although he was always a little wacko. Made every little conflict into high drama. Eventually Y got mad at him—thought he'd been too soft on one of the neighbors. Shulik totally cracked after that. He'd go into these deep depressions, then wild manic episodes, where he'd speak in tongues or go consulting witches. He's been completely loco ever since."

Dudu had stopped dancing, and after mopping his brow with a purple scarf, he began reciting poetry with Shakespearean flair. Shulik's deadly glare hadn't left him for a moment. As we watched, he suddenly spit in Dudu's direction. I gasped out loud, but Israela just nodded.

"He detests him. I understand why." She saw I was waiting for her to explain. "Y got fed up with Shulik's antics and replaced him with Dudu. Shulik was insane with jealousy. Dudu was very young at the time. If you think he's handsome now, you should have seen him then."

"He's quite an entertainer," I said. When I turned back around, Dudu had somehow put on false eyelashes and stuffed his bodysuit with lumpy breasts to transform into instant drag. The audience was cheerfully interrupting the elegiac verses by calling out obscene rhymes.

Israela was watching with rapt affection. "Looks can be deceptive," she said when she saw the confused look on my face. "He's tough as nails, that Dudu. He once knocked out a neighborhood bully twice his size with nothing more than a well-aimed stone. No one ever messed with him after that."

A lute and a slingshot—of course. But what did it tell me? Dudu wasn't just some fantasy of hers; he was right there in front of me, a whirlwind of dance, as real as my own limbs and beating heart. I downed the rest of my Scotch. "Another?" Israela asked, and when I nodded, she hopped up and went over to the bar.

She came back with the bottle, already launching into another story, her dark eyes alight. "I always felt safe with Dudu, you know? Though he was very strict—never wanted me to leave the house." She laughed wryly. "I don't know what right he had to talk, given the trouble he always got into himself. He would travel abroad for all kinds of shady dealings, and then the cops would come by to interview me, trying to link him to smuggling rings,

gun-running—but they never proved a thing. At one point, he got involved
with a neighbor's wife, and shortly afterward her husband was knocked off,
execution style. They never could link him to that either, but it caused a
huge scandal in the neighborhood."

I poured myself a generous measure and took a big slug. "He sounds
dangerous," I said.

"He was a troublemaker, to be sure, but he's calmed down with age."
Dudu was now crooning a romantic ballad in a high falsetto. "I've always
loved Dudu," she sighed. "He's just so talented! You're only getting a glimpse
of it tonight. He composes, sings, plays instruments, writes poetry, acts,
dances like a pro. I was pretty young when he first came to live with me and
still scared from all I'd been through. He would sing me to sleep when I was
frightened. It was like having a fairy godfather."

"I bet Y likes him as well," I ventured.

"They adore each other. Y's the only person Dudu really listens to. He
was the one who first set up Y's office in my house, with the separate entrance
and courtyard. He even framed and hung the *ketubah* there, to remind Y of
his obligations to me. It wasn't much, but Y loved it. I'd always leave him a
meal there, grilled just the way he likes it, and sometimes in the morning the
plate would be all but licked clean. That made me feel so good." She paused,
reflecting. "I think he was around a lot more during Dudu's time."

A scantily clad fortune-teller shimmied up to the table, grabbed my
hand, and began stroking my palm seductively.

"I'll read your future for you," she crooned. "Some very intriguing lines
here. Only ten shekel."

Israela shooed her away with a few shakes of her wrist. "Leave him
alone, Endora." The girl made a pouty face but sashayed away as Israela
shook her head in disgust. "Hard to have a private conversation in this
place."

The Scotch was finally hitting me, washing away the last voice remind-
ing me that this was one of my patients, and a delicate case at that. "Israela,
I don't get it," I said. "I've lived in Jerusalem for years and I'd never heard of
Soreq's."

"You just haven't been paying attention," she said dismissively. "Friday's the only night worth coming to Soreq's. You know Jerusalem. There
are almost no open restaurants and pubs, so it's one of the only places for
non-Sabbath observers to go and unwind. Draws every lowlife in the city."
She scanned the room and smiled mischievously. "You'd be surprised if you
knew who was in here. Politicians, actors, artists, mobsters, even the rabbis
and do-gooders—eventually, they all come to Soreq's."

I sat up straighter and peered around the room.

"You see that table over there?" She flicked her chin toward a group of young, very drunken men shoving each other. "Those guys are Dudu's sons, and they're a volatile crew. You want to stay away from them." It was hard to tell in the flashing lights whether they were playfully roughhousing or in the midst of an escalating argument.

One of them, with delicate features and wearing an expensive silk shirt, was ignoring the melee, fussily moussing his hair. "That's Shlomi," Israela said. "After Dudu's performing career took off, he took over as my caretaker." Shlomi was admiring himself in a small mirror, oblivious to his rambunctious brothers and the surrounding cacophony. "He's a little vain," she conceded, "but at least he wasn't out adventuring, like Dudu or Shulik. He mostly stayed home with me." She watched him fondly as he started flirting with a tall Asian woman at the next table. "Things in the neighborhood were peaceful when Shlomi was in charge. The neighbors would come to visit, not to taunt and harass me, but just to be sociable. They'd ask him to settle their disputes or just listen to him talk about all the latest things he'd been reading and thinking about. He's incredibly smart." She glanced at me to make sure I was listening. "He was the first one to really decorate the house, with luxurious fabrics, precious paintings, sculptures from all over the world. He has exquisite taste. He expanded Y's office, too, and made it a lot fancier." Shlomi was now pontificating to his brothers, who were ignoring him. The Asian woman looked on admiringly, her knee brushing lightly against his. Israela sighed. "It was probably the best time of my life. That's when I started to think maybe I'd have a normal life." She laughed bitterly and drained the last drops of her margarita. I picked up the bottle of Scotch to pour her some, but she waved me away. I poured it for myself instead.

"But you know how Y is," she was saying. "Eventually, he finds something wrong with everyone. He didn't like how cosmopolitan Shlomi was, all the foreign influences—especially the exotic women he'd sneak into the house. Y can be very provincial, you know. And a bit of a prude."

A new song came pounding over the loudspeakers, and Shlomi's brothers gave a loud whoop. I could barely hear Israela. "Y got rid of Shlomi about a year ago, and that's when things really began to deteriorate," she said. "Caretakers have been coming and going so quickly, I can barely keep track of them."

"What do you mean?" I asked.

"All these eccentrics have started wandering through the house—miracle-workers, magicians, soothsayers. Half of them are here tonight." She indicated the feathered mask on the table between us. "That's why I brought the mask. I'm trying to keep a low profile." She glanced nervously around the room. "I mean, it hardly does any good; they all know I'm here." As I followed her gaze, something on the chair next to Shlomi caught my eye. "Lately there have been two caretakers at the same time," Israela was saying. "Sometimes they get along with each other, sometimes they scream at each other and keep me up all night. Some of these guys have been so awful . . ." I was barely listening. What was over there? The strobe lights and booze were making everything in the room swim. I could barely make out the shape, but it was unmistakably familiar.

"But the weird thing is, some of the caretakers whom Y hates the most stay for the longest time. He almost seems to enjoy fighting with them." The song changed again and the lights suddenly stopped flashing. The room was bathed in blue light. There, sitting calmly at the table next to Shlomi and his jostling brothers, was a large wooden doll.

"That doll . . . ," I said.

Israela didn't hear me. "I mean, I know in the early days I really *was* very young and I didn't know much about the world. I wanted someone in the house looking after things, keeping me safe. But now . . . I want more autonomy . . ."

One of Shlomi's brothers pushed another one out of the way, and I got a better look at the doll's face. It was, no question, the one I'd bought for Yudit. The lights changed again and I was able to make out a cocktail drink on the table in front of it.

"That doll," I said.

"But, I don't know, he does have a point," Israela said. I couldn't tell if she was ignoring me or hadn't heard me above the music. "The more chaotic it gets in the house, the more the neighbors start acting up. Maybe I do need protection after all." She stirred her ice cubes with a straw. "And with this horrible intifada . . . how can anyone feel safe?" Then, seeing my face, "What?"

"THAT DOLL!" I shouted, louder than I needed to, even through the music.

She glanced over. "Oh, yeah. That's Ashra's work. Shlomi's a big fan."

"That's . . ." I fought through the Scotch. "I bought a doll just like it. I thought it was one of a kind."

Israela nodded helpfully. "It probably is. She doesn't ever make the same doll twice."

"Then they stole it from me," I said stupidly.

She glanced at the doll again, then back at me. She shrugged. "No way you'll ever prove it."

I felt powerless and unstoppable at the same time. "I want it back!" I felt my voice rising. "I . . ." *I staked my whole relationship with my daughter on that gift*, my brain screamed. *I . . . thought it would fix everything. I . . .*

fucked up beyond my wildest fears. "I spent a lot of money on that doll," I finally managed.

She studied me for a moment. "You'll never get it back," she said gently. "I'd let it go, if I were you. You can't win a child's love with a doll anyway."

"Maybe Ashra would make me a new one. Could you ask her?" I heard how desperate I sounded, but I couldn't help myself. "Aren't you friends?" A look of pure terror suddenly washed over her face. It was gone in a moment, but it sobered me up.

"Israela, what is it?"

She shook her head but she was breathing fast. Finally she said, "I don't think I ever told you about my doll collection." She glanced up at me fearfully before continuing. "Some of them were gifts from Ashra, others I made myself. I often thought about getting rid of them, but I could never get myself to throw them out. I never had a childhood, so they mean a lot to me. But it makes him so furious." She paused. "I mean, there have always been threats, but they've been getting worse lately . . ." She spoke quickly, as though she needed momentum to get the story out. "And the other day . . . I came home to find the dolls broken and scattered around the house." I flashed to the vivid scene from my dream of two weeks prior—of dolls wrestling each other to the ground, shooting each other with Uzis, blowing themselves up.

"You think Y came to the house and broke your dolls?" I asked.

"No, of course not," she said quickly. "It could have been one of the eccentrics who's been wandering through the house lately. But it's also possible that Y sent someone from the Outstretched Arm to do it . . ." She hesitated and then pressed on. "I even thought . . . I know it's ridiculous." She looked at me, her brown eyes full of fear. "I wondered if . . . maybe if what happened Tuesday night, at the pool hall, was orchestrated by Y. Just to scare me, you know."

I'd completely lost the thread again. "The pool hall? The one that was bombed, in Rishon?" She nodded. "What would that have to do with you?"

She looked around, as if to make sure no one was listening, then leaned in toward me. "I was there."

I studied her face, incredulous.

"You were in the pool hall? At the time of the bombing?"

She took a sip of her melted ice. When she spoke, her voice was almost a monotone. "I was in the ladies room washing up when the bomb exploded. That's the only thing that saved me. I don't even remember hearing the explosion, just being violently thrown forward onto the sink and seeing in the mirror the bathroom door behind me blowing right off. I was shaken, but not actually hurt. I made my way into the main room and found the entire club filled with black smoke and dust. Most of the ceiling had come down. Then the screaming began." She took a breath. "I tried to make my way toward where the stairs had been, but the whole area was blocked by shattered glass and debris. You could hear people moaning from under the rubble." She swallowed before continuing. "There were bloody hunks of flesh and body parts everywhere. I could smell fire but couldn't find a way out. And then I saw this woman whom I'd noticed earlier in the evening because she was wearing an old-style flapper dress. But now she was on the floor, under a broken pool table. Her leg was missing, and blood was pooling under her belly. I crawled under that same broken table, next to her, and hid my head in my arms, frozen with fear. I stayed crouched in that very spot for what seemed like hours. There was so much screaming and moaning and wailing and clawing, and then suddenly you'd hear another bit of ceiling or wall come crashing down. I heard the sirens approaching, the voices of police and rescue workers, the barking of dogs, the wounded calling out to be rescued. Through it all, I didn't move or make a sound. Then a policeman finally made his way through the rubble and pulled me out from under that table. Somehow I emerged without a scratch."

"Oh, God, Israela." I didn't feel drunk anymore, but my head felt like it was floating free of my body.

She kept talking, in the same monotone. "They took us all to the hospital, but I had no physical injuries, so I was immediately released. The police then took me in to the station to give testimony, and I was there for hours. It was late Wednesday afternoon when they finally let me go, but I was too dazed and frightened to go home. They wanted me to talk to a psychiatrist, but I refused. I've been staying with a different friend each night." She stroked a spot on her left sleeve. "I was wearing this very dress. You can still feel the dried blood on it." She looked up at me. "It was everywhere."

I glanced at her sleeve. There was nothing visible on the dark fabric.

"But . . ." I flailed around to find a question that felt appropriate, of all the very many crowding my mind. "What were you doing in Rishon? Why were you in a pool hall? Were you alone?"

She looked down. "I was looking for someone," she said. "I thought he'd be there . . ."

There was no point asking who she was looking for, though the pool hall certainly sounded like Y's kind of place. I'd read that it had been an unlicensed operation. Had he been running that joint as well?

"So wait, you haven't been home since Tuesday?" I asked.

She nodded. "That's why I came to see Dudu. He's the one person I trust enough to take me home. I was thinking maybe he'd even stay with me a few days, until I calm down." She twirled the mask on the table. "So . . . here I am."

The weight of what she was saying was still sinking in. Did she really think that Y might have been behind a terrorist attack? I remembered the news report well. Sixteen people killed, dozens wounded.

Was the whole story of her being there an elaborate fabrication? Despite all my doubts, her affect seemed more real, more genuine, than it usually was. Once again I was struck by the conviction that—whatever the nature of the stories she was telling me—the love and fear she experienced were very, very real. "I'm glad you have Dudu to take you home tonight," I said. "We have a session scheduled for Tuesday, right?" She nodded. Emboldened, I leaned over and took her hand. "Israela, we have to start talking, not just about the past, but about the present and the future, about how you envision your life. How to either make this marriage work or get out of it." She said nothing but she didn't pull her hand away. "You're suffering too much," I added. "You can't just keep going like this. Let's decide to start talking about that right away in your next session." She nodded but I could feel the moment had passed. With a jolt of shame, I remembered where we were—a seedy bar—and that I was offering therapeutic insights on the tail of a large amount of Scotch. I pulled my hand away and glanced around the room to see if anyone had noticed. Shlomi's table was empty, and the doll was gone.

Israela was wiping her eyes dry and looking at someone behind me, nodding. I turned to look. It was a tall, very thin man, with dark, spiked hair and a pencil-line moustache, dressed in an elegantly tailored black suit. Was this Y? My heart started racing. Shulik and Dudu worked here, and Israela felt so at home—wasn't it likely that Y was the proprietor?

"I have to go," Israela whispered, her eyes glued to the man in black.

"OK," I whispered back. And then, "Is that Y?" My blood was pounding.

She looked at me sadly. "Oh, Dr. Benami," she said. "Always thinking you're going to see Y."

She leaned forward and put a hand on my cheek, as if to comfort a child, letting it linger there a moment too long. From close up, I thought I could make out the logo of the Outstretched Arm delicately engraved in the thick gold of her necklace.

"Israela . . ."

"I'll see you next week," she said.

She stood up and held the mask to her face, then touched the tight neckband and smoothed her dress. I turned around to watch her take the arm of the man who, I now realized, could only be Bal. They walked straight through the raucous masquerade of Soreq's Pub, making a beeline for the menacing black corridor, leaving me alone, with a throbbing headache, in the sweaty booth that still smelled faintly of Delia.

23

The news of Anat and Tuvya's arrest shouldn't have come as such a surprise. I was so preoccupied by all the odd things happening to me that
the glimpse of Tuvya in the third temple storefront had all but vanished
from my mind. My sister, it turned out, was not just the hot-air balloon I
had always thought her to be; she was a violent terrorist, ready to act on her
deranged ideologies. They had been charged, along with three others, with
belonging to a Jewish terrorist cell based in Samaria, called "God's Right
Arm," which had formed after the murder of five members of a family in the
settlement of Itamar the year before. The group was being charged with the
retaliatory murder of a Palestinian farmer and was also implicated in several
rampages into Palestinian villages that had resulted in extensive property
damage. Hearing the name, I couldn't help but wonder if it might be a West
Bank subsidiary of the Outstretched Arm, but I quickly dismissed the idea
as absurd. All five were being held in administrative detention. Habakuk
was staying with Tuvya's sister in another West Bank settlement.

My mother reacted to the new turn of events with the same impassiv-
ity with which she now greeted all of life's vicissitudes, but my father was
in deep shock, aging rapidly from the cumulative strain. His sciatica was
now so severe that he could barely walk the two blocks to the corner grocer.
Gal was floating in too celestial a realm to be of much concrete assistance,
and without Anat's visits the household could barely be maintained. Thrust,
reluctantly, into the role of parental caretaker, it was I who would now be
commuting up to Petah Tikva several times a week, ferrying in food and
supplies, giving my father, who wouldn't otherwise leave my mother's side,
some relief from his self-imposed vigil.

Tuesday morning, Israela left a message canceling her session. Of
course, she'd need a little space to readjust our therapeutic relationship, I
told myself. Sharing a drink with her had been unprofessional, to be sure,
but the damage was not irreparable. When she came back, we would talk

about it. She had seemed receptive to my suggestion that we begin to address her marriage directly. In that sense, our night in the bar might have actually led to a little bit of progress.

But the following week, when she didn't show up at all, I had to finally admit that my egregious breach of the therapeutic boundary had probably destroyed her trust or pushed her too far, too fast. I didn't know which was more painful—the idea of never seeing her again, or the certainty that this was just another in a long list of relationships I'd broken beyond repair.

That evening, as I walked out of work already half-sunk into the pool of grief and shame in which I spent my nights, I almost tripped on the beggar who worked the corner in front of the hospital. I had managed to avoid him in the month or so since I had dropped a shekel into his gnarled palm, and if anything, he looked even more pitiful and decrepit than I remembered. On a whim, I again dropped a shekel into his palm. I did the same the next night, and the next. Within a few days, he started assembling his rag-covered limbs at my approach, thrusting his filthy, mottled arm out toward me, bowing obsequiously and tossing out a mumbled blessing as I left. I held my breath as he approached, forcing myself not to cringe when his palm grazed my fingers. Parting with the shekel was a painful, forced act, a challenge of atonement I had set myself, I hardly knew why.

It was the end of a long day, two weeks after the encounter at Soreq's. I was distractedly fishing the beggar's coin out of my pocket when someone grabbed my lapel and pulled me into the shadows behind the pillars of the building's entrance.

I put my hands up in alarm, the small, silver coin clattering noisily to the ground. "Take my wallet. Don't shoot," I cried.

"What are you, crazy?" my assailant hissed. "I look like a mugger to you?"

He did. He was so gaunt and wild-eyed, I would have sworn he was a junkie desperate for his next fix. My eyes adjusted to take in more detail: mid-forties, dark skin, and long, delicate side-curls reaching almost to his armpits. A black velvet *kipa* sat high on his head, and he wore fringed tzitzit over a grubby white T-shirt. His thin frame was bathed in sweat, and he looked like he might not have had a proper meal in weeks. Most oddly of all, his upper body was draped in thick, padlocked chains.

His voice was raspy, his tone urgent. "I have to talk to you, Doc. But if the cops see me I'm in trouble." He pulled me closer to him. "Keep your back to the street, stay calm, maybe they won't notice."

I shook myself free, suddenly furious. "You have no right to grab me like that. Why shouldn't I call the cops?"

He stared at me. "It's about Israela. There's no time to waste, she's in real danger . . ."

How was it possible that I could still be surprised, every time? It had never occurred to me that Y might have connections within the ultra-Orthodox community, but why not? There was no sector of Israeli society where his tentacles didn't seem to reach.

". . . before it's too late. Israela's house . . . ," the man was hissing. I didn't need to hear the whole thing again. I had questions of my own.

"Who are you? Who sent you?"

"My name's Yiri. But listen, there's no time for chitchat. Israela . . ."

"Yes, I know," I said impatiently. "Your friends have already told me—"

"I have no friends," he said indignantly. "Don't listen to the others, they don't understand." Seeing my eyes roll, he sighed. "Do I have to explain everything? OK. Turn around slowly, but don't attract attention. Now check out the guy across the street."

On a small triangle of dust and shrub, a cheerful-looking man with a round face and a checkered jester's hat had collected a crowd. He often played that spot. I'd never stopped to watch, but it was some kind of stand-up routine, involving a banjo and some juggling. The crowd was laughing with pleasure, and I noticed three policemen standing at the edge of the circle, sharing in the fun. Yiri noticed them too and pulled me back into the shadows.

I shook him off again. "What about him?" I asked.

"His name's Hananya," Yiri said scornfully. "Him they like. A few jokes, some magic tricks—always with a fake-cheer message. Tells them the world is getting better every day." His voice turned mocking. "*People are all the same inside, if only we open our hearts! Peace is just around the corner!* What a lot of bullshit." He looked in Hananya's direction. "Israela loves him. Every time he sees her he tells her how well the peace talks are going—as if he knew anything about it!"

"So he's giving people a little hope—what's wrong with that?" I asked, annoyed by his mocking tone.

This set him off. "What, are you kidding? That guy doesn't know anything! He just invents happy news to make people feel better." He was no longer whispering. "We just reentered Bethlehem—you see any kind of peace around the corner? You gonna take those strutting UN diplomats seriously, with their cocktail chitchat and self-serving speeches?" His voice was rising steadily. "There's a new terrorist attack every day, each one more brutal than the one before. They have an endless supply of hopeless teenagers willing to blow themselves up to get their seventy-two virgins. We don't have a chance against this intifada, and we never did!" I glanced around to see if anyone was hearing this. "There's no end in sight, and everyone knows it!" Yiri was yelling. "But I just show my face and it's off to the clink again. No one wants to hear the truth!"

"OK, OK, calm down," I said, desperate to get out of there without any more shouting. "What did you want me to know?"

"Israela. She's the most deluded of them all. I'll tell you the bad news *she* doesn't want to hear." He leaned toward me, his black, marble eyes just centimeters from my own. "It's already begun."

I instinctively shrank back from his sweat-soaked stench. "What's begun?"

"Half the house—it's already gone."

"Whose house?" The words were sinking in. "Israela's?"

"I'm telling you, last week," he said, now perfectly calm. "Why do you think she's been missing your sessions?" He leaned in conspiratorially. "There was a big fire—very mysterious. Destroyed two rooms in the north side of her house. She's too scared to even walk out the door. She's so stubborn, if you ask her she'll tell you it's no big deal." He nodded sagely. "But it's just a warning, and she knows it. The rest of the house will be gone by week's end." He threw his hands up in disgust. "She won't listen to me—maybe she'll listen to you!"

I'd been so sure that I'd ruined my relationship with Israela it hadn't occurred to me that she might not be safe, even though she'd told me Y's threats were getting worse. I didn't know what to think. "Y?" I finally managed.

Yiri nodded. "He didn't do it himself, but he sent the bums who did. Do you know how many times he's already told her to change her ways? He's desperate; he can't figure out how to get through to her. She has no sense of modesty, no decency. What does she think, decking herself in gold, putting layers of paint on her eyes? She still goes out every night in her gaudy clothes, meeting up with Bal, living her selfish, dissolute lifestyle. She's like an animal in heat, prostituting herself under every tree in Independence Park. Do you understand what this does to him? He remembers how she used to be, a sweet and doting teenager, following him through the desert with total trust and devotion. That's the woman he wants back! She's forgotten how she loved him, forgotten her marital vows. That's why he sends all his friends out, to give her a chance to repent. But it does no good; she stiffens her neck and doesn't listen!"

I tuned out his words. All I could think about was Israela, in danger and afraid.

"But what do you—," I started.

"I owe everything to him!" Yiri yelled. "I'm in torment watching her treat him this way, defiling the house he gave her, filling it with thieves and sorcerers. I'm desolate, consumed with grief! If only you knew how I suffer!"

He was just like Hesh, another suffering soul whose own misery had somehow become entwined with Y's. But that didn't mean he wasn't telling the truth. I thought of Israela's fear that Y had been behind the terrorist bombing in Rishon. Was he really that dangerous? If he was cruel enough to set Israela's house on fire, might he also be somehow implicated in this relentless intifada?

"The final punishment will be terrible!" Yiri was shouting, and I saw one of the police officers across the street look over. "He'll have the entire house destroyed, the gardens will revert to weeds, the walls will crumble, snakes and wild dogs will roam its corridors!" He laughed crazily. "Do you think Bal will be there for her when her house has been destroyed? She'll be homeless, condemned to live among strangers. Then she'll know who her husband is!"

His chains clanked as he spoke. I looked closer and saw: an outstretched arm menacingly etched into the rusting padlock. "Y gave you those chains to wear? They're not from the police?" I asked, hearing the panic in my voice.

Yiri laughed at me. "What, you think the cops chain people in this day and age? Of course Y gave them to me! He wants me to know what it feels like to suffer as he does. That's what you have to do if you're going to preach ugly truths!"

I imagined medieval dungeons, dank torture chambers, hidden underneath the ornate headquarters that Shaya had described, embedded within the ancient, archaeological strata of Old City Jerusalem.

"You think I like this life?" Yiri cried out. "Always in rags, always on the run, days without a proper meal. I've been in solitary more times than I can count." He glanced over at the cops, who were now talking to each other earnestly. "I curse the day my mother bore me! But what choice do I have? He's told me in such detail what will happen, my bones tremble at the knowledge!"

"But what—"

"I'd do anything to get through to that stubborn broad. I wrote her letters from prison, but she burnt them. When she sees me on the streets she calls the cops!"

"Look, Yiri—"

"It's not just her. I recoil at the evil that flourishes in this land! We're in a constant state of war; the poor are fending for themselves on the street; corruption is rampant. Look at how we've polluted this sacred land! You've seen the debauchery at Soreq's. We were supposed to be a 'light unto the nations'! What went wrong?" His voice was rising again. "We should have never established this state! Why didn't we wait for the Anointed One to bring us home? In our hubris, we tried to force the hand of the Messiah— what good could come of it? I'm tormented by what I see coming!"

"But—"

"If we stay on this path, there will be mass slaughter, a new Holocaust, not sixty years after the last one! Tell me, Doc, why doesn't anybody listen?! Israela—"

I couldn't take any more. "Enough about Israela!" I grabbed his chains and pulled him close. "Why are you all following me around?" His eyes flicked over me, suddenly nervous. "What does any of this have to do with me?" Yuri started to turn away but I pulled him back. "What the hell is going on?" I could hear the hysteria rising in my voice. "WHO THE HELL IS Y?"

He started. I turned to follow his gaze and saw the cops looking toward us.

"Now look what you've done," Yuri said in disgust, pulling away. "Man, you're just as deaf and blind as she is." He hastily gathered his chains in his hands. "Will you at least hear this one thing? Half of her house is gone. Her time is running out!"

With that, he slipped past me and broke into a trot, his chains clattering, two cops following in hot pursuit.

I stood paralyzed in the shadows of the building, holding tightly to the grainy stone pillar behind me, my heart pounding. I hadn't realized the toll that being followed all the time had taken on me. If this is how I felt after only a few short weeks, how could Israela possibly hold up after so many years of threats and abuse?

I closed my eyes and took a few deep breaths, composing myself for the bus ride home. When I opened them, the third policeman was standing in front of me.

"Good afternoon," he said, with excessive politeness. "Your identity card, please."

"What?" I said. "Look, I don't know that guy . . ."

"Your identity card, please."

I handed him the card, and he looked at it closely.

"Please remove your glasses."

I complied, as he compared the photograph with my face.

Seemingly satisfied he asked, "What brings you downtown this afternoon?"

"I work right here, in the hospital." I couldn't keep the impatience out of my voice. All I wanted was to get out of there. "I'm the chief psychologist. Here's my hospital ID. Look, I really don't . . ."

He carefully checked the two names and photos against each other and against the haggard visage before him. "Thank you, Dr. Benami," he said. His excessive politeness was fraying my nerves as badly as Yuri's crazed ranting. I put out my hand for the cards, but the officer didn't move. "Would you mind showing me what's in your pocket?" he said. I looked down and saw the top of a small plastic bag peeking out from my pants pocket. A deep chill passed through me.

"I don't know what that is. It's not mine. He . . ."

"May I see it, please?" His face was as impassive and commanding as his voice.

I gingerly pulled out the baggie, my stomach dropping when I saw what it contained: four chocolate-brown squares of hashish. I had only seen the drug once before, during a high school trip to the Sinai, when a friend had shown me the stash hidden in his shoes.

If you panic, you'll look guilty, I thought. "Look, that guy who was talking to me. He grabbed me." I knew I was talking too fast. "He . . . he must have dropped it in my pocket. I don't know why he would have done that. I've never used drugs in my life."

"Do you know who he is?"

"Well no, I don't. He called himself Yiri. I've never met him before."

"You were certainly talking to him for quite a while," the officer observed. "Would you be willing to tell me what you were talking about?"

"About . . . a client of mine. A mutual acquaintance . . . I . . ."

I was unable to continue. The officer never took his eyes off of me as he radioed for a squad car.

24

I had to find Y. I was in a deserted city, a Jerusalem I'd never seen before. Instead of apartment buildings, there were small stone houses, terraced on the steep hills, ancient and ramshackle. The narrow, cobblestoned roads were slick with rain. I could hear a voice calling out to me, but whatever direction I ran in, the call came from somewhere else. I saw a looming shadow, but when I raced toward it, it spread out and faded out of reach. I was lost among the houses, slipping and sliding on the sharply graded pavement. I turned a corner and a swallowing blackness overwhelmed me . . .

I woke up in a cold sweat and lay on the couch listening to the building creak, waiting for my heart to slow down. I had fallen asleep in my clothes, exhausted after the evening's ordeal.

By the time the squad car had arrived at the police station, I had composed myself enough to create a reasonable story and stick with it. There was nothing so unusual about a drug dealer cornering me to ask about one of my clients or, once he saw the cops, taking an opportunity to dump his stash. It had been a trivial quantity of hash, and my record was clean as a Passover breadbox. No charges were filed, and I was released with deference, apologies, and a warning to be careful with whom I associated.

But who *was* I associating with? Was the Outstretched Arm involved with drugs on top of everything else? The cops had informed me that Yiri was a known criminal. But just because he was probably a drug dealer, and almost certainly an addict, didn't mean he wouldn't have real information about Israela. Had Y really set fire to her house? It had suddenly occurred to me with a chill, while waiting at the police station, that the outstretched arm was reminiscent of a Nazi salute. Who knew what they'd be capable of doing.

I had left the police station and gone directly back to the clinic. Letting myself in with a cringe, imagining what Jezebel would say, I looked up Israela's file and jotted down her address and phone number. I was surprised to see that her "mansion" was on Derech Hevron, a major thoroughfare, with a few old, but relatively modest, Arab houses. I had probably passed it a hundred times. I stuck the paper in my pocket, then carefully locked the door behind me.

On the way home I picked up a pizza— the kind of cheap comfort food that Nava always frowned on—and tried to watch TV while I ate. I had fallen asleep on the couch, with a limp slice of pizza in my hand.

Now, as my heart slowed from my panicked race through the rainy streets of my dream, I thought about the looming absence in Israela's tales. Not once had she said a word of how Y looked—his height, the color of his hair. She had never described being in his presence when it was daylight, when she was fully awake. As far as I could tell, she had never talked to him face-to-face. He was always ahead scouting the route or calling out to her from a mountain, sneaking into his office or sending messengers. "At least I can see him whenever I want," she had said of Bal. "Always thinking you're going to see Y," she had said to me in Soreq's.

No name, no age, no childhood, no face—an eclipse, an all-consuming absence. Lying in the dark, running through Israela's sessions in my mind, it was obvious: Y was a complete fabrication.

But if Y didn't exist, did that mean the stalkers shared the same psychotic delusions as Israela? Who was hiring the caretakers, and who was running Soreq's? Did the Outstretched Arm exist, or was it also a fabrication? The country was suffering under extreme conditions of trauma and stress—could I have stepped into a unique manifestation of spontaneous collective psychosis? Or, the more sinister thought: was there someone actively cultivating it? Someone had been supporting Israela, and someone was now sending the stalkers. Whoever was behind it all had money and power.

Whether or not Y existed, I couldn't shake the conviction that Israela was in real danger. And now, maybe I was too.

I lay on the couch, paralyzed. A fierce wind had picked up and was blowing against the creaking shutters. An alley cat yowled in the distance, its screech magnified by the wind. I had a flash image of Hesh driving through the dark, empty streets of Jerusalem, gleefully targeting the city's doomed, scrawny cats. I pulled the couch pillow over my head and told myself to go to bed.

But what if she really was in danger?

I looked at my watch: 2:07 a.m. I could call her, but what would I say if she answered? *Oh, hi, this is your shrink. I had a bad dream.* I could call and hang up when I heard her voice. But what if she had caller ID?

I flopped on my side and closed my eyes, determined, but my senses were on edge. I saw Ami's long shepherd's robes and heard his deep, resonant voice ringing in my ear: "Whose responsibility is it, Dr. Benami?"

The address I'd jotted down that afternoon was still in the pocket of my pants. Feeling utterly foolish, I got up, put on my shoes, grabbed my keys, and stepped out into a fierce *hamsin*. It was a nasty night, the air yellow with sand. I remembered Gal once telling me, years ago, that *hamsin* winds brought bad dreams. Could it be that simple? But there was no turning back now.

I drove through the empty streets feeling sillier by the minute. Twice I started to turn around, and both times I forced the car back in her direction. I'd just go have a look at the house, make sure everything seemed peaceful and safe, then go back home and go to bed. As I drove up Derech Hevron, I saw an eerie blue light up ahead. My heart started to hammer in fear. As I got closer, I saw that it was coming from a police car parked in front of an empty lot. I was scanning the house numbers, wondering which one was Israela's, and was almost upon the police car before I realized: it wasn't an empty lot at all.

I pulled the car off the road and got out. The police car's blue lights illuminated a pile of rubble—utter devastation, such as you might see on the news after a bombing or, in more peaceful lands, an earthquake or hurricane. Israela's house was in ruins.

I couldn't even imagine what had caused such total destruction. There wasn't a beam unshattered, not a piece of furniture that didn't appear shredded to bits. It looked as if a bulldozer had come and run over the property to ensure that not a single block of stone, not a book, not a photograph, not an artifact would survive intact. Parts of the rubble seemed to have been charred by fire. And then I saw a stirring in the middle of the wreckage.

She was rocking, her hands grasping her knees, oblivious to the howling wind. A female police officer was crouched beside her, whispering urgently, but she seemed not to notice. Her clothes were ripped into rags, one breast partially exposed, her whole body streaked with blood and dust. For a moment I thought her hair had gone white overnight, but then realized that it was covered in ash. She looked drawn and emaciated in the blue light, and every so often she let out a deep moan.

Where were the stalkers now? The caretakers? The neighbors? Her friends, Bal and Ashra? She was utterly alone in her degradation, with only a stranger to comfort her.

No one had yet noticed my presence. A second officer was wrapping yellow police tape around the lot—the news reporters would be arriving soon. The policewoman was probably trying to convince her to accompany them to the station. It occurred to me that I could gallantly approach, explain that she was my patient, and offer my professional services. They would certainly wonder what had brought me there in the middle of the night but would be relieved to let me take over. But to what avail? There was no reason to think she would listen to me or that I could handle the situation better than the police. And what right did I have? I had utterly failed her. The last time I'd seen her, not two weeks before, she had told me how scared she was, and I had brushed it off as therapeutic progress. She had told me of his threats numerous times, and the stalkers had only confirmed it. Not once had I taken any of it seriously. The danger had been evident from the start—the illegal harassment, the threats, the history of battering by a sociopathic husband. Any psychologist with an ounce of integrity would have involved the police right from the beginning. It was my arrogance, my boredom, my apathy, my self-absorption, my desire to be the one she turned to for help and support, that had allowed this disaster to unfold. I had no right to step in now and play the heroic savior.

I looked at her one last time. Silently, I told her that I *did* care, that I wanted to help her, but that I truly didn't know how. I got into my car and drove away.

25

The following day, in the back pages of *Yediot*, I found a small article describing a bombing on Derech Hevron, vaguely attributed to terrorists. No one had been killed or injured in the attack, and only one private house destroyed, so it merited no more than two scant paragraphs. I spent the next few days in turmoil. Was there anything I could have done to help her? Had I been a selfish coward to walk away from her plight? Where was she now?

I came in to work early Sunday morning hoping to find some kind of message from Israela—or even from a stalker—but there was none. For two days I went through the motions of living and working, haunted by anxiety and self-loathing. On Tuesday afternoon I was back from lunch at 1:00 sharp, knowing full well that no one would show. Foolishly, I paced the office, waiting for her to miraculously waltz in the door at 1:10. At 1:15 I dialed her number, knowing there would be no answer. I was playing out the old charade of my life, pretending I hadn't seen what I knew I had seen.

I managed to somehow get through the day, fighting the panic that still fluttered in my chest. To distract myself, I spent every free moment zooming through paperwork, inventing details from long-forgotten sessions, watching the mountain of charts slowly diminish. But every time the phone rang, I jumped, hoping to hear her voice or that of a hospital psychiatrist, a cop, an army officer, an emissary from Y—anyone at all who could tell me what had happened to her. But there was no news at all.

I left the office late. As I dropped my customary shekel into the beggar's palm, I noticed another disheveled derelict lying just beyond him on the sidewalk. Consumed by guilt over how I'd failed Israela, I'd been indiscriminately distributing spare change to anyone who asked. I was digging into my pocket for something to offer the new guy, when I thought I heard a low mumble: "I don't need your money."

I wasn't sure if I had imagined the words. As far as I could tell, the rigid lips hadn't moved.

"Excuse me?"

I watched him this time. His mouth barely moved as he croaked, "I'm not a beggar, like that Job. I don't need your money."

"Are you speaking to me?"

"Dr. Benami."

Another patient I'd failed and then forgotten. "I'm sorry, I don't remember you," I said.

He still hadn't moved but I heard him clearly. "You had me committed. You and the girl."

I looked at him closely—too young, pale, with a beaked nose and thin face made sensitive by long, girlish lashes. And then I recognized him: it was the raving prophet Dina and I had hospitalized on the day of the King George bombing. He was lying stiffly on his side, in rags, immobile, his head shaven, his wispy beard caked in dust, his face frozen in horror.

What had happened to him? "Yes, I remember," I finally said.

His next words came so softly I had to bend down. His lips still did not seem to move. "See how she suffers. She wallows in terror and humiliation."

The stalking, it seemed, would never end. In fact, I now realized, it had begun long before I'd even met Israela. How was it possible that I'd never noticed? I moved closer, into his fetid odor.

"Where is she?" I asked.

"In a pit of despair. In a field of shattered, dry bones."

Suddenly he lurched to the side. Reaching out with one scabby arm, he clutched at a hideous brown mass that lay by his side, brought it to his mouth and bit. Whatever it was smelled even worse than he did. I looked at it closely. He was eating a patty of cow dung. I sprang up, a wave of nausea washing over me.

I steadied myself on a lamppost and looked back down at my latest stalker. Compared to this guy, the beggar, Job, was the picture of sanity and robust health. Many of the stalkers had been odd or unbalanced, but this kid was certified psychotic, with a hospital record to prove it. I could easily go back into the building, grab the first available psychiatrist, and have him re-committed. But I needed to know what had happened to Israela. I forced myself to crouch down again beside him.

"Where is she?" I asked again.

"Dr. Benami, have you ever allowed yourself to know your own despair? Can you peer deeply into the wound? How can you help her if you have never felt what she feels?" I smelled his words almost more than I heard them.

"Tell me where she is," I said, more insistently.

"She was warned, over and over. He had no choice—she would not listen. It has been destroyed, utterly destroyed. Her beautiful house, his love gift to her, in smoldering ruins."

I bent even closer. The smell was overwhelming.

"Where. Is. She?"

"She goes where he sends her." I reached out to shake him, fury temporarily pushing aside disgust. But before I could touch him, he went on. "She is far away, living at the mercy of strangers. She weeps and mourns for the loss of her beautiful home."

I sat back. For a brief moment, I was overwhelmed with relief. She was alive. I bent back toward him. "But is she safe?"

"How can she possibly be safe in a foreign land?" he croaked.

"She left the country?" My mind raced at where she might have gone and how. "Will she be able to return?"

He turned his head just enough that he could look at me. "She will return, Dr. Benami," he said. "In the end, he will always forgive her. After endless suffering, he will implant a new heart in her stubborn, rebellious soul. She will repent of her evil ways, and he will build her a new home more splendid than the first. And he will avenge himself mercilessly on those who destroyed her home."

Yiri had told me it was Y who'd destroyed it—or at least, sent the ones who did. "The paper called it a terrorist bombing," I said.

He was mumbling now, almost inaudibly. "He will destroy them all—her lovers, the terrorists, those who plotted her ruin. They will be annihilated, all of them! Only then will he bring her back, restore her to her glory, instill in her a new heart that is incapable of deception. They will have a glorious future together, but only after she has suffered and repented her ways!"

I wondered if I too would be caught up in the vicious slaughter he imagined.

"Do you also work for the Outstretched Arm?" I asked.

He twisted his neck and pulled down his ragged collar so I could see the tattoo inked into his shoulder blade.

"This organization . . . it scares me."

"It is an arm that is stretched out to those who have fallen," he said. "It will pick you up when you are in need, but it will not hesitate to punish the violent, the selfish, and the stubborn. Otherwise people do not change. Sometimes there is no other way." He turned and fixed me with his chilling, otherworldly stare. "Do you really want to help her? Will you stretch your arm out to her when she asks?"

"Yes," I whispered. "I really want to help her."

There was a long silence. I forced myself to remain crouched by his side, to breathe through his stench and through my growing fear. Was I, too—consciously or not—to become an emissary of the Outstretched Arm?

"He sent me so that you will feel in your very bones how she suffers. So that instead of labeling me and hospitalizing me and shoving me out of your sight, you will look deep into my eyes and see what human suffering is!"

I looked into the desperate, staring eyes, wondering what could have possibly happened in his young life to drench him in such anguish.

"How will that help her?" We were both whispering now, barely moving our lips to speak.

"She will write to you, turn to you for help. If you are to understand what she writes, if you are to help her recover, you must first know her pain!"

I looked at his rigid, dust-streaked body, and my mind leapt to the vision of Israela as I had seen her the week before, rocking and moaning with grief. I thought of the deep loneliness that would descend on me every night in my empty flat, the shots of Scotch that would dull my mind to the ache. I remembered the way I had dismissed him as an incoherent schizophrenic in our first encounter, how I had chastised Dina for listening to his words. Had he been speaking to me, even then? I wondered if I would ever have the courage to lie in my own pain, to unflinchingly eat the dung of my life.

"Thank you . . ."

"Zeke."

The question came before I had time to reflect on it. "Does Y really exist?"

"Every word I speak was fed to me by him. When he does not speak, I am silent. I have no words that are not his."

"If he exists, why can't I meet him?"

"I have seen him many times, but it is not for the faint of heart. Most people don't get as close as I have."

"I understand. But . . ." I didn't even try to hide my desperation. "Can you tell him that I'd like to meet him?"

Zeke turned his head away. "I don't bear messages to him, only from him."

I stood up and started to walk away, then turned back.

"Is there anything I can do to help you?"

He looked at me again, his eyes unfocused. "I am where I need to be. I lie in siege until he commands me to move. When you see me, it will be a reminder of how she suffers. Take it into your heart!"

His eyes suddenly darted upward, over my shoulder. I heard it too—the crescendo of an approaching military helicopter, black against the fierce blue sky. It had become a common sight and sound since the start of the intifada, but this one seemed to move toward us in a beeline, then hovered low, whirring loudly, emitting flashes of light. Zeke lifted his head and turned slowly toward the spinning rotors, eyes wide in terror.

"It's just a helicopter," I shouted but couldn't hear my voice above the roar.

It was rare for a copter to hover so low, and I'd never seen one give off flashes of light before. Perhaps the pilot—a black shadow in the sun's glare—was photographing the area as part of a terrorist investigation? Just as I stopped to wonder why a flash would be necessary in broad daylight, I realized that, of course, it was nothing more than an illusion—the sun glinting off rotating metal. I looked around at the people rushing about on a late Tuesday afternoon, eager to make their way home. Other than the beggar Job—who stared straight at the flashing rotors, his face contorted in pain—no one else seemed the least perturbed by it. And then, as suddenly and inexplicably as it had arrived, the helicopter rose up and flew away. Zeke watched it depart with his terror-filled eyes.

"It was just a helicopter," I repeated, though my voice was shaking.

He lay his head back down on the hard cement, then slowly, robotically, turned over to his other side, transferring the cow dung patty to within easy reach. The bluish arm on his back stretched out to me in compassion and menace. The audience was over.

26

The next morning, on the way into my office, I jumped when the receptionist called out my name.

"Sorry to scare you."

"That's OK, uh . . . Michal, right? I've been a little on edge lately."

"Yes, we've noticed. You remembered my name."

"Well, yes. You've been here quite a while, haven't you?"

She laughed. "A lot longer than you have. Anyway, Jezebel wants to see you. She asked me to tell you to come by her office as soon as you came in."

"Lucky I was in early today, huh?"

She smiled and winked. "We can always cover your tracks if you need. Don't be shy to ask."

Well, that was some change in attitude. Since when were the receptionists on my side? I smiled doubtfully, unsure if she was being kind or taunting, and headed toward Jezebel's office. I had not met with her one-on-one since that long-ago day she had put me on probation. In staff meetings, she was cordial and professional, an attitude I viewed with extreme suspicion. I had no idea what was coming and again felt like a schoolboy steeling for the verbal whip.

She motioned me to sit, her face a neutral mask. At least she wasn't glaring at me as she had the last time we had met.

"Kobi," she said briskly as soon as I'd sat down. "I want you to know that your efforts to improve your work have not gone unnoticed." She smiled stiffly.

"Oh, OK. Thank you," I said.

"The entire staff agrees that you have been more available, more professional, and more pleasant to be around. You have also made good progress on bringing your paperwork up to date."

"Well, I've been trying, but—"

"You come in on time and put in a full day's work. You've even been pleasant to the receptionists. It may seem trivial to you, but it means a lot to them."

"About the receptionists. They've really overloaded my caseload, and—"

"But you seem to be handling it fine. I look forward to the day, hopefully quite soon, when you can be removed from probation and once again resume your full administrative duties." She smiled expectantly.

We blinked at each other for a long moment. "Well, that would be good. I guess," I finally said.

Her smile faded slightly. "You're not sure?"

"Well . . ."

"What is it?"

"Nothing. Of course . . . that would be good."

She took off her glasses, a therapist about to get serious.

"Kobi. As pleased as I am by your improving work ethic, I admit to having some personal concerns about your well-being."

"I'm fine," I stammered. "Thank you. But . . . what do you mean?"

She breathed out a heavy sigh. "There are a number of things, but let's start with the most recent incident. I spotted you yesterday afternoon in earnest conversation with a homeless person lying on the street. Right in front of the hospital, where anyone could see you. He happens to be someone well known to our clinic."

"OK," I said slowly. "Is there some rule against talking with patients outside that I'm not aware of?"

"I'm not here to attack you, Kobi."

"OK. I'm sorry. I know him. I once hospitalized him." A perfectly reasonable explanation. "So what's the problem?"

She looked at me closely, but with sympathy. "It was your face while you were talking to him. You looked . . . desperate."

I didn't know what to say. "That's a pretty strong word," I finally managed.

"Yes, I know," she said. I could see how she must be an incredibly effective shrink.

"Well, we weren't planning a party," I said stupidly.

"Then what were you talking about?" she asked in a deliberately gentle tone.

"I didn't realize I had to report on conversations I have on the street," I replied. I could hear how defensive my voice sounded but I didn't care.

"Of course you don't have to tell me," she said calmly. "I imagine that you were trying to help him in some way."

"And what makes you so sure he wants our help?"

She sighed deeply. "It's always painful to see our patients in distress. But it's part of our professional duty to remain calm and neutral in all such encounters. I know that you understand that." She sat back. "There are proper procedures for finding someone help."

"Well, I'm sorry. I guess I'm a little less sure of all these formulae than I used to be."

"That's what's got me worried. The 'formulae,' as you call them, are the tools of our trade."

"And you never doubt them?" I said, too fast. "You never wonder who they're really designed to protect?"

She nodded thoughtfully. "They're imperfect. But it's become clear to me over the years that they provide crucial guidance."

I was suddenly exhausted. I didn't want to fight, I didn't want to challenge protocol, I just wanted to leave. "Look, I'm doing my job. I'm rushing through lunch to fit in all those extra patients, I'm writing up my case notes, buttering up the receptionists. What more do you want?"

"Kobi," she said, not unkindly. "I know you've been under a lot of stress lately, with your marriage breaking apart"—I winced—"and your mother so ill. I heard that you had to miss your daughter's bat mitzvah—that must have been crushing." She shook her head sympathetically. "I admit that I've been wondering if the stresses of your personal life might be causing you to lose some professional distance."

At this, I laughed out loud. "'Professional distance'—I love that phrase. I used to use it myself, so I know exactly what it means. It means not giving a damn."

"You know that isn't true," she said, her voice steady and calm.

Suddenly I was furious. "What do you know about these patients who you hold so tenderly in your care? Let me ask you something: have you ever eaten cow dung? Can you imagine what it's like to do that? How can you judge them when you've never had their experiences?"

"I'm not judging them, Kobi," she said. "But we have drugs that can help people like that." Then, "Is that what he told you? That he's eating cow dung?"

She was looking at me with concerned sympathy. What the hell was I doing? I was so wrapped up in Israela's web I'd forgotten how "sane" people like Jezebel would interpret something this freakish. If I didn't stop now, I would spill it all—about Israela, Y, the stalkers, the whole outlandish tale. Professional courtesy would get me nowhere; if she heard how literally I was immersed in this story, she would lock me up faster than you could say "schizomania."

"Tell me more," she was saying gently. "What else did he tell you?"

"Nothing—that was it," I said brightly. "You're right. I'd had a long day. I lost my professional distance. It was foolish. It won't happen again." I waited to be dismissed, like a schoolboy, but she wasn't done with me.

"There are other things, Kobi. That day you were swaying and mumbling to yourself in the lounge. And something else . . ." She hesitated, then said delicately, "Obviously, how you spend your time outside of work is no one's business."

"It seems like everything is your business." I sounded like a recalcitrant teenager, but she let it pass.

"You've been seen in some . . . unsavory places."

Was Israela right? Did everyone in town hang out at Soreq's? How come I had never heard of the place before? "You have someone following me around?" I asked, stunned.

"No, of course not. But in some ways, Jerusalem is still a small town. And the girl . . ."

"Delia?"

"She's also known to our clinic."

So that explained how Yossi knew her—I should have guessed. I bit back my indignation and managed to say, calmly, "Thank you for your concern. But I promise you, I'm fine." With all the dignity I could muster, I stood to go.

"OK," she said. I was almost to the door when she added, "There was one more thing, though. I was wondering . . ." I turned. "Whatever happened to that interesting case you had? The one who called herself Israela?"

She knew it all. Did she also work for the Outstretched Arm? Did everyone? As nonchalantly as I could I said, "Oh, she's gone. Her house . . ." I quickly changed tack. "She's not in the country anymore. She was in the Rishon pool hall bombing. After an experience like that, any sane person would leave if they could. I don't think she'll be back."

Jezebel's eyes were piercing but inscrutable. "Did you ever get a psychiatric consult on her? Do you know that she's safe?"

"She's fine," I said, nodding. "She was a bit histrionic, but stable. I considered a consult, but it turned out not to be necessary." I couldn't help adding, "I believe I've filled out all the appropriate paperwork."

"Please, Kobi," she said, a hint of irritation in her voice. "It's just that . . . you never responded to my notes."

"I've been in this racket a long time, Jezebel. I know when I need a psychiatric consult." There was a long silence, in which I tried desperately to regain control. Did my face look as flushed as it felt, my voice sound as shaky to her as it sounded to me? She was staring at me with her unblinking eyes. A hungry shrink, ready to pounce.

"Kobi, if there are things bothering you, perhaps I can help."

"Yes, I'll keep that in mind." I reached for the door again.

"You're suspicious of me, I know."

"Isn't 'paranoid' the appropriate clinical word?"

Her self-control was impressive. "Kobi, I put you on probation for your own good and the good of the clinic. But I've never meant you any harm." She sounded tired. "I'm available to assist you if you are in any kind of trouble or emotional distress."

"Yes, of course. I know that." I forced myself to smile and look her in the eye. "Thank you for your concern. I'm fine, really. I've been doing a lot of thinking, that's all. About life. Questioning things, you know. Midlife crisis." I gave a self-deprecating laugh.

She stood as well, obviously reluctant to let me go. "We'll talk again soon," she said.

"Yes, right," I responded, nodding vigorously. "We'll talk again soon." I backed out of the room for fear of her eyes burning too deeply into my back.

27

A couple of weeks later, after a long day of patients and an exhausting week of juggling work and parental obligations—not to mention the effort involved in dodging all contact with Jezebel—I was driving to the university on Mount Scopus for one of my periodic, now-rote lectures on the coping strategies of children of Holocaust survivors. It had been scheduled months in advance, but I had lost all appetite for the academic jargon and nitpicking repartee. The city had been on high alert for days, with a marked increase in army patrols, road blocks, and police helicopters circling overhead. I turned on the radio to a report on what I at first assumed was the previous day's attack—a particularly horrific rush-hour bombing, on the outskirts of Gilo, of a bus full of schoolchildren. How many had been killed? I'd already forgotten. The previous night, I'd watched video images of a huge bonfire shooting out of the charred bus. It had reminded me, with a grisly jolt, of the recent Lag BaOmer celebrations, and I found myself wondering, once again, what forgotten horrors that bizarre, fire-obsessed festival was meant to both recall and suppress.

But now, something in the urgency of the radio reporter's voice caught my attention. I realized that what I was hearing wasn't rehashed news at all. They were reporting live from a bombing that had only just occurred, moments before, at a crowded bus stop on French Hill.

I turned off the radio and heard the sirens reverberating somewhere nearby. I pulled over, trying to decide whether to proceed. The lecture would almost certainly be canceled, and the road to Mount Scopus would already be jammed with ambulances rushing from French Hill to Hadassah Hospital.

I started to make a U-turn, then impulsively completed a full circle, continuing in the same direction but passing the Mount Scopus turnoff, speeding toward the rising blare of the sirens. I parked illegally a few blocks away and ran toward the noise and the flashing lights. I edged my way through the crowd to the policeman at the barricade, flashing my Jerusalem

Hospital ID, trying to look important and purposeful. Amazingly enough, he nodded me through without any questions, and I found myself in the midst of a raging chaos. All around me, shrieking sirens, twisted metal, the smell of burnt flesh, the sobbing, screaming bystanders. I stared stupidly at a small, disembodied lump of flesh lying on the concrete bench of the now-shattered bus stop before realizing it was part of a foot. There was an overturned baby carriage near a pile of squashed vegetables, and a woman a few meters away screeching, "My daughter, my daughter! Where is she?" Someone asked me a question in English and shoved a microphone in my face, but I pushed it aside as I tried to orient myself to the horror of the scene.

"Hey you!" A medic was pointing at me. "Come here, fast." He instructed me to hold down the shoulders of a flailing, hysterical child so that he could strap her to the stretcher and administer a shot. I stared at her blackened face, the eyes clamped shut, her cries piercing through the din. When she'd been secured and slid into the ambulance, another medic called me over and had me hold an enormous piece of fabric tightly in place over the gushing wound of an old man's gaping belly. *Didn't you need credentials, or at least a pair of gloves, to do this kind of thing?* I wondered, but only for a moment. Next, I was passing supplies to a medic as he worked to revive an old woman. Then holding the end of a stretcher. Then covering a shivering body with a thin blanket. Then shepherding hysterical bystanders out of the way.

An eternity later, the scene began to calm, the worst of the wounded ferried away, and only the cops, the *haredim* scouring the scene for body parts to bury, the cameras, and a large crowd of morbidly curious onlookers remained. The ground was a carpet of blood-stained shattered glass, and the smell of vomit and blood hung heavily in the air. I suddenly thought of my father's words when I had impulsively asked him to accompany me on a trip to Auschwitz several years before: "You can't visit it, like a tourist to a grave," he'd said dismissively. "Without the searchlights, the barking dogs, the rising smoke, the hunger gnawing at your gut, the stench of burning bodies, you can't know what it was like."

Reluctant to just walk away, I was scanning the crowd for more ways to be useful, when I noticed a lanky soldier staring wide-eyed at the scene. He looked naked without his rifle, his olive-green uniform spattered with bloodstains, the blond fuzz on his cheek trembling. I went up to him and put an arm on his shoulder.

"Are you OK?"

He moved his eyes from the charred bus stop to my face and then fell upon me like a just-found child, his head on my shoulder, his entire frame shaking with sobs of terror. Awkwardly, I put my arms around him and felt his entire body convulse. I let myself merge into his trembling form, until I wasn't sure who was holding who, who comforting who. We gripped each other tightly, his sobs unleashing my own, and I felt something deep inside me, some essential piece that had unobtrusively kept me together all these years, break apart in this joint, shuddering sob. I don't know how long we would have remained in this desperate grip, but at some point, too soon, a policeman gruffly shooed us from the scene. The soldier turned his back on me and, head down, without looking back, pushed his way through the crowd and disappeared. Reluctantly, I did the same, stumbling back through the dark streets toward my car.

An hour later, I was home. I stripped out of my bloodstained clothes, scrubbed my skin raw in a steaming hot shower, then sat on the couch, watching the hypnotic televised replays of the scene I had just witnessed. I scanned the victims and bystanders for a familiar face and found myself imagining Yudit as one of the victims. As the dreadful fantasy played itself out, I felt a wrenching laceration in my chest. I thought of the squint in Yudit's eyes when she was wondering if I was pulling her leg and allowed the whole sweet drama of her life to disintegrate into a wrenching absence. I found myself sobbing again, wailing out my grief at her death as if it were real. I ached for the families that would, this very evening, undergo that kind of torment. And I ached with longing for my little girl.

I wiped my eyes, turned off the television, and tried to calm myself down. The ever-silent phone seemed to take up all the space in the room. I was desperate to hear her voice but couldn't summon the courage to dial. What if she answered and hung up as soon as she heard my voice? Or what if she agreed to talk to me, but my voice wouldn't steady enough to respond?

I itched for a drink. I pulled out a glass and reached for the Scotch, but the accusing tone of Shaya came back to me, the stench of Zeke's cow patty, the rage and humiliation in Nava's eyes as she watched the hopes of a lifetime clatter into an empty coffee cup. I thought about the way my father's jowls sagged when he thought no one was looking, the deadness in my mother's eyes whenever food passed her lips, the fury in the scrunched-up face of little Habakuk as he raced around our legs. Zeke was right—my life was a field of shattered, dry bones. But what did any of it matter in the face of such horrors as I'd seen tonight?

In the darkness of my bedroom, my body doubled up into a fetal claw, and strange, animal-like noises began to emerge, unbidden, from deep inside my gut. I clutched my head, pounded at the pillows, screamed out my rage at Nava, at Jezebel, at my hapless parents and lost-soul siblings, at the God-obsessed fanatics who strapped explosives to their bodies. From those excruciating depths, I found myself screaming out to Y. Why did he destroy her house? Why was he so cruel and unforgiving? Somehow my own anguish had merged with Israela's hunched, rocking form; in a way I couldn't quite fathom, the one who afflicted her was also afflicting me. And like her, I was alone, with no one to comfort me.

In the morning, after a tormented, sleepless night, I called in sick. Sucking up to Jezebel was a lost cause anyway; she saw right through me. I returned to bed, seized repeatedly by new, endless waves of raw grief. Maybe it would never stop. I had treated countless patients with severe symptoms of anxiety and depression, every kind of nervous disorder imaginable. I could imagine with perfect precision what a hospital intake worker would write of me if I managed to crawl my way into their clutches. Jezebel would shake her head in sympathy but also quietly congratulate herself on having correctly perceived the severity of my condition. What kind of hubris did we have, assigning people to little diagnostic boxes, pigeonholing human agony? I had hospitalized dozens of despairing souls but now felt that I'd rather die alone in my bed than subject myself to that cool, dehumanizing gaze.

In the afternoon, I finally managed to pull myself out of bed. Hardly knowing what I was doing, I drove to the Jerusalem Forest and started to walk. The sky was an impossibly deep shade of blue, and a warm breeze fluttered through the pine groves. I thought of my brother, shutting out the world with his drugs and his mantras; my sister, with her deluded messianic visions; my father, with his angry cynicism; my mother, in her broken silence. My entire family was numbing itself to a darkness we couldn't even name. I thought of all the truisms I'd imbibed growing up in this tough-skinned little country. *We had always been hated, and we always would be. We have a right to do anything to survive. If we don't keep our guard up, we'll be thrown into the sea.* I was suffocating in the scaly armor in which I'd been reared. It was as if my heart had been encased in layers of extra skin, unable to beat with the fullness of life. But I couldn't live this way anymore. An ancient biblical phrase flitted, unbidden, into my mind: what did it mean to "circumcise" a heart?

I followed unmarked, looping trails for hours until I meandered slightly off-trail for a view and found the ruins of what must have once been an Arab house. It was well hidden from the trail, though just a few meters away. Plastic bags fluttered in the breeze as I wandered over the broken stones, then crouched at the base of the only half-wall that remained, under its empty eye of a window. I heard the deep gutturals of the former inhabitants as they laughed and wept their way through trivial, daily routines, then imagined the morning in which everything lay suddenly broken and interrupted. I tried to conjure up the hatred that could simmer and fester, leading a son, or a grandson, or a great-grandson, to strap a bomb to his chest and rush full tilt toward a bus stop full of old people and children. Heaving sobs overtook me again as I cowered under the wall, ululating wails echoing wildly in the wind. Who knew what other traumas lay even deeper beneath this ordinary little spot of ground? There wasn't a meter of this land that didn't shudder with buried horrors, murders and betrayals and rapes, conquerors and victims converging from every corner of the ancient and modern worlds. I felt as if all the pain of the suffering world lay aggregate under this small, inconsequential ruin.

When the new wave of sobs subsided, I found my way back to the trail, running, trotting, then walking for an hour more until my feet ached and my breathing calmed. I lay exhausted on the rocky ground at the top of a hill, working out the intricate patterns of branches, marveling at the play of light on leaves, mesmerized by the tiniest of wildflowers, by the wing of a fly crawling up my arm. My relentlessly rushing mind had finally slowed to a crawl. What did it mean, in Zeke's wildly deranged vision, to implant a "new heart" in a stubborn, rebellious soul?

When I got back to my flat, I picked up the phone and quickly dialed the number. A few rings and I heard the sweet, soft "hello" of home.

"Nava, it's me."

Silence.

"Are you there?"

"I'm here. Did you get the divorce papers?" Her voice was ice.

"No, not yet. That's not why I called."

More silence.

"Are you OK?" I said.

"I'm fine. Why did you call?"

"I want to talk to Yudit."

There was a pause. "I don't know if she'll talk to you."

"Nava, you shouldn't keep her from me."

The force of her anger stunned me. "Is that what you think? That it's me keeping her from you? My God, Kobi." I could hear her struggling to keep her voice steady. "I've told her a million times that, for better or worse, you're her father, and she needs to come to terms with you. I gave her your number. I told her to at least call you for Passover, to make sure that you would come to the bat mitzvah, but she refused."

I tried to take this in. "But you told me not to come—"

"Don't think I wanted you there; I didn't. But if she had wanted it, I would have never stood in the way."

I felt a fresh wave of anguish flood over me.

"It hasn't helped that you've made no effort at all to contact her in months," Nava was saying. "Even to wish her mazel tov for the bat mitzvah. You pretty much ruined her big day. She thinks you've just forgotten all about her."

But she's all I can think about, I wanted to say. "She never saw the doll?" I managed instead.

"What are you talking about? What doll?"

"I—"

"Kobi, I have no time for your stories."

"You told Yossi she wouldn't talk to me," I said. "I thought she would call me when she was ready . . . I thought if some time passed . . ."

"Kobi, she's a child!" Even through the scorn, I could hear the pain in Nava's voice. "You forgot that you were supposed to be the adult in this relationship? You didn't realize that you were the one who had to make the effort?"

"I did make an effort. I bought her a doll . . . it was stolen . . ."

"You thought you could buy her back with a doll?" Now there was nothing but scorn.

"OK, you're right, I didn't try enough . . . I kept hoping she'd come around . . . I didn't know . . ." I felt humiliated by the weakness in my voice, by my stupidity, felt the tears springing again to my eyes, the fluttering in my chest. *Nava,* I wanted to say, *forgive me, I've changed.* But I didn't really know if I had. The silence on the other end of the line was terrifying.

Finally she spoke. "Will you be home all evening?"

"Yes." I said, hardly daring to hope.

"Let me see what I can do." Abruptly, she hung up the phone.

I soaked my blistering feet in a tub of warm water, staring out the window at the evening's fading light, waiting for the ring of the telephone. What would I do if she didn't call back?

I jumped at the sound of the phone, splashing water on the stained, worn-out rug.

"She wouldn't dial the number," Nava said, "but she'll listen to what you have to say." And then, "Would you please try to be mature about this?" I waited, my heart pounding.

"Hello?" Such a weak, angry, untrusting voice.

"Yudit? It's so good to hear your voice, honey. I've missed you."

Silence at the other end. *Remember, she's only a child.*

"I guess you've been pretty angry at me."

More silence.

"I can see why you'd be angry . . ."

"Really?" she said, with that familiar Benami sarcasm. "You only destroyed my whole family."

"Yudit—"

"You didn't even come to my bat mitzvah."

"Yudit, I'm so sorry. I thought you didn't want me there. I bought you a very special gift, but I guess you never received it. I thought you were too angry to even thank me—"

"You're lying."

"No, I'm not. I—"

"Why did you call?"

"I wanted to tell you how much I've missed you," I said. And then, in a rush, "I think about you all the time. Every day. You know, you're the only little girl I have."

Another long silence. What a stupid thing to say. I felt the sob rising up again in my throat and struggled to keep my voice composed.

"Yudit, can't we talk just a little bit?"

"What do you want to talk about?"

"I want to know everything," I said. "Tell me what you've been up to lately. How was the party? How's school? Are you still on the soccer team? Anything."

She needed a great deal of coaxing, but eventually the words trickled out, about how boring her classes were, the old best friend who she now hated, the new soccer coach who was meaner than the last. Not a word about the bat mitzvah—had my absence really "ruined" it? The voice was apathetic, as if she was only humoring me. I remembered her old rattle of delight at telling Abba every little thing that happened in her life—and, with shame, the fact that I never used to listen to the details. Had I once upon a time talked to my own mother that way? I couldn't recall. Would Yudit ever talk to me that way again?

Shyly, I asked if she wanted to go with me for an ice cream next Saturday night. "I guess," she said. "If Ima says it's OK."

I hung up the phone, sank into the couch, wrapped my wet, throbbing feet in a frayed gray towel, and felt my heart overflow with gratitude. I allowed the tears to flow, but this time it was a gentle stream warming my cheeks. The world was full of evil and suffering, but it was also full of hope and new chances; it was hard to know where affliction ended and blessing began. I wanted to spill my gratitude out into the cosmos but knew there was nothing there to receive it. So instead, I poured out my thanks to the faces that came to mind: Ami, Yiri, Zeke, the whole chain of oddballs sent by Y. And that sad, beautiful, unfathomable Israela, who'd brought them into my life.

28

Two days later a postcard arrived at my home address, postmarked Jordan. The photograph on the front was of an ancient Mesopotamian clay tablet, covered in deeply etched pictograms. The back was festooned with a colorful array of stamps and a cramped, chicken-scratch scrawl.

Dear Dr. Benami,

I'm sorry I missed our last few appointments. Y had my house destroyed, just like he said he would. I'm sure I deserved it, but I cannot begin to describe to you the horror of that night. Some distant Iraqi cousins I never knew about have taken me in. They are reasonably kind to me, although it's terrible feeling like a guest all the time. There are very few Jews left in Baghdad, and I have trouble with the local dialect, so mostly I keep to myself. My hosts have a nice house, with beautiful river views, but I miss my home so terribly I spend most of my days crying by the banks of the river. I don't believe I will ever get over this. I am still numb with shock. Please forgive me for missing my appointments. I don't know if I'll ever be able to return.

Israela

How did she know my home address? Shaya might have given it to her, or Hesh, or maybe even Y. I realized that she probably knew a great deal about my life, just as the stalkers had—it hardly mattered. I was worried now about her safety. Was she really in Iraq? There was no postal service between Iraq and Israel, so someone must have mailed it from Jordan. Did the Outstretched Arm operate in Arab countries? Almost the entire Jewish population of Iraq had left the country long ago, but perhaps Y still had contacts, or even relatives—Israela had speculated that he had been born there. But if so, were they people who would protect her or hurt her? With Bush drumming up the notion that Iraq possessed weapons of mass destruction and increasing talk of an American invasion, she could easily be caught in the middle of another war. The postcard filled me with unease, but I had to trust her to take care of herself; there was no return address, and I could only wait for her to write again.

On Saturday night, I drove into the German Colony to pick up Yudit for our ice cream date. Parking in the area was impossible, and I drove in circles for twenty minutes before maneuvering my way into a miniscule space a kilometer from the house. I sprinted the whole way back, cursing at myself the whole while, arriving almost a half hour late.

I was breathing heavily when Nava answered the door, more from the butterflies in my stomach than from my quick run through the neighborhood. She was wearing a silky, deep-green pullover and sleek black pants, shimmering silver earrings—composed and elegant, as always. Was that a new warren of tiny wrinkles along her temples? If so, it framed her face perfectly, a delicate bridge between her dark hair and coffee-brown eyes. I couldn't keep myself from staring, couldn't find the words for a simple greeting.

"Yudit," she called out, "your *abba* is here." Not "Abba," but "*your abba*"—a fine distinction. And to me: "You're late. She was wondering if you forgot." She turned crisply on her heels and, without inviting me in the door, disappeared toward the kitchen.

I had never seen a woman with such natural grace. How did she manage to always be so beautiful, so artfully put together? Still, she was a little overdressed for a Saturday night at home. Could it possibly be for my benefit? I had a sudden, aching memory of the first time I had woken up next to her, marveling at the delicate pattern of her uncombed hair falling into her un-made-up eyes. Such a long time ago.

I stepped through the door as Yudit came down the stairs in slow motion, a studied tempo of indifference. Her dark, wavy hair, which had always been tied back in a thick ponytail, was now cut shoulder length, like her mother's, and there were two tiny buds visible through her pink T-shirt. Yudit, with breasts.

"Wow, honey, you've grown . . . in such a short time. And your hair . . . I like it a lot."

"I don't."

"Why not? It makes you look more grown-up."

"It gets in my eyes."

"Oh . . . I don't know. I think it looks nice. Sorry I'm late. I forgot about the parking around here. I was driving in circles, looking for a space."

"You're always late." She still wasn't looking at me.

"Well, yeah, I guess. But it doesn't hurt to have an excuse, does it?" I grinned hopefully, but she stared at me blankly. "OK, not so funny," I conceded. "Should we say goodbye to Ima?"

"She knows we're going."

I glanced down the hallway in the direction Nava had gone, realizing with an ache that I might not see her again tonight. "OK," I said to Yudit. "So let's go."

We walked for a few minutes without speaking, bombarded, once we'd turned off our quiet alley, by the restless honking of the car-choked streets. What a contrast to my day in the Jerusalem Forest—how could anyone think straight in the midst of such commotion? Perhaps I should find a place out in the countryside, in one of the small, hilltop communities west of Jerusalem, surrounded by clean air and birdsong. Yudit was walking sullenly by my side. I'd forgotten the physical awkwardness of trying to hold a conversation with a child while walking down a noisy street—did you bend down, in that clumsy, back-crinking way, to hear them and be heard? I realized, too late, that I should have suggested taking her to a movie, a soccer game, anywhere that we wouldn't have to sit face-to-face and converse. I couldn't imagine what we could talk about after so many months apart.

"Do you want to go to Carmel's?" I shouted.

"No, there's a better place," she said. Then, rolling her eyes, "I'll show you."

She picked up her pace, purposefully leading the way, relieving us of the burden of conversation. I was still preoccupied by the brief glimpse of Nava, so gracefully inhabiting our home as if I'd never left. Did it feel empty without me, or did she only feel relieved to have me out?

Emek Refaim was considerably less crowded than it usually would be on a Saturday night and, with the city still on high alert, filled with patrolling soldiers. An ambulance howled in the distance, and I had to remind myself—as I did almost every day—that people still had heart attacks, even in the midst of a brutal intifada. Still, I couldn't shake my apprehension. Perhaps it was unwise to take my daughter on such a public street. Since I'd last been here, a few of the cafés had installed bars on their doors, keeping them locked from the inside, and one even had a cage-like gate surrounding its outdoor patio. We subjected ourselves to a security check, then stood in line at the counter of the new American-style ice cream parlor, Galus, with its thirty-eight flavors and seventeen toppings. Another American *mishugas*—there was nothing from that omnivorous, flat-voweled culture that we wouldn't unthinkingly embrace.

"Wow, a lot of choices," I said, just to say something.

Yudit ignored me and, when our turn came, spoke directly to the skinny, pimply-faced teen. "I'll have two scoops of vanilla, in a cone. With whipped cream on top."

"Two scoops of vanilla? We could have gone anywhere for that," I said, gesturing at the rainbow array. "Don't you want at least one other flavor? Some sprinkles? A little color?"

Her voice was flat. "You don't know anything about me."

I let a few moments pass. Then I nodded. "Have you always liked vanilla?" I asked.

She didn't deign a response, just tapped her fingers impatiently on the counter while her cone was being assembled.

When it was my turn, I ordered the two most unpronounceable flavors on the menu, in a cup, with macadamia nuts, craisins, and rainbow sprinkles. I didn't like ice cream, no matter what the flavor; it was too sweet and hurt my teeth. I would have preferred a glass of wine, a beer, a coffee—anything with a sour or bitter hit. I couldn't imagine what had made me suggest this whole ice cream thing in the first place.

Although there were several free tables, we settled at the counter under the window, side by side, where, if there was nothing to talk about, we could at least watch the people and traffic passing by.

"So, Yudit," I finally said, "tell me about the party. Did you enjoy it?"

She sighed. "Not really. Ronit didn't even come, even though she's supposed to be my best friend. The DJ sucked." All I really wanted to know was if my absence had "ruined her big day," as Nava had put it, but there was no way to ask. "The whole thing was pretty pointless," she was saying. "I don't know why Ima thought it was so important that I have a big, fancy bat mitzvah party. It's not like we're religious or anything."

"But you were into it too," I said. "You put so much work into the invitations, and the decorations . . ."

"I know. It seems so silly now." She examined her cone for a moment. "It was just a party. We ate a ton of food, we danced all those dumb dances, and now it's over. I don't really want to talk about it anymore."

"OK, of course," I nodded. "What *would* you like to talk about?"

She shrugged and started to work on her white-on-white confection. A bus lumbered by, filling the silence with its engine roar. My mind flashed to the torn limbs and gaping wounds that had been haunting my dreams all week. Why was anyone at all walking on the street? Didn't they know there was an intifada going on, have the sense to stay home and avoid busy commercial zones? As if she was reading my mind, Yudit suddenly asked, "Abba, do you think it's safe to be sitting here?"

Had my face betrayed my fear? The last thing I wanted was for her to become as skittish as I had become. "What do you mean, sweetie, of course it's safe."

"But they love to blow up restaurants." She looked around the room. "We're a perfect target here."

"Well, I don't know about that. They have good security here. And anyway, we gotta keep on living."

"Everyone says that, but I don't know," she said. "First of all, the security is useless. They can detonate the bomb right on the street, or on a bus, or just before the security guy finds it. And anyway, just because 'we gotta keep on living'"—she made air quotes with her fingers—"doesn't mean we have to keep on eating ice cream in public ice cream parlors. We could 'keep on living' at home, where it's safer, right?"

"Do you really worry so much about that stuff?" I couldn't decide if I should be proud of her or concerned.

"Of course. Every day. Don't you?"

"Well, no," I lied. "It's still very unlikely to happen to any particular person on a particular day. If I didn't think it was safe, I wouldn't have offered to take you here. And I'm not the only one—look how many people are in this ice cream parlor." We both looked around.

"Not as many as there used to be," Yudit said. "A boy from my class got suspended this week because he brought a gun to school, which was pretty stupid, 'cause what good is a gun if a bomb goes off?" She neatly licked a drop of ice cream off her fingertip. "Turns out, it wasn't even loaded. And anyway, there's an armed guard and security gate in front of the school now; there was no way he wasn't going to get caught." I watched her lick the drips from her cone before each new bite. "Did you know that two people from my school have had relatives killed in the past year? One just last week, right here in Jerusalem, in the Gilo bus bombing. The other was last year in the Dolphinarium disco, but still."

"Wow. I didn't realize you knew someone in the Gilo bombing."

"I didn't know him," she said with irritation. "Abba, don't you ever listen? He was my friend's older brother. But still."

I nodded. She scanned my face, clearly suspicious that I was not understanding the import of what she was saying. "So it *is* likely to happen to a particular person on a particular day. The one from Dolphinarium was my friend Nir's second cousin, but he still talks about it all the time. He was sixteen years old, just a regular kid, and the other one, from Gilo, was only fourteen." Her cone finished, she crumpled her napkin into a tidy ball. "The school psychologist makes us draw pictures every time something happens, to get our feelings out. Like drawing pictures could make it OK."

I nodded, mutely. Was this an invitation to defend the integrity of my profession? Or was she trying to rub salt in my wounds by suggesting that I had abandoned her in a time of rampant violence? When had my baby girl become so cynical? Yudit swooped her free hand around the room. "You see all these people sitting here? They could all be killed any minute, any second. Everyone says the same stupid thing—'you gotta keep living.'"

Was this really what she wanted to talk about? I considered telling her about my experience at the French Hill bombing but quickly thought better of it. I couldn't possibly describe such a scene, especially to a child. And even if I could, it might sound like I was making myself out to be some kind of hero. She would probably think I was making it up to impress her.

Maybe she just wanted some reassurance from her father. What could I say? She was right, of course, we all *were* at least partially in denial. How else were you supposed to live under such unimaginably violent conditions? I began to feel a growing anxiety, a tightening in my chest, as I scanned the passersby for a likely terrorist—an Arab face, a bulky jacket on a warm night. Maybe we really would be blown up, sitting here, awkwardly eating ice cream together. Nava would be grief-stricken and furious, would have one more thing to hate me for. Or what if I survived and Yudit didn't? I'd never forgive myself. I should never have brought her here. We slipped into another long, uncomfortable silence, as I tried to calm my suddenly racing pulse.

"So, Yudit, honey," I finally said, "let's talk about something more cheerful. Is there anything new in your life since I left?"

She snorted, another grown-up sound from her I wasn't used to. "There is, big time, but you wouldn't want to know."

"Of course I want to know. That's why we're doing this."

"Well, OK, but I warned you. I didn't want to tell you on the phone." She took a deep breath but stayed facing out the window. "The *big* thing is that Ima has a new boyfriend."

She was right, I didn't want to know. What an idiot, thinking she was dressed up for me. Perhaps I should have kept the we're-about-to-be-bombed conversation going a little longer—it felt a lot less depressing than this one.

"Oh, OK," I said, unable to keep the strain out of my voice. "Is that why she was all dressed up? Was she going out with him tonight?"

"Uh-huh. To a concert. At Bet Ha'am. Some kind of big deal expensive thing she's all excited about."

What questions were the correct ones for this conversation? "Do you like him?" I tried.

"I don't know," she said. "He's from her dance company. Russian." She pulled her chest up, dropped her chin, and in a deep-voiced thick accent said, "He talks like dis."

I laughed, and she smiled shyly—the first flash of our old relationship I'd seen all night. Encouraged, I continued. "So, you think Ima's happy with him?"

"I guess. I wish he had younger kids. All his kids are grown. I haven't even met them. I hate not having siblings, especially now." She turned to face me. "How come you and Ima never had more kids?"

I started to make a joke and then thought better of it. "Well, you know, with Ima being a dancer, it was hard for her to take off time to be pregnant. That's what she said, anyway. Although she carried you so lightly, most people didn't even know she was pregnant. And she kept dancing, at least a little, right into her third trimester."

"So she could have had one more. It wouldn't have been such a big deal."

"It was to her. A dancing career is . . . I don't know . . . a complicated thing."

"And you? Did you want more kids?"

"I don't know. I never really thought about it. She didn't, and that was fine with me." It was remarkable to hear myself say it—Nava had so subtly and effortlessly called all the shots.

"Well, if she's gotta have a new boyfriend," Yudit said firmly, "I wish she'd find one with younger kids."

I nodded, not sure what to say. I was so shaken by the idea of Nava with someone else, it was hard to concentrate. I needed to be by myself, out in the woods, or with a shot of Scotch, taking it all in. A Russian dancer, fancy concert tickets. Was that what she'd always wanted? She'd always been a lot more interested in culture than I was. We'd spent two weeks in Italy once, arguing the whole time because I couldn't convincingly fake enthusiasm for the numbing variety of *Madonna con bambino*. Feeling Yudit watching me, I tried to eat a spoonful of ice cream, but it had turned to soup. Would it be rude not to eat it? And was it my job to keep this awful conversation going?

Yudit was wiping her already clean fingers with another napkin.

"It doesn't really matter anyway," she finally said.

"What, Ima having a boyfriend?"

"No, not that," she sighed. "I mean people getting blown up. You know what we learned in science class? We only have a billion years until the sun gets too hot to support life on the planet. So what difference does it make?"

What do you say to that? "Well, that's a pretty long time."

She snorted. "We won't make it half that long anyway. Not a quarter that long. There's all these nuclear weapons that they don't even know where they are. Also, the greenhouse gases, we've been learning about that too. All these big cities could flood, including Tel Aviv, I think, even in my lifetime."

"They're teaching you a lot of depressing stuff at that school."

"No, it's just the truth. Even if Israel doesn't get completely destroyed by this war, which it probably will, all the oceans are going to overflow their coasts, or we'll run out of water and die of thirst, or the food and air will be so polluted that humans can't survive. And there's the viruses from Africa. Or something we can't even imagine. I don't know why people carry on about a few little bombings. It's all pretty pointless."

"Well, I don't know . . ."

"Abba, we're stuck on this tiny, little planet, spinning through this huge amount of space, with nowhere to go if things go wrong. An asteroid could hit us at any time. And what do we do? Invent ridiculous new ice cream flavors, throw frivolous parties, and fight stupid wars. It's all so pointless, don't you think?"

She was only twelve, too young to talk like this. I felt shaken, defeated, crushed by her angry eyes. I had failed her terribly. What did she want from me now? What did everyone want from me? "I never really think about things like that," I finally said.

"Abba, what *do* you think about?"

What *did* I think about? What was the endless chatter in my brain all about? And what was the point of this pathetic facade? She would keep testing me, and I would keep failing her. She would never forgive me, and why should she? I had robbed her of the last vestiges of her childhood. I sank my head into my hands, staring down at my purple and green ice-cream soup, frozen with shame. What *were* we doing on this spinning chunk of rock? Was I supposed to have an answer? I should never have called her—she was better off without me. There had never been a more incompetent adult. I thought I could change, but I was the same old failure. I didn't even know how to have a normal, hour-long conversation with my own daughter.

"I guess I'm a pretty useless father," I said, without looking up.

She got up to throw the wad of napkins into a nearby garbage can. I thought she might leave me there, alone in Galus, unable to speak or move, and I dug my fingers further into my skull, trying to relieve the ache. I would sit there as long as I could, transfixed by the psychedelic colors of my inedible cup of American ice cream, until they threw me out at closing time. I could hear in the background the laughing, arguing, flirting, normal-talking people around us. Had they been eavesdropping in on this pathetic attempt at father-daughter communication? Perhaps it was the same crowd that had witnessed my humiliation in Café HaEmek, the same drunken eyes that had watched me in Soreq's leering helplessly at Delia, or who secretly saw me drive away and abandon Israela. Y's emissaries were probably watching me at this very moment, collecting evidence for the next confrontation. The miasma of cumulative horror that I had experienced at the Arab ruin in the Jerusalem Forest returned full force.

I felt her sit down next to me again, could see her legs swinging softly under the table, heard her lick the stickiness from her fingers, one by one. We sat in silence for a long time before I heard her say, "I'm sorry, Abba," felt her head rest lightly on my shoulder, and her legs, pressed against mine, come to stillness.

It was a miracle, like an exotic bird alighting on your shoulder—you don't move, you don't breathe. When she finally sat up straight, I did too. "No, I'm sorry," I said and hugged her head, stroked her hair, smelled and then kissed her forehead, the tears stinging my eyes. I reached over to wipe a small dab of whipped cream out of her eyebrow and she giggled shyly. We sat for a long time, leaning against each other, watching the pedestrians trickle by. When the parlor had almost emptied, we walked back to the house—her house, not mine—in a calm, sweet silence, my hand rumpling her thick, dark hair as we walked. She hugged me good night—"Maybe next time we could go to a movie?" she suggested—and quickly slipped into the house.

I sank down on the porch swing for a few moments—the same swing on which the Ashra-doll, with its atoning eyes, had once patiently sat—relishing the cool breeze of my lost home. At least it still stood, I could still visit it—that was more than Israela had. Somehow, miraculously, Yudit and I had managed to eat ice cream together without getting blown up by a terrorist bomb. I was suddenly exhausted. I promised myself that as long as this goddamned intifada continued, I would never walk my daughter down a busy public street again. Pulling myself to my feet, I slowly walked back to my ticketed, crookedly parked car.

29

The Thursday after my date with Yudit, I came home from work to discover a package slip from the post office. I ran the few blocks to my local branch and only with much arguing was able to retrieve the package from a surly clerk trying to close up for the evening. As I expected, it had no return address but was postmarked Jordan.

I rushed home, eager to open it. But as I turned the corner to my block, all thoughts of Israela quickly evaporated. In front of the entrance to my building, pacing back and forth and smoking nervously—in exactly the spot where Shaya had calmly lounged just a few weeks before—was Delia. I saw her before she saw me and stopped, watching her from a distance. She looked anxious, upset, much as she had that day in Yossi's shop, but less disheveled. Her hair and makeup had been done with care, and today she wore no modest black cape—just a skimpy red shift of a dress. As I walked into her view, her face froze for the barest instant, then transformed itself into sexy, studied nonchalance.

"Where you been, Jewboy? I hate to wait for people." She took a deep drag of her cigarette.

"How did you know where I live?"

"You're in the phone book."

"How do you even know my name?" I was sure I'd never told her. "From Yossi? Or from the clinic?"

She laughed, as if the idea of not knowing my name was preposterous. She nodded to the door, just as she once had motioned toward Soreq's dark corridor. I hesitated. But the longer we stood here, the higher the risk that some office snoop would happen by and report this juicy bit of gossip straight to Jezebel—it would be a good one for the file. I unlocked the door, Israela's package still clutched awkwardly under my arm.

In my flat, Delia sat down on the couch and pulled another cigarette out of her beaded purse. I rummaged for the apartment's only ashtray and placed it in front of her.

"Are you going to get me a drink?" She blew a long stream of smoke into the air and took in the apartment with an appraising eye.

"Well, I can, if you want, but . . ." I was stammering like a schoolboy. A Scotch was all I wanted, but I wouldn't drink if she shouldn't. "Maybe it's not such a good idea," I ventured. "Maybe you shouldn't be smoking either. I mean . . ."

She exhaled in a rush. "What the hell you talking about?" She stared at me.

I couldn't hold the eye contact, even briefly. "Well, I don't know . . . I thought . . . Aren't you pregnant?"

Did I see a flicker cross her face? But then, abruptly, she laughed and took another drag, her red lips forming a practiced circle as she exhaled. "You a bigger asshole than I can believe. Do I look pregnant?" She stood up and thrust her flat stomach forward. "You think I don't know how to protect myself? What kind of shit you talking about?"

What was wrong with me? Delia didn't need protecting. But the hatred in her eyes cut through me with an erotic charge I hadn't felt in years. "I'm sorry. It's just that—"

"It's just that you're an asshole." She shook her head in disgust and sat back down on the couch. "You getting me a drink or no?"

"Yes, OK." Only then did I notice that I was still clutching Israela's package tightly under my arm. I placed it on a side table at the other end of the couch and went into the kitchen to pour two glasses of Scotch with trembling hands

I brought the glasses in and set one in front of her. She was holding Israela's package and examining the postmark closely. She put it down beside her as I entered, a faintly mocking smile on her lips.

The presence of both women in my house at the same time overwhelmed me, and I blurted out, "I guess you know her. From Soreq's."

She accepted the glass and took a deep swig. "Know who? What you talking about?"

"The woman who sent me the package. She knows you."

She appraised me coolly. "There's no return address. How would I know who sent it?"

Before I could respond she said, "You always thinking too much. All Jews are like that. If she's ever set foot in Jerusalem, I probably do know her. Everyone shows up at Soreq's eventually. You'd be surprised. Everyone."

"So you do know her?"

"Aaaah," she exhaled a note of pure scorn. "You never learn nothing, do you? What do you want from me? I'm nobody, don't you get that? How the hell do I know what slut is sending you packages?" She crushed out her cigarette. "Full of dirty pictures, I bet." She took a long pull at her Scotch and stared at me with a hollow expression.

"So why are you here? Isn't it dangerous? I thought you were scared of being deported . . ."

She slowly placed her glass down, without taking her eyes from my face. "I know how much you want to fuck me," she said. One flimsy strap slid off her shoulder, baring the top of one perfect breast. "But you're such a yellow-ass coward." The flintiness in her voice sent another surge of desire through me.

I tried to defuse it with a joke. "So, you do house calls? That's very considerate."

She didn't smile. The strap tumbled another centimeter. "You know what they say. If Muhammad don't come to the mountain . . ."

My heart was pounding, and I was having trouble breathing. It made no sense. Why would she come here looking for me? Maybe she needed a new place to hide. Or maybe Jezebel had sent her, I thought wildly. A kind of entrapment thing? But that sounded more like Y.

I sat down on the arm of the couch, downed my Scotch, and tried to get control of myself by using my most professional voice. "You know, Delia, I was worried about you. After I saw you in Yossi's shop. I thought you were in some kind of trouble."

She never took her eyes off my face as she inched her way toward me. "Maybe I was. Maybe I'm always in trouble." She was close enough now that her perfume was making me dizzy. "Nothing to worry your fancy Jew-head about. You going to fuck me or not?"

I tried to take another sip from my empty glass and then answered honestly. "I don't know. I don't know what you're doing here."

She made another sound of pure derision. "Aaaah. You can't get it up. Is that it?"

Obviously not. "Why are you so mean to me?" I asked.

"'Cause you're an asshole, we already know that," she said. "But this is your big chance with Delia. You going to blow it, Jewboy?"

What was my excuse now? There was none. I had lost Nava forever. Disease? Blackmail? Entrapment? What difference did it make? I reached over and pulled her up and in moments had her dress peeled off, my hands and mouth searching hungrily. And her mouth, too, astonishingly, seemed as voracious as mine. Crazed with pent-up desire and fury, crazed from a lifetime of feckless, aimless wandering, I pulled her into the bedroom and onto the rumpled, unmade bed, pushed into her, roughly, insatiably, inhaled her abundance, her dizzying wet fragrance, her ravenous, icy eyes. I had no idea what she was doing there, couldn't fill myself enough with the reality of her presence. Knowing it was fleeting, an improbable mirage, impossible, self-deluding, perhaps even dangerous, made me want her all the more, made me hungrier still.

Afterward, wrapped in her perfumed, sweaty limbs, I fell into a deep sleep, and yet deeper dream: Delia's thin tattooed rope had come alive, a snake slithering off her arm and onto me, tracing patterns across my body before turning into a thick hemp rope, which was binding my wrist . . .

I awoke on my back, my hands bound to the bed frame by a red, patterned kerchief. I instinctively started to pull away, but Delia stopped me with a glare of command. Then, slowly, dispassionately, like the pro that she was, she went to work on me. I let myself sink into an almost unbearable, exquisite agony of longing.

When I awoke again, somewhere around midnight, groggy and confused, my hands were still bound but I was alone. I panicked, tried to pull free, then called out to her, startled to hear her name echoing through the apartment. It took me a long time to unwork the tightly pulled knots. Rubbing my sore wrists, I double-checked the apartment, but Delia was gone. I returned to bed, burying my nose in the kerchief, in the damp sheets, savoring the lingering scent, drifting in and out of dreams in which Delia aggressively, mockingly, bound my arms in one unbreakable tether after another.

In the morning, with the sun filtering through the still-open shutters, I wondered if I had dreamt the whole encounter. But the kerchief lay tangled in the sheets, a lipstick-stained cigarette butt sat in the ashtray on the coffee table, and my skin smelled of her perfume. Reluctantly I showered, then put up a pot of thick Turkish coffee, and only then remembered the package Israela had sent me. It was still sitting on the couch. Only now, the package was ripped open.

I pulled out the ream of paper, covered in the same scratchy handwriting as the postcard I had gotten the week before. There was a brief note lying on top:

> Dear Dr. Benami,
>
> I don't know if I ever mentioned to you that I write poetry. I've been doing so for years, but much of it was lost in the destruction of the house. I have so much time here that I decided to re-create from memory as much of it as I could. I've also written a lot of new stuff. Maybe this will help you understand my marriage better.
>
> Israela

Downing cup after cup of mud-black coffee, I made my way through the thick stack of poems. One hundred and fifty poems, and not a single one about a sunset. They were love poems, every one of them, dramatic and overwrought. In one line she was extolling Y's splendor, his faithfulness, his strength and passion. In the very next line she was pleading for his mercy, in terror of his wrath and destructiveness. The language soared at times, evoking the jubilance of nature at the knowledge of her beloved. At other times she was wracked with self-pity, quaking in fear and illness, terrified of her neighbors, certain she would die unless he but turned his face toward her. They were beautiful and chilling at the same time.

With the taste of Delia on my tongue, my wrists still raw and chafed, I read Israela's poems with a new glimmer of understanding—the obsession, the terror laced with longing, the thrilling weakness of being bound. When I'd finished the stack, I started through them again and spent the entire day weaving in and out of the poems, in and out of the previous night's memories and dreams.

How far could obsession go? Could you lose all sense of reality in its throes? Many of the things Israela said about Y were impossible. Was it all poetic license, or had she come to believe the unbelievable? I had certainly lost all sense of what was real. Never mind Y—did Delia exist? Or had I imagined our encounter—cigarette stub and all—out of the depths of my desperate loneliness? What were the limits of sane self-deception?

I spent the weekend in a delirious haze of memory and fantasy. Sunday morning, as I dressed to go to work, I searched everywhere for my wristwatch, but it seemed to have vanished. It took a long while of searching before it occurred to me to check my wallet. The credit cards remained, but the cash, all 800-some shekel, was gone. So were the gold wedding rings, mine and Nava's, that had been resting, hers nestled in mine, on the edge of the scratched-up bureau.

Waiting for what? A reconciliation that I knew would never come. Perhaps Delia had better use for them. I sat on the bed and laughed and cried at the same time. Of course Delia would expect to be paid for her professional services. Perhaps she would come back the next time her funds ran low. If she did, I knew I would welcome her again, with open, dream-scarred, insatiably hungry arms.

30

I headed straight home from work every day that week, my heart quickening as I rounded the corner, knowing full well she wouldn't be there. On Friday morning there was another notice from the post office, accompanied by a smaller letter from the Government Ministry for Marriage and Divorce. I laid the letter, unopened, at the edge of the bureau where the wedding rings had once cozily embraced. Here it was, I thought, the dung of my life, and I couldn't even open it to look.

Israela's package contained a long prose poem describing a love of her youth, the voices alternating male and female, surprisingly erotic and theatrical in tone. The style was nothing like the poems she had sent the week before, and the love affair unlike anything she had ever described. Could this ravishing young lover possibly be Y? Unlikely—he had been at least middle-aged when she'd met him. The setting was all wrong as well; this was not a furtive, middle-of-the-night, tent-in-the-desert coupling, but the opposite—a series of proud, sunlit trysts set in the luxuriant growth of orchard and field. I wondered whether the lyrical verse was pure fantasy or depicted an affair she had not dared to tell me about directly. Could it possibly refer to Bal? I read it over and over throughout the weekend, a template of the loves I had known and not known—the steadying presence of Nava, the sensuous thrill of Delia, and the innocent, mythic love that the poem described as "more powerful than death."

A couple of days after receiving Israela's poem, I found myself in session with Penina Mizrachi, she of the knotted, dyed hair and loveless marriage. As she droned on about her cheating, neglectful husband, I tried to imagine her as she once might have been, passionate and vibrant as the young girl in Israela's poem. I searched the mottled creases of her face and folded arms for an innocent, lovestruck girl buried underneath the depression and inertia but could see nothing. I tried hard to listen, to discern what relief she might be getting from this endless recital of despair, but the helpless whine of her voice was grating on my nerves, scratching me dry. For the hundredth time I furtively glanced at my watch. There were ten minutes left to her interminable fifty-minute hour.

"Why don't you just leave him?" I blurted out, as startled as she was by the interruption in her monologue. I hadn't even waited for a pause.

She froze, looking as astonished as if I'd asked why she didn't consider becoming an exotic dancer.

I stripped the irritation from my voice and tried to take on the tone of a concerned older brother. "Why don't you just leave him?" I asked again.

"I can't leave him. I've already told you . . ."

"Yes, of course you have." I struggled to keep my voice kind. "The children. Money. The shame of it. You wouldn't be able to make it on your own. They're all very good reasons."

"I couldn't possibly . . ."

"Do you still love him?"

She stared at me, astonished at the question.

"Did you ever love him?"

Silence. She was breathing heavily.

"From what you've told me, he's been in love with another woman for a long time," I said gently. "Do you think he once loved you?"

Her face was ashen. Suddenly worried she might actually pass out on the floor, I retreated. "I'm sorry. I interrupted your train of thought," I said. "If you want, you can go back to where you left off."

She continued to stare at me. There was no backing off—I was on my own now.

I took a deep breath. "Look, you can spend the rest of the session telling me all the things that make you unhappy, all the reasons you are trapped. But as you say, you've already told me these things many times. I'm not sure there's anything more I can do for you. If you want to ever have a chance at being happy, you will have to leave him."

"Dr. Benami . . . ," she began but was unable to finish the thought.

"My wife left me," I said impulsively. "About three months ago."

Her mouth literally dropped open, and I had to suppress the urge to laugh. A reckless sense of freedom overtook me.

"I guess I'm not supposed to talk about that, but maybe it will help you. I've wondered if I ever really loved her. I think I did, but I'm not sure." Penina was looking increasingly horrified, but I couldn't stop. "She was right to leave. I didn't respect her, I wasn't honest with her. I cheated on her, if you must know. I treated her just like your husband treats you, but even worse. At least he loves this other woman. And now my wife's found someone new." I paused and took another deep breath. "I'm pretty devastated, really. But I can hardly blame her. She deserves better."

Her mouth was still hanging open, but her eyes were more focused and alert than I'd ever seen them. For a brief moment I could see the curious child she had once been before a stifling shroud had descended over her life.

"I really am sorry I interrupted you," I said, feeling exactly the opposite. "And I shouldn't have mentioned my wife. It's against all the rules of therapy. I'm sure your situation is quite different. You can continue what you were saying, but you know, your story . . ." Her eyes widened, but I felt another surge of honesty coming on. "How long have you been coming here?"

"Two years," she whispered.

"Yes, well. It's been a little dull. Don't take it personally. But it's the same thing every single week. I'm going to tell you the truth, because maybe no one else will." I leaned toward her. "Nothing will ever change if you don't leave him."

There was a long silence. I flashed back to the first time Nava had caught me lying about where I'd been the night before. She had tossed our framed wedding photo on the floor, shattering it into a hundred pieces and waking a terrified Yudit, a toddler at the time. After Yudit had been settled back down to sleep, I had held Nava tightly as she cried and flailed at me, admiring the strength in her delicate wrists, perversely glad that she'd found out, promising myself I would never cause her that kind of pain again. The resolution had lasted no more than a few months.

Penina glanced at her watch. "I think our time is up," she said, all but choking on the words.

I smiled at her. "Isn't that my line?"

A tiny smile flickered across her face, then disappeared. She made no move to gather her things.

"You're right, our time is up," I said. "If you prefer, I won't ever interrupt you again."

Silence. Would I have to have her forcibly removed?

"I'll see you next week, Penina."

Slowly, she shifted her bulk to the edge of the couch, then summoned the laborious effort of gathering her overstuffed bag to her chest and hauling herself up to a standing position. Before leaving the office, she turned to look at me one more time. "Sometimes I wondered if you even knew my name," she said, before closing the door softly behind her.

31

After Penina's session, I felt both giddy and mortified. I tried to convince myself that no harm had been done, and who knew? Maybe that was what she needed. Maybe that's what they all needed—a heavy-handed dose of the truth. Tossing the therapy rule book out the window for Israela had launched me on a wild, transformative journey. Why not do the same with the rest of them? Jezebel was already on my scent, and the worst she could do was fire me. And would that really be such a terrible thing?

I tried to behave with the rest of my clients that day, but I struggled to maintain the mask of "professional distance," and every so often I deliberately allowed it to slip. When I left the office, I noticed Zeke lying on his side in an alley across from the hospital, mostly hidden from view, as if respecting my need for greater discretion. I knelt down to tell him about the packages I'd been receiving from Israela, but at the sound of her name he let loose a grotesque flurry of pornographic ravings. I inched away, sneaking a furtive look back toward the clinic to see if anyone had been watching.

The next Friday, a third package arrived. I was prepared for more love poetry but instead found a philosophical treatise. I spent that night savoring every passage, reading aloud, wondering why she had used one phrase and not another. She wrote with wisdom beyond her years, an old soul reflecting on the vanities of life. I found myself meditating on her words as I fell asleep and then guiltily picked up the manuscript for yet another read in the morning. There was something compulsive, and yet deeply pleasurable, in the pull I felt toward her work.

The piece reflected a poignant awareness of human mortality. Given the brutal destruction of her house and forced exile to a hostile land, this was hardly surprising. But what I couldn't quite grasp was whether this hyperawareness of death was making her new circumstances sweeter or more bitter—her writing suggested both. I found myself wondering if it would be possible to be acutely aware of the futility of all endeavors and yet still live life fully and joyfully. What would it be like to savor every moment as if it was full of meaning without deceiving oneself to its utter irrelevance? I tried to imagine my own last moments on earth, drifting away willingly and peacefully, content in the knowledge that my life had no more purpose than a dancing mote of dust.

It was mid-afternoon and I was still deeply absorbed in these reflections when the telephone rang.

"Kobi, you better get over here."

"Gal?"

His voice was shaky, but also more present than I'd heard it since he was a teenager. I felt a long-absent stab of affection. "It's Abba," he was saying. "I came for Shabbat. I went out for a walk, and when I returned he was on the floor, clutching his chest. Thank God I found him." He was talking fast. "The ambulance just came—they're taking him to Beilinson. Ima's asleep in the bedroom, and I don't want to wake her." His voice rose a note, panicking. "Kobi, I'm not sure what to do. Should I wake her?"

"Gal, calm down," I said, trying to process everything he was saying. "You stay there with Ima. Don't wake her. I'll head straight to the hospital. Did you call the prison authority to inform Anat?"

"No, I just called the ambulance," Then, his voice full of fear, "I've been talking to him. I was trying to keep him calm until they arrived."

"You did well, Gal," I said. "Try to get word to Anat. I'm on my way to the hospital."

Before I hung up, I heard him say, "Kobi, I'm scared."

Traffic was light, and less than an hour later I was in the bustling ICU of Beilinson Hospital. When I finally got the attention of a nurse, she informed me that my father had almost certainly had a heart attack. He was in pain but stable, and they were conducting a series of tests to determine what interventions would be needed. Depending on how bad the blockage was, they might have to operate.

He was lying alone in a room at the far end of the unit, his face ravished, his breathing labored, but his eyes alert. He seemed tiny and shrunken underneath the tangle of tubes. I pulled up a chair.

"Kobi." His voice was so frail, and the ambient noise of the room so loud, I had to lean in to hear it.

"Quiet, Abba, you don't need to talk."

"Where's Ima?" His eyes darted around the room, searching for her.

"She's home," I told him. "Gal is with her."

He visibly relaxed. "That's good. Don't bring her here."

"You should rest," I said. "Your body needs to recover."

"I'm dying, Kobi."

"No, Abba, you're not. You've had a heart attack. You'll pull through this. They may have to operate, but . . ."

He made a weak, dismissive gesture. I sat up and stared at the beeping monitors for a few minutes, as if able to decipher their life-determining codes, reluctant to look at him in this diminished state. He'd always been such a proud man.

"Kobi."

I leaned back toward him. "Yes?"

"You're my oldest."

I nodded.

"Hard to believe," he whispered, "but you're also my sanest."

"Not much competition, huh?" He managed a weak smile before his face turned frighteningly serious.

"Kobi."

I didn't want to hear what he'd say next. "Abba, please don't speak. You need to conserve your strength."

"Promise you'll take care of her," he said.

"You're not going to die."

"Promise."

Anything so that he could relax. "Of course," I said reassuringly.

But his face twisted in frustration. "No . . . not what you're thinking . . ." He closed his eyes, gathering his will. "Not in some . . . facility." He spat out the word with contempt. "A proper home. I left you money. Take care of her."

His breath had a raspy tone that terrified me.

"Abba, please don't exert yourself. You'll be fine. We'll talk later when you're stronger."

He looked around, as if about to reveal a great secret.

"I'm ready to go," he said. "I've lived longer than anyone would have thought possible. At eighteen, no one would have bet a dime on my life. Enough."

"Abba . . ."

"It's good you're here," he said.

I nodded and he closed his eyes.

I reached for the cold, shriveled hand and held it, noticing how the tattooed number was now almost completely lost in the deep folds of his wrist. I had loved to hold his hand as a child—it seemed to harbor all the warmth he otherwise didn't know how to share—and would trace the tattooed numbers with my fingers, saying them out loud: 1-4-8-7-2-1, as engrained in my mind as my childhood address and telephone number. I had always wondered why his tattoo was on his wrist, and not on the forearm like my mother's and most others I'd seen. Perhaps he didn't even know why—a bureaucratic fluke. When he was feeling stronger, I would be sure and ask him.

I sat with him a long time, holding that hand, remembering. How he would walk me to *ganenet* Drora's kindergarten. The time he took me bicycle riding in HaYarkon Park. The day he had caught me, just before my bar mitzvah, sipping suavely, or so I imagined, from a glass of his best whiskey. How he had taken the glass from my hand and told me, in the gentlest voice I'd ever heard from him, that I was still too young. "One day," he had said, "we'll enjoy this bottle together."

Suddenly a harsh moan came out of his slackened mouth and his body convulsed. A red light above his head began to pulse and beep, and within seconds the room was full of strangers. I was shoved aside as an army of doctors, nurses, and technicians surrounded him, pumping, injecting, yelling across his indifferent frame. "We're losing him," I heard one of them say, as if from a very great distance.

Alone in a corner, I felt myself begin to rock slightly. "Go in peace, Abba," I began to chant under my breath, warm tears streaming down my face. "Go in peace, Abba, go in peace, Abba, go in peace, Abba, go in peace." For a few moments, it was the only sound I could hear.

"Dear Abba. Go in peace."

32

The shiva was held in my parents' living room, to the roaring, droning soundtrack of their ancient, rarely used air conditioner. My mother slept most of the time, and on the rare occasions when she joined us, it was in her now-habitual state of total silence. She looked forlorn and lost, her hair and clothes disheveled under the inept care of my otherworldly brother, who had moved into the apartment to care for her. Anat and I were there only a few hours each evening, she because of the constraints of her administrative detention, I because of an irrational terror of spending even one night in my childhood bedroom. Anat spent her time cleaning or bustling around in the kitchen, while Gal, who claimed no tolerance for the now frigid air of the living room, sat rocking and chanting on the small, sun-drenched terrace.

Each evening, a few old people with heavy European accents trickled in and out of the apartment. Yudit was unceremoniously dropped off for a few hours on the second night. She sat with me, not saying much, the silence between us surprisingly comforting. But most of the time I sat alone in the living room in deep grief, haunted by my father's presence, ruminating about what meaning might be wrenched from his tragedy-soaked life.

I couldn't remember him ever telling me he loved me, but it now felt as if his fierce devotion was the foundation on which I had always stood. Had I betrayed his deep, complicated, unwavering love? He had invested too much in me, I knew—it had been the blessing and curse of being his oldest, of carrying the name and features of his own deeply mourned father. I worked hard to keep my mind free of his voice or image. If I allowed myself to imagine his drawn face and limping form or hear the weird way he said my name, the tears would sting my eyes. KO-bi, he'd say, stressing the first syllable as if in fear that otherwise I wouldn't pay him any mind. Why hadn't I at least saved one of his messages on my answering machine? It wrenched my heart to think that I would never hear that insistent, Yiddish-inflected KO-bi again.

It was late in the afternoon on the fourth day of shiva, before Anat had arrived, when a thin, middle-aged woman with a long, Modigliani-like face and kind, watery eyes walked hesitantly through the door. She looked about my age, with glints of silver in her short, dark hair.

I stood to greet her. She handed me some home-baked cookies and looked around the room. "There's no one here," she said, stating the obvious.

"It's still early. Most people come after dinner."

"Yes, of course. I'm so sorry for your loss. Where's Hinda?"

"Asleep. I can wake her," I said, glancing toward the bedroom door. "Are you a friend of hers?"

"You must be Kobi," she said.

Her gaze was warm and familiar, but I couldn't place her. "Yes. I'm sorry, have we met?"

"Only once, a long time ago. We were just children." She stretched out a hand in greeting. "I'm Miki." She took in my blank expression and added, "Libke's daughter."

"Libke." A hotel, an explosion. "Oh . . . yes, of course. I'm sorry for your loss as well. It must still be terribly fresh."

"A little more than three months," she nodded. "It was . . . devastating. So sudden, and so violent." She looked at me. "I was very close to my mother."

The weight of our mutual grief was suddenly too much and we both looked away. I broke the silence. "I didn't even know your mother's name until . . . the bombing. I guess we met as children. But I didn't really know . . ."

She heard me floundering. "That's OK," she said. "I understand."

"How did you hear about my father's death?"

"My father told me. He sends his condolences. He would have come, but he's much too frail."

"He survived the bombing."

"Yes. He was sitting right next to her, but he only ended up with broken bones and lacerations. Still, the shock of it all, both physical and mental, has taken its toll. I worry for his health."

"I can only imagine. Were you there as well?"

"No," she said. "Every other year we do seder at my husband's family, and my parents go to the Park Hotel. Had you ever been there?"

"No. I'd never heard of it before."

"It was a sweet little hotel, by the sea. Very unpretentious. More religious than we are, but my parents liked that—it reminded them of seders from their childhood. And they'd developed friends there, people who went every year—most of them survivors." She paused. "So strange to think that such an innocuous little place . . ." She didn't finish. *This is what now passes for small talk,* I thought.

We stood for a few long moments, the silence broken only by the rumble of the air conditioner. I motioned for her to have a seat, set the cookies on the coffee table, and perched myself opposite her on the edge of the couch. As I did, I suddenly realized that the little green soldier no longer hung from the ceiling fixture. Perhaps he had fallen. Or maybe someone had finally noticed and taken him down.

"Are you sure you don't want me to wake my mother?" I asked, just to break the long silence.

"No, don't bother her, it's OK. I was just hoping . . ." She paused again, briefly closing her eyes. "It meant a lot to me that your father came to the funeral," she finally said. "It shows the kind of person he was. He didn't have to come." She looked at me. "I was hoping to tell Hinda that."

"Thank you," I said. "I really can wake her, but I'm not sure there would be much point. She had a stroke . . . shortly after the Park Hotel bombing. Anyway, she doesn't talk anymore."

"What do you mean?" Miki's face showed more than kindly concern— I also saw a flicker of fear.

I shrugged. "We're not sure what's going on."

"Does she know your father is dead?" she asked gently.

"I don't know; it's hard to tell. She's so . . . impassive."

Miki looked down at her hands. She had a nervous habit of chipping at the polish on her short, clipped nails. "I should have . . ." She shook her head and looked up again. "I wanted to tell Hinda how much she meant to my mother."

"I'm sure she knew that," I said.

"No, I'm sure she didn't."

There was another unbearable silence. Finally I gathered my courage.

"How did they even know each other?"

"From Auschwitz. She never told you?"

"No," but that made sense—the heaviness, the mystery. "My father also survived Auschwitz," I said. "Perhaps you know that—although they only met in the DP camp, after the war. He spoke about it often, but my mother never did. Occasionally she'd say something vague about life in the Lodz ghetto or from before the war—about her parents and younger siblings. Not much, mind you. But never a word about Auschwitz. I first heard your mother's name from my father after the bombing." The urgency in his voice on the phone that day came back to me, vividly, and I quickly pushed it away.

Miki was looking back down at her hands. She wore a thin wedding ring on her right hand, and an equally modest ring with a small amber setting on the middle finger of her left hand, which she now began to turn reflexively with her thumb. "My mother spoke quite a bit. I was an only child, and like I said, we were very close. She mentioned your mother frequently. I knew Hinda lived in Petah Tikva. I knew she had three children, all your names, and how old you were. And then we met that one time." She glanced up at me with a half-smile. "You were . . . a little wild. You hardly seemed to notice me. But still, I never forgot that meeting. You're only half a year older than me, you know. I used to wonder what you were doing, would imagine getting together and talking to you. I even heard about your dissertation on children of Holocaust survivors—your father must have been proud of it and told my father. I found it archived in the Hebrew University library and tried to read it." She looked back down at her hands, vigorously working the small, amber ring, and laughed nervously. "It was more technical than I expected."

"It was a lazy job," I admitted.

"Oh, no, I didn't mean . . ."

"No, that's OK. I have no illusions about the quality of my research. I just wanted to get it done." I waved the dissertation aside. "Tell me, how did our mothers know each other?"

She looked down again at her hands. "This ring," she said, twirling the thin band with the amber stone. "My mother bought it for me when we visited her hometown in Poland."

"She took you back there?"

She nodded. "The house she was born in was still standing. It was right on the *rynek*, the central square. Such a beautiful, leafy square—that surprised me. My mother had fond memories of playing in the grass on the *rynek* as a very young child, before they moved to Sudeten. We knocked on the door of her house, but the old couple living there . . . they wouldn't even let us in. Maybe they thought we would make a claim for it." She laughed abruptly at the absurdity of the idea. "We went to the cemetery as well . . . but all we found was bones lying in a field of trash."

"Human bones?"

She nodded. "We inquired in a house at the edge of the field as to what had happened to the cemetery. They said that the Germans had pulled up the gravestones to make roads, and then the Russians dug up the ground to make railway tracks. Children would play with the skulls, but the other bones remained."

"In a field of trash."

"We said *Kaddish* there and left. My mother's family had lived in that town for hundreds of years. It was . . . well, you can imagine."

I could. "My mother would never have gone back," I said. "I thought my father might want to, and I brought it up with him once—but even he would have none of it."

Miki nodded. "My mother was quite brave in some ways. We visited Auschwitz on the same trip. It was very disorienting for her at first. Technically, they'd been in Birkenau, not Auschwitz, but she hadn't realized that. So when we walked into the camp at Auschwitz, she didn't recognize a thing. Those tidy brick buildings—it was all wrong. She was very upset—how could her memory so utterly deceive her? But then, a couple of hours later, when we approached Birkenau, she knew exactly where she was. She started strutting like a tour guide, showing me where her barracks had been, where the latrine had been, where the crematorium was. There was something comforting, for both of us, about her familiarity with the camp." She paused, looking for the words. "It made it a real place, not just . . . a phantom in some featureless nightmare."

I suddenly needed to hear everything Miki could tell me. "What happened between our mothers?"

"They were in the same barracks in Birkenau." I could feel her hesitate, unsure whether to proceed.

"Tell me," I said.

She took a deep breath. "Both of them were alone—they had already lost their parents and siblings. And so . . . they became inseparable. They were almost exactly the same age. They shared whatever scraps of food they had. My mother was from a small town in Poland, but she grew up in Sudeten, where she'd received a very formal German education. She loved German poetry and would try to re-create for Hinda as many poems as she could from memory—Schiller, Rilke, Hesse, even Wagner arias. She would spend hours at it, expounding poetry and explaining to Hinda—who knew very little German—the more difficult words. My mother always said that boredom was the biggest killer in the camp." She smiled at the dark joke. "There was nothing to do all day but think about how hungry you were. So recalling poetry was the game that kept her mind occupied. And while she tried to re-create the verses, Hinda would feed her fake lines, in Yiddish, just to make her laugh. To her dying day, she believed that her friendship with Hinda kept her alive when she had lost all hope."

I couldn't imagine this version of my mother. "My mother was never the least bit interested in anything literary," I said.

Miki shrugged. "Maybe she wasn't. But my mother was, and Hinda needed a friend." I nodded, taking this in.

Miki went on, "My mother had a romantic soul. She'd point out a magnificent sunset mocking them in the sky over Auschwitz, and Hinda wouldn't even look up. She'd say, 'I'm too cold and hungry to look at a sunset.' That's how different they were. But they clung together, like a mismatched pair of socks."

"So what happened?" I asked. "Why didn't they stay friends after the war?"

"My mother always talked about Hinda's eyes. She found them . . . mesmerizing. Is it true that your mother has green, cat-like eyes?"

I nodded. "My brother was the only one to inherit them. Everyone always fussed about it when he was a child."

She nodded, thoughtfully, as if that bit of information solved a profound riddle.

"Miki, tell me what happened," I said. "Please."

She spoke again, more slowly. "They had sworn to stay together and protect each other. They made an oath that if they survived they would consider themselves blood sisters, in every way, for the rest of their lives. They would raise their children as cousins. If one of them died and the other survived, the one who survived would make sure *Kaddish* was said for the one who had died—that her memory, and the memory of her parents and siblings, would live on. You see," she said, "if things had turned out differently, we would have grown up as cousins. That's why I always . . . wondered about you." She wouldn't meet my eye.

"What happened?" I whispered, scared of the sound of my own voice.

"Your mother . . ." She couldn't go on.

"Tell me."

She hesitated, then took another deep breath. "You know that your mother was on the last transport out of Auschwitz."

"Yes, to clear rubble in the German cities during the American bombardment. My father told me. She ended up in Hamburg."

"She left my mother behind." She said this tonelessly, but I could tell how much effort it had taken.

"OK," I said. "But . . . if she was chosen for the transport, and your mother wasn't—"

"It wasn't by chance," she said quickly, trying not to lose her nerve. "There were things Hinda did to get on that transport. She didn't tell my mother . . . what she was doing. But she knew before she left that she would get on and that my mother wouldn't."

I was struggling to take this in. "What do you mean? What did she do?"

"My mother was furious, and terrified. She knew exactly when she was slated for the gas—they were emptying the barracks quite methodically at that point. She pleaded with Hinda not to leave her there alone. They had promised each other that they would stay together, take care of each other, even at risk to their own lives."

"What did she do?" I tried again.

"People did whatever they could to survive. They were desperate." She twisted the ring around and around. "There was a mother who left her own child behind in Auschwitz to die alone—that little girl haunted my mother's dreams for years. But we can't judge them," she said, looking up. "Maybe that mother went on to have a whole new family."

"But your mother—"

"She did judge your mother, harshly. She felt betrayed and abandoned. When the Russians came, she was one of only a handful of survivors, and if they had been delayed even one more day she doesn't think she would have made it." She paused. "But then, years later, she found out that Hinda had survived and that both of them were in Israel. She was overjoyed. She sought your mother out and tried to reconcile." She glanced up to see if I knew this part of the story and saw from my face that I didn't. She continued, "Hinda was shocked that Libke had survived—she assumed that she'd left her for dead. They met once, in Tel Aviv . . . but it didn't go well. After that, Hinda refused to see her. Maybe she felt judged. Maybe she just didn't want to remember. I don't know." Miki didn't meet my eyes. "She cut off all contact."

I had so many questions I hardly knew where to start. "How did you know so much about our family?"

She answered readily, almost relieved. "Our fathers stayed in touch. Mostly for big events—like births, marriages, deaths. My mother always wanted to know what was happening in Hinda's life. She really did think of her as a long-estranged sister."

"My father knew all of this?" I felt a fresh stab of loss.

Miki saw this. "I don't know how much he knew," she said hurriedly. "It doesn't matter now. There's no reason to rehash such horrors."

"Please," I said with a force that surprised me. "I know so little about my mother, and now she's retreated into this . . . this impenetrable silence. My father was the only one who knew anything about her, and now he's gone." I looked at her, embarrassed at the nakedness of my pleading. "Can't you tell me anything more?"

Miki's already constricted features tightened into a hard mask. "Perhaps I've said more than I should have. I only heard my mother's side of things. I don't know the full story. I was an only child, and sometimes my mother confided in me more than she should have."

"And mine never said a thing. Which is worse?"

"There are some tales better left unspoken, no?"

"No," I said. "Do you really think that?"

She looked down at the untouched cookies, embarrassed. "Perhaps I shouldn't have come. You're in mourning, you don't need more shocks. I meant to speak to your mother, not you." She was warm but formal. "It would have meant so much to my mother that Hinda's husband came to her funeral, even if she wouldn't come herself. I wanted her to know what a good man your father was."

The words stung my eyes—"what a good man your father was." It was so obviously true. Why had it been so hard to be close to him?

Miki was still talking, slowly. "I wanted to tell Hinda that my mother never held a grudge. That she forgave her, for everything."

"Please," I said. "I need to know."

"No." Miki was firm. "Your mother can't speak for herself anymore. I shouldn't be the one to break her silence."

"Do you think . . . it's the guilt that makes her mute?" I stammered.

Tears began to well up in Miki's eyes as she picked up her handbag and tucked it under her arm. "I'd better go now," she whispered. "My husband and children are in the car, waiting for me." She glanced uncertainly at Gal rocking and chanting on the terrace before moving toward the door.

33

After Miki's visit, the shiva was over for me. I was shaken by the ominous hints about my mother's past and had little patience left for the formalities of mourning. I had always known that the dark closets of her past were not to be opened, and I didn't want to give in to prurient stereotypes, but—what had she done? I had fantasies of confronting my father about the truth. But I knew that even if he were alive, I would do no such thing.

My father's consoling, rebuking presence hovered over me constantly, reminding me of the night I'd been convinced of Y crouching in the shadows of the flat. But what did that palpable sense of presence signify? Nothing. Everything. Sometimes I felt my father watching me as I ate dinner or lay in bed sleeplessly, a compassionate presence, no longer bitter, understanding all.

But I didn't believe in such things; death was final, was it not? Miki's phrase, and her precise intonation—"what a good man your father was"—kept echoing in my mind. I wondered briefly if Miki had been another one of Y's emissaries, then laughed aloud at the absurdity of the idea. The Outstretched Arm seemed to have little interest in me now that Israela was safely—or not so safely—exiled. My mother's muteness and my father's death were, apparently, none of Y's concern. Back in my flat, I reread Israela's philosophical treatise, groping for renewed sustenance, but her words only left me restless. Where my father's harsh, cynical, fiercely loving voice had once dwelt, there was now an aching void.

It was only a few weeks later that I discovered that my parsimonious father had left a much larger inheritance than I would have ever expected. I placed a down payment on a large Arab house in the Jewish section of Abu Tor, determined to waste no time fulfilling his final wish. The house was selling cheap; it was on the seam where West and East Jerusalem met, and there had been a number of shootings and Molotov cocktail attacks in the area. The house itself was widely rumored to be haunted by its original inhabitants, and it had long been sitting on the market. It was full of odd nooks and charming tilework, not to mention a balcony view across the war-torn valley. Making such a large decision without Nava's discerning eye, on which I had become so childishly dependent, was nothing short of terrifying. But I plunged in and bought it all the same, a forced act of desperation, defiance, and irrational hope.

The day of the closing, as I was getting ready to leave the clinic, there was a knock on my office door. It was Henya, the pious, cookie-baking receptionist. I had never quite gotten over my embarrassment over our strange encounter and had taken pains to avoid her ever since.

"Dr. Benami, I hope you don't mind my bothering you," she was saying. "I was so sorry to hear about your father's death. I hear you've bought a new house."

I nodded.

"I . . . I bought you a little present," she whispered.

"That wasn't necessary," I said. Her milky gray eyes instantly began to fill with tears, and I forced away my own. "I mean, it's incredibly nice of you."

She pulled a small package from the pocket of her sweater and handed it to me. "It's a mezuzah, for the doorpost of your house. One of my younger sisters made it, from enamel—she's very good at crafts. I know you don't believe in such things, but . . . it can't hurt."

"Thank you," I said. "I'll hang it as soon as we move in. It's very kind of you."

She stood in the doorway, staring at the floor. "You haven't noticed," she said.

"Noticed what?" She put a hand on her belly and smiled shyly at me. "Please don't take it personally, but you're not very observant."

My joy for her was genuine. "That's wonderful, Henya. Mazel tov."

Her face fell slightly. "You shouldn't really say that until it's born."

"Oh, I—"

"It's OK," she said quickly. "I usually don't talk about it at all—people say it invites the evil eye—but it was important to me that you knew. I was already pregnant when I saw you that day in the lounge . . . but I had lost two already. That's why I was praying so hard. You see? God does answer prayers."

"I suppose," I said, smiling. If only it were so simple.

"Good luck with the new house," she said, wrapping the sweater around her belly and backing out the door.

I focused single-mindedly on the move for the rest of that intifada-wracked summer. Gal stayed with my mother until the Petah Tikva flat was sold, and they both then moved into the new house along with some family mementos and a few pieces of salvageable furniture. My mother settled into the ground-floor bedroom, laden with her weighty secrets. Gal, though spooked by the voices he heard echoing through the creaking house, took over the attic, strewing it with pillows and rugs and vases full of incense, drowning out unwelcome spirits with melodic Sanskrit chants. There was even a room on the second floor for Yudit, who began spending the weekends with me on a regular basis, a growing assortment of quirky stuffed creatures keeping guard on her bed when she wasn't there.

In the middle of August, Anat and Tuvya were sentenced to three and five years, respectively, and I got temporary custody of Habakuk. He had nowhere else to go, having been declared "incorrigible" by Tuvya's flustered sister. I had little affection for the child, but he was scared of me and went off to school every morning without a word of protest. He took to carrying my mother's pillow around, clinging to it and talking to it as if it were a stuffed doll, and he insisted on sleeping with her, her silence seeming to calm his raging soul. One day he brought home a scruffy street cat who never left, ever hungry, always underfoot, tripping me on the way to the bathroom, purring loudly and rubbing against our legs at the unbounded joy of having a home.

By the end of the summer all the boxes were unpacked, and my mother, though silent as ever, eased her way into the new kitchen, assembling every evening a smorgasbord of unrecognizable dishes with whatever she found in the refrigerator and pantry. Those odd, patchwork meals evoked a new tenderness in me, as if her silence had opened a long-locked door. I took Henya's colorful little mezuzah out of its wrapping—there seemed to be an arm lightly etched on its back, but what did that matter now?—and ceremoniously hung it on the doorpost of my new home. I even rolled into it an expensive parchment that I bought from a shop in the ultra-Orthodox neighborhood of Me'ah She'arim. It was the rankest superstition, of course, but "It wouldn't hurt," as she had said, and I would be needing all the help I could get. Within the course of a single summer I had become paterfamilias to an eclectic assortment of needs, and I stretched to fill the ill-fitting role.

Despite everything that had happened, I still couldn't rid myself of the yearning for Delia. Shortly before the holidays, which came unusually early that fall, I went back to Soreq's one last time and spoke to the bartender—a tall, very black African whose accent I could barely decipher. He had never heard of Delia or Dudu or Bal or Israela and had no idea where any of them might be found. The next day, on my abbreviated lunch hour, I took a taxi to the Old City and trotted down to Yossi's crowded shop. "I don't want anything from her," I told him, "but I moved, and she might not know how to find me." Yossi laughed and gave me one of his business cards, on the back of which I scribbled what I hoped was a not-too-eager note. Yossi promised to give it to her if he ever saw her again. "She hasn't been here in months," he shrugged. And then, in holy-man mode: "The *Shechina* wanders—it is her natural state of being."

After the holidays, Jezebel took me off probation and allowed me to resume my administrative duties. I had made quick progress inventing old case notes, and the chart pile on my desk had shriveled to a respectable height. I missed the drama of Israela's story in my day-to-day life and searched my other patients for stories of equal resonance. Penina Mizrachi never returned to the clinic after my reckless foray into truth-telling, but one day, for no discernible reason, the eight-year-old who had stopped speaking after the Sbarro bombing starting talking again, in full sentences. Was it something I had done? Probably not. It was engraved in our DNA to knit a scar over even the most gaping wound. I was as skeptical as ever about the theories and jargon but comforted myself with the thought that if so many people felt better after talking, I was, in some minute way, at least alleviating, rather than aggravating, the cumulative weight of human misery. It was frustrating work, full of boredom, unavoidable wrong turns, and heartbreaking dead ends, but every so often it brushed at the newly clipped corners of my heart. I made an effort to talk to the other clinicians, about work and about life, and was moved at how willing they were to forgive me, to notice my clumsy attempts at connection.

I was trying hard to change. Was change ever possible? I even developed a guarded affection for Chagall's floating, upside-down lovers—dubbing them Adam and Eve—and treated them as knowing witnesses to the foibles of the supposedly right-side-up world I was striving to inhabit.

The humiliating divorce ceremony was completed in late fall, and Yudit informed me shortly afterward that Nava was engaged to be married to the Russian dancer, whose nickname, I learned, was Dudu. My new heart tottered in panic and grief, then recovered its balance. There were too many things I couldn't understand and couldn't control. I threw away the Scotch, avoided the easy pickups that sometimes came my way, absorbed myself in the details of running my idiosyncratic household, and discovered, in the wells of emptiness that periodically engulfed me, that I could pray even when there was no one to pray to.

There were still a few stalkers, but their numbers had sharply dwindled. After all, there was little point in threats—the worst had already occurred. A man calling himself Shaya, but looking and sounding nothing like the other two men I'd met, bounded into my garden one evening full of extravagant hopes for the glorious reunification of Israela and Y. I listened politely to his rant, then fed him some tea and leftover baklava, for which he seemed inordinately grateful, though he never returned for more. I still spoke to Zeke occasionally. Once, just before the rains of winter began, he seemed uncharacteristically lucid, describing in meticulous detail the new house Y would one day build for Israela and insisting that on days when I didn't see him, he was off visiting her in exile. There was no point disputing the logic of this with a psychotic who consumed cow dung, but despite myself, I was reassured. From what I could glean, she was healthy, learning new things, perhaps making new friends. True or not, it assuaged my guilt.

Then, in January, I was called to a hellish reserve duty in Gaza and returned with a mild limp. I'd fallen on a hard rock while fleeing from a burst of sniper fire, and though the pain in my hip was enough to keep me up at night, the x-rays were clean and the doctors dismissive. I was in constant pain and immeasurably lucky to be alive.

Israela's packages had continued to arrive every Friday morning—she seemed to know exactly when and where I had moved—and they had become the one predictable beat in the haphazardly shifting music of my life. Her literary production was surprisingly varied and wildly uneven in its quality. It included fiction and poetry, philosophy and whimsy, memoir and diatribe. Whatever the quality, I was excited to read this outpouring of creative expression, felt moved by her eagerness to stay connected, wondered why she had never even hinted at her literary aspirations. Perhaps a new environment was precisely what she had needed. She may be sad, I thought, even traumatized by her exile, but it had also unleashed a vibrant, creative force.

I continued to read her writings with meticulous attention, noting every oddity and nuance in the text. With her scratchy handwriting sprawled before me, I thought often of my high school lit teacher. I couldn't remember his name, but I could see him vividly—the round glasses and earnest brown eyes. He had been the only figure in my entire school life who had seen anything positive in me. I had loved dissecting text in high school, had written complex, poetic papers for him, but had done nothing of the kind in the years that followed. Maybe I could have become a linguist, or a translator, or a writer, or a high school lit teacher myself. My father had been right—why had it never occurred to me to pursue my real talents?

On a chilly day in early February, in a steady, prickling rain, I met Yossi for lunch in the Jewish Quarter; with my bum hip, I could no longer play squash. After regaling him with the circumstances of my injury—and just before we parted ways—I ever so casually asked if he knew of an organization called the Outstretched Arm. "What do you want with that rinky-dink out-fit?" he asked, but then pointed the way to their headquarters. "Look for the blue door," he said and headed back to his shop.

It took me twenty minutes of back-and-forthing, but I finally found it. The logo was scratched onto the decrepit blue door, barely visible among the warps and dents. I stood in the soaking rain, strangely comforted, like Libke at Birkenau—it really did exist, was not a phantom of my distorted mind.

I rang the bell, hearing the tinny ping echo inside, but there was no an-swer. I knocked hard, then rang again. The indifferent fruit seller next door merely shrugged when I asked him whether anyone worked there. After one last, long ring, I was ready to give up and go home when a young Ethiopian woman opened the door just wide enough for her to stand in the opening. She was lean and pretty, with a long Abyssinian nose and braided hair.

"Yes?"

"Is this the headquarters of the Outstretched Arm?"

"Who is asking, please?"

"My name is Benami. I—"

"Do you have an appointment?"

"Well, no, but—"

"I'm so sorry, but you will need an appointment," she said with an apologetic, beatific smile.

I couldn't stand the idea of the door closing on me. "Can you just let me come in for a minute and dry off?"

She smiled sweetly. "No, I'm so sorry, but I can't let you in without an appointment. They're very strict these days—especially since the start of the intifada. Would you like an umbrella?"

"No, thank you. That's very kind of you." I couldn't see anything behind her. "Can you please tell me," I heard the anxiety in my voice, "how I can make an appointment?"

She smiled again, radiant and implacable. "I'm sure someone will con-tact you if they want to speak to you."

"But what if I want to speak to them?"

"I'm so sorry, but it doesn't work that way." She started to close the door.

"Is Y there?" I asked desperately. "Or maybe Ami? Or Hesh? Shaya? They all know me. If you tell them that Kobi Benami—"

"I'm so sorry, Mr. Benami," she said with real empathy, "but I'm not allowed to divulge any information about the whereabouts of our staff or volunteers."

"Excuse me for asking, but what's your job?" I asked.

"I'm the receptionist," she answered, her face lighting up, as if she was the most fortunate office clerk to have ever walked the rainy streets of Jerusalem.

"Well, OK. Can you pass on a message?"

"No, I'm sorry, I'm not allowed—"

"Do you have any literature?"

"No, I'm so sorry."

She must have seen the abject frustration on my face because she turned around to retrieve an umbrella from the dark hallway. "Are you sure you don't want it?" she asked imploringly.

I hesitated, then took the umbrella from her outstretched arm.

And then, in late February, almost a year after I'd first met her, Israela sent me a package unlike any she had sent me before. It was a comic novella—a fable about kings and queens, evil-doers and righteous revenge. The American invasion of Iraq was imminent, and my first reaction was surprise that she was composing light-hearted fiction at such a frightening, precarious time. But as I read through the farcical tale, I also realized with growing amazement that the story never even mentioned Y. Of all the works she had sent me, this was the only one to make no reference to him. I was astounded by the discovery, combing through the story a second and third time to make sure I was not mistaken. It occurred to me, with a mixture of excitement and apprehension, that she might actually be getting over him.

Perhaps Zeke was wrong. Perhaps she would never return to husband and home, to the source of so much misery. But who would she be without the overpowering force of Y in her life? The novella seemed clever, but frivolous. If she truly forgot him, would I celebrate her freedom or mourn the banality that would overtake her life? Perhaps she would forget about Y and leave war-torn Iraq, make her way to Europe or even America, and marry an ordinary man, kind and loving. I imagined Israela with a couple of young children, a household to manage, an interesting job. I could see her settling into respectable middle age, discarding with a wry smile the flouncy dresses and old-fashioned shawls of her youth, adopting a sensible wardrobe. She would carelessly shrug off the dreamers that had stalked her, forget the passions of her youth, write modest checks to worthy causes to allay her middle-class guilt. And would that be so terrible? Wasn't that precisely the kind of life that I, as a psychologist, was trained to value and nurture?

It was shortly after I had finished the Y-free novella that a slim postcard arrived.

Dear Dr. Benami,

I hope you have enjoyed reading all the pieces I have sent you. I have some exciting news. Y has arranged for me to come home! He has decided that I have suffered enough and has sent one of his friends to escort me home and help me rebuild my house as it was before. I've been yearning for this for so long that it's hard to admit that a part of me will miss my life by this wide and majestic river. But I have learned so much from this experience and will come back a wiser and humbler person. I know that I will be a better wife!

Now that Y and I are reconciled, I will not be needing any more therapy. Thank you so much for everything you did for me and for reading all my silly writings. It meant a lot to me. I will never forget you!

Love,
Israela

As I read her note, the old anxieties came rushing back. Y must have also read the novella and realized that Israela could actually forget him. Nothing else could explain this sudden turn of events. Hopefully, he would act quickly enough to spare her the upheaval that would follow the American invasion. As relieved as I was for her safety, a part of me had indeed hoped that she was beginning to move on, preparing to lead a comfortable, normal life in a faraway land.

But then I remembered her poems and the single-mindedness of her passion. She had been obsessed with this love for so long—no distance, no exile, no violence on his part would be able to change that. Perhaps if more time had elapsed—but it had been less than a year since the destruction of her home. If he beckoned, of course she would follow.

I was both despondent and relieved that she would not be returning to therapy. Not for a moment did I think this marital reconciliation would last. But my new life was both busy and fragile; I couldn't afford to risk the turmoil that would be unleashed by seeing Israela. I read her letter over and over, lingering over the closing. "I love you too," I said silently. I knew I would never see her again.

A few months later, a new book appeared in Jerusalem, causing quite a stir. It was called *The Book of Y*. The back cover explained that the author preferred this pseudonym because his own name was so long and hard to pronounce, and needless to say, no picture or further description accompanied the blurb. The critics panned the book, calling it disorganized, repetitive, grandiose, an irresponsible mix of fact and fantasy. Many insisted that one author couldn't possibly have written it, arguing that there were too many different literary styles represented and suggesting that "Y" was a composite of many famous authors. Others took great pains to show how derivative the book was, and there were accusations of out-and-out plagiarism. But despite the critics, it was a huge popular success, fueled by wide-ranging speculations on the nature of Y's identity.

I immediately went out and purchased a copy, reading the familiar words cover to cover. The critics were right, of course; it was a terrible mess. But I loved it all the same.

The title hadn't fooled me for a minute. It was, unmistakably, *The Book of Israela*.

Acknowledgments

One night in February 2000, I was visited by The Muse, who deposited the entire first draft of this novel in my sleep-addled mind. The next day I started writing, completing that first draft in six weeks. Thank you, Muse—whatever you may be.

The Muse arrived without warning but not without context. It was my first year in rabbinical school, and Tamar Kamionkowski, professor extraordinaire of a yearlong class on biblical civilization, had let us know that she would accept "something creative" in lieu of a final paper. Thank you, Tamar, for your inspiring class and liberal assignment policies. And many thanks to the committee of the Alice Stein Essay Prize in Jewish Women's Studies for awarding the prize to my proto-novel.

A one-hour conversation with the brilliant Julie Rose was essential to the transition of the original draft into a fully developed novel. Thank you, Julie, for your generosity and insight.

I am so grateful to the wonderful readers I have had over the years: Rafi Blumenthal, Allen Bogarad, Lawrence Bush, Esther Cohen, Melissa Crabbe, James Donegan, Ezra Goldstein, Maurice Harris, Dina Jansenson, Lori Lefkovitz, Steven Lewis, Janet O'Dowd, Dan Porat, Lance Ringel, and Gerald Sorin. Every one of you added an essential spice (and in some cases whole new ingredients) to the final stew.

This book would still be languishing on my computer if not for the encouragement, wisdom, and soul-redeeming humor of my dear friend and colleague Maurice Harris. I am deeply indebted.

Kate Daloz was an amazing editor: incisive, quick, funny, and kind. This novel is immeasurably improved because of her efforts.

I am grateful to Debra Hirsch Corman for her keen copyediting skills; to Matt Wimer and Stephanie Hough for their patience and flexibility as I nudged the manuscript into final form; to the entire Wipf and Stock team for their behind-the-scenes assistance and support; and to Andrew Ramer for the phone call that pushed me over the edge—in the best sense of the phrase.

To my very indulgent friends who have spent years listening to book-related angst and joy—always wondering when and if I would finally send my baby out into the world—I am grateful beyond measure for your love and support. You know who you are.

Last, and never least, my heart tumbles in awe at the Mystery that has brought me to this day.

שהחינו וקימנו והגיענו לזמן הזה